BROTHER OWL

Books by Al Hine:

BROTHER OWL

SIGNS AND PORTENTS

AN UNFOUND DOOR

THE BIRTHDAY BOY

LORD LOVE A DUCK

BROTHER OWL

Al Hine

DOUBLEDAY & COMPANY, INC.
Garden City, New York
1980

ISBN: 0-385-15818-1
Library of Congress Catalog Card Number 79-8966

AUTHOR'S NOTE

I first encountered Joseph Brant in the pages of an interminable novel entitled *Greyslaer* by Charles Fenno Hoffman which I must have read when I was twelve or thirteen and scraping the farthest recesses of attic and bookcase in our house in Pittsburgh. I can remember little of *Greyslaer* beyond vague scalpings and ravishings and the fact that Brant's son was its savage villain, but the character of Brant himself stuck stubbornly in my mind.

Brant and the whole business of settler and Indian, for Pittsburgh is a city with streets named Braddock and Forbes and Northumberland and even Dinwiddie and Gist. And my summers were mostly spent in nearly untouched mountain country where a five-minute walk took me into another world of whispering quiet, an independence of snakes and small animals and virgin timber that my imagination could people with Indian shadows. Brant tall and proud among them.

When I came across a mention of Brant in any history book or dissertation on Indians, it gave a spark to the whole subject, particularly since he was usually (I felt) either maligned or too scantily dismissed. I used him often as a touchstone for testing histories and encyclopedias; those that did not mention him, I damned as worthless; those that slurred him were only a trifle better.

Brant might have remained no more than this to me had I

not, some six years ago, picked up a copy of Dale Van Every's *Forth to the Wilderness,* the first volume of four in his magnificent *The Frontier People of America.* There was only slight mention of Brant in this volume (it stopped at 1774) but much of his patron, Sir William Johnson, and a little of Brant's sister Molly. I waited impatiently for the second volume, *A Company of Heroes,* and was richly rewarded with three sections on Brant. And two more sections in the third volume, *Ark of Empire.* Mr. Van Every had restored my fictional hero to a great figure in history.

Why then have I turned Brant back into fiction?

Mostly because he would not let me alone and, since I am a novelist and not a historian, this had to be the form for my personal exorcism.

I have tried to play fair with historical fact, but character, motivation and many minor incidents are quite my own. Where subsidiary characters have perhaps been wrenched to serve my novelistic needs, I have generally chanted their names to avoid violence to recorded fact. (Most authorities now agree that Brant's father was Aroghiyiadecker: I chose Carrihogo—a possibility briefly mentioned by Brant's first biographer—to make my own man.)

Since Brant is narrator, the attitudes—moral and political and religious—are his, but I confess I have sympathy for almost all of them and no apologies for letting him interpret some events to his own best light. I do not believe he is one iota too harsh on our (and my own) colonial forebears, their greed and duplicity. For the record here, I can again invoke Mr. Van Every, whose *The Disinherited* presents a factual record of our centuries of broken treaties with every Indian tribe foolish enough to trust us.

I plead guilty to many obvious omissions and to foreshortenings necessary to my storytelling. I have not tried to write a comprehensive history of the Revolution in New York State nor a detailed study of the Iroquois migration nor a dozen

other worthy and interesting books. I have simply tried to ex-
press the character of that vision of Brant which has so long
haunted me.

                                                    Rome

BROTHER OWL

ONE

I can remember so much: the blood and screams of the settlers at Cherry Valley as we cut scalps through to hard skull
bone, and cut much else; the scent of pomade and fresh linen
as I walked down Berners Street in London on my first visit
with Guy Johnson; the wet, warm smell of spring livening the
woodlands around Johnson Hall and wrestling with Walter
Butler, his bare torso as brown as my own, and Ganundagwa
watching, her brown belly beneath the British shirting so soft
to touch, and London again with my Lady Frances's body
glaring white in the shrouded dark stillness of the inn . . .

Why, O My Redeemer to Whom each living breath is owed,
do I remember my sister's and Lady Frances's bodies beyond
all I know of Thy word and Thy bounty and Thy salvation
which shall be my life here and forever? Why, when now my
sole and soul's endeavor is to bring Thy word to the hapless
Mohawk, should my head be torn with sounds of pagan
drums and my dry lips tremble on the memoranda of kisses
long past and unsanctified, and my sere loins start again, rising like an old dog before the fire at Johnson Hall?

Is this Thy work or his whose name is Tempter and Beel-
zebub?

No matter, Lord, or perhaps much matter that I should
now, in my own alone twilight, put down the recollections of

a troubled life which has found peace only toward its end, in Thy service, in Thy bosom.

I write this troubled in mind and body only by age; and, for my age and all that I have seen and lived, I am hale.

Hale and sane enough to catch myself out in the first lie of many that may tempt me as I try to record my life. For I write that my life has found peace only toward its end, yet I can remember a very nearness to Paradise when I was a child.

Sir William told me long past that Faith is a vital essence, but should be tempered by laughter against the chill dangers of Covenantish solemnity. A warning I shall do well to hold as I write, for in age it seems to me men like to remember either only joys or only sorrows and forget how cunningly their lives have been a weaving of the two like the purple and the white of a wampum belt recalling the long council, and dancing along with grave decisions.

I do not know how much of the life I led is left for any child now . . . those cathedral forests of lofting elm and chestnut, close-tangled pine and rough locust and brakes of slender white birch where I crawled and then walked and ran and played.

I was born a Turtle, that cautious, well-protected creature being the sign of my mother's people. My father, Nichaus Brant, was himself a sachem of the Wolf people, a wise man, a good hunter and well-heard in tribal councils.

It is necessary now to insist against rumor that what I have written of my parentage is true. Since the wars of the colonials against the King, there have been tales whispered that called me a by-blow son of Sir William Johnson. There have been a hundred other tales lending me a cloven hoof and fangs to frighten children, but it is not of them I speak now.

Had I been a son of Sir William, on either side of the blanket, I should not deny it. He was a great man and a generous scatterer of his seed. There are dozens of men alive this day, both among my own Mohawk Nation here in the north and among the tribes in New York State and among settlers Irish,

Dutch and English who claim proudly and rightly their descent from Sir William.

I should have no shame and the less so because among the Iroquois descent is reckoned from the mother and I am as much a Turtle and a man of chieftain's blood from her had my father been Sir William or George Croghan or King Lewis of the French. But the time and the place of my birth make it clear that my father was truly Nichaus Grant, or Carrihogo in the Mohawk tongue.

I was born in 1742 in the Ohio country where my mother had already been long with my father and his hunting party. At this time Sir William—not yet a baronet, but still simple William Johnson—had been a scant four years in America land-clearing and administering the fur trade in Warrensburgh and managing the affairs of his mariner uncle, Captain Peter Warren of Boston. And further, these were his years of early and close alliance with that Catherine Weisenberg, styled his wife, although such connection did not then or after enchain Sir William from other dalliance.

No, reader, the facts are all against that romantic bastardy so blithely pinned upon me, so accept me as a Mohawk infant, born to Carrihogo and his wife, in a forest clearing below Doshoweh Tecarneodi, or Lake Erie. See me then as a child of trees and swift streams and shadows cut with bright swords of glancing sunlight.

These were years as close to Eden as man might know and may never know again in these our Indian lands so rudely shorn today. How long may it take for great trees to grow again? For the wind-whispered stillness to return? For the huge, shy buffalo to move in hundreds-hordes across grazing spaces thundering and shaking the very earth with their procession?

An old man's mind wanders with memories of grand beauty not seen in a generation. Forgive me.

I grew happily, a whelp in savage innocence.

I think suspiciously of men who claim full memory of their

youngest days for, while there is much that I can call back, I remember little that is exact before my fifth or sixth year. Until then my mind serves up to me only vague blendings of colors and sensations, of blue and dark and brightness, or warmth and cold and sometimes the sharp seasoning of pain. Stirred into them are the stories Carrihogo and my mother, other elders and my sisters and brothers have told me of those first years; and stories like these, told over and over again, have become mixed with the true memories in a blending where borders fade and, do I not catch myself with severe attention to honesty, I believe I remember an incident which is no more than a told tale. Of such blendings may history be, I believe; men weaving together their fathers' and mothers' tales until a coarse-textured baggage of contradicting events becomes a smooth narrative consistent to the friendliest and most patriotic desires of the retellers and believers. If this is so, there may be great knaves of past kings now firmly made into heroes and an equal company of grave and decent rulers turned monsters for all ages to come by the canting tongues of crooked chroniclers.

One such incident as sharp in my mind as if I remembered it and yet, I know, as much spun from stories in tribal castle and longhouse as from recall, sees me alone scatheless encountering a giant owl when I was but two years in age.

A hunter, long with my father's hunting parties, speaks at the fire:

"Brothers! I have seen Small Turtle, Nichaus's son, speak with a bird as big as half a bear!

"I saw him in the beginning-night of the day just gone beyond the mountains. I saw him loitering behind the women and the other children in a small clearing and I saw him with my eyes that can find a spotted fawn in the riverbank growth and I heard him with my ears that can catch the footfall of my brother the wolverine.

"There he sat alone and naked in the grassy clearing and above him was the heavy hammering of wings as there came

from the darkness above an owl as huge and round as one of
Croghan's whiskey barrels, and more, an owl as white as snow
far from any camp!"

Always, here, there were breaths indrawn with wonder
from all around the fire, the wonder fresh even from tribes-
men who had heard the story many times.

"An owl, my brothers, such as man has never seen, large
and strong enough to carry away a camp dog or a child of ten
summers, yet this owl did not touch our Small Turtle nor even
move toward him, but settled gravely upon the earth the
length of an outstretched arm before the infant and looked
upon him with open eyes of yellow fire!"

"Aii-ee!" from around the castle fireside.

"Looked at him, my brothers, and from the sharp curved
beak spoke words in the owl tongue that I cannot speak for
you nor could I understand. And Small Turtle sat solemn facing the great white owl without fear and spoke back words
that were not our tongue nor the Seneca nor Shawnee nor distant Sioux nor any words I have heard man speak.

"And I crouched still where I was, not even raising my gun,
as the owl spoke again and Small Turtle again spoke in return.
And then there was a space of silence before the great white
owl stirred its claws and spread its wings thus far"—and here
the teller always spread his own arms as far as they might
stretch—"and twice thus far and flew up and away into the
blackness of the forest north. And only then did Small Turtle
cry out as one of the women, the party at last missing him, ran
into the clearing and picked him up to return him to his camp.

"And I say, brothers, there is meaning here, and Small Turtle is given powers beyond what we may know!"

"Ai-ee! It is so, it must be so!" And talk would run its way
around the fire, older braves and women and wise old men all
wondering at the story, the more because my tribe of Turtle
had no kith with owls.

Listening myself, I wondered, too. So many times have I
heard the story that I now can close my eyes and see that

great white owl, and yet I have no certain knowledge that I
ever saw it apart from the fire and the storytelling and, for
years after and even now, in dreams.

Did the breaking from my Turtle ties mean all the rending
of tribes in war and migration? Did the whiteness of that
great owl forespeak my coming closeness to the English and
the scorn some of my brothers have that I am less a true
Mohawk than a tribeless go-between, an Ishmael of this age?

Or was it, like the false or fancified remembrances of history I have questioned, simply a story blown up from nothing
to win attention and applause at the evening fire? And meaning nothing . . .

But God has spoken to men of his choosing in many strange
forms from the days of the prophets to this day and sometimes, whether in simple conceit or in hopeful understanding,
I think the white owl was some such sign to me. At the least,
truth or hunter's tale, it was a setting apart and I shall not
know until the Judgment Seat whether I have interpreted and
acted upon it wisely or like a wayward child as I know I have
been in too much else.

I grew happily.

How could a Mohawk child grow otherwise with all the
stretching wilderness for his school and his playground together?

The Indian lands ran west and south and north leagues beyond counting and there was then no question that they were
Indian lands although many questions of whose boundary ran
with another's, of hunting privileges and the like.

My own Mohawks walked proud in peace all through the
valley of the Hudson and into Massachusetts and Connecticut,
and we hunted into Pennsylvania and below the Great Lakes
according to kinship with tribes of the other Five Nations: the
Oneida, the Onondaga, the Cayuga, the Seneca and, later,
when the Five Nations became Six, the Tuscarora.

Beyond, above and below, were a hundred and more other
nations, sometimes enemies, sometimes friends; close and fa-

miliar as Shawnee and Chippewa, strange and distant as Assiniboin and Comanche and even farther nations known not even by name but by dimmed travelers' tales of Indians who lived in blazing heat on treeless plains, of other Indians in great villages carved out of mountains, of small, half-ghostly Indians holding their castles in caves of ice.

But all were, despite blood feuds and cruel wars, in some wise the same people, connected nation to adjacent nation by tribal ties—Wolf to Wolf, Turtle to Turtle, Hawk to Hawk, connected by friendship or by marriage, by treaty palaver and gifts and belts exchanged, and beyond any of this by the sure knowledge that the Maker of Earth had provided land enough for all to hunt and live upon and share freely.

There were white men, of course, but so few and so sparse in their scattering as to give little fear. Some were our brothers, some were our enemies, just as among Indians. There were the English along the coast of what they named New England and south of it. There were French then strong in the north and spread west and then south down the great river. There were Spanish to the south, but of them one heard again only uncertain travelers' tales; it was the English and the French we knew best.

And, of the two, the English we knew better.

For the French had some great hunters and trappers and even Romish priests who could breach the wilderness and live among the tribes becoming more Indian than Indians, yet they never managed so well as the English to set up villages and to keep a community spreading yet still itself a whole and part of its greater whole across the sea. Nor could they contain, like the English, other people—Indian, Dutch, German or Swedish—and make them part of their whole, like myself who still feel today as much pride in being a loyal subject of His Britannic Majesty, a holder of an honorable pension for service in his defense, as in being a Mohawk and a war chief of my own nation.

Here, I believe, after all the more subtle arguments have

been sifted and past treaties weighed, lay the real reason for a greater Indian allegiance to the English than to the French. The easy English pattern of acceptance was closer to an Indian's grasp, especially to an Indian of our Six Nations already familiar with the benefits of loose confederacy bound to common causes. This, too, and the government of the English who had been known in the past to depose and replace a king, just as a sachem grown too old and dangerously uncertain in decision might be replaced for the good of the tribe or nation. While the French King was revered far beyond his human abilities, cocked up into a kind of divinity which even a Pequot or a Pennacock would scorn as merest superstition.

I tell you this to paint the land as it was, not as I knew it, for a child is unconcerned with rulers close at hand, much less across the eye-devouring stretches of the sea.

Still, I had a cloudy knowledge in boasted heritage of such lands across the sea. It was told at our fires how the father of my father Nichaus, himself named Nichaus, had been one of four Iroquois chiefs who sailed to London in 1710 to appear at the court of the English Queen, Anne. And of them none other than William Penn said: "Unless England have the Iroquois as allies, she has nothing in America." Did I dream, running races in the woods, playing with bone buttons on lines scribed in the dust, of England and London and kings and queens and lace and lights carried by gaitered lackeys? I cannot say; the white owl had already set me apart as a stranger child, commanding others without cause yet obeyed, likely to withdraw in the heat of play (especially, I admit, if a game were going against me) to claim proudly rights of privacy and thought.

We played freely all the games of children and games not as different as I have seen ragged tads rapt at in London streets. We ran races against each other, hid and seeked, made up from nothing but collected shells games of intent complexity where each shell or pebble stood for a jewel or an empire beyond the imagining of an adult. Carrihogo, my father, brought for me cunning dolls and toys, but I clung, like any other child, to stones and smooth-rubbed twigs I had found myself and took with me every night to sleep as sacred and immutably my own.

Were these an untouched babe's clue to the Sacrament? Or as simple, aimless choice as the bird or rat collecting his jumbled nest of diversity which had to him one virtue, they were his?

As children we were kept not so close pent as white children and yet in a strange way closer. To the eye of any European visitor, it seemed we ran as wild as young fox whelps, straggling out of camps to wander the forest or field untended. But there was never a time some older eye was not on every younger child, a laddered structure of care and of direction where for every crawling infant there was a toddling child observing him, for every toddler a just older brother or sister or other child of his tribe.

In this frame I learned more of life and the forest world than campfire and shadowed tent and hutment. Carried on my mother's back or stumbling on my own small feet, three paces to my elders' every one, I made long marches following game through the Ohio lands and Pennsylvania, going back some seasons all the long way to our home settlement of Canajoharie in New York, seeing and noting and remembering many scenes and things. Among them one small, perfect space of woodland that lights my mind with all I loved most in those years of innocence.

It was a far distance from our regular hunting, a march that had taken us east and a little south into Pennsylvania. It was a bright spring day as hot as midsummer in the sun, but gently cool where great trees shaded the earth, brown and soft with ages' fall of leaves and needles, green only in small patches nourished by sun and tiny streams that fed the larger creek on whose bank we had encamped. Near to the camp I spent some time at a game I had devised with my sister Molly. I cannot recall its strict rules, only much running and laughing in and out of the irregular brightness of that hot sun, shifted by the sun's own passage and by the movement of wind among the leaves that shuttered light and shade.

We tired of the game at last and Molly went back to the lean-to of pine boughs where she kept her dolls. I sat for a while where we had played, listening to the shrill calls of birds, all the small rustles of forest lives, the splash of that crystal creek as it rushed over and between rocks, caught and launched armadas of bark and broken twigs. Its swift and diamond brightness captured my eye and I, rising from where I sat, found myself following it higher up the mountain. And there I stumbled—quite truly, for a fallen branch caught my unwary feet and almost pitched me into the rushing water— into my perfect vista.

The creek here was split into two channels by a great helter-skelter heap of rock making a peaked and craggy island no larger than a hundred paces all around it. I saw it for a tiny kingdom of my own and crossed the narrowed stream on jutting stones to claim it.

It was not all barren rock, for in some fissures flowers and bushes, fiddlehead ferns uncoiling green from silver-gray, and even a few small trees had found growth, and the stream, throwing small stones against the island shore, had made an outline of pale yellow sand all about it. My nostrils caught the thin light odor, like a cucumber fresh-sliced, that meant nearness of my Turtle cousin the copperhead. I looked with care where I tread and saw one large serpent, near two yards in length, sliding into moist growth from the rock where I had disturbed its lazy sunning.

I climbed to the rock top where I could lie in warmth and survey all my kingdom, and after perhaps an hour some subjects of my realm rewarded my watch. A great, fat she-raccoon sidled from ferns and bushes, uneasy to be abroad in daylight, yet driven by thirst or hunger, looking back over her shoulder every other step, guarding the two young raccoons she had with her, neither of them much over the size of a grown man's moccasin. She stood with them at the water's brink and showed them how to sip from the stream and cuffed them back when they teetered near to falling. With front paws as deft and delicate as any great lady at table, she turned over a flat rock and darted one hand to catch a fat crayfish. Swift-fingered, she tore its claws away, plucked it apart and plunged the bits to wash in the water before she would eat of them herself or offer a sniff and a nibble to her young.

Even as I watched her, I could see the shadows beginning to melt into dusk as the sun took its course down, far away behind the Chestnut Range. There was a sudden touch of chill in the air that matched a moment's fear within me. I had no true knowledge of how far I was away from our camp; there were animals much larger than raccoons in these parts—bears and lynxes and occasionally a wolf with his fellows. Yet I could not feel fully fearful, so sharp was my feeling that this was my own sovereign island where no harm could come. I could not bring myself to leave.

I stretched a little to ease cramped muscles and the mother raccoon darted her head toward me in alarm, but I held so still while she looked that she saw nothing amiss, perhaps just a new-shaped shadow.

Now that night was on its way she seemed surer, more comfortable, and let her children play more freely, toppling into the shallow water with high squeaks. She let them thrash and flounder about before she picked them out, shivering, and licked them toe to tail till they were warmed. Then she led them down my island bank to where a fallen tree made a narrow bridge across the creek and led them across it to the other side. I strained my eyes to track them, but lost all three in the darkness.

Now some fear came back and I was torn. Half of me would have stayed all night on that rocky eminence of this my island, waiting for other animal visitors, other wonders. Half of me shook with the cold, longed for the campfire and began to people my mind with all the scare tales of old lore, ghosts and sharp-clawed monsters of the deep forest.

I rose half to my feet to follow the stream back down to our camp, but then the half of me that was curiosity and arrogance won the battle and I sank back to my watching position.

"Small Turtle!"

I leaped a foot into the air. In all that loneliness to hear my name could only mean a cunning, hostile spirit, some resentful ghost guised as an animal, but using human speech. I stuttered mixed prayers to Manitou-Above-All and to the Great Turtle and all kindred snakes.

"Ho, Small Turtle!" the voice said again. I strained my body to hide within the rock's shadow. "It is your mother. Do you not know me?"

From beside a tree just across the creek a darker shadow moved into some slight light and it was my mother. I slid down the rock side, careless of snakes, and splashed through the creek to clasp her side.

"There, Turtle," she said. "Have no fear. You held yourself well and still the long time on that rock."

"How long had you been there, Mother?" I asked.

"Since before the old raccoon," she said. "Watching my young watching her watch her young." She laughed and led me home.

Growing up, we did more than watch animals. Early we learned to hunt them for the whole forest's populace was our larder and sustenance.

Smiling braves helped us make bows and arrows to shoot from them against our longing for a gun. The use of a bow is a great talent, especially for its silence, but it is not a tittle in comparison with the worst Pennsylvania rifle ever to come from a drunken Dutch smith of Lancaster.

Ah, a gun was all we lived for! Youngest children shot at small game with bows and older youth increased their skill so that archery would always be an art reserved against hard times, but it was a poor and unhappy boy that did not wheedle from his father some kind of gun by the time he was nine or ten.

These children's guns were often as not disastrous. We children got the leftovers—ancient muskets and crude blunderbusses and one terrible old piece of ordnance I remember well with a rusted muzzle flaring out like a bell and a habit of choking its charge and then exploding as soon as anyone peered close to the breech for inspection. It cost the skin from half a dozen young noses, and at least one eye, yet no child into whose hands it came would have thought of trading it back for a bow.

If you have any business among Indians, you will have noticed how many have only eight or nine fingers, how many are deficient of the right earlobe. These are the price paid for old guns in callow youth, fingers blown away by rusted breeches, an ear on the sighting side of the head shorn by a broken lock shot backward.

Carrihogo gave me my first gun and I can feel in my hand now its pocked octagonal barrel and the oily smoothness of its stock against my cheek. It was a flintlock of German manufacture, smooth-bored and with a lock not unlike the English brown Bess musket.

"Let us hunt!" I cried. "Let us hunt now, Father. Where we saw the deer last full moon, or where Guyatango fled from the bear."

"First you learn to know the gun, Small Turtle." Carrihogo pulled me back gently to the courtyard of the castle, where we tarried. "To hold it and to aim it and to load it. Then may we hunt, my son."

"I know all that," I cried incontinent with hunt-lust and excitement. "I have watched you and every hunter these many years. I know all that."

I kneeled and aimed the empty gun across the clearing, sighting on a patch of white stone.

"So!" I said, and with my hands pantomimed a powder

flask, poured in a charge, tamped an imaginary ball into the
barrel, aimed once again and pulled the trigger to produce a
spark, faint yellow in the day's light.

"So!" I said again, proudly.

Carrihogo took the gun from me. He kneeled more deliber-
ately, digging his right knee into the earth, bracing his left
elbow in the center of his thigh as he raised the gun.

He was a slender man of middle height with a narrow
wedge of a face as if the winds and buffeting rains of many
hunting trails had worn away all possible excess of flesh. For
all his slenderness, there was sinewed strength in all his limbs
and a sturdy firmness, especially when as now he kneeled with
the gun as if embedded into the earth, a figure in stone of flint
hardness, his breathing scarcely notable.

"Place yourself firmly, my son," he said. "Remember this always. Better to fall flat and shoot from the ground than to
hurry a kneeling shot and fire all askew."

"But the deer will be gone before I shoot," I argued.

"Not so far as it will fly when you have missed it and tumbled ass-backward," Carrihogo said. "You will practice all this
morning, learning to kneel firm, and then we may look to
loading."

I was close upon tears, but I was nine years old and past
the age of coddling. Carrihogo did not strike me nor even
raise his voice and berate me, both of which I have seen
Englishmen do in attempting to teach their sons. There was
no need for he knew I longed for mastery of the gun as much
as he desired me to master it. With both of us at work to the
same end, the only needs from him were patience and skill
and he, as a hunting Mohawk of noble blood, had both quali-
ties aplenty.

I would kneel and go through the motions of aiming and
firing, and he would kneel next to me and move the position
of the old gun a trifle on my shoulder or against my cheek,
push my elbow forward or back.

I would blurt, "Son-of-a-bitch bastard!" or "Shit!"—for by

then I had met some Englishmen—and try again remembering Carrihogo's exact movements. The sun was still a good space from its meridian when my father was satisfied with my skill.

"You learn quickly, my son," he said, touching my forehead to signal that I should stand. Pride in his voice was part of my reward, but the real reward was his handing me a small powder flask, filled, all for my own for the next stage in my learning.

With him still at my side, I learned how to measure my powder load, how to keep precisely the same measure for known force and velocity, how to gauge my sighting high and low for distant and close targets.

"Cannot a larger load send the ball truer for a distance?"

"It can, my son, but all that learning comes later," he said. "First, learn the simple ways and only when they have become your own nature, as much a part of you as smell and hearing, advance to learn more. It is the town Englishman and the settlement Indian who begins by overfilling his flashpan and ends with a misfire that ravels his face or a burst breech to tear away half his head."

By the day's end I was hitting the rolled balls of whitish clay my father set up for targets as far away as two hundred yards, not with every shot, but with a satisfying frequency.

"Tomorrow you will hunt," he said to me, and I never spent a night more fitful in sleep and filled with various dreams even in later years of peril and war.

I could scarce eat and mother had set aside for me my favorite of all foods as a child, tender young woodchuck well roasted in the coals and beans mashed with trader's meal and salt. No one teased or made sport of me, for those were still years of the old ways of respect and I believe innocence. Older boys, already hunters with their own guns, looked on me with sympathy and friendship for they had known their eve of dreams, and younger boys looked on me with envy and with hopefulness that one, who had just the day before been one of them, was sudden to become a man.

My mother's gentle coaxing saw some food taken and I sat close beside my father afterward at the fire to listen to grown men talk of hunts and war parties and great events and mysteries. It was no special night for anyone but me—not a night of dances or of masks and singing, but there was singing enough within me as I finally left to try to sleep on my treasured bearskin, jealously kept from the itinerant traders.

I had had always more than my share of dreams, from the white owl to a myriad others, and they had all been important to me for none of us of the Six Nations take dreams lightly. I have heard an Englishman speak of a dreamless sleep but I believe only that he has been careless or forgetful. From first awkward steps I was taught to make memory my tool and it has been so ever since, waking or asleep. I have never thought myself a being of such wisdom as to judge whether what the Lord (to me, in those days, Manitou) might send me in the night was less or more important than the brighter, simpler business of the day. I have tried always to remember both that both might serve me. I could write a whole book and many books besides from dreams alone, but the fashion now is for histories of wakeful hours so I shall touch only on dreaming times that match some other apex in my life.

This eve of my first hunt was surely some such time.

I dreamed of water as I had never dreamed of it before.

I dreamed of a hooded man I thought to be my father and when I struck aside his hood there was beneath it the cunning and awesome mask of a caribou man, a doctor of much magic from the north.

I dreamed of a maiden all white and I swear to you at that time I had never seen woman except of my own tribe and nation.

I dreamed of what I thought was thunder and, because I held it in my memory, I knew just four years later at Crown Point to be the sound of cannon.

I dreamed of food I had never tasted but was to taste and savor years later.

I dreamed of letters although in my dream they were but strange and puzzling signs, still years away from the A to Zed I got by heart from the Reverend Wheelock.

I dreamed of my bear fur rent into shreds under me and of the white owl to whom I cried for help and no help came and I woke still crying, and it was dawn and Carrihogo was standing beside me pointing to my gun.

I threw my sobs behind me back into my spurned childhood and scrambled to my feet.

We were five in the hunting party that morning: Carrihogo, Sagoyeh (a Seneca, but of Carrihogo's totem and a stout friend), Billy Painter and Gasunto (two Mohawks who had joined us after long sojourn far west into the lands of the Shawnee) and myself.

It was a cold morning in November and we were led by Billy Painter who had seen many deer in a linked chain of forest glades less than a day's march north toward the lakes. There was no snow, but we carried snowshoes with us and wore leggins, shirts and overshirts and packed blankets, too, against the night. The women had prepared us some food—dried meat and from my mother for me alone crushed berries tied in leaves. I had a moment's thought of pushing the berries back to her—were they not more sweets for a child than a warrior's provision?—but I did not wish to wound the kindness in her eyes and I tucked the packet in with my blanket under my burden strap of plaited bark.

We left the station singing and shouting back boasts of the beasts we would kill and the game we would bring back. Some of the children followed us a mile or more and among them my smallest brother, Daniel, killed a chipmunk with his little blowpipe. It was his first kill—not to include mice about the camp—and he held the striped body high by its tail, swelling with pride centuries beyond his five years' age. We stopped long enough to do a short dance in his honor and Carrihogo told him to save the pelt for our return to the station when we could celebrate the deed properly and combine it with our own homecoming dance and the Bear Dance which was being prepared.

The children turned back, Daniel leading them, chanting and still holding high his chipmunk.

We marched in greater silence now. Through the long morning and well into the afternoon it was country I knew for we had traversed it many times before with the whole party. We halted before fording the Pymatuning to drink of its water and then across the river we struck north, Billy Painter striding more swiftly along narrow darkening trails and into land strange to me.

"Here the deer have run," he called back. Carrihogo nodded. Sagoyeh and Gasunto nodded and Gasunto pointed for me to the stripped, gnawed bark of some saplings and the faint mark of cleft hooves in the softer earth by the trail side. I touched a finger down into one of the tracks and nodded with them. I was a hunter.

Sun slid down behind the trees and there were only its paling fingers to give us light when Billy Painter motioned for silence and all of us tread more warily in his steps, keeping still our breath, as he led us on.

He held a hand open at his back. He stopped still and we all stopped. He moved ahead and all was the even quiet of the forest which is not quiet at all but a murmuring blend of trees moved by the air, of bird sounds and of small-animal whispers. The wind was light but toward us and my nostrils stretched as I smelled quite clearly the smell of deer, of their furred bodies, of their urine and their droppings.

Then Billy Painter let his hand flicker in disgust and waved us on with him into the clearing ahead. Deer had gone, but they had been there as he had said and in great number. The whole clearing was trampled hard as stone by their hooves and there was left in it not even a tuft of dried grass or of withered leaves. Young trees were scarred and chewed bare of bark and slashed by antlers.

We stood at the edge of the clearing and Billy Painter and Carrihogo spoke together, looking at the signs.

"They have had their dance here," Billy Painter said.

"They have had their dance here and they will come back," Carrihogo said.

Billy Painter crossed his elbows No.

"They have eaten everything," he said, "they will find a new eating place."

"True," Carrihogo said, "but they will still come back to dance again. Ask Gasunto; he is of the Deer People."

Gasunto frowned. He was never a man who liked to be forced to a decision.

"They *should* come back," he said, after thought. "It is their dancing place and they should come back."

"So we shall wait near here," Carrihogo said.

Billy Painter nodded grudgingly. Gasunto and Sagoyeh nodded. I nodded, too, although I doubt I had been asked for an opinion.

We settled into a smaller clearing, perhaps a furlong back down the trail, and ate of our camp provisions without the risk of fire to warm them to more appetizing sapor. There was little talk and what there was in low voices.

"We shall hear, if they return," Carrihogo said. "Gasunto will surely hear first as a Deer Person. If they do not return by morning, Billy Painter shall lead us farther on their trail."

I checked my gun carefully, counted my bullets and covered my powder flask as protection from dew or sudden rain or snow before I curled into my English-woven blanket.

There was light in the sky, patterned through the trees, when Sagoyeh nudged me awake. I stood erect at once and packed my blanket, carefully observing his signs for silence. He had pointed toward the trail and I knew that Carrihogo and Billy Painter and Gasunto were already on the move. I made the sign for deer and for Deer Person and Sagoyeh nodded so I knew that Gasunto had wakened first at the sound of the returning deer dancers. The wind was still from the north.

We were halfway to the clearing before I could see Carrihogo and the others stealing in shadow patches along the sides of the narrow way. Even had they made a sound, there would have been no hearing them for the riot from the clearing ahead; there were the deer dancing, their hooves like drums on the hard earth, deeper thumps of colliding bodies and here and again a high squeal not unlike a whinny.

"Carrihogo was right," Sagoyeh whispered. "They have come back to dance. Hah!"

There were more deer coming to the clearing on our very trail and despite the downwind which should have been rank for them with man-smell. I crouched at the side with Sagoyeh as three young bucks, shouldering against each other in their haste, butted past, almost brushing against us; and after them a huge old buck, one side of his antlers shorn of three prongs but still moving proudly as a king, made his way with heavy, angry snorting.

Perhaps he had scented us, but whatever lure it was that drew so many deer to the clearing was too strong for his normal caution. He blundered on up the trail, careless of the whole Mohawk Nation had it been there. I saw him pass Carrihogo and Billy Painter and I saw Gasunto give him a sign of brotherhood as he passed.

I have seen men in war as foolish as these deer, rapt in some plan preconceived and refusing to change even in sure knowledge of peril. Settlers who would not leave a village full in the path of raids. Pipe-clayed English regulars forming the same rigid lines to be shot down again and again. So it was with the deer, Gasunto's brothers.

I cannot tell you why they met so in the clearing or for what reason they danced. Gasunto might have known, but I did not ask then, and there are not many like Gasunto alive today, men of an animal tribe who have kept their brotherhood in anything more than name and ceremony. It is not enough to say, "I am of the Deer People," and to dance the

Deer Dance at the proper time and mix a pinch of powdered antler in one's grog.

Men like Gasunto did all this, but they did more. There were days upon days, added up to moons together, when such men left the fireside and the castle completely and were one with their animal brothers in the wood. When they came back they did not often speak of where they had been or of what they had done, but on the hunt they knew the ways of their animal brothers; and they were brave in the hunt and proud to kill but sometimes sad to see their brothers die. I am not sure it is so today with men and men even, and I know it is no longer true with men and beasts.

The old buck was the last on our trail and after a wait Sagoyeh and I caught up with the others, close against large trees at the edge of the clearing.

We still spoke in whispers although I think we might have shouted and no deer would have heard. My own heart's pounding seemed to me loud enough to reach back to the station.

"Are they all here?" Carrihogo asked Gasunto.

"They are all here now," Gasunto said. He stood proud by a great elm to watch so many of his people in such an important dance.

"Then be ready," Carrihogo said, unscrewing the top of his powder flask.

He made the least motion of a hand before he raised his own gun and then we were all firing.

I saw my first shot strike the breast of a dancing buck and then I was reloading as the sounds of the dance changed from drum-thump to high, choked cries of terror and anger. Deer fell as fast as we could shoot and reload and shoot again. I saw the old buck from our trail clamber over a fallen doe and head for an opening at the far side of the clearing, as I shot another younger buck. The old king, too tough for savory, could live as many more seasons as his tribe allowed him. Fire and load and fire.

Two bucks were locked in combat just in front of me, confused by the shots and the slaughter, each one blaming the other; an easy moral here. I brought the nearest one down and the other fell with it, caught by his antlers.

I looked to Carrihogo and he motioned me leave, so I darted out from the tree and clubbed the second fallen buck with my tomahawk. I struck above one rolling eye and the blade clove through easily to his brain; drops of warm blood spurted and spotted my face and I felt for that second less a Turtle than brother to Gasunto and all the lately dancing deer.

"Heigh!" I heard Sagoyeh cry and I turned and ran for the protection of my tree and none too soon. Another buck smashed horn angrily against the trunk just as I reached safety behind it and picked up my gun again.

The clearing held only a few live deer now, rushing panicked among the fallen bodies of their fellows. Aiming was difficult. I wasted one shot, my first miss of the hunt, but sent another true. Carrihogo downed still another buck and Gasunto sent a missed ball flying after the last of his brothers to flee the trap.

There were a score and six deer slain and lying in the clearing, a heroic toll from five hunters, one of them a stripling, and in only a few minutes of shooting. It was a hunt to tell over again many times.

It was not midmorning yet, but with so many carcasses there was a day's work to be done. Carrihogo had sent Sagoyeh, the swiftest runner among us, back to the station to bring help for transporting the meat. Now he and Gasunto and Billy Painter and I set to work skinning and cutting.

We stood guard in turn over the clearing all the night, first Carrihogo, then Gasunto, then Billy Painter, then myself. The scent of so much slaughtered flesh on any wind would bring scavengers and it was a rich harvest of meat we did not plan to lose for our stores. I woke twice before my own watch at the sound of Gasunto firing at a prowling fisher (and missing it) and at Billy Painter bringing down a curious marten.

I have had many Englishmen ask me, including the writer Mr. Boswell in London, how, without watches or clocks or even sandglasses, we kept track of the time for such matters as these night watches and other boundaried occasions. It is, I believe, a matter of a faculty in Indians and perhaps among other persons removed from civilization which is hardly possible of explanation to anyone brought up in a world of waistcoat pocket chronometers and ornamental mantel clocks. Living without these, we had the course of the sun by day and the moon by night, and besides them our own experience of passing time. Now, grown used to looking at hands traversing a dial, I should not trust myself to split a night into equal segments, but then I knew quite well, as did my father and our companions, how to gauge such division. But it is an art easily lost by ill practice and lazy dependence on cogged wheels and sprung trickery. (For all of which I would not have you think I was ready to give up my own mantel clock of Mr. Thomas of Plymouth, Connecticut, and as handsome and accurate as any English or Dutch clock you might set against it.)

My gun was primed and loaded and at my side. I sat with my back to an aged, shag-barked locust tree at the higher end of the clearing, the piled skins, the meat, the horns and hooves clear to my vision in the light of a half moon. A still night and slow watching.

Two small owls of the kind called saw-whet from their cry flew down to explore the deer carcasses and I threw some pebbles to frighten them away, but lightly and friendly in memory of my great white owl of their tribe.

By my reckoning it was still that time from first dawn that it would take a man to walk easily two English miles.

I set myself to think about guns and if my share of the day's furs might be enough to get a truly new gun from the next trader's visit, one of the rifled bores that kept its ball in truer flight and mayhap some ornament on the metal trim, or a blank space where a graver might etch a turtle or even "Joseph," the English name some had taken to calling me.

It had been at a trader's visit when I was gaping at his wares; needles and spinning tops of bright silver, mother-of-pearl boxes for snuff, glasses that showed you back your own face. I thought I had found all the splendor of the world, but I was eldest of the children crowding around and I held my own dignity and kept them back from touching and plucking at the wares.

"And who may all these be, Chief?" the trader asked me in a jest. "Your tribe?"

"My brothers," I said, for some of them were blood brothers and all were Mohawk.

"Joseph and his brothers, verily," he said, and the other white man with him laughed.

I had no Bible knowledge then, but I liked the "Joseph" sound and told the story to my mother who liked the sound, too, and it was not long before I was as much Brant's Joseph as Small Turtle.

I did not yet know to write my name, but I knew there was a mark for Joseph and I thought it would look mightily grand cut into the lock of a clean new rifle. My eyes were still open, but my thoughts were not with them.

I do not know how long the intruder had been at the venison. All I knew was that suddenly my eyes came into focus and away from my geegaw dream and it seemed a great beast was rending our precious meat, throwing torn and bloody chunks from side to side as it plundered and feasted.

I plucked my gun from where it leaned, leveled, aimed and fired. A wild roaring split the air as I blew the lock and poured in a fresh charge, trembling rammed a ball to place and aimed again, shouting into the din: "Carrihogo! Gasunto, Billy! A lion! A painter!"

I had made a hit on my first shot, but only a wounding hit. The enraged beast snarled and wheeled about the meat and then, at the sound of my shout, turned toward me and charged.

I swear it seemed as immense as a bear coming at me but I held myself firm and let off my next shot full into it. Carrihogo, gun in hand, was rushing toward me. Gasunto and Billy Painter were not far behind him. I had fallen quickly to one side as soon as I had fired, for even a dead painter with claws extended can maim and kill whatever it blindly strikes.

I had shut my eyes tight awaiting the rending impact.

I opened them on Carrihogo's broad laughter.

"A lion!" he said. "Brothers, see how Small Turtle's ball has shrunk the mighty painter. Billy, view your brother turned tiny." I let my eyes open fully and follow Carrihogo's gaze. The beast I had killed was no more than a woods lynx, a spotted, stripe-whiskered cat no longer than an arm's stretch.

I mumbled apologies and asked forgiveness for waking weary hunters before their time.

"Not to worry," Gasunto said, checking his own laughter. "Older braves than you have seen small beasts grown great at the end of a cold night watch."

"And it is a fine pelt," Carrihogo said. "A fine pelt all your own that should bring a good return from Trader Shiras or one of Croghan's men."

My spirits rose as quickly as they had fallen.

"Enough for a gun?" I asked.

"With the rest of your share it may be," Carrihogo said.

Sagoyeh was back before midday with a party of ten men. We had already cut saplings and branches for them to bind with the bark rope they brought and make carriers and skids for the hunt's yield. We helped them load and pressed our march and reached the station for an evening feast and, as Carrihogo had promised, we danced for my brother Daniel's chipmunk and we danced the Bear Dance and we danced for my first hunt and we danced for my lynx which made it the easier for me to bear Carrihogo's telling several times how I had cried "Lion!" and "Painter!"

There were other hunts before the first snow flew that winter and I killed a bear on one hunt and finally did see a mountain lion (it was Weenanah, a Mingo of the Heron Tribe, however, who killed it) and had many adventures, but none so deeply burned into my memory as that first hunt.

The first snow was light, but the wisest man of our party, old Bundus, a Mohawk of the Beavers, who knew weather well over three score years, shook his head and said that the winter would be cruel. Carrihogo with Sagoyeh and perhaps half a dozen others was determined to hold the hunting territory along the Ohio, but he agreed to old Bundus's recommendations that the rest of the party, the women and the children and braves to travel with them, were better off returning to our home castle of Canajoharie.

Castle was the name the English had given to our permanent settlements, part peaceful community, part fortress, that dotted the Iroquois country from Albany to the west. Our two chief Mohawk castles were the Upper Castle at Canajoharie and the Lower Castle less than a day's march south at Fort Hunter.

I had been at the castle other winters before and I looked forward to the bustle and excitement of its people and to the comforts it offered. Yet I was torn, for the hunt had changed me and I did not fear the harshness of winter if I could be sure of spending it with my father and his braves bringing down more deer, even buffalo and above all the marten and mink and ermine whose skins were so prized for barter.

But Carrihogo had decided and there was no argument. With my mother and my sister Molly and my brothers Daniel and Canadiora and Ganeteh and other children and women and braves, I set forth back to Canajoharie. One piece of good fortune: Trader Shiras had come by our station soon after my first hunt and my lynx pelt along with my deerskins had purchased me the new rifle, a beautiful gun of the Tower Lock type with a stud for attachment of a bayonet at its end. I do not know whether I owned that gun or it owned me, but with it I held to my right to march with the braves on the journey home and arrived in early December at the castle, as assured a warrior at ten as I have ever thought myself since, nay more so.

The Canajoharie castle was a fine place with well-built longhouses for different tribes and segments, a clearing post for news of all the nations, of wars and raids and hunting north and south and west.

A family lived more closely in itself here than in the forests. We listened to long stories from my mother and other women and some old men. All the children were earnest listeners to any tale of war or of animals and ghosts, but I found myself together with Molly (three years my elder) in special fascination with stories of the Confederacy itself, of how the chief and sachem Hiawatha brought the five first nations into a league that gave them strength and honor more than any single nation before.

Molly would take out all her dolls (and a vast store she had, rag and wood and bone and three china-faced figures from the traders) and call them her own confederacy, the which, she said (I can remember the quaintness of her gravity, for she was then just a plump, small girl, but she sat in the firelight as stern as Chief Hendrick), was "bigger than the Six Nations, and of it the Mohawks are always best, and it is greater than England or France or Spain."

"And I am a war chief!" I egged her on.

"You are a war chief," she allowed me, "but I am queen like the English Anne."

Our brother Canadiora (to die the next year of a pest) hooted laughter, but I cuffed him since I saw no joke and easily believed everything Molly said. For she not only retold tales, but she listened to me when I wished to tell her my dreams and fears and some things I thought too light or too strange to bear to our mother.

I gave Molly some help too in the only matter where I ever knew her to be lost, in times of thunder and of lightning. In all other affairs, even as a small child, Molly was as fearless as any war party pine-tree chief, but the rumble of thunder in the air, the rolling of its echoes among our mountains, flashes of bright skybolts and their kindred balls of spinning fire which I have seen trim all the bark from one side of a high oak tree—these reduced her to the most timorous and helpless of creatures. Such times I let her roll herself into my prized bearskin, covering even her head, and I petted her trembling shoulders and soothed her with every kind of talk till the storm was over and she might uncoil and become once again imperious queen.

Though I missed Carrihogo, I took in his absence some part of being man of our family, and this made me proud and glad, teaching little Daniel to hold the gun I had put aside for my new rifle.

Also I was glad to be at Canajoharie, for the winter was quite as cruel as old Bundus had predicted. We reached the castle before the first heavy storms, but providentially, for after we were installed in our longhouse there was no ceasing to storms for day upon day. Snow was higher than my head around the longhouses and, where open fields gave scope to wind, it drifted into hummocks ten and fifteen feet high where castle cattle stumbled and froze and died and not a few Mohawks with them.

There had always been some hunting from the castle, but it had not been a necessity most years. At Canajoharie our people farmed the land and kept kine and pigs so that the hunt was, as in England where lords chase stags and foxes, a sport and not a staple. With the snows of this winter, it was again a harsh need and my new-blooded talent in demand. Early mornings I would strap on snowshoes and go forth with older braves over the crusted white for whatever game we could find. There were no deer and few large animals of any kind that had not either fled the snow or gone to winter sleep. One hunt we did flush a sleepy, furious bear, which was great good fortune. More usually we were happy and grateful for the handful of big-footed rabbits we could kill and for other small game and birds.

The hunts were hard and treacherous with snow crust that gave way often even under wide snowshoes. I saw one good hunter die when he crashed through a house-high drift and it took us, a party of seven stretched in a line and holding on one to the other, all an afternoon to reach him and drag him back too late to the slippery surface. I saw other hunters lose toes and fingers to the frost and came near losing a toe myself one freezing hunt of three days' length. When I got back to the longhouse—three rabbits and a lean muskrat to show for my pains—the great toe of my right foot had no more feeling than a lump of putty. And after I had handed over my bag and set to cleaning my gun, it then began to throb and burn so that I was ready to slice it from the foot and had even a knife in my hand to do this when Hockasute, an elder chief wise in medicine, stayed me and as I gnashed my teeth bathed the whole foot in snow-water for an hour and more till the throbbing abated. It was a day and another day more before it left off aching entirely, but, thanks to Hockasute, I still today have five toes on each foot.

And along with the hunts the blazing fires in the longhouses and the dances of every tribe and special dances to placate the wickedness of the weather and ask for an early spring. For such paganism I should ask forgiveness, I suppose, did I not, O Father, know now enough divines who hold my ignorance in those days as good as primal innocence. And I have met others who say that because we sang to Manitou as One God, a mysterious Maker of earth and man, we were not far from true faith and a sight better than ancient pagan Greeks and Romans with their statues and dirty temple abominations; I appreciate their rationale, Lord, but I know (as do Thee) other rites of ours not so simple nor so clean and for these I ask Your forgiveness in the privacy of prayer while I forbear to trouble the Noble Savage philosophers with unsavory details.

Beyond all else perhaps I remember that winter best for being the time I first saw Sir William Johnson.

We had heard already of William Johnson, of course, even in the West. We had heard of him as a fair man and a trader and a clearer of land for farming who still was an Indian friend. Soon after, we heard of him as a man taken into our own councils, adopted as a Mohawk and by no chief less than Tiyanoga, Chief Hendrick himself. He had been adopted at this very castle, bathed and scrubbed in the Mohawk River, painted and made flesh and bone with us under the name Warraghiyagey, Man-Who-Does-Much. He spoke the Mohawk tongue and bedded Mohawk maids and had built his new home, Fort Johnson, only a brisk morning's march from Canajoharie. The English King George had made him Superintendent of Indian Affairs and he was among the few men dealing with us whose word was as good as the word of another Indian. And yet, though he spoke Mohawk and held rank among us, tales told he was as little like an Indian as could be—loud, laughing and crying as the spirit moved him, no more given to the dignity of a chief than a clown.

Oh, yes, we had heard of William Johnson, but it is one thing to hear of a notable man and another to meet him.

He had sent grain and other provisions from Fort Johnson to aid us during the hard winter. Now, with the beginning of spring thaws, he came himself.

Snow and ice were melting, but it was still a cold day of March and he came to Canajoharie with a longish coat of buckskin over another long surcoat of good green velvet (but faded) with brocaded trimmings at the neck, buckskin breeches and high stout boots. He was a tall man, almost six feet (a good two inches over my own tallest growth), with gray-blue eyes lively yet deep-set in a comfortably fleshed face. Mostly he wore a wig, but I remember that first sight of him with his own brown hair still dark and worn long, a little in Indian fashion.

He walked among the longhouses with sachems at his side

and talked constantly, about mischief the French were stirring up by the Great Lakes, about plans for spring planting, about a lame boy of eight (a nephew of Gasunto's) whom he wanted to take back to Fort Johnson to see a white doctor, about the sharp tongue of his woman Catherine, about one of the Schuylers (great landowners to the east) who had been drunk three days on end as Johnson's guest.

"Fuddled with grog, fuddled with grog, damme!" He roared laughter telling the story. "So he'd his eye on a rosy little serving girl, fresh from Sussex, and I fed him more wine and more brandy and let him fondle her upon his lap. Betimes, his head began to fall on his chest, so I had two of my braves carry him up to bed, but not with the pretty wench. No, brothers, I kept her aside for myself and bedded down next to the patroon old Becker's squaw, Miranda, the ugliest woman white or Indian between Boston port and Kittanning.

"So he wakes in the morning, more than some queasy you may guess, but remembering the wench and feeling warmth next to him and he with the swollen pecker of a night's carouse, hah! He reaches over and finds himself face to face with Miranda.

"Screech? I've heard a brave with a tomahawk into his head whisper by comparison. He was out of bed and down the stairs, still in his long nightshirt and ready to fly into the snow.

"I held him back and soothed him down with a claret cup. He still believes the drink sent his sight askew and he chose Miranda as a beauty. They tell me back in Albany he's drinking nothing stronger than tea and canting chastity at every church service."

The tall man doubled with laughter till tears formed in his eyes and the sachems laughed with him. It was not so often you found a white man who told scurrilous jokes on his own people. Johnson told hardly any other kind of joke and told them on everyone—Indian, Englishman, clergyman, trader, captain of soldiers and on himself.

". . . and the fresh Sussex wench I thought I had to myself," he wound up his tale, "I found two nights later spread on the pantry floor and entertaining a party of your young bucks, Red Head!"

The chief, Red Head, allowed himself a thin smile as Johnson doubled into fresh laughter.

"Now, about the stores"—he unbent and spoke as soberly as if no anecdote had intervened—"the corn should be brought to higher ground at once. The Mohawk is rising visibly. By tomorrow it will be at the sheds . . ."

I tagged along, listening with other boys and a few girls old enough to have tricked themselves about with beads and oiled and plaited their hair in hope of attracting the superintendent's lickerish eye.

I understood less than half of what he said but it was good to listen to so tall and splendid a man with such a riotous outpouring of words. I had no thought then that my life would be linked with his nor, I believe, did my sister Molly, but I noted that she stood near enough to watch and hear when Sir William spoke.

It was spring and I was ready to return to Ohio for more hunting with Carrihogo, but the chiefs of our longhouse ruled otherwise.

"It is time you knew something more than hunting," Red Head told me. "There is planting and care of cattle and much else a man should know. These are strange times, and a boy growing into them cannot learn too much. Besides, you are a Turtle and you have neglected your tribe lore; this much I know from your mother. You and your brother Ganeteh must sit with Gray Diamond and grow to be worthy of your sign."

Gray Diamond was an important Snake Person and he sat solemnly many mornings with Ganeteh and myself telling us the power and meaning of the Turtle and of all his kindred from the harmless bright green grass snake to the rattlesnake whose marking was Gray Diamond's own sign. And of all the turtles whose slowness is the slowness of wisdom, who can shut out the world from their armored homes and who can break a grown man's wrist with one jaw snap when they are aroused. And of a myriad lizards in every rainbow color from dazzling red to yellow and green and purple, living silently by stream banks and under rocks and noting all that passes them, good and evil, and surviving long after all has passed.

These were my people among the animals and it was Gray Diamond who helped me to their wisdom. I told him my dreams and he helped me with them, too.

Most of my dreams, when he had unfolded them and set them against their proper meanings, were simple, but some were not. I told him my dreams before the first hunt and he furrowed his forehead and drew anxious lines in the ember dust of his fire.

He did not like the dream of the caribou man I had thought to be my father.

"Not father," he said. "Not father, but son, Joseph. And, because the caribou is as far as possible from the Turtle it is an evil dream. I see blood and sadness there, but I can see nothing clearly."

Nor did he like the dream of the rent bear fur and the white owl that could not help me.

"It is another dream too far away from me," he said. "You should not have dreams like that, my son."

"But I cannot choose my dreams, Gray Diamond."

"I know that well," he said, more kindly. "It is my own ignorance I rage against. For your white owl is all enemy of the Turtles, yet from dream and story is your friend. Little wonder the bear robe is torn, but what its tearing may truly mean is beyond me."

And he only shook his head when I told him the dream of the maid so shiningly white.

So, though I learned much from his teaching, it also troubled me.

We were mostly at the castle for the next two years. My sister Molly had in a matter of months shed all her girl-plumpness and young men, braves and English traders and some officers commenced to swarm near her like spring flies to a comb of honey left on the board. This pleased her some, I think, but she encouraged no one and seemed to practice holding herself unusual straight and talking much with wives of chiefs in other tribes who came to visit the castle.

When Carrihogo, on one of his visits home, spoke of a Miami chief as a staunch ally to France, Molly raised her head and said: "O my father, I think he is but playing with the Joncaires till he gets the powder they have promised. Then he will take his braves far back for he is a man most fearful of war."

Carrihogo twitted her for talking beyond a girl's knowledge, but when he was next home he admitted all had come about as she had foretold.

"I find I can learn much from talking to my own sex," she said. "Just here at Canajoharie I have met knowing women from as far as the grounds of the Cherokees."

"It is as desirable for a good woman to know much as for a foolish woman to know nothing," Carrihogo said, pleased with her subtleties.

She was still close friend as well as sister, and me too she pumped for any news I heard of our people in the western lands. And this I enjoyed, and having more instruction from my father when he was home, but the castle began to weary me.

Boys slightly older could enjoy sampling the rum brought in by Dutch or English (all against the pleas of the chiefs that it was an evil corrupting our people to sloth and maniac revelry) or could entertain themselves with girls (for before marriage there was great freedom in respect of copulation; adultery after wedlock, however, might still be rewarded with whipping of the woman, sometimes to death). But I was too childish to have a taste for spirits and not quite curious enough to try myself with a woman, so I had long black spells, what English call "the dumps," of sitting sullen wishing I were anywhere else, doing anything else than what I had to do at the castle.

Some planting I learned and a little of caring for our domestic animals. I learned the time of moon for best planting of corn and how to dry it and store it in pits or sheds when it was harvested. I learned how to make a slow fire, the best of hickory, for the women to smoke and dry meat. I learned to help a cow in difficulty birthing and some balms of wild plants to soothe their sore udders.

I learned almost everything that interested me not at all, but I accepted it because it was my elders' law.

That fall there was a flaring up of excitement when one of our hunting parties stumbled upon a ranging band of seven Hurons with two Frenchmen among them fomenting disaffection to the English Crown and general mischief. Our own party was of only four braves and they hurried back to the castle and a larger force put out, I among them.

We caught up with the Hurons below Scanadaga Lake, surrounding them quite easily as they tarried over camp in a small valley. There were twenty-three in our band and we raked the valley with fire, killing two Hurons and one of the Frenchmen before they threw their weapons to the ground and surrendered meekly. There was cover, even in the valley, where a real warrior might have hidden and worked his way out no matter how many guns leveled by a foe; I do not think a Mohawk party would have been taken so easily.

Three others of the Hurons were wounded, one with an arm half falling from his shoulder. We drove them back before us to Canajoharie with the boys younger than myself, four gunless youths who had been allowed to tag behind the war band, throwing stones at them and gibing at their clumsiness. And it is true that the brave with the shattered arm was a ludicrous sight, shambling and tripping from side to side, gouts of blood spurting when his one good arm lost its grip on its wounded mate. To his credit he did not cry out, but he fell and died from loss of blood before the homeward trip was halfway done and the boys were unhappy, cheated of further sport.

Nor did they (or any of us) have the usual pleasure of testing our remaining prisoners with any trials of torture at the castle. No sooner did word get to Fort Johnson than Sir William was among us with a band of English soldiery, taking them away for questioning and later (as I learned) for exchange against some of our own braves held in captivity by the French. Sir William, being Sir William, did not cheat us entirely; himself a Mohawk of the nation, he knew we had been looking forward to a feast with the torturing so he paid us for the prisoners with food and drink from his own stores and with squares of English cloth (each one large enough for a good shirt) for every member of the war party.

Our Huron trespassers, according to fireside rumor, were more than an isolated foray. War talk was stirring all along the verge of English influence. There had been peace between France and England since shortly after my birth but papers signed in Aix-la-Chapelle had no great currency in the Mohawk Valley. Even while I fretted at Canajoharie, French and their Indian allies had leveled the English trading post at Pickawillany on Lake Erie and fortified its site into their Fort Presque Ile. And elsewhere too were there troubled councils and lawless raids from side to side for cattle or guns or strategic land or sheer devilment.

That first war, ended at Aix-la-Chapelle, had been an eight-year squabble over the succession to the throne of Austria, a European matter stretching its tentacles of fire and death all across the sea to our continent. The new war brewing now in 1754 was a pretty reversal of the first; it was the boundaries between French and English claims in America that sparked its tinder into flame on battlefields of Europe and as far a distance as Plassey in India. In Europe it was styled the Seven Years War for its duration; in America it was the French and Indian War, I know not why since Indians fought on either side. Wherever, it was to shift old alliances, shake men's minds and hearts, realign vast boundaries on either side the ocean.

Concerning land closer to home, we had worries beyond any great policies of France and England. Philip Livingston, of that family as prolific and devastating as the locust, was with his brother William once again pressing a claim to possession of our castle territory. A score of years back, he had cozened three braves, far gone in drink which he had treated them, to sign a paper ceding him not only Canajoharie itself, but all the arable land about it. The signers had no right to make any such conveyance, even had they been paramount chiefs (which they were not), and Philip Livingston was baldly using his position as New York's Secretary of Indian Affairs to loot the very tribes entrusted to his care, but he still held the document valid and had even sent surveyors (a treacherous breed) to measure off the land secretly by night. Sir William, as Superintendent of Indian Affairs for all the colonies, protested and held off the Livingston claim, but every now and again Philip or William Livingston made effort to press it through. It was as if, visiting London, I had got a fuddled drayman to sign me rights to St. James's Palace and then bribed and bullied a court of law to hold the agreement binding.

I listened and I was not so young that I did not find it in me to think some on what I heard. As to the French rumors, I had no doubts to trouble me. The Six Nations, and especially the Mohawks, stood with England in any such division. It was to the English Queen Anne that my grandfather Brant had made his visit with the other chiefs and it was to the Georges that followed her we held respect.

The Livingston matter was different, for there were other Englishmen who used the same tricks against us and, often as not, such tricks were upheld even by Englishmen more honest and decent. Yet I knew Mohawks I would not trust behind my back and it seemed false to set a different standard for other men.

Thus were two different trains set up in my growing mind. One, the consideration of large national interests, England and France, the colonies' own special claims, the role of our Iroquois Confederacy in all. The other, the matter of land I could see and walk upon being Indian or English, free and open for hunting and communal tillage or closed by English laws of ownership against all but one man or family.

The thought of ownership was as clear to Europeans as it was impossible of understanding to most Indians. For as many centuries as most kingdoms of Europe could count recorded history, Indian tribes had roamed and warred and had a living from the rich land without any more need of boundaries than loose treaty agreements over hunting rights. To protect himself, an Indian must learn something of the strange new doctrine of landholding, yet do so while still keeping faith with laws and traditions of tribe and nation. Hard thoughts brought to bubble in a boy's troubled mind.

I was twelve now and in the spring Carrihogo came again to Canajoharie and I would go with him, first to the great council at Albany, then back to the Ohio hunting grounds.

Chiefs from every tribe and nation had been called to the conference which was the whole boiling over of both the French and the Livingston matters I have mentioned. Hunting chiefs like my father were important for their intelligence of what was afoot in the Ohio lands and the Canajoharie sachems to contend claims like that of Livingston. In addition there were representatives of Crown settlements come to settle their own boundary rivalries. Both Massachusetts and Connecticut laid claim to the same parts of land as did Pennsylvania and New York. Royal charters, drawn up by men to whom this whole continent was but an ill-made map, had as little substantiality as a man's breath on a cold looking-glass yet carried all the immutable authority of English law.

I had thought our Canajoharie castle was a settlement of some size and complexity, but it was nothing to prepare me for the vastness of Albany. I had sat listening at more than one council, but they were children chattering in a corner to compare with the Albany deliberations. I had seen carousing when a trader doled out rum for pelts, but I had seen a sober congregation at meeting house against the boozing, shouting, cursing, vomiting routs of this June and July.

John Lydius, sometime an aide of Johnson's, now more a double-dealing opponent, had set up one whole house as dispenser of spirits to any Indian who would drink and most cordially to any Indian (never matter what their rights and connections with the question) who would confirm the Connecticut claim to the whole Wyoming Valley of Pennsylvania. (I had no dreams of that valley while I tarried in Albany, no hint of its linkage so unjustly with my own reputation.)

No farther from Lydius than I could throw a small stone, the trader Conrad Weiser had a grogshop of his own where he got actual signs on parchment of tipsy Indians deeding him (for £400 squandered as quickly as he had paid it over) the whole expanse north and west of the Susquehanna River as far as it might stretch even to the western sea. All this being fantasy and comedy to write about, but acted out as seriously as if such promises and claims were real.

Among the royal agents there was argument and attempts at some common action. Mr. Franklin of Pennsylvania put forth a scheme for a federation of all colonies and modeled it most closely (giving credit as he did so) on the institutions of the Iroquois. "It would be a strange thing," he told his fellow Englishmen, "if Six Nations of ignorant savages could be capable of forming a scheme for such a union, and be able to execute it in such a manner as that it has subsisted ages and appears indissoluble; and yet that a like union should be impracticable for ten or a dozen English colonies." Johnson stood with the Pennsylvanian in the matter, but it fell to pieces in the bureaus of London politics.

Of Indians, it was our old Chief Hendrick who spoke most and best and to the principal point; to wit, was our support of

England to be a matter of all devotion and no reward, of blind loyalty to a power which took happily its profit from our hunting and trapping but would not support us with the forts and forces we had to have to hold the French and their Indian allies at a distance? He was of our nation and too proud a man to use blackmail, but he raised the question clear: How long could the Iroquois League continue staunch with England did England make no effort to cement the bond? If William Johnson were given full power for Indian dealings, he said, there was some hope. Without him, there were nations of the league already half beguiled by the French who could turn all the way.

I believe my father had some doings with such talk. I know he was closeted long with Hendrick and Johnson, telling them of what movements he had seen to the west. And his warnings had rude confirmation for before the conference was done there was news of the French rout of young Captain Washington's ill-managed forces at Great Meadows and their unhindered erection of Fort Duquesne at the forks of the Ohio.

Here first I saw Sir William's devotion to bringing chiefs and tribes and nations together without either crude bribery or the threats of force popular with other English leaders. He showed as much care and understanding of some petty jealousy between Oneida and Cayuga as if it had been a king's treaty written on parchment. And, with all such cares, finding time to pat my boy's head and ·say to my father: "A fine whelp, Carrihogo. Your own fighting blood, I'll vow!"

I took this compliment deep into me to treasure and ever after at Albany Sir William stood a little taller and finer in my eyes. And ever after that.

The best that the conference accomplished was a consolidation of Johnson's position. For the rest, it ended as much a shambles as it had begun with even Chief Hendrick taken drunk in Lydius's groggery and signing concurrence of the Connecticut claim.

Between this folly and the French victories, Sir William was in a black mood. He bid farewell to Carrihogo and other chiefs at the same time he sent a sobered and rueful Hendrick off to Philadelphia to undo his tipsy penmanship.

"Season of folly, brothers," he said. "Young Washington has let his own gluttony for fame lead his head into the French noose and now every tribe from Moncton to Ottawa will be supping with the Joncaires, ready to sign blind treaties with a winning side. We must do what we can to check this tide, my brothers. The King's government moves like a gut-bloated bear in winter for all his coat of arms carries a lion. We must buy what time we can till I have enough force to take the field in earnest." He bent his gaze on Carrihogo and other war party chiefs. "Harry the Frog-eaters where you can and when, brothers!" he said in a shout. "Smite them hip and thigh as the Holy Scriptures entreat us and scalp both them and their renegade redskin partners. Fire and gun and hatchet, brothers! I shall be dancing the war dance at Canajoharie, but I shall expect blood on your blades before I even reach the castle!"

Carrihogo shouted agreement and I shouted with him. We left at once, by horse, for the castle and stopped just long enough to gather arms and provisions before going on west, a war band of thirty braves, myself the youngest with one Gabriel, a Christian son of Red Head, fourteen, nearest to my age.

Carrihogo set us a fast pace and kept us to trails not likely to abut with French or Huron parties.

"Here are enough of the Six Nations to protect our boundaries," he said. "We might gain a scalp or two for the King's bounty and our own fame, but William Warraghiyagey's needs are more important. We will shame the French on their own borders and among their own allies."

We turned south below Cattaraugus Creek and soon after came upon traces of another party. Carrihogo's sharp eyes caught the lightness of small twigs broken from tree trunks by passersby brushing against them.

"There have been travelers before us," he said. "Now look carefully and listen carefully. The new French fort at Picka-willany is only a day's march away. Let your eyes be every-where, brothers."

And before we had marched another hour, it was my old hunting companion Gasunto who discovered the marks of a fire just a few paces off the trail. It was a day or more gone since its use, and it had been covered for concealment with some fresh earth and leaves but not skillfully enough to elude Gasunto's perception.

"These shavings are cut as the Oneidas make their fires," Carrihogo said, stirring the ashes with a stick and pointing to some unburned traces at the embered edge. "Yet I had thought we would find Hurons here . . ."

"I have seen in far hunting some Ojibways build a fire just thus," Gasunto said.

"It is Huron," said a brave. "It is Huron from the broad leaves used to cover."

"I have seen Shawnee use cover of broad leaves," another brave said.

"Not to cover fires," Gasunto argued. "Perhaps to cover their own dirt?"

"Do you mean, brother, that I cannot tell shit from ashes?" the brave was indignant.

Another warrior, very old and wrinkled, pushed forward.

"You are all wrong, brothers," he said. "It is a fire of Mingos traveling with women. Mingo women keep their fires thus, always a neat circle."

The discussion went on and on. A Mohawk will not inter-rupt a man who is speaking (unless he be gone in drink or anger), so much time passed with no real decision. I read in the journals today and hear white men (and even some old Indians) talk about the Indian faculty for telling at a glance how this arrow must have been fired by a warrior of that tribe, this fire built by that particular nation, this belt strung by such-and-such a wampum artificer and I am constrained to quiet laughter. I have been on so many trails with so many parties in just such a situation as the one I describe. And always there have been a dozen to twenty different opinions of signs along the trail, and always, when the hunt or the raid is over, the story is retold in some wise like this: "Then did the great hunter Hoohaw look at the fire and say: 'It is a band of Mingos that have passed here less than two hours ago—five braves, two women, two children and one gray goose. The oldest brave has a sore on his right cheek from poison of the oak and we will find them camping in the northeast corner of Salt Lick clearing roasting their goose.' And so it came to pass."

The braves were still arguing when young Gabriel cried "Heugh!" from the edge of the clearing where he had been pissing into a clump of ferns.

No one paid him attention except myself for I was wearying of the long talk.

"What?" I asked.

"Heugh!" he cried again. "Look with me, Joseph. I think I've found a sign better than shavings."

He pointed at a round ball, the precast bullet for a rifle, lying by the ferns.

"Carrihogo!" we called. "Gasunto! Look!"

It took them a moment to break off from their deliberations and in the moment Gabriel and I could see clearly on the ball the three-leaved stamp of the French flower that marked many of the balls used by King Lewis's *couriers du bois*.

"So, French and Huron," Carrihogo said. "They cannot be far. Let us move on swiftly, but silently. We can march into the night and catch them unawares."

"Let them wake tomorrow morning without their scalps," Gasunto chuckled.

Carrihogo split our party into two parts and, to Gabriel's and my disgust, we were put into the slow-moving second part for carrying the bulk of provisions.

We marched all the night and when we caught up with

Carrihogo and his band there was sunlight touching on the mirror of Chautauqua Lake and beside it two dead Frenchmen and seven dead Hurons, all nine of them greeting the morning as scalpless as Gasunto had predicted.

Carrihogo described in detail how he and his men had sighted a wisp of campfire smoke from a mile away, had then stolen without a sound upon the sleeping Hurons and their French friends and slaughtered them before they could know whether their wounds were dream or reality. I know that many Europeans think nothing of a martial encounter that does not begin with a roll of drums and alert confrontation on both sides, but for sensible economy there is much to be said for our Iroquois tactics.

I had always had pride in my father, but I had the more then and of a new kind, for I was seeing him a chief and a wise leader in matters of life and death. I marked each word that he spoke describing the raid, where he and his men had taken cover, how wide a gap they left to cover before they made their rush, and like details. All this wisdom of Carrihogo's was to serve me much advantage later and to be used to his honor.

Carrihogo and Gasunto debated whether to leave the corpses as a warning or to hide them and keep our secrecy so much the longer. The latter decision was taken and Gabriel and I helped gut the bodies for easier sinking in the lake. We filled the hollowed bellies with all the small stones we could find and sewed them up again with bark lacing. It took us half the morning, under Gasunto's direction, to float the bodies on joined logs to where the lake waters were deep enough for concealment and there to topple them overside. Booty was divided fairly and I got from one of the Frenchmen a fine silver ring with an amber stone, several knives and a good blanket.

The water burial done, we pressed to the nearest large camp we knew friendly, a hunting station mostly of Mohawks, but with some Oneidas and others allied in trust with us. Not every brave was convinced of the English cause and I know some who supped with nearby French and leaned a ways toward their blandishments, but our arrival—with nine fresh scalps and extra packets of plunder—did much to strengthen faith in King George.

Had there been English action in force in that summer of 1754, I promise you the French might have been rolled back beyond the lakes and down well past Kentucky by Six Nation strength alone. A few other raids like ours had set the tinder alight in men's hearts but tinder needs fresh wood to feed on and the fresh wood promised, armies of English troops, lead and powder and presents, stayed distant rumor for too long and Indians grew weary of waiting.

Still Carrihogo kept his word. We stayed west all that summer and into the next and carried on swift raids that had the French uneasy and ill balanced. I killed my first man, and then my second man and other men till I no longer counted except to take care of guarding scalps for bounty payment.

The first man was a Frenchified Oneida whom I shot from behind a scramble of stones that marked the ruins of some long-dead settler's cabin. The Oneida wore full war paint (which was not so common in these running raids as in a true war between Indian nations) and charged fearsomely at my flimsy redoubt after he had let off his gun (a French musket and a piece with no true aim when I later tested it). I held as still and solid as Carrihogo had taught me, but the Oneida did look frightening, white and red lines along his face and his breast a blazon of magical scribble. He had a small ax in each hand and threw one ahead of him, charging with the other held head-high. The thrown ax nicked stone close enough for a chip to cut my ear, but I held my aim firm and squeezed my trigger.

It must have been the intensity of my excitement that made everything turn slow just then, a phenomenon I have noted since yet never quite so vividly. I could even see the pale yellow spark from my lock with a measurable pause before the

detonation. And then the checked stride of my attacker, another pause before I saw the black dot precisely in the center of his brow, black and then spreading darkened red as ichor mingled into his war paint. He clattered with his ax not a foot in front of me and I crouched forward with my knife in my right hand, catching his hair in my left and cutting the swift part-circle that let the scalp come off easily as I pulled.

I remember it well, but, although it has its sharpness as a picture enhanced by danger, it has none of the exultation of my first hunt or even of some other hunts. To kill in war is part of a business and there are accountants all down the line, from the agent paying for the scalp to gray-fleshed, thin-lipped men at sloping desks in London, adding their columns of death on death, scalp on scalp, taking neat care on the figures to prove an inch of advantage here and there to one king over another.

There have always been riddles here for me, O Lord, and none of them solved yet by my most diligent study of Thy word. I know Thou hast been, in Thy time, a God of war, but when it was a simple matter of Thy chosen people against idolators and worshipers of Moloch and the like. But what are war and killing to a Christian, when both armies claim Thy grace and have chaplains calling opposite causes God's choice? Such thoughts never troubled me then, but writing of early blood and conflict, they cloud my mind, uneasy questionings . . .

Slowly bestirred, England was offering some response to all the pleas sent back to London by Sir William, by Governor Shirley, by Benjamin Franklin, a dozen and more other worried and responsible citizens. We were still west when the first messages came that the great English Army had arrived. Sir William had ridden to Virginia to meet with General Edward Braddock who brought with him confirmation (not needed with the Iroquois yet important to the colonial Englishmen) of Sir William as general of all Indian forces against the French. He tried to persuade General Braddock to make his march north and against Fort Niagara, but the general's orders had been set in London and were not to be changed, no matter what the advice of a man like Johnson. No, Braddock must march against Fort Duquesne, a stronghold more prestigious than consequential. Captain Washington would lead a colonial force along with Braddock's English regulars and we could only hope that the Virginia surveyor's knowledge of the land might guard his general from too great errors. Sir William, having done what he could, spurred his horses back to Fort Johnson to cement his own frontiers.

There is no profit in retelling poor Braddock's disaster. Colonel Washington (who has no longer need of credit from me) did his best to explain that wilderness warfare was not always well fought in formed ranks, but his words fell on deaf, brave ears. Along the Monongahela, before he came even in sight of Fort Duquesne, General Braddock took a ball in his chest and watched a mere few hundred Indians slay more than half his fine fifteen hundred troops and most of their colonial outriders.

Sir William Johnson held his confederation together, but he was sorely pressed. A runner panted into our station in late August with messages that Sir William needed us and we packed light for a swift journey and ran the long trail back to Canajoharie. It was more like an armed fortress than the heartlight settlement I had left the year before. Hendrick and other war chiefs were riding back and forth from councils at Fort Johnson to councils at the castle and belts of wampum were as common as peddler's pots and pans, each one signifying a reminder of some past pledge or a new one. Sir William was back and forth with the chiefs and as often pelting away to Albany on his favorite roan to superintend there further muster of colonial militia. For, though it was an "English Army," Johnson's command was a force of frontiersmen and, after Braddock, we all thought it the better for that.

Sir William had no easy task for there was bickering and rivalry in every colony and through every segment of the King's forces, a foreshadowing of worse divisions to come. London was far away in miles and even further in true understanding of frontier problems. The King's ministers seemed to take delight in sending by each new ship some new official whose powers contravened or contradicted one another. In the name of the same King, one man would offer an Indian nation friendship and payment and arms while another was seizing Indian lands by cozenage or force and both were begging for Indian alliance against the French.

Carrihogo sat long with Henrick and Sir William the night before we set forth again, a small party this time (no more than ten) to precede the main body and scout information both by spying out and by capture and torture. Sir William attached much importance to intelligence, and from as many sources (one to be checked against the other) as possible. He was himself at the castle to bid us good speed, and this because of the greatest change of all in my absence. For my sister Molly was now the mistress of his great house at Fort Johnson!

It gave me a strange feeling, loss mixed with pride and a bewilderment that the sister I had lately joined pranks with, climbing trees and running chases through the fields, was sharing a grown man's bed. Carrihogo had told me on our way home, and a friend later said my face was hooded with a darkness between sorrow and anger, but I do not remember this. I am sure I had a touch of grief at knowing my favorite friend and sister no more at the longhouse, but I cannot say, at that time, it had any larger meaning.

Like everyone within his radius, I knew of the appetites and energies of the squire of Fort Johnson and Molly was now sixteen and an unmarried maid ripe for some adventure. There had been dozens of other Mohawk girls who had caught Sir William's eye and had either warmed his bed at the Fort Johnson dwelling or dallied with him in the dark of a castle longhouse. The most of them had settled down with honest mates after and with no monstrous fuss about their liaison; we Mohawks took such matters in the sensible pace of day to day. If I thought anything for myself it was that Molly might draw me to her lover's attention and I might be rewarded with one of the new powder horns I had seen lately from England.

But in the castle the talk was that with Molly and Sir William there was more than his usual light dalliance. She had moved entirely from Canajoharie to the mansion and taken with her her finest robes and beads and other treasures. Sir William's German woman, Catherine Weisenberg, had been sent back to exercise her shrewish tongue alone in Albany.

There was other talk and none so fine, so that I had to bloody the nose of a lad from another longhouse who prated that my sister had sold herself for gain and without love. There were to be many other such stories through the years and many another fight with envious tongue-waggers, red-skinned and white both, who took delight in libeling that which they were too coarse to understand. Did they expect Sir William's consort to live like a pig and dress like a bond-woman? But most such rumors and squabbles lie far ahead of this homecoming when I had not leisure to digest or reason out all that these news of my sisters portended.

Sir William clasped Carrihogo to him and gave him once again his instructions as to what to look for. Then he reached and clamped my thin boy's shoulder in his powerful handgrip.

"Molly's brother," he said. "She speaks of you, son. Stay to your father's heel and you'll learn much on this journey. And when you return, we shall talk of what you've seen—you and I and Molly—and perhaps of much else."

Then he was turned away at the longhouse door, shouting to the Dutch boy who held his horse, and we were running again, but east, and more northerly, on Carrihogo's swift heels.

I see now difficulties in the writing of a personal history that I had not dreamed of such evenings as I have lost myself in the skill of Mr. Fielding's lusty playfulness or Mr. Smollett's quite as lusty crankousness. For anyone who has had anything happen in his life or who has any original thoughts (likely borrowed thoughtlessly from the past but no less seeming original to the thinker) believes it would be quite easy for him to write a book, had he but the time. And here am I, enough time set aside, embarked on such a writing only to find it as full of unexpected dangers as the spring rapids of Sacondaga tumbling toward Fort Edward.

Am I to cover a hundred more pages with marches? Am I always to be writing, "And then we set forth north, and then we set forth south, and we were four days, or five days on the trail?" What I began as some kind of reckoning to do with my immortal soul is like to become a surveyor's ledger. A pox on it! If too many of my days have been spent heel-and-toe to-and-fro, it is no need for me or you to measure every step. Let me try to record only what may have some meaning.

Sir William's strategy was to build quickly a stronghold at the southern end of Lake George to hold this natural route against the French, whose own fortresses at Ticonderoga and Crown Point above were gates ready to swing open and unleash disaster on New York State and the whole open New England country south and east. There were men felling trees and planing them by the lakeshore, others throwing up earthworks while colonial militiamen patrolled uneasily about them. Should the French strike through before Fort Henry were finished there was small hope of holding them out of the richest colonial heart.

Ours was a mission to detect the least French movement that might threaten Sir William's fort. Even scalps were not so important as news and its swift delivery. Carrihogo led us almost to the shadows of the new French fort at Ticonderoga and we camped there, changing our sleeping place each night, for many days, watching King Lewis's troops at drill, watching their tame Hurons playing loud games of lacrosse, and never setting off a shot or giving in to the temptation of lifting some hair from a *courier* or an Indian strayed alone from the fort.

"I could have his scalp so quietly not even a squirrel would hear," Gabriel pleaded once with Carrihogo.

"You will be paid well enough without the scalp," Carrihogo said.

"I know, but there is honor as well as bounty in a scalp," Gabriel argued. "Not even a bird will cry out; I can use the ax most quietly, elder brother."

Elder brother was a little imposing from a fifteen-year-old to a war chief, but Carrihogo kept his rein.

"We deal with men, not birds, younger son," he said. "When your scalped Frenchy does not come back, these whole woods will soon be swarmed with Hurons and French both and we will be forced to flee far beyond where our eyes may be of aid to Warraghiyagey."

We kept hidden days more until one hot and insect-humming August day Carrihogo pointed out to us a lone Huron leaving the fort and taking a narrow trail southwest.

"There is a brave will not be missed in the fort," he said. "He goes back to his own camp and may not even be expected there."

"I can have the scalp?" Gabriel whispered quickly, running a scarred finger along the blade of his hand ax.

"You have spoken for it. You may have it," Carrihogo said. "But there are things I want from this brave first. News and words of the French plans. When he has spoken, you will have your scalp."

"But no brave will give such word," I said.

"No brave should give such word," Carrihogo said, "but this is such a one as I have been hoping for. The brave who stays by the French to fight would never talk at point of knife, but the brave who grows restless and leaves early to seek his woman and warm fire—he may talk."

"Will they not hear him scream at the fort?" Gabriel asked.

"Wahtehnah and I will catch him silently," Carrihogo said,

nodding to a mighty hunter from our castle. "And when we question him, it will be far back in the cave."

Carrihogo and Wahtehnah left and moments later returned dragging between them their Huron prisoner, a brave between twenty-five and thirty, bare except for a string carrying belt. We held converse to its minimum until we were safely into the cave, a winding cavern safe past even shouting distance of the French fort.

"Any cries beyond the cave, a hunting brave will take for night bird or trapped varmint," Carrihogo said. "He's a flabby brute." He nudged the prisoner forward. I had lighted a taper and we wound around turnings in the cavern till we reached a space broad and wide as a tavern drinking room and fissured in its ceiling so that one could keep a fire without smothering.

"Flabby, maybe," Gabriel said, "but what a prick!"

Indeed, he spoke true, for the Huron's member was as huge as any man's I have seen before or since, and it was difficult to keep one's eyes on any other part of his anatomy.

"Big man, big prick, little man, all prick," Carrihogo said with stubborn pride. "We are not here to try his privates, but to open his mind."

He ripped off the cloth and leather with which he and Wahtehnah had gagged the prisoner and shoved him down against the cave wall.

"Build a fire, my son," he told me.

"I speak nothing," the Huron said, but there was sweat already rolling from his flesh.

I took some tinder from the Huron's pack, not to waste our own, brushed it into a small mound and set it to smouldering with my flint. From the stores we had left in the cave, I added several slender dried branches and soon had a fire dancing through some larger pieces of wood.

"When do the French plan to leave the fort, brother?" Carrihogo asked. "And by what road? And to what purpose? Three small questions, and you may go home to sweet food and a cunning wife." The Huron knew as well as we did that

there could be no likelihood of his leaving the cave alive, but
Carrihogo was a stickler for the proper form in questioning.

"I speak nothing," the Huron said. "The English eat shit
and what they have left over they feed to the Mohawks."

Carrihogo smiled appreciatively and turned a small stick of
hardwood in the fire. When its end was glowing, he thrust it
into the Huron's right eye. The Huron reached a hand helplessly to soothe the burn and Wahtehnah kicked it away.

"When do the French plan to leave, brother?"

The Huron caught his lower lip in his teeth to keep from an
unmanly cry and said nothing.

Another brave withdrew his stick from the fire and worried
the wound Carrihogo had made. The Huron flinched but
spoke no word.

It was a long evening and tedious to any but such special
souls who take delight in reading about torture. I have seen
too much of it to adjudge it anything but a sorry necessity in
wrenching information from those brave or preternaturally
stubborn spirits who will not give it. I have scars of my own
for not speaking so I may bear witness from either side of the
fire. It is a business as old as man; I have read since that the
Jesuits used it to make converts of Jews and Moors, and the
Jews and Moors to exact confessions from Christians. There
have been times when it has excited me but as I grow older it
is just another entry in a catalog I would as soon put aside.

There were six or seven more logs on the fire before the
Huron broke and he did so only when both eyes were gone
and he as riddled with burnt holes as a sieve of skin.

"Six more days and six more nights," he choked out. "They
march then if Baron Dieskau's troops are all together. They
will lie behind cover on Wood Creek where they know the
English will march and they will mow them down as they did
Braddock and all his army." He had to repeat the information
three times over before Carrihogo was satisfied and honored
him with the mercy of a cut throat.

"Six days gives us time," Carrihogo said, kicking the body

away from the fire. "We leave tomorrow to give Sir William the word. We leave in two parties, lest one of us may end like this meat here." Gabriel had taken his scalp.

I poked the fire to order for a slow night's burning and settled to as soft a spot as I could find. I could hear Carrihogo and the other braves snoring except for the one who had taken a guard post at the cave mouth. Gabriel nudged against my side.

"Do you think there might be medicine in that dead Huron, brother?" he asked me.

"What medicine?" I said. I had not eaten the heart of a fallen warrior (and I have never done so), but I knew the custom and at that age could see nothing more shocking to it than any other vicissitude of life and death. "He died betraying his friends; there is not much medicine in such a heart."

"I was not speaking of the heart," Gabriel said. "Pah! He died a coward, but a coward with such a prick, brother!"

"Agh, you are a buzzard-child!" I said, disgusted yet amused.

"If you do not want to share," Gabriel said with some dignity, "you could hold your peace about what I may do."

"Do what you will," I said, already half asleep.

I did not wake to watch. I do know that I stole a look before we left the cave and that poor Huron's scrotum was as empty of its cods as a thrush's nest when children younger than Gabriel have been collecting eggs. And I do not say Yes or No to superstition, but I know that Gabriel from that day on was renowned in beds all through the Mohawk country, white beds as well as Indian. Be sure I make no recommendations but only tell the things I have seen and guessed and their issuance.

We found Sir William and his forces with Hendrick and over four hundred Iroquois below Fort Lyman where our news made us heroes.

"We can press through before Dieskau leaves his fort," Sir William said.

But Hendrick, his vast, fat body hunched over the fire, shook his head.

"His Indians are already in our land, Warraghiyagey," he said. "Let us put up defenses here while we can. I had not thought to hear my brother make plans to walk into the same trap as Braddock."

"Damn me, if I ever said any such thing!" Sir William protested. "We'll advance with care, mighty brother, and split our forces into three parts so none can be so easily trapped. Thus." He drew lines on the earth, showing three different bands advancing north by different roads.

"No, brother," Hendrick said. "Thus the French will destroy us surely." He picked up three sticks. "Together we have some strength," he made as if to break the three sticks and they held firm, "but apart we are weak." He withdrew one stick at a time and broke each one easily, throwing the halves into the fire. Sir William frowned, but held his silence in thought.

"All right," he said. "We stay together, but keep your Indians spread wide, scouting ahead and at the sides."

"Perhaps," Hendrick said. "Let me sleep and hope a dream may guide me. We will counsel together again when I wake."

Two young braves helped tug Hendrick to his feet (he carried so great a weight now that he could scarcely walk unassisted and had to ride a broad old wagon horse on any long journey or war march) and went with him to his quarters.

"We will decide something in the morning," Sir William told Carrihogo, "something, surely." His face brightened for a space. "Molly is well," he said. "Well and beautiful. She would even have come with me, but I persuaded her she might serve better keeping the house in order and sifting any rumors that might come from the castle. She salutes you both." He clasped Carrihogo to his breast, then me.

We went out into the stirring camp and for the first and not the last time in my life I drank rum and drank too much of it and made myself drunk and wild and sickly in that progres-

sion. On a daunt I had tasted rum before and been ready to
spit out the burning liquid soon as I had proved my mettle.
This time, I do not know . . . so much was stirring and the
rum and the wildness were a part of it that I could not deny.
Carrihogo had left me to myself and I spied an old castle visitor, Captain Deliverance Gibson with a pannikin of spirits
among a ring of friends, white and Indian. When he passed
me the ladle, I sucked all its contents down and handed it
back for more. My eyes bled stinging water, but I held off
choking. The captain roared with amusement and gave me
another helping.

"The young brave's ready for his first battle," he said.
"Drink deep, Joseph, and damnation to the French!"

"Heugh!" I said, and finished the second ladle.

I don't know what properly the tipple was, likely some
home-brewed poison from a back alley in Albany. It was
harsh and burning, but I swallowed and held it down and felt
it turn about and probe warmly in my belly the while its subtle vapors stole back upward through my body to invade and
conquer my mind and make jerky puppet strings of the ten-
dons that controlled my limbs.

"Damnation to the French!" I cried the captain's toast in a
high, loud giggle and held out my paw for a fresh ladle. And
got it.

The fire we drank around was suddenly warmer to me and
an ugly Onondaga across it seemed to be my best and oldest
friend.

"Longoh, you old son of a bitch!" I cried, throwing an arm
about his shoulders.

"I am not Longoh, but Horn-Biter," he corrected me, but in
good humor. Among older men who enjoy their drink it is always a delight to see a younger man drunk for the first time
and I confess I must have presented a comic sight, thirteen
years old, naked but for my belt, some war paint of the trail
still on my face, hiccoughing and lurching around the tipplers'
circle.

They let me sponge on them for a few more rounds by which I was reeling and as happy to seek other companions as they were to see me leave. I do not remember much else of that night except as it was told to me by others for it has been a pattern of my drinking, when I do exceed my capacities, to have a merciful curtain ring down over my recollections, else probably I should always be too ashamed to drink again.

I seem to have stolen a braided mask from some pack and to have put it on and played at being a fiddler's trained pig about several other fires where anyone would treat me more rum for my antics.

"Very lifelike you were, too," Gabriel told me, "grunting and making as if to wag your little curly tail."

I shuddered.

"Bring me more water," I asked him.

I had come awake, sweating in the sun where I lay in the main passage between tents and huts, an ox wagon creaking as near my head as a hand's breadth, my breath stinking and my stomach aquake, my brain trembling with a phantasmagoria of many-colored dreams. Gray Diamond had said that the dreams come in sleep after drinking are no more to be trusted than the waking actions of a drunken man, but this did not stop the dreams from disturbing me. My old white owl had been back, but waving his great wings and croaking anger; I saw the rent bear robe again and the same dream of the caribou man which frightened me more than ever.

Gabriel brought me more water, kindly. He had spent the night sober with a Seneca girl and all he had for the morning was an agreeable lassitude.

I drank until the burning had retreated some and doused my face and breast and shoulders with what was left from Gabriel's gourd.

"What is Hendrick's word?" I asked. "What did he dream and when do we march?"

But Hendrick had dreamed nothing that gave him any aid

in judging the battle plan and he would not order his Indians to move without such provision. Warraghiyagey cursed and argued, but there was no moving the old sachem, and without him there was no moving the force.

We stayed in place two more days till Hendrick had a satisfactory night of dreams. He was ready to move with Sir William so long as the forces were not divided. His dream had been of corn cut by a husbandman, and the corn had been set in the rude shocks of the French manner, so it was a clear omen for our own victory. Yet Hendrick was not fully happy; there had been a sudden rainstorm after the shocking of the corn and he thought the husbandman struck by a lightning bolt. He was still grumbling, but he let his braves lift him and set him on his horse next to Warraghiyagey's.

The two chiefs moved forward together, a picture from some splendid mythic tale of old war heroics, so different, Hendrick in a skin jerkin intricately beaded and a feathered crown atop his great bulk, Sir William in a red regimental coat, thin then and light on his steed. Yet they looked alike, for Sir William had blazed his face with lines of the same war paint Hendrick wore. I envied and admired both, not favoring one above the other, and wanting their glory combined for my own.

The whole force moved north, more than three thousand colonials and Hendrick's four hundred-odd Iroquois and there must have been two hundred more of camp followers, women, traders, curious children.

Hendrick kept silent, still far from content of his choice.

"We shall break them in battle and shove them back to Ticonderoga," Sir William kept crowing.

"They are many, brother," Hendrick said, "and Baron Dieskau is a great captain."

"We shall break them," Sir William repeated.

We were not yet to Fort Lyman when a scouting party burst into our march to say that Caughnawagas were on the road ahead and had looted a supply wagon bound for the fort.

"We can catch them while they're still plundering," War-raghiyagey cried. "Great brother, hit them with the lead force."

Hendrick sat stolid on his lumbering gray horse.

"With my own Indians in the lead force and your colonials I have still only five hundred," he said. "If they are to win a battle, they are too few. If they are but to die, they are too many, brother."

"If my brother knows fear, I shall lead the sally myself." Warraghiyagey spoke softly and Hendrick knew he could make no delaying answer. He smote his old horse on its side and gave a cry and the whole forward army, colonials and Mohawks mixed and I with them, surged up the trampled roadpath toward Fort Lyman and the new Fort Henry.

What we found ahead was a tumbled provision wagon with its two oxen killed and a few Indians still dredging its innards for loot. They slunk into side shadows as our first columns came into sight, parting to make way for Hendrick who rode quietly and proud down the middle.

As he reached the head of the force, a cry came from the sheltered forest: "Who passes here?"

Hendrick reined his horse to a stop and answered: "We pass here as we have always passed, the Six Confederate Indian Nations of America."

There was no other sound but some creaking of leather on horses and the breathing of the men about me. I fingered my powder horn and loosed its top; my rifle was ready for the first shot, if need be. I heard Hendrick's words, grave and fine in the voice that had swayed a thousand councils for onto fifty years, sounding in the stillness and echoing back from the wooded roadside.

A few Caughnawagas came from their cover and huddled in a circled group. One stepped forward to reply in a voice higher than Hendrick's and seeming another, poorer echo.

"We are the Seven Confederate Indian Nations of Canada," the speaker cried. "We stand here together with the army of our Father, the King of France, to fight his enemies, the greedy English. We have no intention to quarrel and trespass against any Indian Nation. We desire you keep aside from the English lest we find a blazing war between ourselves."

It was the conversation of high councils and Hendrick's meat and drink. He cleared his throat and made a dignified reply, stating that it was the greedy French who had moved into land not theirs, that the Six Nations stood as ever with their English brothers yet wished no war with other Indians. Would the Caughnawagas join the Six Nations and march with Hendrick and Warraghiyagey, whom they knew well, there need be no blood spilt on this path.

It was a good speech and I heard it already thinking the Caughnawagas would be swayed. But there was a young brave behind Hendrick who was known for short temper and weak judgment. I saw him raise his gun and was ready to shout, but before words could leave my lips he had put a ball into the Caughnawaga spokesman and now there was rattle of gunfire everywhere and the whisk of arrows from the forest.

I kneeled and fired into the trees and saw Hendrick start in his saddle, hit by a Caughnawaga ball, before his frightened steed clattered down the road and off. I took quick cover and searched around me for Caughnawaga war paint or French buckskin, firing and reloading and firing. The Caughnawagas got a volley into the force still packed on the road, but no more than a first volley. We melted man by man to the sides of the trail and retreated keeping careful cover.

I have read histories of battles and it is no surprise to me that they are but seldom written by the men who have been engaged in the actions chronicled. If you are worth your grog and shilling as a soldier, you cannot take time in combat to note fine shadings of tactical skill or even your own deployment. To my memory, the battle was all of a solid piece, from the first reckless shot at the Caughnawaga chief to its end at our fortification by the lake. Yet I know very well there must have been a reasonable hiatus to allow us to get into position and I believe I did eat and drink and give natural relief to bowel and kidney between the first retreat and the second, longer battle stand.

What happened that gave us our precious breathing spell was a disagreement between the Caughnawagas and Baron Dieskau. They had returned to his French troops with the story of their skirmish and the baron had ordered an immediate advance to take advantage of the coup. But the Caughnawagas wished to tarry; they had three Mohawk braves prisoners and they wanted time to burn them as was the custom. Baron Dieskau swore and kept on crying: *"En avant!"* His Indian allies replied that perhaps they would rejoin the baron later.

In a rage, already held up by an hour or more, the baron advanced without them, ordering his well-drilled and cleanly uniformed French troops down the road where we saw them coming and, from behind our wagons and trees and other cover, cut them down in pat vengeance for the Battle of the Wilderness earlier in the year.

Warraghiyagey took a French bullet in his hip, but by the time he fell there was no longer doubt of the battle's outcome. Carrihogo and I helped carry him to a tent where Dr. Fry dressed his wound and told him he should stay, but he insisted on returning to the breastworks. His good resolution was stronger than his limbs, however, for he quickly found himself become too stiff and painful to move and we took him back to where he could rest on a pallet. Felled in body, he still directed the action in mind and spirit, advising Captain Eyre on the best use of his small cannon, inquiring again and again of Hendrick who had not been seen since the Caughnawaga shot had struck him and his horse had bolted off the road.

Warraghiyagey was still lying flat when two colonials and five Indians pushed Baron Dieskau in through the flap of the tent. The French commander had been shot through both legs and dangled between his captors like a beautifully colored blue-and-white toy soldier, discolored with spreading red stains from the waist downward. The Indians began clamoring immediately for permission to take the baron off and burn him before he lost all consciousness; they had fought hard and lost brave comrades and it was the least of natural rewards.

I was of two minds myself. It would be a splendid thing to see so great a chief as Baron Dieskau at the stake, but I had been long enough among chiefs white to suspect that there might be different rulings in European warfare and my suspicions were correct.

Sir William reared himself up painfully and forced me to help him from his bed and cede it (and the surgeon) to the prisoner. Propped by me, our general dressed down his lieutenants.

"You shall have prisoners enough, and other chiefs among them, for merriment and feasting of many days," he said. "But this general belongs to me and to King George. Had I been taken, he would have kept me from the Caughnawagas for himself and King Lewis. Know this, brothers, and know it well."

There was grumbling and more argument, but the group at last retired, not so much convinced as needing to seek further council from their fellows outside who were, doubtless, already discussing where to set the stake and what kindling to use.

The baron rolled an eye and winced as the surgeon probed.

"I think those fellows of yours were regarding me with some lack of compassion, General Johnson," he grunted in quite fair English.

"Compassion!" Warraghiyagey snorted. "They wished to spit and roast you like a rabbit, sir, and are threatening to desert me if I do not yield them such permission. But feel no uneasiness. You are safe with me."

He had no sooner said the word "safe" than a new bustle of Indians shouldered into the tent, the original captors reinforced by others, and the argument began again. It was all in

Mohawk, quite incomprehensible to the baron, but I noted he kept a firm stare on all faces, seeking any clues to his final disposition.

Warraghiyagey covered the same ground as before and added some promises of rum and powder and Fort Johnson hospitality. The Indians eyed Baron Dieskau and saw a man obviously wounded beyond the point where he might offer much entertainment and so there were finally nods of agreement with Warraghiyagey and then one brave went over to the bed to shake the baron's pale hand.

"All safe!" Sir William repeated, as though the argument had never been in doubt. "Help me out, Joseph. I'd see what's happening for a spell."

What was happening was a battle finished and a total victory for us, the first time on this continent that a force of colonials and Indians, unaided by any British regulars, had met and routed a trained army of French under a famous commander who had himself been captured. There were broadsheet ballads printed and sung in London to praise brave Will Johnson and with Warraghiyagey as fortune's favorite, acclaimed leader of colonials and Indian allies together, the English tide seemed at a flood which should sweep all easily before it.

It remained only to break through Ticonderoga and press on to Crown Point, both bastions well within our reach.

Had not Sir William been wounded, had not so many bickering rivalries broken out all afresh between New England colonials and New York colonials, had not our own Six Nations been so discouraged into tardiness and half-heart.

How much of history is written in despite of "ifs"!

If Sir William had been whole he might have rallied all his forces then and there. This, I think, was the major factor in the sullen stalemate that followed our great victory, but there were other matters: Hendrick most importantly.

He had been lost, and it was not for more than a day after that we could piece together like a torn jerkin the sorry story of his end. After his horse had left the road he had fallen from it and stumbled, wounded and reeling with his great weighty bulk, into the forest beyond, the ancient power ebbing from him, his silver mane caught in brambles, his piercing eyes the prey of mites.

I have thought of him, almost seen his staggering image, reading the English play of *King Lear*.

As he blundered he fell into the fire circle of a Caughnawaga campsite and there women and children rushed at the tottering apparition and put out his eyes and clumsily took a contemptible patch of scalp from that old head that had looked on queens and princes; there he died.

And with Hendrick dead there was no single chief who could sway the Six Nations. We were still a confederacy, but we spit at each other and bickered as badly as the colonials themselves. We Mohawks held true to Warraghiyagey, but other tribes were quick in sending belts to him and to us signifying their withdrawal from the wars and damning English and French alike. And so the battle that might have been a dawn turned to a twilight.

And yet this very twilight was to be for me a kind of dawn.

"Let Joseph come with me," Sir William directed Carrihogo. "He has a gentle hand at helping a sore body, and Molly'd like him for company. A space at my household may teach him some things he has not learned in the forests."

I waited Carrihogo's answer, keeping my face stiff not to betray all the pictures I made behind my eyes of gleaming new pistols from England, of downy beds, of mirrors and brass buttons and every glimmering lure I'd ever envied in a trader's pack. And past all the boyish greed, a happiness at thought of being with Molly again.

Carrihogo did not answer at once. I believe he knew his answer immediately, but, as a chief and a man of some substance, waited to find a proper frame in which to place it.

"We are already one family, Warraghiyagey," he said, when he did speak. "You have my daughter to wife and at her breast your son, my grandchild. I have fought beside you this week in battle and three of my sons have fought beside you, too. This boy is one of them and if it pleases you that he go back with you to Fort Johnson rather than with me to the castle, let it be so. In my heart and in your heart they are the same place as is any place you dwell or I dwell, friend and brother."

Thus did a new life begin for me, the lessons and associations that were to shape my destiny and even the destiny of my people.

But I could not and did not know this then. I saw pleasures and baubles and pressed my father's hand in thanks and helped Warraghiyagey into the litter we had made from supple boughs on a gun carriage that two bullocks might pull back to Fort Johnson.

TWO

What does a person see first, moving from one world to another? For this is what I had done, much more so than in later years traveling to London or Paris. By that time I had seen more than one world and was, in a wise, prepared for anything, although not, as you shall discover, beyond amazement and disappointment.

But this was a change of worlds for a youth of just passing thirteen. I had fought and hunted with men and killed my enemies, but all as part of a life that was Mohawk from my still-boy's-name of Small Turtle to the way I ate my food to the set my mind took for itself in the forest at night.

From this to Sir William Johnson's manor house, furnished as I had not believed even a king lived. The roof made of lead sheets carried by ship all the way from England. The dining room with its long table laid with silver implements and food served in dishes so fragile they broke at a simple fall to the wide-planked polished floor. Sir William's own office room with a desk ornately carved where he sat flanked by shelves of books from Boston and London; pages of philosophy, pages of religion, pages of cunning engravings to show how a mill might harness a stream or wind to grind corn. Beds! I think perhaps beds most of all, with deep eider mattresses and coverlets of woven cloth in every pattern and all of a softness not to be believed. Treasure! Treasure! Treasure everywhere!

Then what does a person see first, moving from one world to another? I cannot answer, for it seemed I saw everything at once and was overwhelmed and would likely have run back to the castle had it been anyone to greet me at the main door but my sister Molly, dark and wise and slender, still wearing her Mohawk robe, quite coolly in command and control of all these mysteries.

"Joseph!" she kissed me warmly on either cheek. "How is he?"

"Molly, lass!" Sir William called from his litter. "Come see me hale and lazy. The Frenchmen couldn't hit me *there!*"

His voice already sounded a well man.

"Come kiss me!" he called. "And bring me my whelp!"

Molly smiled and ran to his side.

We ate that night at the table in the dining room. It was never what the English call "a small family dinner" at Sir William's board. And you shall see why as I list now the most important members of the household. Sir William and my sister Molly first. Then Sir William's children by Catherine Weisenberg: John, Ann called Nancy, Mary called Polly. William of Canajoharie, a son near my own age by a Mohawk woman who died in birthing; his Mohawk name was Tagcheunto. Daniel Claus, Sir William's secretary, a dry, hardworking young man who (Molly said) had ink instead of blood, but still had heart enough to be smitten by Nancy Johnson. Guy Johnson, a nephew of Sir William's. Peter Johnson, Molly's firstborn. To these add a whole hubbub of Sir William's closest lieutenants, from George Croghan to John Butler and his son Walter, constantly coming and going. And besides these, other guests like, on this first evening, Reverend Prouty from Massachusetts and the sachem Red Head.

Everyone talked at once. I sat silent and a little shocked, for I had had thirteen years of training by tribal fires where no one interrupted a speaker young or old until he had finished all he had to say. But Molly, and even Red Head in these surroundings, were as rude as if they had been English-bred.

Molly would show me the persnickety operation of a fork at the same time spooning succotash into the infant Peter while saying proudly to Sir William: "Did the Caughnawagas not collapse as I told you, Will?"

"They did, Moll, but how you knew—"

"I'd had it in messages from their women. I knew their hearts would not stay firm in war."

I smiled, reflecting and basking some in her own pride.

This was my same sister, but with every facet heightened like a jewel shone to its finest luster. Now all the childish games she had played with me, her fancies and her stories, had come together in the Molly of Fort Johnson, my scampering tag partner a grown maid who might have been a queen, so confidently she moved in these grand surroundings, so surely she spoke of policy and war.

The Reverend Prouty kept asking Sir William if he did not think the Indian—"Our Red Brother," he would say, looking a little nervously at me and at Red Head and at Molly and Tagcheunto—was not ready for salvation in the Church of England.

"Damned well ready and more than ready." Sir William pounded the table toward the reverend. "But I tell you, Prouty, you shan't catch a single savage soul till you're ready to dive into the wilderness alongside savage bodies like the canting Congregationals." And, wheeling to Red Head without a pause for breath: "We'll have to do something about Squashcutter's widow, hey? Too hot a little vixen to be left untended, brother. Find her a brave before she has the whole castle turned into a bawdy house! If young Joseph or William here were a mite older I'd marry them off just to keep all that ginger in the family."

"She's fat," Molly said. "She's fat and old."

"Hey, how the girl rises!" Sir William was delighted. "Tell Captain Noble she's fat and old, Molly, for he's making extra trips every day past the Beaver longhouse."

There were cups passing along with the food, but I had not

outlived the memory of my experience at the camp and drank naught but spring water. By dinner's end, the older men were merry and the talk went on in the broad living room where Quacko, one of the Negro slaves, threw fresh logs into the broad fireplace and we younger children pushed dogs and cats aside to make room in its warmth.

I fell asleep right there and Quacko carried me off to my bed, in an alcove room my very own. I last remember Sir William's voice, still booming, and Molly's soft, happy laughter over some randy jest, and the fire warmth all enclosing without the drafts of air from under tentskins or through logchinks . . . How ever did the wealthy English stay awake past dinner? . . .

I woke in full terror, dreaming I had been trapped in a pit dug by Abnakis for the great brown bear of the north and was trying to scramble out before their party came back and carried me off for torture. I could hear their braves coming with rattle of drums and clatter of arms equal to all Baron Dieskau's white-and-blue army. My heart pounded loud as their drums and it took minutes before I realized I was sunk in the deep soft bed of the Johnson mansion and the war sounds were Kitchener ringing the bell he used as a signal that breakfast was ready for the household and for the visiting Indians camped at the skirts of the green lawn.

It was probably Reverend Prouty who helped set my feet upon the path of salvation, unlikely instrument though he may have appeared. He was a dour man for the Church of England, but he had a singleness of determination that attracted my respect even as it to some degree repelled my emotion.

You could have made a good copy of Reverend Prouty out of divers thickness of rope for he was thin and stringy all over, from twisted brow to furrowed neck to gnarled wrists and knees and ankles. He had said grace at dinner simply by waiting out everyone else's loudness. At breakfast he did the same, a harder task with a larger feeding congregation and all at varied stages of their meal. But he held a hand above his rope neck until there was a grudging pause.

"O God, the King eternal," he said in his dry voice, "Who dividest the day from the darkness, and turnest the shadow of death into the morning; drive far off from us all wrong desires, incline our hearts to keep Thy law, and guide our feet into the way of peace; that having done Thy will with cheerfulness while it was day, we may, when the night cometh, rejoice to give Thee thanks. Give us grateful hearts, our Father, for all Thy mercies and for the food before us, and make us ever mindful of the needs of others; through Jesus Christ our Lord, amen."

There were a few muttered "amens" from converted Indians and from English at the board. I did not notice, for my own heart had taken flight at the first words, words which even in Reverend Prouty's drone had a singing and an imagery beyond council oratory or campfire song.

I should not pretend, O Lord, to any flash of light like that You vouchsafed Saul on the Damascene road. I do not think that any true religious fervor struck to my marrow. It was a simple bemusement with a beauty I encountered in phrases. ". . . turnest the shadow of death into the morning." I listened to those words and relived a thousand mornings from the shores of the Great Lakes to that hard winter at the castle and saw thin light bringing me back again and again from dark sleep that had been the rim of death. There was in these words a hint of knowledge, not just of man but of more than man beyond anything Gray Diamond had taught me. I was far from Thy Grace or any understanding, but Reverend Prouty's dry recitation was the thin entering blade of Thy wedge, else why do I remember his prayer even today?

I have lived to see grander houses than Fort Johnson but none I think so rewarding to the helter-skelter explorations of a young boy. The main house lived up to its double persona of mansion and fortress. Not only were its stone walls stouter than many a frontier bastion, but its front was helmed by a long, low, thick stone wall with a half-roof slanting upward to deflect either arrow or bullet. For all the time I knew it it was never manned for war and was instead a convenient overflow for Warraghiyagey's tide of guests and a magnificent setting for us boys to play.

The house behind it was as spacious and gracious as I have tried to convey. There were a dozen other slaves in addition to Quacko and Kitchener, mostly blackamoors. These and some white indentured servants lived in various outhouses. Other farmworkers scattered in dwellings farther afield. And despite their great number, none were idle.

Cooking and serving of meals was sometimes kin to catering for an army. I have seen as many as a dozen large crates of limes alone arrive in one shipment from the West Indian islands to serve Sir William's taste for cool drinks of lime with rum or gin. And every inch of the great house was constantly to be scrubbed and polished and waxed for there was never a night of carousing so late or so wild that either Molly or Sir William would forgive dust or debris in the house the next evening. I have seen a party of giddy braves, ably abetted by their host, smash a whole wall-long hardwood settle while wrestling in the living room and come in from the fields the afternoon following to see the same room shining and spotless with a brand-new settle against the wall.

There were Sir William's own farmlands and added to them the affairs and accounts of the hundred and more other farms in his suzerainty.

Daniel Claus, working in Sir William's office, had hardly time to cast sheep's eyes at Miss Nancy for the bills and deeds, remittances and accounts, piling up on every side and higher piles yet of correspondence with London, with other colonies, with all the ramifications of waging His Majesty's war upon the French. Along with all the letters came and went emissaries of every style from sachem and milord to colonel, captain and clerk, devouring Sir William's serious converse during the day and drinking his frivolous company

into the night to the tunes of Blind Kain, the Irish harper Sir
William had brought from his homeland and who plucked
sobbing or laughing strains from the tall woman-headed harp
in the great room those unpredictable evenings he might be
sober.

With brotherly and boyish pride it never occurred to me
those first years to question that Molly held a place in importance beyond any other woman who had engaged Sir William's affections: was she not my sister and the daughter of
Carrihogo and my mother and of chiefly blood?

All this was true and meaningful, but more meaningful
were Molly's actions in not resting on an enviable heritage. I
have seen many maids of as good family as our own become
do-nothing squaws immediate upon the sanction of marriage.
In some wise they have felt the mere accomplishment of licit
copulation should mark an end to all endeavor in their lives
and they have settled into a slovenly round of demands upon
their husbands and complaints when the husbands, paying the
bribery of servants and jewelry and fine dress, are found seeking satisfaction in bed with less nagging partners.

With Molly all of her life with Sir William was a delight
and not the least of it her involvement in his business and his
politicking. As a woman of the Mohawk, such pursuits came
naturally to her. She sat with him at many councils and those
at which she did not sit in her person she heard fully from
him afterward. Her own Turtle ties and the Wolf fellowship
of Carrihogo found her kin in every tribe around us and such
as she could not cement firmly to Sir William's ends, she was
able either to hold neutral or to be informed of their other alliances.

Her power and influence with Sir William were no secret
and it was sometimes amusing to observe staid gentlemen of
the Virginia tidewater (where there was little social commerce with Indians) making elegant legs at her and changing,
in midsentence, speeches rehearsed to flatter an ignorant in-
digene into the language of adult diplomacy. There were

those who tried to bribe her and got short shrift; Molly wished nothing for herself save greater honor for her lover and neither pelf nor cozenage could turn her to a decision against the interest of Sir William (or the Six Nations, or King George).

She had her own callers and her own councils, no less than Sir William's. She had an instinct for honesty and fair dealing in men and could laugh and talk without restraint with men like Mr. Franklin and later his bastard son William, and honest, unlettered George Croghan. The same instinct drew her into an armor in the presence of insincerity and double-dealing, but this armor was so compounded of politeness and womanly grace that a Livingston or a Schuyler might leave a meeting preening himself on a social (at the least) conquest and never know her true feelings except when, later, he might find his plans rebuffed.

She taught me how to write my name, Joseph Brant, in clear, good penmanship, and she tried to teach me some other letters, but there was never time. I learned to make out a few words and names, hers and Sir William's, New York and Canajoharie and Connecticut, but I learned them only as signs, not for their combination of letters; this knowledge, anxiously as I strove for it, was not to come to me yet. I had enough to master all at once.

Molly showed me the general workings of the estate so that I might act as a guide to visiting colonials and Englishmen and even lead them sometimes to the cattle and translate as best I could between them and my own people. I was brash and eager and hid my own uncertainties in makeshift glibness so that I gained considerable unearned reputation for skills as an interpreter. I did keep honesty with Molly and she pooh-poohed my worries.

"You learn more even while you pretend, brother," she told me. "You have always wished to move more swiftly than a turtle. Keep your head clear of the cobwebs of Englishmen's fears and worries. You were born a Mohawk, to move in a straight line."

I wish I could have studied her advice and kept it. Herself, she did. I believe it was one of the charms she had for Sir William that, unlike many an Indian wife of a settler, she never fell under any glamour of English ways of dress or other fashion. When occasion insisted, she could wear a London ball gown with the fairest and even tread a London dance, but most other times she dressed as a Mohawk princess and was the rarer and more beautiful for it.

Better than teaching was the time she found to ease my homesickness and to comfort me when I had done some simple thing all topsy-turvy and suffered the laughter of John Johnson or William, or the more wounding laughter of the girls.

Sometime in this first year at Fort Johnson I had my first joy of carnal knowledge of a woman, but I cannot, for the best of brain-racking, recall when or where or with whom. I am sure my deficiency here offends every canon of romantic writing and can only plead that it is truth, not bashfulness, that checks my pen. Truth and another of the small-great, great-small things that set Indian aside from European. For I do not think I have ever met an Englishman who did not remember his first bedding of a wench (and very few Englishmen who did not enjoy describing it in detail as the bottle passed around the table) and I do not think I have ever met an Indian who did remember his, or if he did, was willing to share its reminiscence with a ribald company.

A strange difference, for I believe we Iroquois treat our women better and give them higher position in our nation and in our families than the English do theirs. Yet in this vital matter of the sexual act, we are less excited and see no extraordinary triumph in the number of women we may have entered or in explicit recall of the manifold enjoyable variations of the act.

I suppose a native African in those regions of vast desert

remembers each drink of clear water as a distinct delight. Well, we of the Iroquois have never been parched for sex and without esteeming it too lightly still do not set it off in special mystery apart from food and drink and fire warmth. Life is a combination of all these comforts and it seems a tangled life that must keep perhaps the best comfort of all in such a mixture of isolation and adulation.

I can know that my first wench must have been in this period because I do remember other encounters. There was Maple-by-Water, daughter of a Seneca sachem, who tarried with Molly at the house many weeks and used to meet me evenings in the cool shade of the new blockhouse. She twined with me breathlessly and told me she would live with me when I was older and a great lord just as Molly lived with Sir William. We played at such plans and I pushed her harder into the matted grass saying: "And we shall do this in a grand coach! . . . And in a feathered bed! . . . And with four blackamoors holding candles to light us!" until we were happily exhausted with love and dreams. She went off with a young fur trapper from Albany but my heart was not broken (as is the fashion in English books) for by that time I was bouncing merrily with Katie Scanlon, an Irish lass with long red hair and skin as white as milk, who tread the spinning wheel for Molly (and she was a maid when I first had her; I do remember this and believe she was the first maidenhead I broke).

Katie was not given to dreams. She enjoyed the act of the moment (and of every moment she could find) without embroidering any future upon it. In these most agreeable ways, she seemed more a Mohawk than an Irisher and, such is the perversity of the male in mating rut, I harbored more likelihood of wishing to make her my spouse than I ever did of Maple-by-Water. Some such outcome might have ensued from our games had not an unfortunate accident intervened.

It came about when we were concentratedly at it in the shadow beneath the mansion stairway (it was afternoon and

Sir William gone to the castle for some council, Molly gone with him). Katie, all agiggle, had hoisted her long skirts above her waist at my first grope and reached into my small clothes to grasp my already rampant parkin. I was into her with a will, her sturdy legs clamped about me as I prodded lustily, when I felt the sharp slap of a ferule on my bare shoulders.

"Vile abominations!" creaked the thin voice of Reverend Prouty, come silently into the house on one of his frequent visits. He kept the thin stick raining blows with even distribution upon myself and upon the bare thighs of poor Katie, by now shrieking with dismay.

"Whore of Babylon, Daughter of Gomorrah!" he cried. "Pagan beast and Romish bitch!"

Katie, her eyes rolling with fright, tried to twist away and from under me and I, quite as anxiously, attempted to withdraw from her and revenge myself upon our interrupter; minister and friend of Sir William he might be, but I was a brave of chiefly blood, blood the further inflamed by passion, and I would have killed him on the spot had I been able to turn and face him in fair combat.

But I could not. I was wedged into Katie unbreakably and she was caught upon me painfully and firmly. We were like two rutting mongrels, such as I had often laughed at, caught in a concupiscent vise and yelping helplessly in their dilemma.

I screeched with anger and pain, Katie shrilled and wept, Reverend Prouty continued to cane the both of us and Katie added her own small fists beating at my chest and face.

Quacko came from the kitchen, attracted by the commotion, laughing the rude, uncheckable laughter of his black kind. And on his heels other of the household servants, standing about in a jeering circle as Father Prouty went on with his chastisements and orations.

"Sins of the flesh!" Thwack! "Lewd posturings!" Slap!

It was blessed Kitchener, although laughing himself as heartily as anyone, who went back to the kitchen well and returned with a basin of chill water which he threw upon Katie and myself. The drenching worked some spell on the binding of our privates and we sprung apart, rolling into the gaping crowd. Katie was on her feet and off to her quarters in the sheds by the large barn, a flutter of sopping skirts. I was away as quickly, into the woods nearest the house, Prouty shouting after me in his high, coiled voice: "And Sir William shall hear of these Philistine revels! Woe unto Israel! Woe unto Canaan!"

I was sore in mind and body, my shoulders and buttocks from Prouty, my face and chest from Katie's fists and my poor manly member from the terrible squeeze to which it had been subjected. All these I could bathe in the nearest flowing stream which gave me some surcease, but the pain and confusion in my mind was not so simply balmed. I lurked in the trees all that night chasing satisfying fantasies of scalping Reverend Prouty and dissecting his privates while he still breathed, conversely of taking a long march north and north and north, past all the French and all the Chippewas and beyond the Cree to find a land all my own, yet even when I had settled here, lone lord of plains of ice and white snow, I could hear reaching me the echoing laughter of Quacko and Black Rosemary and fat Seven Opossums and all the rest.

With morning dawning I found my steps come back within sight of the great house as hunger touched my belly. There are those Europeans who would see me already corrupt in more ways than the licentious, for to them a lone Indian in a forest has only to bend down to catch a hare, rub two sticks to light a fine fire for cooking, and feast to his gut's content. Perhaps it may be so (certainly it is in their books about my people), but I had been a hunter since before I was ten years yet had usually depended on food kept for me at castle, camp or fort. I might have caught some animal that morning (I did eat some few berries), but I was not of a mind to set up crude housekeeping on my own. My belly rumbled and my thoughts were full of the breakfast table at Fort Johnson. Yet my shame was still too strong to venture forth.

Shame and I admit some fear of what Reverend Prouty might have told Sir William and of what Sir William's own thoughts might be.

So I crossed my legs beneath me and sat hungrily at the edge of the wood, watching kitchen smoke, in my head hearing my friends ask for another plateful of oatmeal and more baked venison and beans and fresh, foaming milk.

Perhaps I should have fled north, I thought.

But then I descried a bustle at the door of the house and a knot of figures coming out with one in their middle—Sir William, I surmised—making gestures toward the forest. The group split into twos and threes and I knew they were looking for me.

I feared, and I wanted to be found, both at once. So I sat stiffly, saying to myself: "What Manitou wills," and vowing that if I made no motion to attract attention it would lend some kind of meaning as to whether I was found or not. In this way I could accept discovery with every punishment it might entail or that lack of discovery which would be a sign to take up the banishment I had contemplated.

I must have sat so for better than an hour before Tagcheunto and two young braves from the field crews stumbled on me.

"Here he is, father," Tagcheunto called Sir William. "I found him! I, Tagcheunto, found him and claim the crown you offered."

And lower of voice, to me: "Don't fear, Joseph. Warraghiyagey is not in anger."

His words could not soothe me. I remained crouched in silence until Sir William himself came to my side, fine in a golden-brown velvet surcoat specked with burrs from his own searching.

"Leave me with the lad." He motioned the others away and when they hesitated made the motion sharper, a chopping of his hand that left no doubt and they backed sulkily out of earshot.

"Now, lad," he said, placing a hand on my shoulder (I cringing from his touch), "what's the glory in giving such a fright to me and your sister Molly?"

My words would not come straight either in Mohawk or in English for I had no clear idea of what I wanted to say except to ask the impossible, that time turn back to before the ill-starred mounting of Katie.

"Reverend Prouty . . ." I said. "I was with Katie—"

"With Katie and in Katie like a thumb in a glove," Sir William said. "Humping every maid in the fort the minute I turn my back . . ." His words were scolding but his tone was not harsh.

"It was not that way, Father," I tried to explain. "Not because you had turned your back, Warraghiyagey. We had been at it before."

"So," he said severely. "Humping every maid in the fort whether I'm there or not. Right under my nose, for all you care in your prick-proud youth."

"And old Prouty came on us," I stumbled on. "And he beat my shoulders and lay a curse on us so we could not come apart until Kitchener broke the spell with fresh water—"

"Spell, my Irish ass!" Sir William snorted. "D'you suppose Prouty's been laying spells on every mingy cur that's ever been caught in a bitch? Use your noggin, Joseph. You've had an accident that might befall anyone and is the nightmare of any coistrel-minded gentleman as I can testify. Now, up on your feet and come back to the house. The sooner you've faced your music, the quicker the rabble will be to forget the tune."

"You're not going to punish me?" I asked, getting to my feet as he had bid me.

"If I did, I'd have to punish every man with more than lard between his legs, and myself as bad as any," he said.

"You are sure it was not a spell?" I asked, starting to follow him.

"You and Katie caught, a spell?" He began to shake with

laughter and held himself with one hand against a tree. "Mohawk and maid in a self-made vise," he stuttered through his laughter. "Ah, God help us!"

I was still not at ease in my mind.

"The Reverend Prouty spoke of abominations," I said. "Sins, lewd posturings?"

"Easy, lad," Sir William said. "Prouty's as good a parson as the church turns out, but trust him not concerning what the Psalmist calls the way of a man with a maid. Trust no parson thereby, Joseph.

"If you want guidance, I'll risk being branded a Dissenter or a Bibliolator and tell you to go to the Book itself. Look on how many wives the patriarchs had, and see that there's no prohibition against humping save when the act is adulterous. Remember that, my boy, and you'll have a merrier life and one without soul-tearing."

"I don't think I ever want to stap a maid again," I said soberly. "Not ever."

"Here, now," Sir William said, "that does smack of blasphemy! You've seen my old hound Finn, caught in the morning in some yelping bitch and going to it in the afternoon as blithely as if nothing had upset him. There's your model, lad, else the race should die out. May take you longer than Finn, but that's a burden of humanity. I can recall my first clap and it kept me chaste well beyond a month. That, I should think, might be a fair limit to any wholesome man."

And it was as Sir William had said and I have never forgotten his words nor have allowed myself to be frightened from a free bed by any preacher's canting.

And more than the wisdom in his advice was his sympathy toward me and his accepting me his fellow in folly as well as in esteem. There are many great men of the world who may raise one to friendship with a compliment or bribe one's pride with medals and honors, but there are few like Sir William who can forge a shared bond from ridicule and humiliation.

I bore grimly the jests and snickers of the household for

weeks. I tried to find poor Katie and, when I did, I even made some overture to plighting a troth between us, but she was more wary of me than I had been of her and would have none of me. I think a man may rise above scorn more easily and quickly than a woman. My sister Molly helped find Katie a fair indenture with a family in distant Germantown by Philadelphia. She served there, gained her freedom and later, as I learned, wedded an English sergeant and returned with him to England where she may be living to this day with no one of her neighbors ever to dream of the afternoon she found herself clipped to a Mohawk under the stairs of Fort Johnson.

The Six Nations had yet to recover from the death of Hendrick, so great a chief that he had held them firmly welded up to his death. Little Abraham was neither warrior nor sage enough to take his place and Sir William had to work his hardest wearing two hats, the cocked model of his commission from the English King and the feathered bonnet that marked him a Mohawk chief.

His busy occupations included me and I was glad for activity and frequent trips away from Fort Johnson made more easy the dimming of my disgrace with Katie. I was fourteen and quick of mind and had the beginnings of some skill at diplomacy. I had not yet enough English to deal with colonials comfortably, but I knew almost all the tongues and dialects of the Iroquois Nations as well as many other Indian tongues, so Sir William was free in using me as both interpreter and agent on some of his missions to the west. I went sometimes by myself, sometimes with Carrihogo or others, to test the temper of the tribes and to use what argument Sir William gave us or we could wield ourselves to keep them with England.

Our journeyings and messages brought far chiefs to the Canajoharie castle for fresh councils. I have had some experience in dealing with men and with parties in my own life, but I cannot know from what reserves Sir William drew the energy to keep in balance all his affairs in these years. I could not remember every council, every swing and returning sway of allegiance, but I remember certain critical times. The council where after many years and many efforts Sir William brought back the Delawares to friendship with the Six Nations in a speech quite worthy of Cicero or Marc Antony or any Roman orator.

For generations we had considered the Delawares no better than bondswomen miming the manly arts of war and hunting and, for our scorn, they had sided everywhere with our enemies and vexed us despite their very slight prowess. But now, for England's sake and for our own, Warraghiyagey wished to bring them and the Shawnees into peace and friendship. So he spoke for long hours and took the gamble of calling the Delaware men and braves in open council and, at the end, the Six Nations upheld his welcome and the Delawares, for that time at least, sat down with us as a fellow nation and sheered away from their flirtations with the French.

But no sooner had Sir William managed this than his colonial brothers in Pennsylvania and New Jersey set to war with the very tribes he had been soothing and a whole new series of troubles were begun.

As a small child I remember a fright of swarming mud wasps on the bank of a creek below the lakes, and how I ran, after plugging one hole, to another and no sooner had plugged it than the buzzing creatures were upon me from some other place till I gave up and ran howling to my mother who plastered my bites with cool mud from the same bank and they healed. So was Sir William with all the divers tribes and the various rival colonials, except that he never gave up and ran off howling.

Let one alliance be cemented safely and sure as sunrise a settler gang would fire an Indian family, and as soon as that might be settled some brave would rape a colonial daughter, or land be stolen. I had a hard loyalty to Warraghiyagey and the Crown then and I am still a loyal British subject, but as I look back I must admit that there was often little to choose between settler and Indian, between King's man and lawless trapper, between some Frenchmen at their best and some Englishmen (at their worst). Mad years of war and lunacy. Hendrick dead. Red Head dead, too. False chieftains bolstered by colonials or other Indians for their own ends.

But if anyone should think that all my life at fourteen was fornication and high war and politics, let me disabuse them.

I am sure I had more responsibility (and I think more sense) than any boy, Indian *or* English, may have today, but I was still more boy than man and the most part of my strivings were those of a boy. Take the matter of young William Johnson whom I have generally called by his Mohawk name of Tagcheunto to distinguish him from his father.

From my first day at Fort Johnson we had been friends, but we had been rivals, too. That day we wrestled and, with the weight as well as the skill of a few extra years, he was able to best me. I made it my resolve to throw him fairly and put more of my spare hours into wrestling practice than ever I set aside for my letters or any other learning. And in a week or two I challenged him again, this time before Sir William who took great delight in the prospect of our match and insisted on having it held on the sward in front of the house with a full audience.

So we wrestled again, but Tagcheunto had been studying the art just as I had, so he kept all his earlier advantage and threw me just as easily.

Our bouts became part of life at the fort, and in every one of them Tagcheunto won. It meant so much to me that I should win, partly because Tagcheunto was Sir William's son and I think that was a position I at once envied and would have overcome. Our rivalry made us both expert at the art and I can say with honesty that, after I had attained the best of my growth at sixteen, there was no other wrestler in the Mohawk Valley save Tagcheunto who could put me on my back. The two of us became famous in the towns and farmsteads and in harvest seasons we were called to put on shows of wrestling. I have somewhere in a trunk an old handbill, scratched out by some Saratoga or Schenectady clerk: "WILLIAM OF CANAJOHARIE & JOSEPH BRANT, FAMOUS MOHAWK INDIAN WRESTLERS will exhibit their skill at Norman's Barn, on the Thrashing Floor, Saturday Evening, COME ONE! COME ALL!"

And nights like that were grand for William, even when his affection for rum had begun to get the better of him, was as canny a wrestler as you would ever see. We would ride to such a fete together, borrowing one of Sir William's horses, and be met at the inn of the town by whatever farmer's son had organized the evening (generally with the offer of a purse, not knowing we would have wrestled for sheer pleasure seven nights a week). He and his committee would stand us our dinner and we would take care to sup sparingly against the nausea that a clenched belly could yield later and I would try to moderate Tagcheunto's tilt toward the decanter as those townspeople who had wagered against us would try to encourage him.

After the feast to the fray.

Our gladiatorial arena might be an open common with spaces marked off on the grass or the floor of a vast Dutch barn. In either case we had an audience of a hundred or more crowding about the wrestling space before we even arrived so that we had to shoulder our way in with pats and buffets and congratulations and many an offer, especially to Tagcheunto, of a swig of rum or apple brandy.

Into the ring as our host shouted to the crowd his mixture of announcements and our introduction.

"Reward, hear ye, two pounds for a sorrel mare with a white star blaze on her forehead, strayed from Goodman Neuhauser's pasture. And tomorrow morning the noted Methodist preacher, Brother Jeremy Aldrich, will give his famous sermon, Salvation's Call to Thirsty Hearts, in the Assembly Ground on the bank of the Sacondaga. And now the event that brings us here, fellow townspeople, an exhibition of wrestling skills by the celebrated Mohawk Indian Wrestlers, William of Canajoharie and Joseph Brant."

Though Tagcheunto was quite half English as Sir William's natural son, the sound of "Mohawk wrestler" enhanced his art to the audience and he had given up protesting it. At our introduction, we would bow and then let the master of ceremonies continue.

"William and Joseph will challenge singly any man who thinks he can throw them. Together, they will offer to hold their own against any *three* men who may challenge. And they will finish the evening with a match between them to display the finer points of the ancient art of wrestling and such tricks and refinements as have been added from Indian lore."

The action was always slow to start, but at last some hulking hay-pitcher, goaded by his fellows, would enter the ring and indicate either Tagcheunto or myself and the first match would be on.

We would touch shoulders, the yokel and I, and then ordinarily he would attack me with a bull's rush of fury, hoping his weight might topple my slimmer form. Such assaults were easy; with a sidestep I would let him half pass and then catch an arm or leg and throw him. Generally the force of his own rush would topple him so heavily that all wind was knocked out of him and I would pin his back to the ground.

It was much the same between Tagcheunto and his opponents. Rarely did we meet a really good wrestler and then the enjoyment, as a change from tumbling heavyweight dunces, was as much a pleasure for us as for the audience.

The climax and the best point of the evening was always the final exhibition match between Tagcheunto and me. We gave an instructive show for ten minutes or more of holds and balances and feints and then got down to an actual trial of strength and skill; but no matter how much practice, no matter how I grew, I ended twice out of three times (and often the whole three) with my back to the ground and Tagcheunto victor.

Yet it never came to the point where I accepted his victory as inevitable. Every bout, before it started, was in my mind at last the one where I might triumph. And because I believe there is nothing we do without design, I hold this refusal of mine to be discouraged not mere stubbornness but the lesson I was meant to learn from all our wrestlings.

And, after the match, it was usually off to an inn or a friendly house to tipple and with good luck to get off with a girl, ending with my helping Tagcheunto home most times since not only did I drink less but my head was stronger than his, though Trust must know some nights when it was he who had to guide my own unsteady steps.

And there were, all in these same years of growing, times I wished nothing to do with anyone, including Tagcheunto and Sir William and even my beloved sister Molly. I wished to leave the house, not for a return to the castle but to pace with my own thoughts away from any other human.

Sometimes I thought, at other times I savored my solitude and the green space all about me. Parsons and women, I have found over many years, are unable to understand this simple, mindless act of communication with the universe. "What were you thinking about?" they will ask and ask again, brows dark with disbelief should you answer, honestly: "Nothing."

Yet it is not only possible but I believe most desirable that a man should have moments of refreshing mental emptiness and at no time are such periods more needed than in the years of youthful growth. How many hours I have squatted by Scots Creek, beginning perhaps by following the darting course of a trout in its shallow waters, ending, as the philosophers now name it, mesmerized by the glint of light on the current, my mind as washed as the contoured stones that had already sunk beyond vision and become a part of the blessed blank induced by sun and water in a head so teeming with dreams, ambitions, wonders that it had to be cleansed or turn from sanity.

When a man's body is vexed with fever or congested with phlegm, the trained physician drains away a moiety of blood for its relief. When a man's brain is heavy and crowded with the pain of growth, should he not likewise ease its pressures?

For there was more to my thoughts in those years than ambition to pin Tagcheunto in our wrestling. I was already old enough to stand on my own as a hunter and a warrior and I could see manhood full before me with problems more complex than hunting deer or planting corn or even engaging in campaigns against the French.

It wracked my young and puzzled brain to grasp the fact that although all the lands from one sea to the other were not diminished a single measured foot, yet the coming of Europeans had already set about foreshortening this vastness. The easy flow of tribe and tribe from one hunting ground to another could not continue in the European mode of land ownership.

All but the most stupid Indian could see these changes, but the wisest of our sachems thus far had found no solution for them save uneasy and changing alliance with whichever French or English spokesman offered us the most beguilement in surety of holding our own territories. And yet I cannot remember any one of such agreements, whether they were dubbed royal treaties or pacts with different states or simple oaths sworn one man to another that was not breached on one excuse or another by the European. It became no longer a matter of finding an Englishman one could trust, but of choosing between any number of Englishmen which one might cheat you least. A sorry record and one that shames me as an English subject myself, but nonetheless a true record.

I could throw my ax in bootless anger into a tree yards away, railing inside my head fruitlessly against these changes, but I could not stop them. In this, at least, I claim more wisdom than many of my fellow Indians, even fellow Mohawks. For too many of us, seeing the change and hating it, could find only two paths of resistance, either to war against the Eu-

ropeans or to give up the struggle in a proud Indian silence
and accept the end of ourselves as nations of free men.

I have thought on both ways in my time, and to speak truth
I found delight in a dream where with gun and bow and
tomahawk I could see my people wading in white blood as a
giant confederacy of tribes drove French and English,
Spanish, Swedes and Dutchmen into a surf whose green
stained red with their life's fluid. And then, the last European
driven down the bloody sands, we took back our own land,
feasted and fought with each other in the old brave way,
hunted and tilled our crops without the busy prattle of traders
and surveyors drunken on their visions of fences everywhere.
But ever in this dream there came sight of fresh ships landing
from the sea, of more whites with cannon huger than any seen
yet, wave upon wave of them, until they again inched forward
into the forests and brought their countinghouses and their
fences and all the rest of the changes that could not be turned
back.

And I have chosen the other side, at times, the side of pride
(which may well be our people's curse) and refusal to engage
in a struggle so purse-bound and petty and unwarriorlike. Too
many times I have stood with arms folded in scorn and accepted a hundredth lie from an American representative, a
thousandth to-be-broken promise of borders to be observed.

And this variety of acceptance as fruitless as warlike resistance. For the European will be willing always to let the Indian keep his pride so long as it does not interfere with imported greed. Rare is the man from across the sea waters who
does not care more for the figures in the ledgers, for the lines
inching ever forward on the map, than for whatever he may
call his self-respect. Yes, I have heard them boast and laugh
over simple theft of land from my people, congratulating one
another on their cleverness without a flicker of shame. It is as
if I were to preen myself because I had cozened a toy from an
infant without fair return. And I tell you this *is* Shame and
Evil! This is Abomination and Deceit! For the toy, and the

land, are worth nothing, and the decency of a man's immortal soul is worth everything. Else . . . else there is no meaning to life, nor to life after death, nor to Thy word.

I grow sore angry and bitter and incoherent even now in what should be my calm age.

And I thank Thy grace the more for Sir William Johnson who taught me there might be another way between these two extremes. In him I met for the first time a man who refused steadfastly to draw a line of difference between Englishman and Indian. When he was made one of the Mohawk Nation he *became* a Mohawk, not just another white with an entertaining Indian anecdote to regale his friends. So, when he took me into his household and later gave me commissions for his King, I could count *myself* an Englishman yet nonetheless a Mohawk.

And this was not the most of Sir William's importance to me, for he was different in other ways from the English landholders and the Dutch patroons we knew. Like them, he was a man fond of wealth and especially fond of holding land, but he seemed always to value people higher than land or gold. In this way he was truly the first Englishman any of us could honor as Chief.

His land was held fairly and never, insofar as I know (and I believe I should have known any exception), by theft or chicane. And no sooner did he come into possession of a piece of land than he set about improving it and improving the lot of his people along with it. He took good rent and shares and tillage from all his land, but first he helped his settlers make possible the cultivation to yield such bounty. He was never a really bookish man, yet I cannot count the times I saw him, not just in his study but often walking or riding, with his nose deep in some volume newly arrived from England detailing better care of land and the tending of animals.

Yet he could drop all this at the first rattle of a war drum and be painted and dancing at the castle, ranting the call to battle.

Which was important to me especially and to his other Mohawk brothers for it let us know there need be no great split in a man between the fierceness of a warrior and the sage counsels of a chief in peacetime.

These were hard thoughts for a boy, but necessary, and, even so, they were by no means the only burden of my mind, an endlessly wound palimpsest, as I think it, with all these thoughts and hosts of others written upon it, the important and the trivial, some writ over others in a scribbled maze I must now work my best to untangle into any reasonable order. Reasonable: it is held that the brain is the organ of reason, but if it be such a disorganized palimpsest as I have said it may be just as much an organ of unreason. I have come now to hold the brain but another tool in man's mechanic store, like the great muscle of arm and shoulder, which can do good when good is its instruction, but may do evil, as the arm may smite another to death, when evil guides it. Hence the easy road by which I came to a belief in the Soul, if in no other sense than as a name for what pilot guides brain, muscle, appetite and all the rest. And, if the Soul be not held in a true course for salvation, the actions of all its minor engines, however skilled, will lead only to disaster and destruction.

Thoughts so serious were tempered by lighter thoughts. Of these, the lightest and most pleasant concerned Ganundagwa, my next younger sister to myself, and promising a loveliness matched only in my memory by Molly and by my still most beautiful spouse, Catherine.

I have spoken with easiness of maids, but Ganundagwa was more to me than the frolicsome liaisons with such other girls. She was not, let me make clear at this onset, my true sister, for such relationship, whatever lies you have read concerning Indian customs, would have banned for us any amorous connection. She had been adopted by Carrihogo and my mother some years before when her own parents had been lost to a swift plague of an illness between catarrh and the bloody flux. She had come to live with us at the Canajoharie longhouse

and then, chosen as a protégée by Molly, moved to Fort Johnson where she attended my sister and learned some English
graces from Polly and Nancy Johnson.

Strange to tell, it was following my debacle with Katie that
I began first seriously to notice Ganundagwa and to be noticed by her. Alone almost of all the household she held off
joining in the jokes about my plight that continued weeks
after. For this I might have blessed anyone, but it was easier
to bless her with her heart-shaped face so often merry yet re-
strained against the bawdy jests concerning Kate and me. She
stood straight and was slender, something not always so true
of our women, and her breasts, still small and firm, hinted an
enticing abundance to come. I found myself thinking of her
every time Blind Kain sang to his harp any of those many
English songs that praised "celestial globes" or "milk-white
orbs." Milk-white was, of course, an imported foolishness for
Ganundagwa's skin had the scarlet-tinted tan of certain roses
and I should not have traded it for all the snow-white, milk-
white, lawn-whites of all the English and Irish balladeers
combined. Her eyes were gray in the light of day and turned
to black when evening came. She wore her black hair sometimes plaited and bound in Indian fashion, at other times in
the combed-out and curled elaborations that she and Polly
and Nancy took turns practicing upon each other. Seeing her
of an afternoon's stroll with Molly, bare feet and legs bare to
the thighs, a cambric shirt loose above knee leggins, you could
think her an Indian lad ready for first hunting. Seeing her the
same evening, after dinner at the great house, turned out in
lace and colored muslin with a fretted comb set in her hair,
you could only believe her a princess of some fine nation in
Araby or the true India. I lost my heart, but feared to speak
anything to her. I had recovered enough from the sad affair
with Katie to have tumbled another girl or two, but this was a
recovery only physical. I still felt my cheeks hot when anyone
mentioned, however innocently, such words as clinched or
caught or stuck, or even trapped. And, ours being a farm and

hunting society, you may imagine how many times a day I so winced.

I had no way of knowing that she also thought of me with love since her pride would not let her speak first and with my shame there was little chance of my speaking ever. So I continued to steal glances at her and she, as I learned, stole glances at me and, as I also learned even later, Molly and Sir William watched both of us and smiled quietly in company and hooted together with laughter in the privacy of their own bed, wondering how long our mute courtship might stumble on.

But for the fortune of our being in the same household, it could have stumbled on indefinitely and come to nothing. But we were so often together in the normal course of every day that opportunity found its way to break the deadlock. It came one afternoon, on the cushiony grass before the house where Walter Butler and Tagcheunto and I were wrestling in half seriousness, half horseplay. Walter, older than Tagcheunto, was slighter of build and I could best him as often as he did me though it never gave me the satisfaction I should have had from pinning Tagcheunto. Still, this afternoon I was above my best form and I took one fall out of three from Tagcheunto and then, engaging Walter, pinned him to the sward three times in a row and speedily each time. There were watching us Nancy and Polly Johnson and Ganundagwa and Enoch, a new black slave, and some others, but all I heard at the last fall was Ganundagwa's silver voice crying: "Oh, a fine throw, Joseph! Splendid! Splendid!" above the patter of other approval.

I rolled away from Walter who was raising himself ruefully on an elbow.

"Enough!" he said. "I have work to do. Tomorrow will be another story, Slippery Turtle."

I gave him a hand to his feet. Tagcheunto had already gone off toward the stables; it was past time for him to ride to Warrensburgh and join his drinking companions. Nancy and Polly had risen and were brushing at their skirts, a gesture they employed habitually as a mark of gentility whether there had been any possibility of dirt or none. Enoch was turning to the kitchen, the others amove in other directions, and Ganundagwa alone sitting still on the little grassy terrace.

I see the scene now as if in a painting, every figure in it clear and caught in their half or quarter turns away, but the whole painting composed by some master who without slighting any other part of it still kept the viewer's eye fixed on that slight, bright-eyed maid with her own eyes fixed on me (Figure of a Savage in the Foreground) in candid praise.

And I still do not know how there happened to be a space of time where we were alone there on the lawn for Fort Johnson was never much of a site for solitude. Yet alone we were. There was only the stretching green of the grass and the touch of a setting sun to light it and myself and Ganundagwa.

"Thank you," I said, turning toward her clumsily and full of almost every other thing to say.

"It was a clean throw," she said, a little breathless as if she, too, had been at wrestling. "Oh, you were splendid, Joseph!"

I could not find further words, but I kept my course to her side and took her by an arm and found the two of us walking together away from the house and past the bakehouse and into the shelter of some trees.

Now, if I were ever to write a book of advice to young men in the years of courtship, I should devote a whole chapter at least to the rhythms of a man and a maid walking together. There is the maid with mincing gait who teeters every other step to rest against you and this means, not as you may believe, an equal desire for amorous sport but a foretelling of more inane coquetry to come: with a maid walking in this manner, either desert her quickly or trip her into the nearest bush and have her despite her protestations else you win only a millstone about your neck and long winter evenings of her asking "Do you really love me?"

There is the more forthright walking together of a maid like Kate who would glue herself to one's side and walk as part of your body, but only so far as the nearest possible spot to make two backs together. And this, though in no wise serious, is wholesome and decent to my mind.

And there is the lady's walk, a set distance apart no matter what the terrain or the pace, a touch-me-not marathon that I suspect does not even end at the altar, and one experience of this should be warning enough for any man.

My walking with Ganundagwa was none of these, but the type of instant bodies' communion that comes seldom in any lifetime. There was as little of boldness in it as of flirtation. It was only something I can call acceptance on both our parts, a togethering as if we had been walking thus since before time and would walk thus—be thus, beyond time's end.

We stopped and stood in the shadow, her arm still in mine.

"I have been watching you every evening," I said to her. "And every other time I saw you, but I have been afraid to speak."

"Why?" she asked.

I could not answer with anything better than the balked grunt given as an Indian's total language by writers who should know better.

I shook my head in vexation.

"Because of you and Katie?" she asked. Now that we were together, she had no longer need for pride or diplomatics.

The hot burn rushed to my face and I nodded and tried to turn away, but she held my arm and would not let me out of her gaze.

"You are foolish, Joseph," she said. "Very foolish for a hunter and a war-blooded brave. Could you not see that I watched you, too?"

I stammered something. I was amazed and off my balance: Walter Butler could have thrown me easily then and there. And I was more amazed that there was a person here, this girl

I had watched with such longing and delight, who could speak the word "Katie" without a trace of smile or smirk.

"Had it been with a Mohawk girl," she went on calmly, "the trouble might never have happened."

I turned to her now and kissed her, first her cheeks and then her yielding, opening lips. To kiss had not been an ancient custom among Indians, but we had learned it and found it much to our liking.

When our lips had parted she spoke again: "And even if it should happen with a Mohawk girl, I would not care if I was the Mohawk girl. I and you, Joseph."

To tell the truth, what we fell to then was not a very successful bout of love. I was clumsy and still half frightened with my own good fortune; Ganundagwa was a virgin and had less than great enjoyment from the piercing of her veil. Yet I remember this coupling beyond any others for there was in it a strange tenderness mixed with violence on both our parts and a sharing beyond most acts of sex that I believe is the meaning of that obstinate word Love, so tortured between poets and parsons and philosophers. For it is this Love which, added to the act of sex, makes it important beyond gymnastic expertise else old lechers would never lack for partners and young lads weak with longing would sleep forever alone or with other lads.

It must have been over in five minutes and both of us were lying there, laughing and crying in each other's arms.

"If you knew how I had waited, Joseph," she said as I was saying: "If you knew how I had wanted you, Ganundagwa." And we collapsed into laughter again.

I am grateful for all the poets and balladeers since, for all I can remember almost every moment with Ganundagwa, I have not the words for them and so find it convenient to refer you to whatever madrigal or sonnet that stirs you and makes you remember your own best, lost love. This is what poetry and song are for above all their other virtues.

We went back to the house and that evening at dinner my

sister Molly caught my eye and smiled and, strange to say, I smiled her back without even a trace of blush-warmth to my cheek. I wished only to feast my glances upon Ganundagwa, coiffed and English-dressed for the meal and as beautiful as the pagans' Helen or Aphrodite.

Lovers cannot tell how newly they glow with requition of their love for they have already seen each other in that magic glow the Scots call glamour. Lovers are capable of believing they share a secret long after everyone within their circle has seen and noted and probably discussed in some detail their embodied metamorphosis.

I do not recall when or precisely how we learned that our sweet secret was a public property, but the revelation was not so bad since all the public involved approved almost as deeply as we did ourselves. And all the public seemed to know, as much as we did, that ours was not a transient folly, but meaningful love.

Molly was as joyous as we were, for Ganundagwa was the apple of her eye and I was her favorite brother and in truth she may be said to have planned (at the least, hoped for) our alliance. By the time I turned sixteen and Ganundagwa fourteen, the plans we had started to make in our trysts, only half coherent, were fleshed into actual prospects. Sir William was as pleased as Molly.

"Marriage helps give a man bottom, Joseph," he told me, pacing by my side on a walk through the orchard. He was ever a great believer in "bottom," that mysterious substantiality which sets a man of value apart from his more feckless fellows. "And there's no prettier maid than Ganundagwa, unless it's our Molly. I see no virtue in waiting. I've talked with Carrihogo and I'll help him dower the maid worthy of your station, my son. I only wonder, looking farther ahead than need be, whether it might be best you marry in the Church as well as Indian fashion."

This question was still open when I left with other guides early in the summer to accompany the English regulars under

Colonel Bradstreet (some two hundred and fifty soldiers) and their three thousand colonials against Fort Frontenac on the far shore of Lake Ontario. It was familiar country and an easy march, our Mohawk guidance and the presence of the colonials protecting Colonel Bradstreet from the worst excesses of a Braddock. The French gave up with no great struggle, but I learned a little more of the arts of modern war and for my own part in combat added something to my reputation as a fighter and a leader.

England had begun to regain the favorable flow of a winning tide in war. Sir William Pitt, in London, had nagged and harangued the motherland into more forces and more money for the conflict on our side of the ocean, and now the fall of Fort Frontenac drove another splintering wedge into the power of France. A fresh spirit of victory and enthusiasm stirred all through the northern colonies.

With some of the colonials and the rest of the guides, I made a quick journey back south, buoyed on the way by these great stirrings and by thoughts of Ganundagwa.

I left my fellow guides at the Canajoharie castle and went on alone, my feet flying, to Fort Johnson.

And found that Ganundagwa had been buried less than a week after I had gone north.

It was Sir William who told me, a man who would never turn tasks of bitterness to others. He met me at the front of the house where he had been ready to greet me for a day, ever since the first rumors of my return had reached him.

"Boy, boy," he clasped me to his breast.

"Greetings, Warraghiyagey," I said, curbing impatience. "Where is Ganundagwa, Father?"

"Sit down," he said, leading me into the great room. "She's gone, Joseph. With Manitou or in Heaven, angel or dust. She's dead, boy."

There was nothing brutal in his shortness. It was kinder than times I have seen since when I have heard men and women masking and putting off announcement of disaster.

I felt tears on my cheek and heard the rasp of sobs from my bosom as if another person wept.

"I do not believe it, Father," I said. "I just left her. I have held her in my arms not months ago."

Sir William held me, a warrior back from a great fort taken in combat, as if I were a child, but he could discover no more words for me. "Molly!" he called and I saw my sister come down the staircase and the look of loss on her face took from me any hope of fighting the truth.

"She fell to a fever, Joseph," she told me. "It was over in two days and three nights. We had William McCampbell come from Schenectady to bleed her, but it did not help. You know how swift it can be . . ."

I nodded my head against her breast where she held it. We Mohawks die quickly of the strange fevers and agues which the Europeans have brought to our shores with them along with greed and surveyors and rum and all the rest.

It is as well I was not yet a Christian for it was a blow that could have shattered a fresh faith.

I have seen much death since then and heard many pawky efforts at condolence from Christians both lay and divine. The sorriest thing I think to tumble from human lips is placing some hideous blame upon God, saying: "He loved her (or him) so much that He would have her (or him) with Him in Heaven." This, when some poor soul has choked out life in an agony of bloody coughing or had the crab gnawing at bowels for months. To make Him seem ridiculous does service neither to God nor man. I teeter often near heresy on this question, but I cannot help thinking there are some things still can wound God as well as us mortals.

What else I took from this tragic experience was a deep knowledge that the good of life may be as transitory as morning's dew or a blossomed flower. This has never left me. Then, as a young Mohawk, bred in the old ways, I had been able always to accept death as a fact of existence, a necessary end to every life. But what had happened with Ganundagwa's passing was more than another death; it was a loss of part of myself, something new-grown that counted more than a limb, something I had treasured for being as permanent as my own soul. And that, too, had proved to be as easily taken from me as any child's toy. Never again would I count on any pleasure lasting. It was a lesson that came close to deranging my mind, but, once learned, it has protected me well through my life and enabled me to stand through many vicissitudes otherwise too harsh to be borne.

They tell me I lay abed almost a week refusing food and any drink but a sip of water now and again, my eyes closed most of the time, not against light but against a present that held no Ganundagwa. With them shut tight enough I could lie still and re-create moment after moment, hour after hour, day after day, from memory.

On the sixth day, Sir William came into the room and beat a tattoo on the foot of the bed with a new crop.

"Up, Joseph," he said.

"Warraghiyagey, I cannot," I said. "Without Ganundagwa there is nothing."

"There is no nothing in life, son," he said with severity but with the great understanding he could bring even to a chiding. "There is only more and less, and how much less I have heart enough to imagine. But you do her memory no honor by moping and mourning." He struck the bedstead again. "Damme, Joseph, you had months of happiness. Remember it and be grateful. Now, get up."

He gave the bed a final thump and walked away without turning to see if I stirred. I think, if he had turned, I might have stayed and lain in that bed till Death took me, but the sight of his broad back, his blue cheviot coat stretched taut across it, the vitality of his stride were more than I could resist. I dragged myself to the side and sat up and called Kitchener to bring me food which I vomited as promptly as I ate, but it sufficed as a step to return to some kind of life.

It would be a tribute to Sir William's power of persuasion

as well as to my own sanity to report that, from that rising, I was once again myself, but it was not to be so swift a recovery. When, now as I write about her death in distant recollection Ganundagwa still has the power to make my hand tremble and my pen blot these pages, how much the more was I an invalid of love and loss at the very time?

Once I was up and about, I spurned the help of Sir William and even my dearest Molly in favor of seeking oblivion with Tagcheunto in his habitual carousals. With him I rode from wrestling match to wrestling match or simply from tavern to tavern, embroiled in boozey fights in which I can take no pride except that a stunned noggin often drove out the memory of Ganundagwa. But only for moments.

One night in Rensselaer I drank with Tagcheunto and some townsfolk and a few colonial militiamen. I ran my usual gamut in my cups—morose to start, then flushed and giggling foolish at the stupidest japery, jigging on the tavern floor, and then quick shift to sorrow and to anger.

I had achieved this last dismal mood when one of the village louts saw fit to bait me, some careless remark I should have passed over at any other time. I was so drunk I never could say whether it was a general slur against my people or something more personal, but it had me in a split-second at his throat, feeling great pleasure in the sweat-moist softness of his white flesh under my clenching grasp.

I moved so swiftly that full minutes passed before the other carousers even knew what was happening. And then they could hear the racked whisper of his choked breathing and see his features turning purple gray as I kept my pressure on his windpipe with my right hand and with my left forced back his head, the bleared eyes popped in agony, toward breaking his neck. And I should have succeeded in so doing had not the other drinkers, even Tagcheunto joining them, prised me loose and held me firm while my prey fell like a boneless sack to the filthy floor.

"He's dead!" I heard someone say.

"Nay, there's a trace of heartbeat left," in another voice, and Tagcheunto shouldering me out of the door and coaxing me onto my horse and to ride away.

For, though drunkenness might serve among Indians as an excuse for murder, there was little such reciprocity among the colonials when an Indian slew one of their people. Tagcheunto kept me away from towns over a week while my victim, his injuries complicated by fever and some affliction to his lungs, hung between life and death. He recovered at last and I could rejoin communal pursuits, but the story of my brawling stayed even more alive than he and grew in the telling. "Brant's temper" became a byword and my victim, in different versions of the tale, was swollen to a dozen men or shrunk to an innocent child I had torn limb from limb in drunken wrath. Thus was seeded, in drink and riot, a legend that followed me ever after.

There were some months of such senseless search for an artificial anodyne before I could come back to staying at Fort Johnson, at putting my talents (whatever they were) to better use than brawling and blind dissipation. No one, neither Molly nor Sir William, chided me or pressed me through this time. Molly told me that she had been more than once tempted to do so.

"But Sir William held me back," she said. "He knew so much, Joseph, of how men may be led but seldom forced. 'The lad will grow tired of a thick tongue and a roiled belly,' he said. 'Would I could hope the same for Tagcheunto. But Joseph must grow tired himself; do we try to guide him, he'll resist with a fine combination of Indian and youthful stubbornness and take all the longer. Leave him be, Moll.' And we did leave you be, and he was right."

Sir William called me into his study one late afternoon when I had been behaving more like a human being and less like a fury for a week or so.

"You've come through it, Joseph?"

"I think so, Father," I said. It still sent a sting through my heart even to speak of Ganundagwa's loss thus obliquely, but I owed him an answer.

"I lost a lass once," he said, no longer looking at me but across his desk and through the open window to the snow outside. "Not so bad as death, perhaps, and perhaps worse, my lad. It was for what they called an 'unsuitable connection' that my family shipped me out of Ireland and to these parts. I stayed blind, stupid drunk the first week of the voyage and thought my heart would never mend, either for the loss of the lass or for the banishment from my own land. And now, this valley is more mine than any part of Ireland and Molly sweeter than any dream of the past. I say that truly, lad, but some evenings Kain can sweep his strings and sing of a Galway colleen and I find my eyes misting. We are peculiar beings, Joseph."

He brought his eyes back to me.

"There is much work for all of us," he said. "My son John is learning much and my nephew Guy is becoming a man of capability, but this is not enough. Neither John nor Guy, for all their closeness, have come to my own feeling for the Six Nations and I doubt they ever shall. Poor William can only wrestle or drink. This is the gap that you may fill for me, Joseph, if you can and if you will. I have been able to serve His Majesty as a bridge between Englishman and Mohawk without ever being the less a loyal subject. I shan't live forever. You may be able to serve him in the same way without ever being the less a Mohawk."

"But you are young, Warraghiyagey," I said. It is not our Mohawk custom to speak ahead thus of death and it made me uncomfortable.

"And I may stop a bullet or an ax tomorrow," Sir William said. "Or fall to pox or plague. No, Joseph, I have spent twenty years building on this continent and I must plan to keep what I have built from falling to ruins. Will you work to be my other self?"

"I will do what you bid and what I can, Father," I said.

"Good," Sir William said and told me his needs for inspection of the two new forts, the one at the Canajoharie castle, named Fort Hendrick in honor of our fallen chief, the other at Kanadesaga (now called Geneva), held for us by the Senecas who would admit no English garrison but wanted their own ability to defend it.

"You've seen enough fighting to have a sound eye for weakness," he said. "You will go to speak for me, cementing friendship and assurances of the King's strength, but observe as you speak and let me know how well defenses stand. The castle is close and safe enough, I think, but unless we are sure of Kanadesaga, we may have to hold back plans for other forces."

He told me much more in detail and reeled off names of chiefs and their wives and children for me to remember in his messages.

At the end he had me repeat the most important points and was pleased that I could do so without fault.

"Get powder and what other equipment you may need from Claus," he told me. "The sooner you can be off—"

"Tomorrow," I said proudly.

On snowshoes it took me better than two weeks, almost three, to reach Kanadesaga and there, for all my youth, I was Sir William's man and treated with full respect as I gave his messages and made my own careful inspection of the log fort. It had been built sturdily three years before and it stood stout save for a blind spot to the southeast where a longhouse cut off view of the approaches. Two Skunks, the Seneca war chief, was agreeable to my suggestion for setting a war watch in the longhouse and that solved that problem. I feasted and took council for another few days before turning home.

I came home by way of the castle where I found, as I knew, Fort Hendrick to be strong and well manned. I stopped with Carrihogo and my mother and she took pleasure in treating me, Sir William's chosen agent, as her Small Turtle of old, cooking me special dishes and scolding some the state of my belt and leggins. Carrihogo had me sit with him and other chiefs by the fire, proud to let me share in grown speech of import, the old subjects of land and treaties, English and French.

My feet dragged in the short final lap between castle and Fort Johnson, my mind nagged by my previous homecoming to death and loss and despair. I feared almost to face the door of the house. I knew my mother and Carrihogo were in health, but what if I hailed Sir William and no one answered? Or he came to tell me of Molly's death?

But Sir William smiled at me from behind his table-desk.

"Hail, Son-Who-Has-Traveled-Far," he spoke with an Indian formality, yet drolly. "What is your word?"

"My word is good, Father-Who-Does-Much," I matched his speech. "Kanadesaga stands sound and Fort Hendrick could balk the French King himself. Two Skunks sends you long life."

Thus we got through the greetings approved between men of gravity and importance and I realized that behind his smile Sir William was offering me some measure of "bottom."

"Sit, lad," he motioned to a splat-back chair, "and tell me more."

I put my rifle against the wall, made myself comfortable and told him all I had seen and done.

He nodded attentively when I explained about the Kanadesaga blind spot and its solution and narrowed his eyes when I told him the nagging impression I had that the Senecas, while in no wise turning to the French, were weaker in their allegiance to the Crown and even to Sir William.

"Yet you think they will hold the fort fast against the Joncaires?" he asked, stabbing little marks with the plumbago pencil on a paper before him.

"For now, Father," I said. "What I tell you is only a hint from my heart, nothing seen with my eyes."

"Eyes and heart need both be sharp," he said. "This is something we must talk of further with Molly. I have a strange bequest for you." His tone had changed abruptly and I could not analyze whether it was serious or in some wise mocking. I felt, recurring for the moment, my fear as I neared Fort Johnson of death and loss. A bequest meant death: had I been right in my premonition?

"Parson Prouty died," he said, and my heart was light again. "Most of his small estate he left to charity, but he particularized that you, Joseph, should have this prayer book." He reached into a drawer and drew out a worn but sound volume, leather-clad and on its cover in flaking gold print "The Book of Common Prayer."

"Don't ask me why," he said, now open in his smiling. "I had never chosen you as one of the Reverend's favorites."

I held forth my hand and he placed the book into it. I felt its light weight, but there was a sudden extra burden on my palm beyond expectation, beyond mundane measure. Thy sign, O Lord!

"Died of the spasm last fortnight," Sir William said. "Sudden, but easy, the happiest way for a man to pass beyond."

"I would look at the book and think," I said, speaking as much to myself as to Sir William. Too many different thoughts and sensations were abroad within me.

"Fine," he said, almost absently, already turning to paper on the table before him. "We shall talk together with Molly after the evening meal."

I took myself to my room with the Reverend Prouty's prayer book and all my considerations.

I had seen as little as I might of Reverend Prouty after the debacle with Katie. Time had eroded my bitter impulse to kill him upon first sight, but I think he sensed a mite of my savagery and was as willing as I to keep distance between us. Yet, warring with this, was a small but strong belief that, however dry and unpleasant he might stand as a man, yet he held some magic, some secret that I would share. So much for Reverend Prouty.

Beyond this, another fact had troubled me deeply. I had,

before setting out against Fort Frontenac, made those precautionary rituals common to any Mohawk, a small sacrifice and a burning to Manitou and my own Turtle protectors against harm for myself and my loved ones. And I had come back from that mission to the death of Ganundagwa.

Before I left for my mission to the forts, I had done nothing, in part because of hurry but in at least equal part from loss of faith. Yet from this last mission I had returned not only whole myself, but to a whole community of family and of friends and to the bequested holy gift of Reverend Prouty.

Could I doubt some significance to this?

I sat on my bed and studied the book, turning its pages and searching for help. Some words I knew and could make out in the small print—God, Good, Sunday, Prayer, Burial, Sick—but the much greater part was a mare's-nest thickness of mystery with, ever and again on a page heading, some word of such strangeness and power that I could have cut my right arm to know it then and there: Sexagesima, for an example.

All I could be certain of was that it was a book of prayer and devotion and that it had been words of prayer in Reverend Prouty's wrung voice that had moved me before and troubled me ever since. Staring would not help me, so I set the book aside with my own store of belongings and called Kitchener for a bowl of water that I might wash and prepare for the evening meal.

We talked, as Sir William had planned, afterward of the Seneca fort and of my feelings.

"Did I not tell you Joseph was wise?" Molly said to him. "I have my own reports of the tribes at Kanadesaga and of the rest of the Seneca Nation and they are as Joseph has said. It is nothing one could pin to ground with an arrow, but it is there still, a lessening of their tie to us and to the King."

"I sent Two Skunks a belt by Joseph," Sir William said, thinking while he spoke, "and promise of cloth and powder in the next wagon we send out. What else to do, lass?"

"If I felt they were wavering to the French . . . ," Molly said. "But it is not that, do you think, brother?"

"It is something different," I said. "I can give it no more name than the lessening of ties Molly makes it."

"So for now, I think we are safe," Molly said.

"For the plans against Niagara?" Sir William asked.

She nodded. "But I could wish you were not off to war yourself, my lord," she added.

"And would you love me as a fireside chief?" Sir William snorted.

"I would love you as you," Molly said. "I am no longer a young girl who must be impressed over and over by her brave's courage. I know the man I have." And she looked at him long with the warmth that always gathered between them.

"Then why not leave things as they are?" Sir William said with a whole new harshness in his voice that I had never heard in any exchange with my sister: it was not just harshness, but a pleading that was near to anger.

"Because things that must be done should not be delayed," Molly said, and her voice too had changed and was the voice she might use in council, covering the voice of warmth and love.

"What?" I asked without even knowing my own question.

"Nothing, Joseph," Molly said. "Another matter."

"Yes," Sir William said. "I think we agree to stand as we are on the matter of the Senecas. We go against Niagara as soon as Colonel Prideaux may be willing."

"And I go with you?" I asked.

"Of course," Sir William said and smiled a dismissal and an end to my share in their discussion.

"One other thing," I stayed my parting.

"What, little brother?" Molly asked.

"The book Reverend Prouty left to me," I said. "It is a new treasure to me, but it is a treasure unlocked. I cannot read it and I thirst to know its meaning."

Sir William welcomed the change of subject.

"Right, lad," he said. "You've come by the English you have all helter-skelter and without its writing. Molly, what shall we do?"

"You know I've little writing myself," Molly said. "Joseph may need more than I in times to come."

"John has his letters fairly," Sir William said, "and Nan and Polly enough to pounce on every new romance. And, Lord knows, Dan Claus is as good as any minister. I can help myself, but my time is overburdened."

I listened, eyes alight, while he and my sister put together plans for everyone to help me with my letters.

"It will still be helter-skelter," Sir William said, at last, "but it should be sufficient to get you on your own road. Perhaps later we can bring a school to the house."

And after this I could accept his dismissal in good spirit, going from him and Molly at once to Daniel Claus, he none too delighted that I should interrupt his time with Nancy, but willing, when I told him it was Sir William's wish, to find time every day to help me with the English letters. And Nancy, herself always a good-humored maid, said she would spell out words for me when Daniel was away.

Thus I was, after so much careless catchpole learning, set upon more education at the age of seventeen.

I attended to other duties, too, and went about local businesses for Sir William, but now in my spare time I waited for a moment Daniel might help me, or John or Nancy or Polly.

Daniel Claus was the best teacher; the rest helped, but made a game of the whole thing and were neither strict nor persistent. Daniel sat me down with slate and scriber and had me copy every letter, over and over till I could have formed it with my eyes closed, and to say as I wrote its name and make some of its sounds. He would not let me even try to read from my prayer book at the first.

"That's your goal, Joseph," he insisted. "You'll spoil it rushing at it half cocked." I was reminded of Carrihogo and my hours of dry-firing before I was allowed to load my first gun with ball and powder, so I agreed with the reservation that I might steal peeks at the prayer book sometimes alone.

I cut my tender learning teeth on childish verses of John Bunyan and Isaac Watts. I felt shamed at the time for I knew that these simple rhymes were meant for children scarce beyond infancy, but I have since had some gratitude because I believe this first training has made it the easier for me to read now and enjoy verse for adults. Too many men, well schooled as they may be, I have met who can read only an account book; the very form of verse distresses them and sets them off from both delight and instruction that might otherwise be within their grasp.

Now was the time when Pitt's strategy and all Sir William's careful welding of the tribes to English alliance would come together in a final campaign to crush the French. There were three parts to the master plan: General Wolfe with his force of near ten thousand would batter Quebec from the sea; other land forces would at last strike Ticonderoga and Crown Point; a third force would strike by land and lake water at Fort Niagara. And this Niagara attack, to come first, was to be Sir William's chief concern.

There was one strange necessity before we set forth upon Niagara, and it harked back to the secretive exchange I had heard between Sir William and my sister Molly the night of my return from the forts. Catherine Weisenberg, thin as a kindling twig, cough-racked and sick to death, was brought by litter from Albany to Fort Johnson.

She arrived late in the afternoon and was taken at once upstairs to rest, with Mr. McCampbell, the physician, staying at her bedside alert for any critical alteration of her racked straddle on the fence between this world and the next. Father Cotton, of the Anglican church at Warrensburgh, came soon after she did and had dinner with us. Sir William sat through the whole meal in dark and sullen silence while Molly tried to keep speech moving as if this night were no different from any other.

I caught her aside after the meal when Sir William had gone off to his study.

"Why is that woman here?" I asked. Like anyone else in the valley I knew her for a whining shrew and termagant, a hatchet-faced terror these many years whatever she had been to Sir William in bedded bygones. Even her children, John, Nancy and Polly, had no kindness toward her and kept from her room this night.

"She is here to be decently married, as she deserves, Joseph," Molly said. "Sir William mislikes the idea, but it must be done. If she dies unmarried to him, John is only another bastard among all the rest, and on Will's death everything he has put together will fall in a tangle of lawsuits and petty greed."

"But *you* are his wife!" I blurted. "Let him marry you and leave Peter his heir."

"To hold his life's work together," Molly said soberly, "his heir should not be in any part Indian. Believe me, little brother, for I have thought long about it. I am of your blood and we know that we can take care of our own. It is not so with John, nor with Nancy or Poll who should be able to marry men of their choice without carrying the brand of bastardy. I have had my own hand in helping Will strengthen his holdings and his renown; it is as much to my desire as to anyone's to see them cemented firm. Enough."

She turned away from me and I could see a glint of sorrow at her eyes' corners, but her head was held firm with resolution. From the doorway of Catherine Weisenberg's room I heard Mr. McCampbell's discreet cough.

"I believe now," he said, when Sir William came out of his study.

"Call Cotton then, Joseph," Sir William directed me.

He spoke in a low voice with Mr. McCampbell. Above their murmur I could hear Catherine Weisenberg's complaints croaking from inside the room. "All the pother for a poor sick woman. Any decent man would have come to me . . ."

I found the Reverend Cotton in the great room and led him to the bedchamber. It was lit but dimly by candles when we had lamps aplenty and I thought it was as if Sir William, however he had given in to Molly, had no liking even to look upon the woman he was taking to lawful wife. She still croaked her grievances, a frail wisp of womanhood barely outlined under a quilted coverlet, till Father Cotton hushed her.

"Stay by the door, Joseph," Sir William ordered me. "We need no interruptions nor audience in this affair."

So I stood guard, watching the hall and also the bedchamber, and listening.

I heard Father Cotton rustle the leaves of his prayer book and at once realized it was the same as my own.

"Dearly beloved, we are gathered together here in the sight of God . . ."

I felt the same familiar shiver from the day of Father Prouty's grace, and it grew as the service touched more splendid portions: "I require and charge you both, as ye will answer at the dreadful day of judgment when the secrets of all hearts shall be disclosed . . ."

I resolved, then and there, never to take woman in marriage without this particular magic incantation. And I have not.

"Now get her out of here!" Sir William's order broke the reverie into which I had fallen. With Mr. McCampbell superintending, Catherine Weisenberg Johnson, once again raising her croak of remonstrance, was bundled into her litter and carried out of the house for the trip back to the town where she soon died.

I slept badly that night and had more troubled dreams than in many months, all the familiar ones recurring and new dreams of uncertain, misty dissension. I dreamed of bears, never a good sign for a Turtle, and my white owl returned in one dream but this time it brought me no solace. I was glad for dawn and a day of laid-out duties.

For now everything was bent to the Niagara expedition. I
look back now and see our start almost as a comedy, dead serious as it was then to all of us concerned. But here was General Amherst forbidding any instruction to the Indian allies of
what their role would be, and here was Sir William knowing
full well that no Indian would follow a blind order from anyone and thus countermanding his commander at every council. And here was I, doing Warraghiyagey's and Molly's bidding to guard any chief from dropping a word of our plans,
and all the time quite sure that everyone from Joncaire to
wandering Seneca brave knew our goal as clearly as we did
ourselves.

General Amherst was an amalgam of arrogant ignorance
and surprising intelligence. In the field he was as capable a
commander as King George ever had, yet in almost every
point where his planning touched the Indian alliances he was
as foolish as a barnyard goose. A man of pride and sensitivity
himself, he could not see that equal pride and sensitivity
might belong to any man of darker pigment and this was his
most obsessive blindness.

We set out in late spring, fine weather for marching, and
made our way to Oswego. We had some days' wait there, by
the lake waters, for our provisions to arrive and to allow time
for the assemblage of our fleet, a curious flotilla made up of
every small craft, from our hundred Indian canoes to bateaux
able to mount small cannon to rafts and whaling boats from
far.

We hugged the coast as we sailed west, more to satisfy
Colonel Prideaux's belief that there could be such a thing as
secrecy than in any hope of hiding our fleet from hostile eyes.

We brought our boats to shore early July on the shore by
Four Mile Creek, just that distance from the French fort. No
enemy held us off and we were settled in a well-protected
camp before Captain Pouchot even learned of our arrival.

There began a siege which was more a duel of wits between Sir William and Pouchot than any conventional mili-

tary operation. Using every sachem with blood or totem ties to the French Indian allies, Sir William embarked on a barrage of belts and promises and oratory more deadly than a cannonade. Colonel Prideaux moved his artillery into place, but Captain Pouchot did not tremble for he counted on a forest suddenly come alive with shooting, scalping Senecas and Chenussios.

But I had been carrying, with others, Sir William's cunning talk among the tribes, especially to two Turtle brothers who stood high as Chenussio war chiefs. Before the first shot was fired, the whole Chenussio gave Pouchot notice that they had no stomach to be embroiled in this battle and evidenced their firm decision by burning down the French trading post.

Captain Pouchot saw himself now outnumbered, but loosed some missions of his own. He sent Kaendae, a Seneca chief as eloquent as bibulous, into our very camp to plead with all Indians of the Six Nations against supporting the English cause.

It was here, I am sure, that Sir William showed his shrewdness for he made no effort to turn Kaendae away or to have our English sentries fire on him as he approached our camp. Indeed I think he purposefully kept Colonel Prideaux in midnight darkness as to what Kaendae's mission was. He even saw to it that rum was set before our distinguished visitor to lubricate his tongue as he made speeches to cozen our braves. I sat by the fire and listened as Kaendae raked up old (alas, true) tales of Indians betrayed and killed by English settlers and sang in praise of all the French were willing to offer us. But Sir William made no speeches against him and left him free and unmolested.

So the more Kaendae spoke, the greater Indian suspicion waxed. It seemed a simple matter. If there had been any substance to Kaendae's promises, surely Warraghiyagey would have been busy chasing him from the fireside. That Sir William said and did nothing was the best surety that Kaendae must be lying. We listened to him and smiled and even sent back to the fort with him three of our chiefs to parlay in person with the French.

Pouchot smiled with glee, as I heard, when Kaendae brought our chiefs into the fort, but his face fell with every sentence they uttered for they spoke only recommendations that their Seneca friends desert the French. Pouchot had neither Sir William's patience nor his foresight. He halted our chiefs before they had finished their speaking and insisted on blindfolding them (against all that they had already seen) before hustling them from the fort. And every Indian was surer than ever that the French promises held only emptiness and that security lay with the English.

Happily, Colonel Prideaux's engineers got their cannon within range before the impatience could do any serious damage among the tribes. The thunder sound of the guns enlivened Indian blood. Kaendae was still moving between fort and camp and reported that a shell in our first firing had fallen directly down Captain Pouchot's chimney and come near to blowing him up in his bed. We gave Kaendae more rum and sent him reeling back to his masters to tell them what stories God knows.

We had our own worries for, in that same first salvo, a cohorn exploded before firing and struck Colonel Prideaux fatally. He lingered only moments, not long enough to make any instructions on the ticklish question of the chain of command.

While Indians cheered and shouted that evening, Sir William argued with the English officers. Captain Charles Lee claimed he should take Prideaux's position, but Sir William pointed to his own commission from the King as colonel in charge of the Six Nations and would not budge from his right to assume command.

Sir William kept the cannon firing and pressed the trenches closer to the fort, but Pouchot stood brave and stubborn, still hopeful of assistance, no longer from his Indians but from a force of a thousand Frenchmen and two hundred new Indian allies under Captain Charles Aubry.

In this position, Sir William took the risk of striking out to halt Aubry before he could reach the fort and he made his move none too soon. Our forces had no overwhelming superiority but we carried the field. I took seven scalps in the battle, four French and three Seneca including that of Two Hawks, a brave I had once hunted with, but I felt no qualms of fellowship when I found him running at me with an upraised ax.

With Aubry routed, Pouchot surrendered. Sir William took the fort in the King's name but handed Pouchot back his sword in respect for his bravery. Most of the French were allowed to depart without much excess of looting or torture.

After the battle, I stood in a short ceremony with some other young braves to take new war names as is sometimes our custom. A man may, if he likes, carry one name from cradle to death. It is more common that he will have one birth name, then pick up one or more other names for happenings in his life. I was both Small Turtle and Joseph Brant (or Brant's Joseph). Now, for a name to carry in battle, I chose Thayendanegea, or Sticks-Bound-Together.

Sir William walked with me alone about the landside rampart and congratulated me, little on the scalps I had garnered, much on my work with the Chenussios.

"There are a hundred men around you, Joseph," he said, "who can lift the hair off a skull and the better part of them are dunces and will remain so though they put together scalps enough to make a longhouse rug. There are only two or three who come close to you in subtlety and this is what I should advise you to cultivate."

There were battle cries still ringing in my ears and the smells of blood and powder, so I did not take his words well.

"But I do not wish to sit at the fire like a squaw, or at a desk like Daniel Claus, Father," I said.

"There's no danger you will, son," he said. "Have trust I know you that well. But in such rare moments as you are not knee-deep in blood, continue your learning."

He forced me to laugh with him and we went back to Captain Pouchot's quarters where Sir William was bedded and opened a bottle of claret and then another and I ended by helping him into that bed our first artillery fire had nearly blown to bits.

We had won Niagara and so moved forward the first step in a campaign that was to see the French forts at Ticonderoga and Crown Point fall.

Boast as I may of my memory, the year from the Niagara siege is a jumble of so many happenings that I cannot even try to record it in any decent order. There were events that stirred my blood and engaged my interest that may be petty and meaningless to everyone else, and there were great moments of victory in the French war that moved me slightly or not at all.

I suppose I remember best the great council Sir William called of all the tribes at Detroit. I had had some work as messenger and emissary and I was to meet Sir William and John at Niagara but news I heard sent me hurrying to meet them earlier. A Huron of Turtle kinship had told me there were bad belts circulating among all the tribes north and west, calling on them for an attack against English outposts and settlements across the whole frontier. I do not give in easily to rumor, but this brother's word was grave and he had a reputation for truth. I took a canoe with Tagcheunto who had come with me, and we struck across Ontario, risking rough water, to Oswego from where I made my way to those Chenussio totem-mates who had been helpful before. This time they were less cordial and it grew plain that it was the Chenussios who had begun to pass on the bad belts and also that the belts had been thoughtfully received by many tribes angry at increasing settlement and usurpation of hunting grounds. I wished I had Molly to palaver with for hers was in some ways the best mind of all of us (even including Sir William's) on tribal matters like these, but there was no time. I sent Tagcheunto home to convey her the news (half certain she had it already from her own sources) and left to catch Sir William's party at Onondaga.

On the trail, just before reaching Onondaga, I met with two Mohawk braves I knew from the longhouse at the Canajoharie castle. I had guessed true; the news was already there and at Molly's behest they bore good belts from the castle asking that Sir William abandon his plan for the council, so far away and amid so much danger, and return to Fort Johnson to mend his own defenses.

We burst in upon Sir William and John in the longhouse where they were drinking with two sachems, one a Seneca, the other my old hunting companion Billy Painter, grown gray and stout and solemn, but still bright of eye.

"We have word, Warraghiyagey," I panted, "bad word of bad belts against the English." My Canajoharie companions flung down their own belts before the three men.

"Catch your breath," Sir William said. "Sit and have drink."

We gulped our rum gratefully and then had to catch our breath all over again from its choking fire.

"Now, tell me more, Joseph," Sir William said. "I have had great, world-trembling rumors from my lord Amherst, but when you bring the same news I shall consider believing it."

I told him what I had heard, first from the Huron brother, then from the Chenussios. The two braves from the castle gave much the same story underlined by Molly's opinion of its gravity.

Sir William drummed his fingers on the worn-smooth table board and held out his glass for John to fill again.

"We have the same word from General Amherst," he said, after a swig at his glass. "He writes full of alarums and excursions in one sentence and in the next ignores the whole business because he cannot believe the peril of Indian warfare, even after they defeated Aubry for him." He snorted and drank again. "And Molly and all the chiefs at the castle would have me turn home and I suspect General Amherst places as little importance on the council as he does on Indian war . . ."

He looked about the table, from me to John to Billy Painter to the two braves.

"What would you have me do, son John?" he asked.

John looked down into his own glass as if there might be an answer there.

"I think it is clear, Father," he said, and repeated: "I *think* it is clear. Molly and the wisest chiefs counsel your return." He looked to me and to Billy Painter for support. "A hunter does not stick his head into a lion's cave," he said.

"And you, Joseph?" Sir William asked.

I had not expected to be called upon and I started like a guilty scholar caught with his lesson unprepared. But this was no lesson, these were hard facts I had been asked to answer.

"I do not know, Warraghiyagey," I said after I had thought. "If I did know, I would be you."

For some reason my reply made Sir William laugh and with the gust of his laughter the whole table brightened from its grim consideration of a moment earlier.

"Perhaps you will be, Joseph," he said. "You, John, are right, as Molly is right, only so far as you go. There is one reason a man may stick his head in a lion's cave and that is to find if the inhabitant of the cave is really a lion or only a fox taking tribute from the lion's reputation." Billy Painter smiled; Sir William spoke of his people and with proper deference.

"But—" John interrupted.

"No, there is none," Sir William said sternly. "By God, son —and Joseph, you listen, too—this is a matter of bottom and it can't be scamped. I've worked twenty years to reach the place where I can talk in council to tribes like the Ottawa and Chippewa who've always sided with our enemies and you think I'll let some bad belts from the Chenussios frighten me back behind the walls of Fort Johnson! Billy, what do *you* say?"

"I say my brother Warraghiyagey is right," Billy Painter

said. "He must have a look in the cave to find what animal lives there. Perhaps it is only a skunk."

"Remember not just what we are doing, but why," Sir William addressed John and myself. "Now let us all drink till we're stupid and in the morning I shall make up a message to soothe Molly. She'd have seen the truth herself if she weren't carrying my child."

John had the bottle tilted and we were happy to follow Sir William's instructions and example. I have no count of the number of times I put that great man to bed, but this night was not one of them for Billy Painter put me to mine.

The braves left back for Canajoharie and we the other way to Niagara. Sir William sent belts ahead to certain Seneca chiefs that they might meet him there and give him opportunity to set plans in motion before the Detroit council. But when we reached Niagara there was nothing to greet us but more scolding messages from General Amherst and three bedraggled Senecas, no one of them near the rank of sachem, with a meaningless wampum belt signifying nothing. Sir William scorned even to accept it and John worried mightily.

"I deal with chiefs or with no one," Sir William said. "If I take a belt like this before Detroit, I've drawn my own teeth. See to the boats, John."

We took twelve large boats and a few canoes and spent some days fitting them for the journey. It was just before we left that a Mohawk runner reached us with word of pestilence at the castle and around about it. Molly was as yet untouched, but my mother had been carried off to death in fever and delirium.

I walked away to make what small rites I could this far from home. I had seen my mother little in the years since I had started to become a man, but now I could remember too much for my ease, all the long years of care and playfulness. I found a turtle by the riverside and marked its shell with my knife, making her sign and, in our superstition, giving her some chance toward another life.

"Well done, Joseph." I started to hear Sir William's voice for he had come upon me as silently as any other Mohawk. "You do well to remember her," he said.

"I wish I had seen her more," I said, "and I wish I had Father Prouty's prayer book with me to read the Christian words for death. I can make out much of it now, Warraghiyagey, but I left it at the house for I fear to lose it."

"Perhaps I can help you, Joseph," he said. "I remember some parts."

He stood for a spell in silence and then spoke as we both watched the marked turtle waddle and then slide away into the river.

"I am the resurrection and the life, saith the Lord: he that believeth in me, though he were dead, yet shall he live: and whosoever liveth and believeth in me, shall never die."

"Thank you, Father," I said.

We were away the next morning in dreadful winds and high waves. We were on water two miserable weeks before we reached Detroit, a fine fort bravely situated on the river's curve. On the bank to greet us were good, honest George Croghan and a whole host of braves he had brought with him from the Ohio country. A good omen, it seemed to me.

Captain Donald Campbell, the English commander, was a portly, friendly, blinking man, uncorrupted by General Amherst's directives and swollen even beyond his considerable girth with pride at having as guest Sir William Johnson, the hero of Lake George and Niagara, His Majesty's Supervisor of all Indian Affairs. He led us to good lodging inside the high stockades that contained not merely a fort but a whole city with shops, churches and wide streets.

Though it was an English fort now, you still heard much French spoken for many of King Lewis's traders and *couriers du bois* had not permitted defeat to move them from the homes they had set in the wilderness. Most of them had made some clumsy profession of allegiance to the English Crown and our officers did not incline to fret at their loyalty or lack of it. There were good men, shrewd hunters and woodsmen among them who were valuable to the land even though they might secretly foment trouble to its government.

"I'd have them all run out," John Johnson said as we sat at dinner with Captain Campbell. "There's men here as dangerous as the Joncaires. It's like allowing a rattlesnake to share your hearth."

"Or sticking your head in a lion's cave," Sir William said dryly. "You have a persistence in never carrying a thought far enough, son John. Drive them into the forests and you light a hundred fires against King George. Keep them here, busy with industry, they will soon find the clink of earned coins headier than loyalty to Paris. Right, Captain?"

"Oh, right by dozens," Captain Campbell agreed. He had little tricks of speech preserving what fashionable cant he remembered from London. "Right by dozens, Sir William. And, if I didn't agree with your reason, our French settlers have additional attractions." He pushed his pudgy hands from out his lace-trimmed sleeves and sketched in the air a female form, copious of breast and slim of waist before a lyre-swelling roundness of rump.

Sir William smiled broadly. "Their women?"

"The most handsome in the world," Captain Campbell bragged. "Clean as kittens, not a fire ship in the lot. I've arranged a ball tomorrow night in your honor, Sir William, and a round dozen charmers to grace it."

"Then we'd best not get full fuddled tonight," Sir William said, putting a hand over his goblet as Captain Campbell's orderly made to replenish his drink. He winked at John and myself. "You, too, my lads. Keep your ballocks limber and your brains clear."

We went to bed early. I shared a room with John Johnson and we talked a little before falling into sleep.

Ever since the night Catherine Weisenberg, his mother, married Sir William, he had held some distance from me. We had never been so close that this became an embarrassment of novelty but there was a difference though perhaps not apparent to any onlooker but which I felt and knew myself. This night, whether from weariness of the journey or after so long a trip so close together, he broke the barrier down a little.

I was hanging my shirt on a wooden peg.

"You bear me no grudge, Joseph?" he asked and startled me.

"For what?" I asked.

"Over Molly," he said, and for a wild moment, so loose were my thoughts, I thought he meant he had been in love with my sister. There had been others approached Molly at the house and to no avail.

"No," I said, "but why?"

"Because Sir William saw the light of righteousness and had himself wedded to my mother," John said. "Had he not, there could have been a wedding with Molly that would have left me a bastard, and Nancy and Polly with me."

I laughed in relief and understanding.

"I don't think Molly would have stood for such injustice," I said. I saw no need of telling him that the marriage was as much Molly's work as any bolt of righteousness to strike Warraghiyagey.

"I'm glad," he said, meaning grateful, and he made me shake his hand in the English fashion.

"Father would have me learn to take his place," he said, after we were both abed, "and he tries to teach me. It is not so easy, Joseph, to be son of such a father. I'd enjoy the wealth and the position, but to hold the whole frontier in my two hands and persuade Amherst from his mischief and keep the lords in London happy, I'd never do it."

"Rest easy," I told him. "Times will change." I did not embroider that I thought for the worse. "The marriage ensures that you'll be Sir John one day. Is not that enough?"

"It should be, I reckon," he said and sighed and turned on his side to sleep.

Thrice in the night I heard him twisting in his bed and cry-

ing out in a low voice from his sleep. I think this was the first
I realized that Englishmen might have dreams, too, and be
worse off for the lack of any teaching to assess them.

The morning we were busy from cockcrow, hearing
Croghan's reports and talking with his chiefs, getting a picture
of the tribes here gathered, Potawatomis, Ottawas and Hurons
in their own stout castles just outside the fort.

Sir William broke off such deliberations late in the afternoon to have time for shaving and dressing for the promised
ball. There was a store of extra clothing in one of our provision bateaux, and we were all able to present ourselves as
gentlemen worthy to grace such a grand social occasion. Sir
William had a plum-colored longcoat of velvet over plum
breeches and a beautiful cunningly designed waistcoat showing golden flowers on a field of pink. John had a velvet longcoat, too, his a bright blue. I unpacked a yellow jacket of
brushed wool that Molly had given me and wore it with new
breeches of garnet wool and a plain waistcoat of mulberry
velvet.

I think the three of us, when we entered to the dance floor
with Captain Campbell, already beading with sweat in his
heavy red regimentals, looked as civilized as any of the
French gentlemen guests.

Captain Campbell had been true to his word. There stood
against the wall across from us his promised dozen of French
maids, dressed as if Detroit were Versailles. They were a rainbow of colors, their panniered skirts separating them so that
the mere dozen covered a whole wall of better than forty feet.
Some were brown-haired and some were ruddy and some
were fair and some had locks as raven as my sister's, but all
were comely and dressed to perfection, not only of clothing,
but to the last tendril of headdress.

Sir William strode to the middle of the line and bowed at
the hand of a slender, straight, dark-haired young woman. She
smiled and I saw her amber eyes bright with the honor and
her own pride as she stepped forward gracefully and took Sir

William's hand. The small group of musicians, a spinet, two violins, a bass viol and a trumpet (from the military band) struck up their tune. I found myself facing a small girl with hair as yellow as my jacket. "Mademoiselle?" I said, and she stepped forward for me, chirping a torrent of soft, birdlike French words that might have been Hebrew for all I knew. I saw John moving to the floor center with a tall young woman and then gave myself up to the intricacies of the dance which I had studied often enough at Fort Johnson with Polly and Nancy for my strict tutors.

I had been to balls of a sort before, but this was the first really large and splendid one. And my little partner was pretty and charming and exciting to the appetite of a young man cut off a month and more from feminine companionship.

I told her: "Nix Francy" when we started our dance, the mixed phrase from the *lingua franca* of the fur trade to let her know I had no understanding of her speech. She giggled and changed to a halting English that was every bit as diverting as her native birdsong. She explained that her name was John, which was a great oddity to me since I knew not then that the French so pronounce Jeanne, and I told her my blond friend dancing yonder was also named John, so she giggled again and swung breathless at my arm's length as the music quickened.

There was wine served at a long table near the musicians and, at another table, a vast variety of different foods. We helped ourselves to both fares and then she assented to walk with me out of the hall and in the shaded grounds about it where bushes had been planted to offer a handsome vista by day and comfort for lovers by night.

I guided her behind one such cluster and placed a kiss to her lips which she returned vigorously, a small giggle still bubbling past her lips even while we kissed. Never before or after did I meet such a maid for giggles and squeals and for making them aphrodisiacal. I tried a hand beneath the formidable array of her skirts and was surprised to find no small clothes at all.

"Ah, sor!" she said, still giggling. "You shall disrespect me so."

Before I could phrase my denial she had sunk back beside the bush and pulled her skirts high enough to accommodate me.

"You are a fine man," she told me, clinging to my arm as we went back to the hall. "Ow many times the nights?"

"We shall see," I said, for the first time a small degree intimidated.

I danced with her again and with several other ladies and came back to her for another dance and another stroll outside. When we returned that time, she introduced me to a tall man with the look of a woodsman about him, her father. He shook my hand and, looking neither sour nor pleased, took her by the elbow, saying: "That's enough for one evening, *ma petite.*"

"*Ah, hélas!*" my blond little "John" giggled in farewell.

"You had the little Cardin," Captain Campbell twitted me, coming to where I stood with John Johnson at the wine table. "She's as fine a piece as any in these parts, Mr. Brant, for the doing of it, but Sir William has stuck with the prize of the ball, for beauty and for wisdom."

"I see he has indeed," John said somewhat dourly.

I looked with them and Sir William was whirling by to the music with the same beauty with whom he had opened the festivity.

"Mlle. Curie," said Captain Campbell. "Angelique. Her father, Antoine, is the leading trader of the region and as much taken into our tribes as Sir William is to yours. And she with him. They say she goes on Indian trails and sits in their councils. I cannot vouch for that, but I do know she's a better interpreter than any man at my command."

As if they had known we spoke of them, they glided to a

pause near us and Sir William fetched her wine and introduced her to me and to John.

"Angelique Curie," he said. "My son, John, my Mohawk brother, Joseph."

He spoke in Mohawk, having no more French than I, and she greeted us in Mohawk with a little lisp of Huron or Ottawa to it.

"A fine ball, Captain," Sir William complimented our host, "and the girls as beautiful as you promised."

"Girls?" John blurted. "But you've only danced with one, Father."

"I choose the best to do homage to all her sisters," Sir William said, and translated his speech to Mohawk for her.

"And I choose Sir William, the leader, to do homage to all brave Englishmen and cunning Mohawks," she told us as they rejoined the dance.

"I mislike it," John muttered. "He sticks his head in the lion's cave and finds no fox, no lion, but a lioness."

"She's a fine girl," I said, "but I doubt she'll eat Sir William."

"I'm not thinking of her destroying him," John said, "but if he grows 'fatuated he might think on marriage."

He had been long at the wine table else I doubt he would have spoken such fantasy to me.

"I can hardly believe that," I said. "There is still my sister."

"Oh, he loves Molly," John said, impatient, "but he makes his own laws where bedding is concerned. With my mother dead, why shouldn't he marry again? And you say Molly won't wed him . . ." He lurched, put his glass down and went seeking a dancing partner.

I danced the next dance with a merry, dark girl who spoke quite as good English as I did. When I suggested we take a stroll she shook her head gently.

"Do not confuse yourself that Mademoiselle Cardin is the pattern of every lady here," she said. "With her, love is as much an affliction as affection, Mr. Brant. I should not say all the rest of us make a graven idol of chastity, but the freest would require some longer courtship than a whirl around the floor and thence into the bushes." I could take her rebuke in good spirit, for Mlle. Cardin had slaked any immediacy of lust.

I got my new partner wine and introduced her to John and then saw that Angelique Curie was standing alone while Sir William spoke with Captain Campbell and a Frenchman dressed in well-cut silver-gray broadcloth who I learned was Antoine Curie.

Moved by her beauty and by the curiosity John Johnson's worry had stirred in me, I presented myself to her for the next dance, making my speech in the most formal Mohawk of the council fires.

"I am honored, Mr. Brant," she said.

She spun lightly at my direction in the figures of a reel and I felt, even this short time, a strength from her and an intelligence along with her charm that I had not known of another woman beyond my own sister Molly.

She was friendly and courteous, yet she spared no word as we talked. There was no sentence that could be damned as impolite or prying, all stood within a genteel interest in her partner, and she had from me before the music stopped the number on our mission, that we knew of the bad belts but were not sure whom to blame and would have had more but for a wakening caution in me.

I parried these inquiries as best I might, but found my dancing duel less easy for me when Mlle. Curie shifted her speech to talk of my sister. I could defend Molly to any man's insult—the accusations of everything from stealing Crown gold to unfaithfulness—but a woman's feline hints and probings were not amenable to such direction as I had used with men.

And, in truth, Mlle. Curie's feelings toward Molly, as subtly revealed that evening, were more a respectful envy than any crude derogation. She wished to know how high the both of us might sit in offering Sir William advice and whether Molly condoned his notorious liaisons from blind love or cool policy.

"I think, Miss Curie," I said finally, after turning aside a dozen such darts, "my sister behaves very much as you might yourself enjoy to in a position of power and trust beside a man you would love."

"I had heard much of you as a warrior," she said as I led her back to Sir William. "I can add to that that you are, young as you may be, a coupler of some discretion with your bravery."

"And I believe all the praise I have heard of you, Mademoiselle," I said, "not merely of your beauty which is clear to all who look, but to your subtle wisdom." I felt forced to ring in this note as payment for Molly and for her "cunning Mohawk" phrase when we had met for the word she used, in Mohawk, may mean either learned or devious and I had held some thought she did not mean it wholly as a compliment.

Sir William took her from me and into a dance. I joined John, alone and morose again with his wine.

"She is a fascinating woman," I told him, "but I should not fear that she'll be your stepmother."

"God will you're right, Joseph," he said, not much consoled.

But I made up my mind and kept to my belief even when we saw Sir William lead Angelique off the floor and out one of the doors. That she was beautiful pleased him, but I believe his chief interest was in what he could learn from her of the belts.

And I felt just as certain that Angelique was no Mlle. Cardin, or even one of her slightly more resistant sisters. I had, as you may well guess by now, enough converse with the fair to have some gauge of their propensities. Angelique I could judge a treasure worth any man's winning, but for that same reason a treasure to be won fully and fairly. She would intrigue Sir William, but he would halt short of any real alliance; there were too many irons in his fire to bring in yet another so hot and so likely to jeopardize the organization of his life. Besides, in an odd manner, she was too close to Molly to

threaten her, as a man with a fine bay mare in his stable is
more likely at a horse fair to have an eye for gray geldings or
a black stallion.

I could explain none of this to John, so I did not try. When
the ball ended with Sir William and Angelique still absent I
helped him, for he was stumbling drunk by now, back to our
quarters.

I heard Sir William return much later, whistling like a
young swain on his way down the hall and was glad that John
was snoring deep in drunken sleep.

I had thought Sir William would sleep late, but he was very
soon calling us and sending a soldier to bring George Croghan
to him and a handful of chiefs solid in his trust. We all sat
about in his room while he dressed with care for the council.

The only time he mentioned Angelique was not by name
but when he said reflectively: "I learned a little last night, a
little that points to much. I could wish General Amherst had
some appreciation of how much intelligence is arrayed against
our governing these parts."

Only when all our conferring was done, when Croghan had
told the last tittle of his store of information, and I myself had
been pumped dry of all I knew about the Nations and individual chiefs at the council, did Warraghiyagey relax again.

"We shall have a fair observer at the council," he said. "My
dancing partner comes with her father to hear the speeches
and to judge their weight."

John held back what must have been a true Niagara of
questioning and only grunted.

"Help me fix my stock, Joseph," Sir William said. "I must
be as correct as the French King himself and as straight as a
Mohawk war chief for this day's work." I rucked the white
lace about his neck and tied it neat in back.

The council was held on level ground under the sky for
even the ballroom could not have contained a part of it. There
were tribes from hundreds of miles all about, strange accents
I could hardly follow. It swam in an atmosphere of dark sus-

picion and distrust. No Indian there but knew that it could herald some act of irrevocable defiance of Sir William and the Crown. When it began I saw it as a scene of a lion's cave, but Warraghiyagey was the lion and there were scavenging dogs and wolf packs arrayed all around him, waiting slavering to bring him down at the first signification of weakness.

I saw Angelique and her father seated on a small hillock surrounded by Hurons and some of those same Senecas who had ignored Sir William's belt for a meeting at Niagara. I saw Guyasuta, by now known surely to us as the real begetter of the bad belts, tall in a circle of his own Chenussio fellows, one of them my own Turtle brother and informant who gave me not a glance of kinship. It was a strange, impressive gathering together.

Sir William was a lion and also a gamester ready to throw the dice in a game to which he had staked everything. He had left the surety and comfort of the Mohawk Valley to deal here in the west with tribes never predictable in temper or allegiance, nations as long devoted to the French as the Iroquois had been to England. His power and prestige in our own tribes and nations close to Fort Johnson had long been accepted unchallenged; another man would have found these laurels enough to rest on. But Warraghiyagey was no such cautious gambler. Whatever he might accumulate, this was but wherewithal to wager on ever larger ventures. I have seen men like him playing at hazard in the gaming clubs of London, calm in demeanor, yet burning of eye, placing whole familial estates against the turn of a card. These men gambled only with money; Sir William had all the King's American colonies for his risk.

A Huron sachem opened the council, throwing a green belt of peace to Sir William and speaking a grand, hollow speech of good will. I saw Angelique smiling and Sir William smiling, both for opposite reasons, for I am sure she smiled to think these Huron words were cozening the great chief of the English and the Mohawks while Sir William smiled knowing such bombast could only serve his cause.

Without raising his voice in anger, without even pointing out a single Huron lie, Warraghiyagey made his own speech. He thanked his Huron brothers and made gracious greeting to all the other tribes. He noted that the greatest council before, three years earlier, had been held at Canajoharie "in the shadow of my own longhouse and its protection." Now, he told his audience, a score of whom would have taken his scalp without even asking for a bounty, the blessings of peace had come upon America and he could travel all these hundred miles to meet here in Detroit at better convenience to his western brothers.

Oh, there were some small matters of dissension, he noted, such as always might occur among even the closest brotherhood. There was the business (a hint of laughter underlay his speech) of some bad belts, sent by misguided malcontents among tribes quite certain to ignore them. Had this not been an honest council among men of probity and honor, he would not even mention such a foolishness.

And, while the Hurons were still nodding on his words, he asked, in just the same voice: "Who sent these bad belts, brothers?"

There was a hush across the whole gathered company.

And Warraghiyagey repeated softly but insistent: "Who sent these bad belts, brothers?"

The Huron sachem who had made the first speech was forced to stand. "Our brother óf the Chenussios," he said and pointed his finger at Guyasuta.

"Ah," Sir William said, still as soft as a man talking to a maid, and I wondered at that moment whether the whole council was in some wise a courtship of Mlle. Curie.

"Ah," he said. "Now we know it is our brother of the Chenussios, but still we know not why."

Guyasuta, a conniver but a brave man and his own master, got to his feet to speak.

And from this moment the council was all Sir William's for, as I have learned since, once you force a man to justify himself unexpectedly he will stumble and stutter no matter how true he may believe his cause nor how correct his actions.

I could almost feel for the Chenussio chief as he strung sentence after sentence in a poor necklace, saying first that the belts meant no evil to Sir William and then that the English must be driven to the sea. The council heard him out, but this was Indian custom rather than conviction.

Then a Huron rose to deny anything Guyasuta had said of his people's consent to the belts. And one Ottawa contradicted him and another Ottawa the first. Sir William kept himself from smiling openly. I saw Angelique looking from her father's side with discomfort but a new respect for the English chief she had danced the night with.

Sir William himself set an end to the wrangling. As if it were no more than the pettiest of squabbles, he made a speech in thanks for the agreement of all nations there, a sincere acknowledgment that there were Indian grievances with good grounds against some settlers, and an infinite promise that all might be worked out well. He called me to his side to give orders for liquor to be brought for all who thirsted. There was the next day and the day after that for the real meat of the long journey, private councils with individual chiefs.

I sat with him through most of these and observed him disarm even Guyasuta, telling him like a father speaking to a son of the evil the other Indian nations would work upon the Chenussios if that tribe kept up its acts of mischief. "Indians should settle the quarrels of Indians," he said, "and that they shall do, but I hope you may be wise enough to keep from such war of brother against brother."

Guyasuta bowed his head. He saw the falseness of his actions, he told Sir William, and he was not fool enough ever to repeat them.

"I cheer your wisdom," Sir William said and made him gifts

of a wampum belt, two fine blankets, some leggins and whiskey.

It went thus with other private meetings. Warraghiyagey was never such a fool as to follow General Amherst's direction to threaten Indian nations with English might. Instead, he held (I know now to my own sorrow, yet with no lessening of respect for my mentor) nation against nation in this case, even tribe against tribe.

The western tribes had been held to the King's Peace. Hurons and Ottawas, Chenussios and many Delawares still had discords and disaffections. What Sir William had won, as usual, was time. No frontier may ever be an easy, peaceful region, but the outcome of Fort Detroit ensured the end of these particular bad belts and gave assurance that there would be no rising against the white men in this year.

There was another grand ball to celebrate the ending of the council and here Sir William danced again with Angelique, but even John had lost some of his fear. For this ball it was she who seemed to be courting him.

I did not watch Sir William's actions overmuch. My little giggling friend "John" Cardin was once again in the ladies' line and I stole another walk with her among the ornamental shrubbery before her father, just as at the first ball, neither frowning nor smiling, took her home. I believe now he rationed her a fixed amount of dalliance as a hunter might let a hot bitch run one night of the week, but keep her kennel-pent the other six. Whatever the arrangement, I enjoyed it. And I believe John Johnson had some satisfaction from the girl he had favored most the first gala, but he never gave me the easy confidence of Tagcheunto or other wenching companions. Even then, at nineteen years, he had wrapped about him some of the heavy dignity he used ever after to disguise his lack of what his father would have called real bottom.

We took another day and a half to pack and then sailed toward home and I have never seen such a change in a man as in Sir William. I had not thought, through the council days and the nights of dancing, how tight he must have held himself against important effort. Now that the business was over, he turned, huddled in greatcoat and blankets in his bateau, an aging man and ill.

"He has the bloody flux," John told me in alarm. "He shits twice every hour, all liquid and in pain, but he will not let me ask for help."

It was a wicked but a common ill and I made Sir William drink a tea of roots and leaves I compounded from stores Molly had provided. This potion eased his shits, but he still shook from chills and worried me more than I could let John know.

After the tea cure, he had me ride in the same bateau.

"I've been an old stag playing at young buck, and I'm delivering the price for my play," he said, and I had then a suspicion that Angelique, at the last ball, had abandoned her defenses.

We spoke more of the council itself and the standing of the Indian nations.

"There was right as well as wrong in Guyasuta's belt, Joseph," he told me, "but you know that as much as I do. The nations *must* hold together, but it is our task now to find a way of holding them thus in peace and with England. I could bring them together in war, so could you or Guyasuta, but such coalitions have no meaning. Yet war is the only banner that excites them."

We found horses at Niagara to speed our way home. At Oswego, we got word that Molly had been delivered of her child, a healthy girl, and Sir William broke out all that was left of our wine and rum to celebrate and had the bloody flux again, it taking me two more days, still traveling, to stem its drain upon him.

"I'm grateful, Joseph," he said, "and I think I've a way to prove it."

"There is not need for proof between father and son," I said.

"Mayhap there is a way," he said. "Your letters, lad."

"They have been coming better," I said, and indeed I was proud that I could write some dozens of words without reference to any lexicon.

"They'll come better yet," he said. "I've decided that you should go with William of Canajoharie"—so he always called Tagcheunto, as if in pride at not hiding his parentage—"to the Reverend Wheelock's school at Lebanon, Connecticut."

"So far from home!" I said, returning then from a journey of six hundred miles.

"You'll learn better and faster there," Sir William said. "And some figuring as well as letters. And a grounding in the religious speech you're so fond of, even if Eleazar Wheelock is a needle-nosed Congregationalist."

"Tagcheunto will be with me?" I asked, seeking some security.

"He's been nattering about an itch to learn the arts of surveying," Sir William said. "You've heard him enough. He thinks it a magic he can use to outwit the land-grabbers and, at worst, it may help him make fairer settlement for his friends."

We galloped to the gates of Fort Johnson the next day, I riding half out of the saddle with fullness of the news of my own future. I had an extra long embrace for Molly, whose hand I could see plainly in the decision for schooling, and I told her so.

"Some truth, Joseph," she smiled, "but Sir William needs no prodding where you are concerned. You know not how often he talks of you, and without any prompting from me. Have you not a gentle kiss for your new niece?"

I bent and kissed her newest babe, Elizabeth, ashamed that my own joy had made me forget congratulation.

I took a fresh mount to ride into Albany after Tagcheunto and dragged him from a tavern with the news of our educational adventure. He was excited enough to stay sober two weeks after.

Back at the house, I slept that first night in deep exhaustion, but not so deep as to banish dreams. The great white owl returned, and in this dream it seemed to me his broad wings signified all learning and the gates I would be opening with my wisdom. I thought so much of learning: I still do, but know now there are many locks it cannot open, doors sprung only by Divine Grace.

〰〰〰 THREE 〰〰〰

Traveling to Lebanon, Connecticut, was much more for me a journey into *terra incognita* than the long trip west to Detroit. I had not thought to be shocked, but I was by the difference in the whole countryside. It had by now (in how short a time!) become completely a white man's land so that even our valley with its towns and settlements were wilderness by comparison. What few Indians one saw about were timid, skulking fellows, little better than slaves, squatting by tavern doors waiting in hope of some menial job that would yield them pence for boozing. I know now that this impression was of no total justice; there were here and there in every county some of my brothers who had held to positions of respect. But I must write what I saw and felt then and it was severely depressing.

"Wait till I learn my surveying," Tagcheunto said. "We'll drive them back with fences of our own, a language they can understand."

He had some belief that surveyors' rods were sorcerers' wands and the whole mundane business of measurement and mapping a sort of spell. No one could disabuse him of this notion and I had long given over trying.

Townsfolk gawked at us at every stop for food or drink, but they were cheerful enough to take our shillings. I thought of an old story of a Mohawk doing no more than suddenly appearing on the main street of a town and, at his sighting, the whole population, English and tame Indian alike, running shrieking behind their walls in terror. There was none such total panic at our progress this late summer of 1761, but there was still a healthy respect in the suspicion these people held of us.

I tried to anoint my homesickness with some pride in this, but I failed. I felt, in that valley of smug settlement, bereft and far from all that was dear to me, a feeling I had never encountered however far I hunted or traveled on a mission for Sir William. This was far different, not so much that the countryside disquieted me, but because on this journey I was for the first time abroad for my own pursuits. My further education, it was true, would make me more valuable to Sir William, but this was not my final reason for the pilgrimage. It was a mission to serve my own ambition, to help me into what mold I hoped might aid my own vague, strong plans of being a great man. And this made all weigh more heavily on me for no man has so severe a master as when he works for himself.

Tagcheunto was silent, but I suspect he carried much the same burden. Years now he had talked, in his cups and out, of his yearning to master surveying. Now Fate and Sir William had plucked him from the tavern and said: Go do so, and the rest would be his own success or failure.

"We could reach Lebanon today," I said, reining to a pause and then slackening my reins to leave my horse drink at a small creek.

"If we press on," Tagcheunto said, dispiritedly.

"Or we could camp here," I said.

"We could," he said, bound to be of no help.

"So let us," I said. "One last night under sky before we become the pupils of the eminent Reverend Wheelock."

"Good, brother," Tagcheunto smiled, happy I had made a choice for him. He slipped off his horse and tethered it near the stream where it could both drink and graze, and I did likewise.

It was a still, clear night, none the best for hunting, but we managed to kill two hare and Tagcheunto skinned them while I found dry wood for a fire. We roasted bits of the meat and ate it with hard bread from our packs, washed down with some Madeira Sir William had sent with us.

"Give some to Pastor Wheelock," he had said, "but drink what you need on the way." With Tagcheunto's thirst we were fortunate that there was one bottle spared at the end for our teacher.

We lay on our backs and I looked at the stars pricked out distinctly in the cloudless sky and counted all the visible constellations by their Mohawk names and then ran back again through the English names. I tried to shake my mind so that it might meet the morning and Reverend Wheelock in some order, to put in proper place the advices I had had from Sir William and from Molly and from everyone at the house; for all were busy helping us away, wishing us Godspeed and giving us advice on how to behave in a school and town no one of them had ever seen. Even black Enoch, lately made free by Sir William and married to a plump Wappinger squaw, pressed an excellent jackknife to my hand. "They will no doubt take away your gun, Joseph," he said, full of a solicitude that touched me, "but this you can keep hidden on your person. Among Connecticut Yankees a man should never chance going wholly unarmed."

Sir William had been less warlike, but frightened me as much as I am sure he meant to hearten.

"You want your letters, Joseph," he said, "and you'll have them to the exact degree you're willing to sweat for them."

"I am willing to work, Warraghiyagey," I said with dignity.

"I said sweat, not work, damn it," Sir William said. "I know you're not a shirker or I shouldn't be sending you, but there will be more than work to endure. You're a man of nineteen years with your own war name won fairly in the field at Niagara. But you're being set to lessons generally learned by children not far beyond wetting their beds. That's bullet you've got to bite, and bite over again every day you're there against your Mohawk pride."

"I see," I said, now troubled.

"You don't," Sir William said, "but you will, and when you do you may remember my caution."

Molly made great to-do about my departure, half her time telling me how great an opportunity it offered, the other half fussing over me as if I were not her brother but her babe. I think the birth of Elizabeth and the death of our mother worked together in her for a motherliness never so common to her nature. We had always loved each other, but with more equality of spirit. She kept packing my saddlebags with small comfits and giving me advice on everything from avoiding sleep under a full moon to keeping my fingernails pared and clean to make a good impression upon gentry. Now, at the least excuse, I would have leaped on my mare to ride post-haste for all the dithering she wished to put on me.

But there were no signs, no least excuses. My sleep was light but sufficient and my dreams of no great significance.

Tagcheunto and I brewed tea from the stream water and broke our fast with it and our hard bread. What bread we had left I crumbled and left for birds and any small animals to repay the slight but welcome stretch of forest for the hare we had had of it.

We reached Lebanon before noon, a small, neat village of wooden houses in the simplest style, one post station that doubled as inn and doubled again as tavern, a white spired church where we found an old man, the sexton as I got to know, who directed us to the celebrated Moor's Indian Charity School.

It was a large enough house with lawn about it, but I felt a sinking disappointment. I do not know what I had expected, but somewhere in my mind had lingered stories half heard of Englishmen visiting Sir William who had been at Oxford or Cambridge. I must have wished to see some assemblage of different buildings and of teachers in holy orders swanking along paths in flowing robes. We found a lesser house than Fort Johnson, and a handful of Indian youths, looking dour and chastened in gray nankeen shirts and breeches, sitting on the grass.

We threw our reins over one of the hitching posts at the fence and advanced upon the house with more bodily confidence than either of us felt in our hearts. A spare, brown-haired man in black longcoat and gray breeches came out the house door to meet us. It was Eleazar Wheelock.

"We wish to see the Reverend Wheelock," I told him, taking him for some factotum of the man himself.

"You see me, young man," he said, plainly but with a trace of humor.

"We have a letter from Sir William Johnson," I said and handed him the missive which I had close in my jacket pocket in full readiness.

"Oh-ho!" he said. "Let me puzzle it out before looking at the letter. You must be Joseph Brant, and, if you are," he turned toward Tagcheunto, "you must be William of Canajoharie. Have I guessed right?"

We admitted he had and the spirit of our meeting began to thaw.

"Then come in," he said. "Rest your weary bones while I read Sir William's instructions." We followed him into the house and to a spacious room where he motioned us to a settle while he took his chair at a table and cracked the seal of Sir William's epistle. He read with attention, looking up now and then as he did so.

"Good!" he said, folding the letter and putting it under an iron weight on the table. "I am happy to have you as scholars."

He reached across the table and swung a small handbell.

"Samson Occum who is a Mohegan and already ordained a minister of Christ will show you your quarters and tell you of our rules," he said. "You will dine with the rest of the scholars and take the afternoon to get your bearings in the town, then sup and to bed. Tomorrow, I shall talk with you and learn where you stand in schooling and what instruction may befit you."

Fast on his ringing an ugly young Indian came into the room, bobbing in a bow toward the table.

"These, Samson," Mr. Wheelock said, "are our new scholars, Joseph Brant and William Johnson of Canajoharie. Show them sleeping room and acquaint them with our government here."

I took an immediate dislike to this professional underling and Tagcheunto did, too.

"Mohawks," Samson said, leading us from the room and down a corridor. In the word he managed to distill all the tame New England Indian's fear and envy of our invincible people.

He took us up a narrow stairway and into rooms above the ground story where rows of beds stood together.

"This is full," he said, and, looking into another, "this is full."

"We have not come all the way from Canajoharie to share a longhouse," Tagcheunto said.

"Have you the means to justify your pride?" Samson asked, rubbing a thumb against its forefinger.

I felt in my purse and separated a sovereign from the other coins.

"More than enough," I said, showing it to him.

"Ah," he said. "Then there *is* this room at the end that I have kept my own, but has beds for two more."

It was a decent chamber. I did not relish Samson as boon companion, but better one of him with us two than to have bunked among six or eight strangers.

We put our bags next to our beds and Samson intoned the Reverend Wheelock's rules which were not so tight or infantile as I had feared although they made Tagcheunto frown. There were set hours for meals and religious services and there was a ten o'clock hour to be in bed. There were instructions as to clothing, mostly a surety that cock and balls be covered, as if we were naked savages.

We took some clothing from our bags (I shook out the same handsome jacket I had worn at Captain Campbell's galas) as further evidence (if our respectable traveling garb had not been enough) that we owned more than breechclouts and string belts. Samson admired our possessions and lost some of his stiff superiority stroking the soft stuff of my coat.

There was clangor of a bell which made Tagcheunto leap in surprise; it startled me, too, but I held myself calm to give no extra advantage of Samson.

"That signified our midday dinner," Samson said. "Follow me down to eat and meet your fellows."

Meals were served in a long room at the side of the house and there were at the plank table better than a score of Indian youths of every age from eight to twenty-five.

Samson showed us seats and took his own place at the table head. He pounded his pewter mug for a moment's silence and made a general introduction of us to the table.

"Thayendanegea, Joseph Brant," he said, "and Tagcheunto, William Johnson. You may work out names as you come together in study and recreation. Now, in the Lord's name, let us be grateful for the food we eat and every breath we draw, amen."

There was a chatter of "amens" all around the table and Pastor Wheelock's scholar flock set to eat with as much appetite as if they had been hunters back from a long and arduous trail.

Samson had used our Indian names before our English ones, and I was to notice that this was a pattern of the school. In a kind of protection, all we scholars fell back among ourselves to Indian speech and formality even when we came from nations that scorned each other. We all (or mostly) admired Pastor Wheelock and his teachers, but there was more wall between scholar and teacher, Indian and white, here at this very school founded to bring the two together, than in most frontier settlements. I believe honestly that I spoke as much English back at Fort Johnson as here in Lebanon outside my classes. But what I spoke in my classes was more correct and when wrong forced into shapes of correctness and this was my main purpose beyond whatever high ideals the school's benefactor, Mr. Joshua Moor, may have had in his mind.

The school had been begun by Pastor Wheelock and this present house and land had been given by Mr. Moor, and both saw the venture as a training place for Indian missionaries, all of the Congregational meeting, to embrace a faith which they would then carry to their fellows in the forest. But, aside from Samson Occum and some few others, we scholars had come to the school less for the light of God's word than to improve ourselves in man's arts. I make this admission, Lord and Redeemer, not arrogantly but to keep my testament true. What I desired (as Tagcheunto his surveying) was an ease in English which would help me, not only to decipher the beauty of the Gospels, but to speak equally and with force in any commerce with English or colonials. And I also sought all I might learn or observe that could make me understand the white man better and to borrow or steal such of his lore and ways that could be useful to my own people.

Set in a scale against Salvation, these seem and are paltry aims, but let my reader remember how little I still knew of God's word and will for man. Taken in a true light, my aims were ambitious beyond those of most men, white or red, for I had sketched an outline of myself as leader and savior (forgive the word) of my Mohawks and all the Six Nations.

After the noon meal, some scholars went to classes, others sported at games on the grass, some had chores to do for Mr. Wheelock, some ventured into town. Tagcheunto, naturally, was for joining this last group and I went with him to watch that he should not be carried away by the temptations of the tavern. We found that the town had made some effort to put conditions upon serving spirits to Indians, but, as always, the prohibitions were more hopeful than effective. The tavern owner kept his front room respectable and sold rum in jugs and bottles out the back door to anyone who could come with the needed few pennies, Indian, Englishman, Dutchman or donkey. Pastor Wheelock was not fool enough to be in ignorance of this and he countered by trying to serve enough hard cider and ale at his own board to make the temptation of the tavern unnecessary. This was a seemingly sensible measure, but in truth it benefitted only scholars like myself who took drink in moderation. The ones like Tagcheunto who had fallen in thrall to spirits would never have enough even putting the tavern store and Pastor Wheelock's ration together every day.

We got back to the school, Tagcheunto only tipsy, in good time for supper. A short, flat-nosed youth called to us when we entered the house: "*Ave, Josephus! Ave, Gugliemus!*"

He was Lame Crow, a half-breed Abnaki of fifteen, one of the few scholars studying Latin and bound to show it off at every opportunity.

Mr. Wheelock set a fair board, nothing so sumptuous as Sir William's but beyond the fare at nearby Tisdale's Academy, a well-thought-of school for gentlemen's sons that drew students from as far away as the Barbados. We supped and drank the hard cider and afterward walked all in a company to the church and heard Pastor Wheelock discourse for two hours on Ebenezer. He had much reputation as an inspiring preacher, but, unless he were reading from the Scriptures themselves, he set me to sleep better than any tisane Molly had ever brewed against insomnia.

The next morning we were routed early from our bed by that raucous bell and had our meetings with Reverend Wheelock.

Tagcheunto had his talk first and came from it downcast, but with no opportunity to speak with me for Mr. Wheelock was at his back, beckoning that I should take his place for my own meeting.

"So, Joseph," he said, when I had sat down, "you would learn English to read the Bible and spread God's word among the Mohawk."

"Not wholly," I said, determined to be truthful and not to cant and toady like one of his Pequots or Schagticokes. "I have come to be of some use to Sir William Johnson in his affairs and I hope to be of some importance in the councils of my nation. Can I master English, I shall be better in both spheres."

I watched his face sharply for the disapproval I thought must come, but instead he smiled.

"Sir William wrote that you are a young man of probity," he said. "He judged right. God's will for you will be carried out no matter what you promise or what I plead, so I'm just as happy to have you speak truth. You will start classes this morning with Mr. Smith who teaches the alphabet."

"The alphabet I know," I said. "A, B, C, D, E—" and would have chanted all to zed if he had not rapped the table to stop me.

"And I had studied out the Hebrew letters in my teens," he said, calling "Aleph, Beth, Veth, Gimel, Daleth!" in the deep tones of a black magician. "But when I sat to a desk at the academy," he said, "I had to learn them again in their way, and you must do the same with English. Mr. Smith is a patient master and can help you, but not if you are to bridle at the first rules."

"I am sorry, Mr. Wheelock," I said, and I remembered what Sir William had said and felt a little better.

I went to the schoolroom and Tagcheunto was there before me, his face an ell long as he crouched behind a desk made for an eight-year-old.

Mr. Smith, a young man simply but elegantly dressed, greeted me and found me a space near Tagcheunto.

"We will find a way of getting you proper seats tomorrow," he promised, "but we seldom have had warriors placed among our beginners."

The statement drew some of the humiliation away.

The rest of the morning, shrill voices of the small scholars next to us sounding in counter to our own deeper responses, we explored our letters, in their order and separately by sound, then drawing them on slates. It was easy for me, and also for Tagcheunto whose mind was quick when he was half sober and who had absorbed more than he knew at the house from just looking at books and the inscriptions beneath pictures.

But he pulled me aside up to our room to protest.

"I kept telling him I came only for surveying," he said, "but he tap-tap-tapped on his table and nodded yet said I had to have my letters first. What kind of school is this, brother? He steals Sir William's money to humiliate his sons!"

"He is right, Tagcheunto," I calmed him, or tried to. "The surveyors must write down what they measure, and in words as well as numbers. And they must read books that govern the use of their tools. I think it is so with everything. The English and the French have made their language into a key without which we can unlock nothing. That is why I am here to learn, and you, too."

"If you say so, brother," he said, mollified but by no means happy, and we sat in silence, thinking of home, till the bell called us to the noon meal. And then back to Mr. Smith.

So our days went, with games in our spare time and drinking in the evenings and Tagcheunto and I did some wrestling which greatly entertained the town when we set on their asses the biggest young men from Tisdale's Academy who were not popular with the townspeople for their affectations of lordship.

With Mr. Smith's help I was soon through repeating my alphabet and had gone swiftly through the baby books of verse and proverbs. He gave me of his own time without stint and beyond the classroom and I shall be forever grateful since he put into my hands, after we had exhausted primers, *The Pilgrim's Progress* of John Bunyan.

Mr. Bunyan captured me from his first sentence: "As I walked through the wilderness of this world, I lighted on a certain place where was a den, and I laid me down in that place to sleep: and, as I slept, I dreamed a dream." He could have been writing his words only for me, my forest world, my fears and hopes and temptations. I read on, the first night I had the book, deaf to Tagcheunto's and Samson's pleas to douse my light, and I think I almost expected to meet in the pages my own great white owl.

I was so deep in my studies and then in my infatuation with *The Pilgrim's Progress* that I turned a dim eye to Tagcheunto's increasing troubles.

The third week we were at the school he reeled back late at night and sorely drunk. I helped him to bed, steering his puke to the chamberpot, while Samson sniffed in disdain from his cot and whispered direly of punishment for so grave a breach of scholarly decorum.

Mr. Wheelock summoned Tagcheunto to him the next morning and rated him for his boozing and said had he been any other student but Sir William's son his action would have had him sent home at once. But he would keep him on with the promise that Tagcheunto should do no drinking in the town and confine himself to the beer and cider at our meals.

Tagcheunto made the promise, and indeed it should not have been hard to keep for anyone but him, for I got up from many of my meals wobbly on my feet and with a fine hazy glow to my head. But Tagcheunto was one of those to whom all spirits, and even simple beer, are but a fuse to light a whole arsenal of drunkenness. Had Mr. Wheelock offered him a dock to the ocean with rum ships from the Indies making fast there every week, Tagcheunto would have been found, eventually, wandering up from dock to find a tavern and add to his bibulous supply. I know the illness and its dangers to those it strikes well (too well, as Thou knowest, Lord) and I cannot blame, but only weep.

My Mohawk brother tried and it hurt my heart to see the

torture of his efforts. Three weeks he kept his faith, but shook and shivered in his cot those nights. The fourth week he brought back a jug from the town.

He nursed it carefully and made it last several days and seemed to be improved in health and behavior. At least he no longer woke us in the nights with shouts from twitching dreams. I took my knife that Enoch had gifted me and held its small, sharp point against Samson's throat to explain what he could look forward to did he carry tales of Tagcheunto's secret cellar to a master. So things went passably well for another fortnight.

But the jug from the tavern that had lasted a week now served for Tagcheunto only two or three days, and at last there was a new jug every night and no concealing his condition from Mr. Wheelock who sent a Schagticoke boy to say he wished to see him in his study.

Tagcheunto left the door open and I had no shame (he was my friend and fellow Mohawk, was he not?) in loitering near to overhear.

"You have broken your word, William," Mr. Wheelock said.

"Who, sir?" Tagcheunto asked. He was drunk as a fiddler's bitch that very moment, but he kept his feet without swaying and spoke with a forced clearness.

"You have been buying spirits in the town and boozing them beyond your promise and far beyond my patience," Mr. Wheelock said, tapping ominously with his nail.

"Not spirits, sir," Tagcheunto defended himself with clumsy cunning. "I have had a heavy phlegm upon my chest, sir, and have been forced for my health to take heavy dosages of purl." Said purl being a vile mixture of warm beer and gin.

"Purl me no purls," Mr. Wheelock rose half out of his chair. "You've been blind drunk these past five days. Mr. Starret informs me you refused to fetch his horse for him. Even Mr. Smith, as kindly a man as ever was born into a sinful world, tells me you fall from your chair in class. Sir William sends you here and contributes good money to our cause of trying to turn out scholars and gentlemen, and how do you behave?"

Tagcheunto swayed a little and blinked at Mr. Wheelock owlishly.

"I know what a gentleman is," he said. "A gentleman has *others* fetch his horse, and a gentleman drinks when he pleases. And I can do these things without your schooling, sir. So I bid you farewell."

He made to turn in military fashion on his heel, but the dignity of his departure was marred by his stumbling into the corner of the table and having to stifle a "Damn!" as he staggered from the room. I took his arm and helped him up the stairs where I packed his bags for him.

"Tried, Small Turtle, I tried," he said.

"I know you did, Tagcheunto," I said. "And you have much English now. You can learn the rest of surveying at Fort Johnson."

"No," he said, choking back a hiccough. "I'll never learn it. It's a white man's art and let them have it and be damned."

Samson, to do him credit, had Tagcheunto's horse waiting.

We touched each other's hands to our foreheads and he rode away. I had had time to write him a note for Molly and for Sir William in my much improved hand and in it I tried some to shield him from full blame. He had better not have come to the school at all and that was the size of it.

I looked with no happiness to the night with Tagcheunto, so long my closest friend, gone, and only the pious Samson for companion, but Mr. Bunyan helped me much. The pages took me within themselves and made me one with Christian on his progress and with Mr. Great-heart, Mr. Holyman, Mr. Dare-not-lie and Mr. Penitent as they sallied to meet the Monster. And it came upon me, after I had put down the book and just before I slept, that I was finding in words something of what Tagcheunto sought in booze, and my newfound compulsion not so openly unfortunate yet just as deep and mayhap deeper in me.

The routine of the school contained my life after Tag-cheunto's departure. There were some diversions, but not many. It took me a long time, hard endeavor and a good part of the allowance Sir William sent me to make friends with a lass who worked at the inn, making beds and scouring. This was no great romance (no more for her), but it sufficed for the siphoning of that appetite. And I wrestled some still, with success but without the rowdy pleasure I had always had with Tagcheunto.

Samson found another roomer to take Tagcheunto's space. This was a slim and very clever Nipmuck boy of fifteen named Beech Stalk, but he liked other men better than girls and I have never been too easy with these persons. I chased him twice out of my bed and did my late-night reading, with Mr. Wheelock's permission, downstairs.

We celebrated the Savior's birth with extra services at church and much singing of the old carols from which I took much joy, singing lustily with the others *On Christmas Day in the Morning* and *Christmas Day Is Come* with its merry chorus of ding, dong, dings. The last carol, being a favorite of Sir William's, had me homesick again and I stayed so over the two days we had to mark the holiday.

Then it was back gladly to work. I had left the class of younger children behind and schooled now with the first class both in numbers and letters, a senior student in everything but specialties like Greek and Latin and Hebrew.

I made no Indian friend. Their tame town ways repelled me and they, in me, stood fearful of the "wild Mohawk." So that the closest I came to a friend was Mr. Smith whom I grew to know better and respect more the better I knew him. He was from a family of much wealth, but had vowed to devote his life to the church and most of all to good works among the Indians.

When I felt I knew him well enough I spoke to him about the differences in Indians and his danger in judging Mohawk and Seneca and other tribes still true to forest ways by the sample of mealymouthed young hypocrites assembled in his classes. He took no offense, but was happy at a door open, through me, to new knowledge and I judge this one mark of a really educated gentleman as much for its rarity as for its honesty.

His plans were for a long trip the coming summer out into Ohio land, there to preach the Gospel wherever he might find an Indian to listen. This was my childhood hunting ground, so we talked long into nights about its terrain, its perils and its people. Before spring had softened the air, we were speaking of making the journey together with me serving him as interpreter and guide while he continued my instruction. The plan seized all my imagination and even moved into my dreams. I remember one dream where I saw myself preaching to a circle of Indians stretching beyond where my eye could count them and on one side of me as I preached was a huge old turtle and on the other my owl.

Mr. Smith wrote for permission to Sir William, a note so flattering that I blushed when he made me read it. Mr. Wheelock would give us his blessing. In June we would leave with an extra packhorse and full provisions for engagement on the Lord's work.

I had been able to make out much of the Bible by now and the words were as singing and brave as I had hoped. But I cannot say I was yet a Christian though I styled myself so to please my mentors.

I liked all I read and almost all I heard (such times as I stayed awake at sermons), but it was a liking of the mind, not of the heart. And an easy liking for a Mohawk. I think any Indian may respect the tortures of Christ's Passion better than most white men, and surely those wandering, bloodstained, perplexed and peevish Israelite tribes are more our brothers than most of the men who preach the Word! But it was this much and no more, and yet quite enough to kindle my expectations of journeying with Mr. Smith.

I had come back from making purchases against the trip in early May when Mr. Wheelock called me to his study.

I thought he would be having more advice for me regarding the mission, but he handed me a sealed letter and he had its twin open before him.

"Sir William asks your presence at home," he said. "He does not say why, but I doubt he would make any such change unless it were important. And he sent this letter I have given you from your sister. I'm sorry, Joseph. I know you counted on the mission with Mr. Smith and he counted on you, but a man's plans are sand in a whirlwind."

I thanked him and hurried to where I could con my own letter. Molly wrote in a mixture of English words and Mohawk signs and she did not write long, but it was clear and urgent: "Trouble with the Detroit tribes. No little trouble, brother. Guyasuta and Teedyuscung's son Bull and every other sachem with heart more weasel than lion. You are needed sorely, Thayendanegea." And I knew it was truly serious for she would not otherwise have called me by my war name.

I left that night, packing only what I needed most and my Bible and Bunyan and giving Samson and Mr. Smith leave to divide what I left behind among the scholars.

I rode fast and stopped for the shortest of naps and for food, but even so I began to hear rumors at every step: all the nations of the west had come down upon the frontier and slaughtered every settler; rape; fire; murder and savage torture. And traversing this sea of rumor, I, as an Indian and a strange one, was looked upon with something less than friendliness. At Pig's Tail, where I crossed the Housatonic for the Webatuck country, some settler shot at me as I forded. I took the hint of his bullet splatting the water by my horse's side and spurred on toward Johnson Hall, my new home I had never seen finished for Sir William and Molly had not removed there till after I had gone to Lebanon.

It was a new house, but a most familiar scene with Indians

camped all about the yard before and behind it, a Highlander sentry at guard at its road gate and the front door clogged with officers, sachems and gentlemen from Albany. Daniel Claus ushered me right into Sir William's study and I checked the shock I felt at how much my foster father had aged in nine short months. He pulled himself partly from his chair to greet me and it was clear the effort cost him some pain.

"Joseph, lad! I'm mightily glad you're back," he said. "Daniel, call Molly."

Daniel went on his errand.

"My son-in-law, you know?" Sir William hooked a finger at Daniel's back.

I said I had heard and also of Guy Johnson's marriage to Polly and said how fine the new house looked and we talked thus of nothing till Molly joined us. She closed the door behind her.

"It's true, lad," Sir William said, after Molly and I had embraced. "I don't know what you've heard, but almost everything is true this time. And happening under my nose."

"You could not have stopped it," Molly said, and to me: "Will's been a sick man, his liver hard as a rock, and he blames himself for every spark of fire in the whole wilderness."

"Sparks of fire!" Sir William said. "It's a conflagration!"

It was the old plot of the bad belts all over again, but this time come to life and action in many tribes, some of them of our own confederacy. Guyasuta of the Chenussios had once again been the begetter, but this time he had done his work more stealthily and there had been no great council where Warraghiyagey might have pulled his teeth before they bit. An Ottawa war chief, Pontiac, had laid siege to Fort Detroit; Delawares under Captain Bull were ravaging in our own hunting grounds; the Potawatomi were marching on Fort St. Joseph; the Senecas playing with old friendship for the French.

Such news and much more had been gathered by Molly

and by some of Sir William's own scouts. And we sat there—a sick man, a young woman and a boy fresh from parson's schooling—to plan how to stem the whole tide.

"There's George Croghan, thank God," Sir William said, "and he can hold most of his people off, at least in neutrality for the while. And Henry Bouquet in Pennsylvania may march quickly enough to save Fort Pitt. If Detroit can hold out long enough . . ."

"It's a strong position," I said, remembering the high stockades and the well-stored sufficiency within them.

"If Guyasuta and Pontiac can bring together all the tribes they've sent belts to," Sir William said, "there is no position strong enough. My enemies say I fight for land or for wealth, and it seems to me now I've been fighting only for time. If we can hold off the Senecas and the grumbling confederate nations till we have a victory or two to display, then they'll swing back to us as easily as they list now to France and Pontiac."

"We have called all the chiefs I'd be willing to trust," Molly said. "You must save your strength to talk and argue with them and keep them from any declaration."

"Aye, love, I can do that much, I think," Sir William sighed. "I'd sooner be on the war trail, but my liver cries 'Bed!' louder than my heart can answer 'Battle!'"

"Detroit is important"—Molly changed the course of our talk—"but so is our own front garden. I speak of the Delawares raiding near us. It must take some months for any changes in the west, even with best hopes for Bouquet and forces to relieve Detroit. To any watching Indian eye, we shall suffer in those months if there is word that Captain Bull and his mixed-blood band of renegades are burning and scalping as they like."

"You are right, Moll," Sir William said. "But Bull and his crew are the harder to pin down for they're not even a tribe. I could spare enough men from here to squash them like glutted mosquitoes, but I don't know where to swat."

"Could that be my mission, Warraghiyagey?" I asked.

Molly darted me a glance of thankfulness.

"To find where to swat?" Sir William thought aloud. "I don't like the risk, lad."

"He is my brother Thayendanegea," Molly said, "and I do not savor risks for him either, Will, but I should sleep with even less comfort if I knew he were shirking a needed duty."

"Well," Sir William said. "Perhaps . . ."

"They move below the region where my face is best known," I said. I might never have been to Mr. Wheelock's school as I spoke in an old enthusiasm for the stratagems of war. "To insinuate into a mixed-blood band should be no difficulty when Captain Bull must be glad of every added able hand."

So we made plans.

Sir William had to ride away that evening to a meeting of landholders at Warrensburgh and we said him good-bye at his stirrup in a chill drizzle of rain. Molly and I dined alone together and I took to my bed early, the table wine compounding my weariness from my traveling.

I woke to a wild wailing screech and the apparition of Molly at my chamber doorway. I reached to the floor by my bedside for the ax I had lain there, visions of an attack by some marauding band, of fire or sudden death chasing one after the other through my sleep-fuddled brain. Then I heard the rumble of thunder and recognized poor Molly's tribulation.

"Joseph!" she was wailing. "Small Turtle!"

The wise woman who had finished planning cool strategy with Sir William and myself that afternoon was reduced to the trembling, girl-child sister I had shielded from storm fright in my old bearskin years before.

"Calm, Molly," I said. "It is only a storm. Thunder harms nothing and the lightning that strikes is never seen."

"I cannot . . ." she tried to speak, but her chattering teeth passed only incoherence through her lips.

"Here, my sister." I stripped the feather-stuffed comforter from my bed and held it out to her. She grasped it gratefully and rolled it all about her so that she curled on the floor near me with her head concealed in its soft protection.

Outside a teeming rain struck against Sir William's fine glass windowpanes and more thunder crashed and rumbled with lightning pointing flamed fingers down between the thunder roars. I sat on the side of my bedstead and stroked the frightened bundle that hid my sister, soothing her with the same childish phrases, that Manitou would send us a rainbow in the morning, that rain was a benefice to all Turtles, all the rest, that I had used to reassure her in camp stations and at the castle.

A little after dawn the storm had spent itself and Molly poked her head uncertainly from her cocoon.

"I am ashamed," she said, "but it is a fear I have never mastered, brother."

"Thunder cannot touch you, Molly," I said, as I had said so many times before.

"I know that, Joseph," she said, "but I know it only when there is no thunder. Will has told me, and Dr. Franklin has told me, and Gray Diamond told me when I learned my earliest Turtle lore. And I can nod and believe them all, but the first storm sound from the sky chases all such knowledge away. Now you will tell Will and he will laugh at me, and I will laugh at myself till the next thunderstorm."

"I shan't laugh," I promised her.

I stole back some little sleep after she had left, but I thought, before sleep claimed me, that all men have some fears, and perhaps it is better and simpler to fear a thing outside oneself, like Molly's terror of the thunder, than to carry fear and uncertainty of what may lurk inside the soul, this fear that sometimes steals over me no matter what the weather.

Sir William and Molly and I kept our plan secret among the three of us and gave out to others, even the most trusted (for they had tongues capable of sliding), that I was being sent once more to palaver with the Chenussios. Since I had done this before (indeed my war name means Two-Sticks-Bound-Together from my bringing them back to our camp at Niagara) the story was accepted by all.

I left on horseback with full packs and took the road I should have taken to the Chenussios. Molly had made arrangements with Carrihogo, aging but still active and alert, to meet me before the castle and take the horse.

We had not been together for many years nor even seen each other for the last, but it made no difference. Our time was short.

"You are well, son?" he said, taking my reins from me.

"I am well, Father," I said. We made farewell signs as we went our separate ways.

A mile or two into the forest, I stripped my clothing and wrapped it into a bundle which I could wedge in a cave cleft I knew. There was two or three days' hard moving ahead of me before I would come into country where Captain Bull had been recently raiding, but I desired to run no needless chances. And this extra time on the trail would help bring me back to ease with my own near-naked hunter's body and a oneness with that nature I had deserted nine months.

I wore only a small clout for a hunting Indian's grudging decency on encountering whites and a string belt to hold my powder horn and bullets, my ax and a small provision pouch. I carried my rifle (not my best and newest, but a sound enough gun, worn and pitted in keeping with what might be expected of a tribeless wanderer) and walked and ran that whole first day without much pause, my weariness a delight in my return to this free old life.

I could reflect while running and with some shock that this was the first such true freeness in half a dozen years. I had hunted in those years, but always with parties, and I had traveled far but always in company and in company as often as not of slow-moving English soldiers. It swum my head happily to be once more a lone Mohawk, swift and silent and deadly on the trail.

This will always be a part of my being, no matter how old I grow, how heavy or how slow. Chief Hendrick, riding to his death, may have seemed to a watching colonial soldier an ancient tub of lard, but I had seen him that day with my eyes of a Mohawk youth and I knew, however he might lumber on that old horse, he was a brave racing to battle. Now, on my way, I saw again him and Sir William as they rode that day. I think, in most times of war, this was the vision always with me.

The first two days I ate sparingly of my provisions and made a fire only the second night and that a little one guarded of its smoke. The third day I saw from my trail a small farm with a man and woman working in its field. It was a good site to commence making some impression of my new character.

I left the trail and took shelter of trees and sparse bushes till I could be between the couple and their house. I crouched and made a hasty daubing of some war paint to my face and then emerged from my retreat with the loud, high, blood-chilling Mohawk cry of war, my rifle pointed at the startled farmer.

"Spare me! Spare me!" he keened most pitifully, but I saw him edging toward the spot, five yards or six down the furrow, where he had left his own gun.

"Stand where you are or die!" I said in throaty English. He stood while I scooped up his gun, and his wife, a thin, sorrowful-faced woman, gibbered.

"Powder, lead, food," I said the words as if the tongue were strange to me and made signs as well. They stumbled ahead to their wretched one-room house, a hovel Sir William would have scorned to quarter a slave in.

In the house I tied the man up tight on a rude, teetering chair and made signs that no further harm would come to them if his wife fed me well and gave me the powder and lead I had demanded. She scurried to do my bidding. I added his powder flask to my belt, crammed some sheet lead to my pouch and sat at the table to stuff my mouth as crudely as they might expect a godless savage's table manners.

While I ate, I quizzed them in mixed English and Mohawk for word of other Indian marauders. Yes, they had heard of such and from their descriptions I was sure it was Captain Bull's band.

I grunted repletion without thanks and tied the woman before I left, but lightly enough so that an hour's work or less might set her free. They had a tumbledown shed a little distance from the house. The wind blew away from it, so I set it afire to lend better verisimilitude to my role as raider and also, I own, for some inner satisfaction of my own.

Their news fitted the rumor Molly had given me, that Captain Bull might be making his own fortress of the old, abandoned castle at Canisteo. It was nominally under Chenussio sovereignty which fitted Guyasuta's hand in the conspiracy. I went back to forest trails and pondered my best approach. I could simply walk into the castle and offer myself for a member of the band, or I could let them capture and convert me. The latter had more risk, but seemed the more convincing.

I was within an hour's walk of Canisteo the next day and I kept my every sense sharp against sound or sight of other Indians. The trail I tread showed signs of much use. My heart beat loud. I walked more slowly and it was not long before my ears caught the faintest rustle of pursuing braves, just now and then a cracked twig or a footfall, the sound of good hunters less careful than usual because on their own ground.

I found it one of the hardest things in my life to walk ahead without looking back. How did I know they would wish to capture me alive? Perhaps all I would ever know would be the thunk of an ax in the back of my head and quick death.

My morbidity was ended when there came a clutter of sound to my rear and strong arms pinioning my own even as

I spun to face my enemies. They were three braves with just a few lines of war paint on their faces, all three well armed with good rifles and sharp axes.

"Brother," I said, giving up struggle against their odds. "I harm no man, why do you molest me? I am a simple hunter and my only wish to feed myself and find a skin or two to sell the trader."

They spoke no word and I admired Captain Bull's training. They gave a grunt betimes, leading me ahead of them to the castle, handling my rifle and the gun I had taken from the farmer, but this was all.

Canisteo overlooked its river which gave it good defense from the east. Its other three sides were protected by a combination of log palisades (in ill repair) and a natural rock escarpment.

I was led before Captain Bull, a brave of bulk and tallness. He insisted on a long ritual examination and even some small torture, but they were (as I had hoped) not over suspicious of me. My possession of the farmer's gun and horn, both burned with his name, counted for me and they had heard of the firing of the shed which was another gallant mark in their eyes. I was a strong and putatively brutal warrior and they could use another such. So, with only a few burned toes and one finger broken (I smiled fixedly through this performance though the snapping of the finger sickened me a little in my belly, and gained much honor), I was made a warrior of Captain Bull's band.

In the weeks that followed my first impressions were quite confirmed. For all the deterioration of time, the castle was still a strong position, but its main strength was Bull himself. He kept his band in good order, but he had no lieutenant capable of command in his absence. Could he be drawn away, any small and disciplined detachment could take the position.

Harder than any torture was being forced to sit silent while these slovenly bandits entertained themselves at their fire with scurrilous tales of Molly and even of my own self.

"They say she's a barrel all her own hidden in War-raghiyagey's cellar," one oaf said, "filled to the brim with gold and jewels."

"And not just from him, either," leered another. "She sells her favors to the rich patroons when they visit and then splits the profit with Sir William."

"No Indian gets an audience with Warraghiyagey until he's greased Mohawk Molly's palm."

And so on.

"Have you ever seen this Molly?" I ventured once.

"Aye!" one scowling brave claimed. "A pockmarked wench actually, but she has strong Turtle magic to swim men's heads and fire them to lust. Sly. Sly, the whole family. I watched her brother Joseph wrestle once against a Dutchman of eighteen stone and the boy made some witchman's sign and threw the farmer to his back for all his weight."

I swallowed such talk and in between it garnered the news I needed and set afoot my own sly, witchcraft machinations.

Molly had named me a trustworthy Cayuga who hunted in that area and would see that messages got back to her and Sir William. I laid a plan and sat upon it for hatching and sent her word of it. I could not count on receiving any answer; this were too dangerous under the best auspices. I could only reckon the time I had allowed in my message, a week for it to reach Molly, another week for preparation, a week more for any armed force to come near the point I had prepared.

I had begun to think out my plans from the moment of capture (and this thinking had proved some diversion as they burned my toes). I began to speak them as soon as I was accepted into the company. I had noted on my journey a fine farmhouse somewhat in isolation and now I took this memory for my bait and embroidered it until the house became as grand as Johnson Hall, yet as vulnerable as the farmhouse whose shed I had tindered. I painted a dozen maidens in residence (for there was a lusty streak to these bandits) and a curing house full of hams and smoked venison and claimed I

had crept close enough to spy a cellar laid down with wine
and spirits from wall to wall. Then, as good as any novelist, I
made up a tale of lying by a window and hearing the house-
holder and his two stout sons explaining to the women that
they had to go on a trip to buy agricultural implements. But
they were sure the farm would be safe, for they were leaving
two trusted slaves with guns. And I described two decrepit
old slaves scarce able to lift a rifle and my listeners laughed
and nudged each other with delight.

"We could take it with five men," I said, "but we would
need another ten to carry back all the booty."

From this speech on, my difficulty was in restraining them
from marching at once and Captain Bull's in finding men who
would stay and guard the castle in the absence of the raiding
party. I was able to make my sore toes an excuse for delay
since only I could guide the band to a place that existed only
in my mind. Bull at last cowed a score of his most raggle-tag-
gle followers into agreeing to stand guard. We set off with a
band of twenty just twelve days after I had been captured,
too soon for my peace of spirit.

I held the march back as much as I could, but this was not
too much since I had to keep a name for bravery and I could
not well do this and at the same time plaint about my sore
feet. As often in campaigns, it was an accident that slowed us
and saved my schedule. Just past the Cohocton we skirted
farmlands and the sight of one lonely but large cabin was
more than the party could resist. Now I was truly torn for I
had no plan to be part of killing the very people I had set out
to protect, yet I had given myself such a character that I
could not back away from murder. I argued that the prize
ahead was so much greater we should not risk it by untimely
action here. Bull was wise enough to support me, but he had,
as too often with Indians, no real command power and we
were overruled; the final argument against us being sight of a
woman's petticoat hung drying from a yard post.

So we moved silently on that unsuspecting cabin in the late

afternoon, having taken time to watch two men come back to the house from their fields.

They kept no watch so we crept to the very door and threw it open before they knew our presence. The two men had not time to reach for guns. Bull's braves were upon them with knife and ax and they were lying on the floor in endless sleep before they could have heard more than their women's first screams. Both women were comely (to begin with), one fair and one with reddish hair. Our party crowded one after the other into the room as the first-comers began their sport, stripping off the women's clothes with shrewd knife slashes, taking some care at this point not to cut or spoil their skins; their long hair would be there for the taking at any time. They cried out in God's name and begged mercy in English and in Dutch and in a mangled sort of Indian dialect, but there was no mercy that evening.

Captain Bull had first choice and took the fair one, disdaining any help to hold her and bending her screaming back over the table where she had been having her dinner, squeezing her plump breasts with his huge hands as he swived her to his glut. Two other braves held the other woman while a third entered her, spitting in her face and hissing insults in Seneca as he had his pleasure. Then others took the places of the first and the screaming died away to sobs and even little moans of near to pleasure. I felt my own prick rise under my clout, but I held away for to have a woman against her will has never titillated me so greatly. When all had done with her, Bull let the two braves first into the cabin have the scalps and we set to looking for loot.

There was not much: two guns, a paltry store of powder, some knives and some women's baubles. I spied a little door off the main room and opened it. It gave on a small, low-ceilinged room holding only a cradle and in the cradle there slept an infant as peacefully as if no riot had been churning in the house. I stepped out and let the door shut behind me as softly as I could.

"Nothing there," I said. "A privy, a white man's trough to shit in." I think I might have fought them to save the child, but I was believed and my companions had found some wine and were drinking and amusing themselves by slashing aimlessly at the dead bodies of the two men and two women.

I found Bull and persuaded him to leave before any visiting settler might stumble on the scene. My real fear was the child might wake and cry, but Bull took my false reasoning and we darted away into the night and on our road. I said some silent prayers, both to Manitou and to God the Father, that the child might be found before it died. This night I could do no more.

The raid delayed us, not just the time of raiding, but boozing that night on the trail and all sleeping well into the next day. I now felt some hope of success for my plans and the poor four people who had died might have been the saviors of ten times their number.

We came near the Susquehanna two days later and I took council with Bull, asking that I be allowed to go ahead and make sure of the farm and its position. He weighed my request but decided against trusting a new recruit so completely.

"Yellow Legs will go with you," he said. "Two are better than one." I was prepared for some such precaution and had my plans for it, and I was not too displeased for it was Yellow Legs who had led off the rape of the red-haired woman and had most reviled Molly by the castle fire.

Yellow Legs stayed close after me across the river. I led him up the far bank and on up a wooded hill. There I looked below before I beckoned him to have his own vista for I wanted the last sight of his life to be the company of two hundred militia and Indians ranged in camp below. There was a grunt of amazement that turned to a gurgle as I cut his throat with my razor-sharp knife as neatly as a woman killing a dog for dinner.

I slipped quickly down the camp side of the hill and

identified myself to a sentry. Within the minute I was at the fireside of an old friend, Andrew Montour, George Croghan's best right hand as Croghan himself was Sir William's. He had been at the Hall when Molly received my message and had volunteered to lead a party against Bull. I told him in few words the disposition of Bull's party and he had detachments moving to surround them before I finished speaking. He took another detachment with me across the river where he had trumpet and drum sound a call. We stood in our position there ten minutes; it took no longer than that for Bull to try the trap and find it without an escape. He came out with seven of his braves, weaponless hands high, and surrendered to us. The other braves our flanking platoon routed out later, and Montour went on to clean out the outlaw castle with no loss of life to any of his company.

I went along with Montour, and then back with him and our prisoners to the Hall. Canisteo was no major battle, but it served, as Molly and Sir William and I had hoped, for a pivot in Sir William's dealing with the unpledged nations.

Sir William was still ailing and our arrival with captives brought color back to his cheek. He scolded Captain Bull before assembled chiefs of a dozen tribes and sent him off in irons to be prison-held as a hostage in New York port.

I stayed only long enough to pack again and go south with Montour to join Colonel Bouquet in his march to relieve Fort Pitt.

Meaning more to me in my heart than the relief of Fort Pitt was this journey's opportunity to find again that sheltered island in Laurel Ridge that had captured my soul's delight in boyhood.

I walked alone up the course of the mountain stream and it shocked me to find how quickly with a man's stride I passed the distance, so far in my memory, to where the creek divided to protect my island kingdom. But it was boon to all my war-weariness to find that pile of rocks, their skirting shore of sand, even the cucumber smell of a brother copperhead, all the same.

It would have been too much to have spied a stray raccoon and I did not, but I lay some time on the same rock from which I had watched that solicitous mother, and refreshed my spirit with recollection and with merely watching the clear rushing of the stream over stones no doubt worn somewhat in the years' passing, but still the same in my fond eye.

I had seen so much of things I could not love—lands encroached, fire and blood and double-dealing—but I made to myself some kind of solace that so long as this glade stood green and clean and untouched there might be hope of good in a wicked world. I styled myself a Christian and did so with honesty, but I felt no contradiction that before leaving my island I said an old Turtle spell for its preservation. I was at the commencement of a period of wild confusion in my own head that lasted almost ten years and saw me, less a wanderer on the land, but more an Ishmael in my soul.

It may have been the swiftness of change from Mr. Wheelock's school to masquerading as a godless bandit with Captain Bull, it may have been the dazing thump I had on my head at Bushy Run that had me babbling delirium while I still marched for two whole days, it may simply have been a culmination of all my worrying dreams, my ambitions and my clear sight of Indian fighting white man and I, an Indian, with the whites.

All I see now, looking back, is a mortal in the years of young manhood suffering all the greensickness of youth and stretched upon a rack of the spirit beside.

I moved to a house of my own at Canajoharie and I married.

Christine was a small girl, slender and comely as I always admired, and I think I married her because she puzzled me. I met her and tried to tumble her, and failed. Now, had I married every maid who said me No I should have a harem of as many wives as some Arabian monarchs. It was the how of her

No that puzzled and intrigued me, for she said she liked me well but still would not sleep with me (or anyone) this side of marriage. For, she went on, she was a Christian and her father had given up many chiefly rights (he was an Oneida) to preach God's word. So she said and so she stood and I could not get her from my thoughts while I was away. I came back and tried her again with the same result. She let me fondle her and kiss her and took much delight and, to change Mr. Dryden's song:

> But when we came where pleasure is
> She *ever* would say Nay.

So, possessed by what demon I know not, I took the Holy Eucharist for no better reason than lustful curiosity and asked her father for her hand and married her before a Christian altar.

We had a wonderful night in bed and she woke before I did to begin the day chiding me for where I had strewn my clothes, for something I had said carelessly against her mother, for the fact that our bed had a mattress of chicken feathers and not goose down and how many other women had I known before marriage?

I took the last question first and tried in honest innocence to make some tally.

"Sixteen," I said. "Mayhap seventeen."

She threw herself down and buried her face in the bed but you could still have heard her screeching from one end of the castle town to the other as she called me lecher, ravisher of virgins (I could swear there were no more than four in the whole sixteen, seventeen), bloody Mohawk pagan and other unkind epithets.

I have wondered since then how many men could truly say why they married. It is as solemn a sacrament as christening or burial, yet we enter into it often (as I did with Christine) from mixed and trivial causes, a vague dis-ease with the pattern of our lives, a cunny-struck madness for some maid who will not say Yes without the ceremony, for some woman of rich dower or other importance, or because a pregnant wench is crying (or her father threatening). Those marriages fixed on true love and Christian love as well must be as rare as blossoms in midwinter. With all our tribulations, I have had the fortune of such marriage with Catherine, and I think Molly and Sir William, with none but an Indian bond, had the same, but I search my mind and all my friends and these two are all I can believe in.

Poor Chris! It was a stormy marriage all the way and all her strength was in railing at me for otherwise she had ill lungs and general weakness. We had two children, Isaac and Christiana. Christine kept a neat house and I enjoyed playing with our children, but she ate in clothes and furnishings every shilling I got from Sir William (who was a generous man) and from the Crown and, besides our time in bed, she sharpened her tongue upon me every waking hour. I had in Canajoharie six fine rooms not counting the kitchen and a storage shed, but I spent as much time at the Hall as there.

Sir William was well only fitfully. He had got a knighthood for John and moved him to Fort Johnson in hope his son might take over some of his load, but Sir John was better fitted to playing the squire's importance than to shouldering the squire's responsibilities. Guy Johnson had managed to take some of the burden of dealing with Indians, but only the least part of it. William of Canajoharie could not help himself, much less his father. Sir William invented duties for Tagcheunto to keep him as far from home as he might and sent much money to pay fines for drunkenness and disorder.

So I had work to do, helping Molly when Sir William had to stay abed. Taking his orders and transmitting them to others, Indian and English, and making more than several decisions on my own. Beyond Molly and Sir William and Carrihogo (now so old as to be but a doll propped up at some councils) there were few who called me Joseph any longer. I was Thayendanegea, a chief and a war leader. Everywhere, that is, except my own home.

Christine shrilled if I left her when I went to the Hall, and scolded me when I took her with me if I spoke to anyone else. I bought her gowns to match the finest robes of Nancy and Polly and she accused me of trying to turn her into a strumpet.

We had a great ball at Johnson Hall the spring of 1767 with a few favored Indians and all the finest gentry, English and Dutch, from up and down the valley. Christine, for once, was awed enough to hold her tongue in public.

There was dancing and Sir William led off with Molly, but sat on an upholstered couch after that dance for his illness was coming back upon him. I danced with Christine every other dance, almost enough to slack her accusations of desertions, and others with Molly and the Johnson girls.

Christine had gone off with Polly for dispersal of the punch bowl's tax upon her bladder. I knew better than to dance with any charmer in her absence, so I found myself a drink and took it to a chair next to Sir William's study door. I heard speech from within and could not help but follow it.

"Come, Moll, give us a kiss," I heard.

"Don't play the fool, Philip. I brought you here to show you the deed that's contested. Look at it, not me."

"And who would look at a deed when they might do some deed with you, Molly. Don't fool with me, lass. The whole world knows the old man's a crock, and you're young and lusty yet."

There was sound of a scuffle and a smart slap before my sister's voice: "I had rather sit alone with Sir William's ashes, and all that I can remember of joys with him, than an eternity of tricks with your stiff parkin, Mr. Schuyler." I heard her move. "Sir William's paper knife is not the weapon I would choose, but it will do. Get out! Get out! Get out!"

I saw Philip Schuyler, a man I had known from campaigns against the French, a good soldier and a great landowner, backing out from the study with a red mark from Molly's slap still burning a brand upon his cheek. I saw no duty to speak more to him, but rushed into the room to my sister.

She leaned against Sir William's desk, his blunt letter knife in her hand and her bosom heaving in the English-style dress she wore that night so that I could fathom Mr. Schuyler's abandon. I had never seen Molly my sister weep for anything save thunder, but she was near it now and I held her fast in my arms and let her shield her face away from my eyes.

"Ah, God!" she said, in cursing learned from Sir William. "Ah, God, that randy patroon and how many others think I have no more interest in Sir William than his prick. I, who have been as proud to be a segment of his mind as a sharer of his bed, who have lain awake with him long after humping to think plans to save the frontier."

I held her and felt her heart's flutter slow from its anger.

"Are all white men so, Joseph?" she asked. "Did you learn aught of that at Lebanon? Do they think every one of us with a red skin mere puppets of our passions? I know my Will does not, but he is one in a thousand, in a thousand thousand, a milliard, however they count. Ah, brother, I feel soiled."

She stood away from me and her face changed from sorrow to a smile as curved and wicked as a sword. "I would have," she said, "Phil Schuyler's head for a football, cut from his arrogant body to kick about the Hall like a toy. And, if Will should ask me: 'What is that?' I could reply: 'Some cheap knickknack for my womanish pleasure.'"

I would have gone then and taken an ax to Philip Schuyler and brought his head back to my Molly and she knew this and clenched my arm.

"Enough, Joseph," she said. "There will be other revenge and time for it one day. Now let us forget all that has passed. Will you dance with me?"

And we tread, hand in hand, the most stately of minuets.

Sir William ailed and rallied and ailed again. It was another fortnight before a runner from Molly had me out of my bed at home (Christine, you may be sure, shrill in protestation) with word my foster father had had another stroke. I threw on clothing and hurried to Molly and found Sir William stretched rigid on a couch, lifted from where he had fallen to the floor. He had had such strokes before, but this was the worst and I could hardly trace a beat to his pulse and his face was parchment.

Molly spoke of calling apothecaries and surgeons from as far as need be, but I told her this was foolish; Sir William had had all the English physic he could stand; there only remained our own medicine.

"The springs," I told her.

So she agreed and we called other chiefs and braves and we loaded the helpless man to a litter and set out, perhaps a hundred of us, to take him to that stinking water close on the Massachusetts border that has great power to heal ills. It should have been two days' journey, but we reached it in a day and a half and I wonder now what amazement we may have caused onlookers along the way, seeing this long procession of the most stalwart Mohawk chiefs and in their midst, borne gently aloft, a gray old man in a litter swaddled in white sheets.

At the springs, we tilted his litter into the water, sheets and all and, as the waters lapped about him, he came back to consciousness.

"Where am I?" he asked, and saw me. "Joseph"—with a smile—"is this some circle of hell, and, if it is, how be you here?"

I smiled as I might have wept and told him his illness and our measures.

"Do not talk, Father," I said. "Do not spend yourself. Let the waters do their work."

So we kept him there three days and into the waters every day and our wisest medicine men scoured the woods for roots and herbs to implement his cure.

Sir William walked away from the spring and marched the

road home with us and, although he had some other spells of sickness, there was none again so close to death before death itself. And, if any reader still scorns the value of the springs, I can note that Molly bore him Mary, Susanna and Anne in the years after this adventure and there were, as usual, some other children in the valley that could call him father.

I went back to the castle and Christine and every time she coughed she asked me did I care more for Sir William's health than for hers. In truth I should have had to answer Yes, but do you know any husband who might have such courage? And the smallest child, nursing a clay doll, could tell you that the springs had virtue only for ailings of kidney, belly and groin and were no use against the racking fever and the crab-constriction of the lungs already consuming Christine.

I think it was that same year I joined the lodge of Masonry Sir William had encouraged a friend to bring up from Pennsylvania. I shall not spill its mysteries: the reader who is himself a Mason will know their strength and value, the reader who is not may take my word that this association has been important through all my life next only to faith in the Lord, my Salvation.

And I went with a more vigorous Sir William to Oswego where Pontiac made final surrender after all his sunderings of the frontier. I talked with him and found him to my surprise a man worth much respect, wrongheaded in his goals, but as troubled as I myself with our times of change and desolation to the Indian.

We took an easy pace back and I had good opportunity to talk, as of old times, with Sir William.

"The Six Nations should hold what they have," he told me. "This land is vast enough for English and Indians and even French, though I'm not sure London would thank me for saying that.

"But you can't hold it in the old way, Joseph. You must teach your people to till land and make something of it. An Englishman will think twice of stealing a plowed field, not at all of taking a hundred times the same acreage in wilderness. Remember that."

I nodded and stored the thought.

"This country is so great it can be anything," he said and reined his horse and I stopped, too. We were at a gap in the mountains and could look back to land sloping evenly toward Lake Ontario, its halo haze a distant cloud, and ahead on up to mountains imperial in their rugged, tree-clad height. "Anything, Joseph, my son," he said most softly and fearfully.

"Townshend's Acts will be harder to repeal than the stamp business," he said, veering with his quickness to another tack. "If Pitt had not been ailing, he might have found some guise to sweeten them. But all us old men who love the colonies and England equally are sick. Is there no way of telling the Boston hogs and the New York swine"—so he generally spoke of the Adamses and their merchant counterparts in New York port— "that taxes pay for their safety?" He was talking as much to the trees by the trail as to me, but his words stuck.

"They'll see, after a month of arguing, the need for a shilling spent to keep militia active from Ligonier to Fort Pitt, but they won't see the other shillings that keep King George's fleet on the seas, saving their ports from the French. They won't see the indissolubility of the Crown's interests, that a penny in Flanders is a penny for Philadelphia and the obvious reverse."

He trotted on in silence for a few minutes.

"And London is as stupid. Damn!" he swore. "They take reports of an Amherst as gospel and treat me and Franklin as amiable freaks to be honored yet never overencouraged." He stared gloomily at our path as his horse picked its own way beside mine.

The trail widened into a clearing where a small stream took a stiff descent in a little waterfall and the sun at that moment, as if to counter Warraghiyagey's despond, broke through clouds and bathed this little space with shafts of light, turning the tumbling water to a shower of diamonds.

Sir William took a deep breath, so deep that I could hear it. "But it's a good life for all of that, lad!" he cried and spurred his horse and I clattered after him, the two of us down the trail well ahead of our train, galloping and careering like two young braves on a first ride in the forest, I twenty-five and my lord somewhat over fifty.

To home, I found Christine in worse temper than ever, plaguing me near to distraction, but by now I knew, from our own wise men and confirmed by English physicians, that these frenzies were the nature of her illness. It seems that ailments of the lungs are febrile not merely in the body but in the mind, and the victim races in fury against a doom he knows he cannot stay. So I tried my best for gentleness and patience, borrowed money of Sir William to satisfy her new whims, let her scold me as she would and tried to find some solace in the children.

Such patience was hard bought for this was still in my years of confusion. What relief I could not find in work I had from an increase, slow and painful, in my understanding of religion. Some men, I know, are blessed like Saul with a blazing revelation, but I am convinced that most of us come much more gradually to any real faith, hearing only the words first (which is why the Scriptures say in St. John I:1: "In the beginning was the Word") and the words not made flesh till long travail.

And this travail is not an even path, but one of ups and downs and digressions and backslidings like that of Christian in Mr. Bunyan's allegory.

We had ministers and missionaries in and out of the castle and from Christine's being herself daughter of a preacher, ours was often their house of hospitality away from their homes. I had thus good opportunity for long talks with Anglicans (my first and still true faith), with Congregationalists and Moravians and many others. But the sad thing was that all this talk, instead of allaying my mind's bewilderment, only roiled it worse. I even took my problems to Sir William, but he was a man of so much different mold that he could neither understand nor help me much. He had long left the Romish faith of his infancy to become a staunch Anglican, but I think he could just as easily have stayed Roman or turned Quaker (if either of these had been the faith of his society) without himself changing a whit.

"Give God his tithe," he told me, "look your fellows in the eye and deal with them honestly, Joseph, and you'll strum a harp in heaven beside archbishops. That's enough to know, son. All the rest is scribblers' arguments."

I could not take it so easily, but I own the nearness and friendship of ministers, especially Dr. Stewart from Fort Hunter, helped me face and accept poor Christine's death.

Coming to Christine's death I have read back over what I had written about our marriage and it makes me feel a cheat although I cannot think how to change one word of it. It is only that my living longer has given me the power to chronicle events and associations without contradiction from anyone else concerned and, however I try for truth, it is my eye and my memory and my conceit that must color every word I write. I feel this the more, looking at lines I have put down about Christine's shrewishness, for I remember also in the last week before she died I would have sold myself as a bond slave to have heard her just once more berate me for some imagined slight or shout at me to buy her a new comb or robe.

For the last week she turned about entirely. Every line of her face softened to a gentler beauty and she wanted only to hold my hand close as I sat on the side of her bed and tried to amuse her with aimless talk and gossip of the castle.

"When this spell has passed, you shall see how good a wife I can be, Joseph," she said, and then sobbed a little that the spell should not pass except to death and had my vows to watch carefully over our children, vows I kept how poorly you may read later.

She had little pain (for which I was thankful), but a wasting weakness that devoured her in the space of that single week so that, at its end, she weighed no more than a girl-child of eight or nine and I carried her slight body when the breath had gone from it down the street to the house of John Bandy, a medicine man, for confirmation of her end. Dr. Stewart came up from Fort Hunter to say her burial service. I walked for a month or more thereafter like a man in a dream. I put the children in her father's house where Dorcas, her younger sister, took their care.

It was Dr. Stewart who shook me out of these dumps and suggested I remove to Fort Hunter where I might help him with the work of translating the prayer book and some of the Gospels into the Mohawk language. This was the kindly reason he gave, but he confessed later that he saw me lost in the castle where every byway, every friendly face reminded me more of Christine and sharpened a pain of loss that should have been growing less.

A strange thing, for it was not love of her that fed my loss, but some hatred of myself, knowing I had misled the lass, married her without the depth of feeling she deserved and always proved out far less than whatever paragon she had hoped for. I had some consolation of religion here. It is a hard thing for any man to explain to another, for this consolation was not a matter of explanation of Christine's death or absolution for my failure with her, but a coming and going warmth of community with God, that never stayed with me long, but always long enough to promise an eventual infinity in its healing strength.

Move I did from the castle to the Fort. Sir William had as much business for me at one as at the other, though these years I was a desultory missioner to his pursuits. I found a good price for the Canajoharie house and could thank Christine's demands for the excellence that had increased its value. I took a dwelling at Fort Hunter with a room for my own study, a bedroom of my own and a large bedroom where Dorcas could stay with Isaac and Christiana.

It was a good community in and about the Fort. I busied myself with Dr. Stewart on his translations and also gave him some help with the school he had established for both English and Indian youths. George Croghan had settled by Otsego Lake and I was often a guest to his house, listening to his tales and his grand plans for the future. It was there I met Lieutenant John Provost, a regular officer of Swiss descent, who had married Croghan's white daughter Susannah and had his own house across the lake. If I noticed Croghan's Indian daughter, Catherine, it was then only as one of many children playing about the manor.

It was John Augustine Provost who made the immediate and most heartfelt impression on me. He was a young man of my own age, handsome and of good bearing, son of a general, most excellently educated and a fine soldier. I had so long sought a true friend, and Lieutenant Provost seemed an answer to my unspoken prayers.

No European I have spoken with has ever been able to understand the meaning to an Indian of "the one true friend." Englishmen may have many friends, some close, some not so close, and so have we, but they have nothing like our idea that each man should have one friend apart from all the rest, more than even a brother, truly another self. Such a friend I had not found and I felt the lack. There had been times I had hoped that Tagcheunto could hold this place in my heart, but even when we were closest rum had his loyalty beyond anything he could give another human. And by now we had drifted apart to mere acquaintances.

Then I met Lieutenant Provost. It was at dinner at Croghan's board and he seemed interested to hear me speak of Mr. Wheelock's school and my experiences there, also my thirst for reading and the pleasure I had had from the few volumes I had read, naming Bunyan and some of the simple verses.

"Tracts and trifles!" he said. "You must look at the library I have collected here. I've John Locke for gravity and Mr.

Fielding's *Tom Jones* for frivolity and verses all the way from Mr. Dryden's translations of Horace and Publius Virgil Maro's *Aeneid* in its own Latin."

O, could I have but transported Samson Occum there to overhear an English gentleman-scholar speaking with me with such equal familiarity!

I launched a spirited defense of my beloved Bunyan and, long after others of the party had left the table, we sat there over our wine arguing whether moral messages might help or hinder a work of literature, and the nature of Inspiration in Art, and many other weighty matters.

After that night I was as often a guest at the Provost house as at Croghan's, and more at both of them than at my own hearth which Dorcas kept smart and neat and where I still enjoyed to play with my children, but which had none of the books or the heady conversations I reveled in at the lake side.

There is warmth in remembering this time, but a little shame in recall of all I neglected for what I thought to be the most important bond in my life. I did business for Sir William, but managed to keep it from taking me away too far or too long and he, with the wisdom that marked all his dealings, neither questioned nor pressed me. I took my proper place in some councils though not so many as I should have.

It was not a time of inactivity, yet all my activity aside from being with Lieutenant Provost, was a sleepwalking without involvement of my deepest self.

John Provost was all I had ever thought to admire in a blood brother. He was a brawny sportsman and hunter and what joy to be on the chase with a man who, after bringing down a deer, could stand by it and quote in Latin as he viewed the green vista around us: *"Diffugere nives, redeunt iam gramina campis arboribusque comae."* Which are words of the poet Horace Flaccus saying: "The snows have been strewn and retreated; even now grass comes in the fields and leaves upon the trees."

His was a wedding of learning and action which I looked

for as much in a friend as I hoped for its achievement in myself. I borrowed all his books, one after the other, and read them and preserved them against stain or tear for the treasures they were. I think the sole time I ever lifted a hand in anger against my tiny darling Christiana was when she plucked at the volume I was reading of Jeremy Taylor's *The Rule of Conscience* and came near to ripping a page.

John Provost was also a Mason and we attended the Lodge together, making a treat of the short journey to Warrensburgh and staying the night at the inn there. We could have gone on to stay with Molly and Sir William at Johnson Hall, but I did not wish to share my blood brother with anyone.

I called him that, blood brother, and he would smile and say: "You are my blood brother, too, Joseph." I could not know the words meant no more to him than an English declension of friend. And I am glad I did not know for I had, unspoiled and wonderful, close on three years of seeing him every week I was at the Fort, and of living as part of him, beyond my own concerns (for blood brotherhood is its own cure against selfishness) for all that time.

It was in 1772 that Lieutenant Provost received orders to leave Otsego and report for full military duty in Jamaica.

He showed me the letter, as I thought for grievous commisseration, and I put a hand to his shoulder and had already blurted: "Oh, my brother . . ." when I saw that his face was alight with pleasure and anticipation.

"I'll have a command of my own within the year," he said. "And a sunny clime with slaves at no high price."

I held myself from saying: "And what of your blood brother?" but the thought was in me.

Still, I could not expect an officer to rail against His Majesty's orders and I clung to a belief that my friend was perhaps masking his own sorrow in the English fashion of diversion, by making great emphasis of other aspects. This was a frail hope and unbuttressed by any special word to me which he might easily have given in the weeks before he sailed. I waved him and Susannah away in the morning, helping pack their bags and trunks on a post carriage. John left me some of his books, but in a careless gesture and what he left were none of the best.

I counted days against his arrival. Three weeks to Jamaica, another week to be settled, three more weeks for a letter to return to me. I gave two full months and no letter came. I had myself, the very day he left, scoured the Fort traders for the finest and most expensive regalia of furs in the Mohawk manner that might be had and sent them after him, sparing not a shilling (not a guinea would be no exaggeration) to be sure they reached him by swiftest boat. And I gave eight weeks for this and there was still no letter.

Good George Croghan noticed my unhappiness and tried to cheer me, but I could not be cheered. I had accepted many things in life, but I had not thought betrayal by a blood brother would be one of them.

I can write this now without heaviness of spirit or blame for my somewhat friend. I had made the mistake of judging an Englishman by Mohawk measure and I was not the first or the last Indian to do so to my disillusion. A foolish mistake of youth, a more ridiculous mistake for myself, a man of thirty years.

But I had no such philosophical consolation then. Only an ache and a burning at what I felt was treachery. Dorcas tempted me at meals with tenderest dog and venison cooked in honey, but I had the least of appetites and shrunk my weight from thirteen stone to under eleven.

My mentor and companion Dr. Stewart at last forced me to meet with him in his study and in a flood of words long dammed I told him all that troubled me.

He listened to all I would say and had the wit not to chide me for childishness (the worst mistake Englishmen and preachers make most often with my people), but showed some sympathy and even understanding, comparing my passion for blood brotherhood to certain customs of ancient Greek and

Roman warriors. He even offered to make himself ("Poor trade though it may be," he said, smiling) a substitute and a new blood brother, yet understood without chagrin when I did not accept his tender.

I think I would have moped months more, but I had other worries. Poor Dorcas had begun to show every sign of a swift-devouring consumption, just as had Christine. She was a good woman and a tireless foster mother to Isaac and Christiana and there seemed to me only one payment I might make her before she, too, was carried away: to have her bound to me in legal and sacred matrimony.

In my sorrow over Lieutenant Provost's leaving I had taken refuge in her bed . . .

No, for God's sake let me speak some truth in my narrative. You, reader, must know me well enough by now to catch me out in such a simple lie. I had been sharing Dorcas's bed all the years we had been at Fort Hunter. None but the most bloodless bluenose could conceive a man of my age and well-recorded itch living under the same roof as a bright and pretty lass like Dorcas in any kind of chastity. And Dorcas was a girl of human appetites herself.

We had never spoken of marriage, but her illness struck some chord of conscience. I went to Dr. Stewart and asked him to see us wed. He shook his head sadly and said that the rules of the church forbid marriage between a man and his wife's sister. I countered that Dorcas had been only half sister to Christine, but he would not budge, not even when I shook my Bible at him and quoted chapter and verse in the marriages of the patriarchs where such a union might easily have been deemed more blessed than marriage with a strange woman.

So I threw my eye about the Fort and found a German minister, an easygoing Moravian called Father Yount, who came to the house and made us man and wife. Dorcas died the next week, but with a sweet smile and I have never regretted this excursion into a sacrament explicitly forbidden by my church.

Blows of fortune toughen a man (I do not dare claim they improve him) as the caustic of tanning toughens leather.

I took Isaac and Christiana to Johnson Hall, where Molly was glad to have them scampering with her own brood and where I once again was able to defeat morbidity by plunging more deeply into Sir William's affairs.

Sir William was bound to sail to England and rejoiced to have me at hand.

"You've been shirking your duties," he told me, "hiding at the Fort with parsons and burying your nose in books. You have a position in the Nations, Joseph, and you can't turn your back upon it. I'm sorry about the girl, but I'm glad you're set free again. I can trust Guy to sit in my study while I'm gone, but I need your eyes and ears and a strong hand and above all these a sound head in the west."

It was so good to hear him talk again, to relish his old quick command of far-flung affairs and his faith in holding the frontier.

"The Townshend Act's repealed," he said, "just as I told you. All but that petty Stamp Excise, and, if my words have any weight with our friends in London, that, too, will be annulled. We're just at the beginning, my lad"—I could have been sixty and still my lad to Sir William—"of a Britannic America that will have the old country proud of her."

Then he came to details of the troubles, and I wondered at his confidence and good humor. Our Iroquois Confederacy, at Fort Stanwix, had ceded southwest lands to settlement though such lands were truly Shawnee and none of ours to partition in any treaty. I had opposed the cession at the time and myself been opposed by other chiefs who felt the move was the only way of preserving our own Six Nations in their land. Now settlers were crowding into the rich land by wagon after wagon and Pittsburgh (no longer just Fort Pitt) was like to become another Philadelphia. Shawnees were not slow to take ax and fire and to call other nations to their side.

"Try to hold off the Delawares from any alliance," Sir William told me. "The Mingos, too, and the Wyandota, but above all the Delawares for they seem a bellwether ram for border mischief."

This was to be my mission, to help hold tribes apart. My recent years had been years of confusion, but there had been hard thought in all my misty maunderings. This was not *my* mission, so much I admitted to myself. But it was a trust put on me by Warraghiyagey, an old man to whom I owed not only much myself but who was husband to my most beloved sister (O Molly, had you been a man there need have been no search for a blood brother!) and protector of her children, and himself a Mohawk chief greater than any since Hendrick. I said I would do all he bid me.

We bid Sir William farewell for his voyage and Molly warned him with broad winks against the whores of London ("Our simples, Will, are proof only against American clap and pox, and you remember that") and then Molly and I sat down in the great room and supped solemnly, missing Sir William, missing Blind Kain (long ago killed in a drunken brawl in Lancaster) and Ganeteh who had died the year before, and Tagcheunto far away, and our mother. The handsome room with all its English furnishings was full of ghosts.

"Warraghiyagey looked to be hale," I said.

"He is, brother," Molly said, "but he is past youth and I cannot persuade him to take the ease he needs. Every time he leaves for a journey, I do not know I shall see him return."

"He will return, sister," I said, "this is a feeling I have too strong for falseness. He has put himself too far into our land for his bones to lie anywhere else."

She smiled a little.

"And you, too, will be leaving," she said. "I spend my life saying good-byes. Many times I have cried out without sound that I was born a woman, and then Will takes me to bed and

I'm glad." She paused to sip her wine, and when she spoke again it was Sir William's councilmate.

"There is a Mingo chief you should know of," she said. "He can tell you much. Johnny Two-Bottle he is named, so bring him rum as a gift more meaningful than any belt. You may ask of him at Lyman Dilworth's below Pittsburgh on the Ohio."

I left the day after and I was three months among the western people misliking everything I saw but obedient to Warraghiyagey's wishes and I kept the Shawnee fires from spreading.

Ah, but it was a dolorous region! There were some settlers stout and true folk, but the opening of the Ohio Forks had been a magnet for every clod of white riffraff. These did not homestead farms, but clustered festering in rabbit-warren settlements. They held all Indians freaks and ogres and their heroes were the like of Captain Cresap, most celebrated for killing unarmed squaws, and the foul Girty brothers who were quite "democratic" in slaughter of anyone helpless, red or white, but whose Indian killings gave them haloed fame.

I had one night's camp by the Mahoning River with a Shawnee sachem who had come to treat with me regarding Mohawk aid he must have known I could not offer.

"Where are we to go, brother?" he asked when I had told him how firm we stood with England. "The settlers swarm like gnats and the game runs before them so that a man cannot hunt his old grounds and find more than a woodchuck. When they fight, they kill women and children without mercy. Now that we have learned their ways, we kill one woman and the whole militia comes alive against us to punish our unheard-of savagery. We scalped once, brother, to show a trophy of war, the hair of a brave killed in fair battle. And they have turned scalping into a tally where any hair with a shred of flesh to it counts so many pennies from the King.

"Where are we to go, brother?"

"Our lands still stretch beyond the setting sun," I told him

(I still believing this then). "You cannot build an earthen dam in swift water. Move beyond their present reach, brother, and make yourselves strong there. Then, should their greed move them on, you may stand firm as you never can here."

"Do not tell a Shawnee to run, brother," he said sadly. "We have never collected our wounds in our backs and we will not now."

I got back to Johnson Hall in time for the grand council of the Six Nations forthcoming at the castle. I had done Sir William's work as he would have, but there remained work of my own with our own people.

I had some special pride that Carrihogo, my father, in his age sat beside me and he and I together bespoke an Indian past that ran back to his father, that Nichaus Brant who had voyaged to Queen Anne's court. So no man, whether he agreed with me or not, might listen without a certain respect.

I spoke long at the council and tread as narrow and slippery a line as ever man had to balance upon. I could not betray Warraghiyagey by turning Iroquois allegiance toward the beleaguered Shawnees, but I had to use all the eloquence and all the reasoning God might grant me to impress on every nation of our union the need to keep the settler hordes held back at the banks of the Ohio, that line agreed upon by us and by them at Fort Stanwix but already breached a dozen places.

I talked with Molly and with Guy Johnson after the council. Guy fretted some at things I had said, but when he had left us Molly gripped my hand tight and said: "You spoke well, brother."

"I would not go against Warraghiyagey," I said unsurely.

"You did not, and you could not," Molly said. "Is not my Will a Mohawk, too? No, you were right, Joseph."

So I slept better and without some of the dreams of blood and division (that bearskin rent again!) that had dogged my sleep on the trail home.

Sir William himself was back from England not long after me and he called me to talk before he was all unpacked.

"I hear you've fomented riot and rebellion among the Nations, Joseph," he said, but in the style I knew of old for his humor. "You'll become the John Wilkes of the Indians, my lad, and there's worse things you could aim at."

"I saw things on the Ohio that troubled me, Father," I said, "and I had to speak them. We betrayed our brothers the Shawnees at Fort Stanwix, and we are paying for it now."

"There was no other course open at Stanwix," he said severely. "Would you have had the Mohawks grant *their* land to settlement? The Shawnees are not of the Confederacy. There is still land aplenty left them west of the line."

"Which they must wrest from other peoples," I said.

"And is it not always thus?" Sir William asked.

"Then why do we have laws at all?" I countered and we were at it hammer and tongs.

We were none so far apart as we sounded and by the time our talk was through late at night (Molly had come in with some posset of milk and sherry with nutmeg and spoke her own mind) Sir William was as firm as I for holding the Proclamation Line and I had given up the Shawnees who were lost anyhow by past agreement at Fort Stanwix.

I stayed at the Hall, working as Sir William's secretary and taking some pride when I helped him write a long dispatch to Lord Dartmouth that spoke for the necessity of holding boundaries as firmly as I could have pleaded myself.

Spring quickened the land again. Isaac and Christiana bloomed, the former now a likely lad of ten and I took pride in teaching him, as Carrihogo had taught me, to sight and load a rifle, though I think I had been more patient.

Sir William had his times of weariness, but he still walked younger at sixty-two than many a man of forty. We had a splendid ball at the Hall late in June to welcome summer with an orchestra from the best musicians, both military and civil, of Albany. Sir William danced till dawn threw more light than our tapers. I came close to keeping pace with him, but my dancing I interrupted when I found a farmer's daughter who knew other figures than those accepted on the floor; I was feeling more a natural man again. Even Molly, usually merry though abstemious at these gatherings, let herself become tipsy and sang a Mohawk chant to the whole company.

July entered that year of 1774 hot and moist and oppressive. On the tenth Sir William had a packet of dispatches from Boston, all gloomy with the outcry in that city against the tea excise and a harebrained move by His Majesty's ministers to supersede the Massachusetts Assembly. He shook his head and clucked at the news as he read it to me, but assured me that our friends in London would enact swift countermeasures.

I accompanied him to a council of the Nations and he alluded to the Boston troubles as he spoke to the chiefs. "If there are troubles," he said, "they will be as temporary as those over the Stamp Act. The King, your father, is not a fool for all that some of his ministers might be better attired in dunce caps than in cocked hats." The sachems all laughed. "To the King, you are his faithful children," he went on. "Remember how he has protected you in the past, and whatever summer squalls may blow, do not be shaken out of your shoes." There was more laughter and crowding to clasp his hand and hug him. The King, however great, was far across the ocean; Warraghiyagey was here.

And by that evening he was dead.

He fell of a fit in the afternoon, shaking and cold to touch and unable to speak. I sent a brave on horseback to Fort Johnson and Sir John killed his best bay hurrying to his father's side. He had a remount of a farmer and reached the Hall before Sir William expired in Molly's arms, still unable to speak, his pale head, wigless and scrawn, lolling on her lap.

There were Indians of every tribe gathered all around the house, on the lawn, perched in trees and on the roofs of all the outhouses. When I stood in the doorway and told them of Warraghiyagey's death their outcry, simultaneous from every throat, was such a ululation as might be heard in Albany. The Six Nations had lost a great chief, the frontier had lost its molder.

We waited the funeral some days that the most notable mourners might have time to make the journey. I helped, with Guy and Sir John, with Tagcheunto returned sober and stricken, with Brant Johnson (another son, no kin of mine despite his name) and Molly's Peter (now a man of twenty), with Daniel Claus, with Robert Morris of Philadelphia to carry the coffin from the Hall to the church in town. There must have been half the valley with us, Molly and her eight children with Nancy and Polly, other women, naturally or legally related after them, then the whole swarm: Mohawk chiefs and chiefs of all the other Six Nations, great landowners like Robert Livingston, chiefs of other nations and tribes, patroons and a myriad of small farmers and servants, those people to whom Sir William was as much a king as His Majesty George III.

I stood beside Molly in a front pew and heard the words of the service.

"I am the resurrection and the life, saith the Lord: he that believeth in me, though he were dead, yet shall he live: and whosoever liveth and believeth in me, shall never die."

I held my eyes closed and I could hear Sir William's own voice and see a small marked turtle sliding into the muddy shore waters of the riverbank near Niagara.

"I would have died with him," Molly said, dry-eyed now but still holding my arm.

"I would, too," I said, "but I do not think Warraghiyagey would ever have taken such acts as tribute."

"No," she said, clenching her hold on me. "No. Some of these others, perhaps all, may forget him save as a name and passer-on of an estate, but we are left heirs to his hopes, Joseph. You and I, to support each other for what we remember of his wisdom and greatness."

"Can we hold his hopes?" I asked, a grown chief, but chilled that moment and fearful.

"He would only ask we try," she said.

I signaled for a carriage and drove her back to the house where Sir John and Daniel Claus were already arguing about the disposition of Sir William's great padded resting chair.

I do not enjoy remembering all the petty details of greed and chicanery that followed on my foster father's funeral. The broad pattern to suffice for any reader not a lawyer or some other brand of jackal. Sir John avid for every honor and sorely humiliated when Guy Johnson was named Indian Superintendent instead of him. Daniel Claus reading over not just the will but every scrap of paper he could find to make sure he and his Nancy got their due. Poor Tagcheunto quickly drunk and galloping about the manner shouting: "I am a King's man!" Guy Johnson, nervously licking his long fingers, the best man of the lot, calling on Molly and me for details of administration.

I tried to see that Molly and her children were dealt with fairly and I think I did so, though Molly had turned all Mohawk and would scorn to argue over anything. "I am a chief's daughter with a mother of chief's blood," she said to everything I asked her. "I can take care of myself and of my own, Joseph."

In the many councils, small and large, now called, I was no longer Joseph but always Thayendanegea. There had been ambition in all my dreams, but now I found my people looking to me to lead them and I trembled, but not before them or where anyone could note.

Sir John might be baronet and Guy His Majesty's Indian Superintendent, but neither of them could take Warraghiyagey's place at a council fire.

I was in my thirty-second year and called upon by rude circumstance to fill the shoes of Warraghiyagey who had been to me always more than mere mortal.

FOUR

In the English style I was now secretary to Guy Johnson, Indian Superintendent, as well as commissioned captain (half pay unless on active duty) in His Majesty's forces. In the Mohawk style I was Thayendanegea, a full war chief and a high sachem in all councils. The Confederacy that had looked so fine to Mr. Franklin had deteriorated into a rotted belt with frayed strands and thin patchwork mending dangerous gaps. My hope would be to make it whole again and, if possible, to enlarge it among other tribes to give our people some coherence against any who would encroach our lands. The tribes had to be knit stronger to one another before anyone might speak of a total armed Indian strength. Yet where would we find time for such delicate knit work?

There was more discord than ever among whites and I did not know whether to count this good or bad for the Indian cause. Groups calling themselves Sons of Liberty (and gilding their name by tarring and feathering anyone who disagreed with them) were meeting openly all over the valley. Sir John stayed rigidly aloof from such goings-on, but Guy and Daniel Claus attended some meetings and came back much concerned with what they called open treason.

"If we had soldiers in enough quantity we could scotch the whole business now," Daniel ventured.

"We have the militia," Sir John said.

Guy barked a scornful laugh.

"You'll find better than half the militia on the side of rebellion," he said.

We four sat glum. I did not tell even my superior, Guy, that I had been approached privily in conference with no other than Philip Schuyler, sounding me out which way the Six Nations might turn if it came to open war between the libertarians and the King's government.

I had temporized with him and he had temporized with me. I knew that the loudest hotheads among the Sons of Liberty damned him as a King's man, and I knew that loyalist supporters thought him no friend to England. I allowed him to leave with the feeling that the Iroquois would weigh both sides before coming to any bound decision, for I had begun to see some opportunity of playing loyalist against Liberty man for the best treaty we could win. I guessed from his talk that he put his personal fortune in the same scale and was waiting to see whether the King or the so-called Continental Congress might make him the better offer.

The eruptions of Liberty in our valley came early in 1775 when ardent Sons of Liberty called from village square to country meeting house that every man should declare himself for King or Congress. There could be no doubt for Sir John and Guy and Daniel; overnight they became hunted men in their own homeland. As for me, I had still to hedge for time and I felt I could do this better in the company of my old friends. There would be enough Mohawk chiefs left in the valley to keep some balance of official peace between our people and the newly styled Americans while I sought from the King's men what concessions they might be willing (or driven) to give us above Congress offers. It was no more just a matter of the Proclamation Line which Congress had promised us in perpetuity; now there seemed chance of improving that boundary and even restoring something of their own to the Shawnees.

Still it cost me to leave the land where I had grown to my

manhood. I stood aside gloomily while Sir John packed his best silver to be shipped to Canada; he would stay in the Hall, under a parole, but he felt his best treasures safely away. I threw my own lot with Guy Johnson, to speed with him to Montreal.

I shook Sir John's hand and promised I would see him soon again. Then I took my ax from my belt and stepped to the splendid stairway. Before Sir John could remonstrate I struck three deep blazes into the shining dark mahogany of the rail.

"If you are forced to leave, brother," I said, "and any Indians come this way thereafter, this is a sign they will respect against pillage and burning. Take it as a small scar set off against a fatal wound."

With Guy, some other King's supporters and better than two hundred of my best Mohawk fighting braves we made the march to Montreal. Ticonderoga had fallen to colonial regulars and there were indications of other advances toward Montreal and Quebec itself. There were a score of stout pockets of loyalist devotion and word of ships bringing fresh British reinforcements, but there was no way to separate rumor from fact, hope or fear from concrete accomplishment.

Montreal was the first great port I had encountered in my life and all about it fascinated me, from its thick walls and great houses and multitude of shops to its docks at the river, where I saw more ships than I had dreamed might be gathered in one place, dingy trading vessels being loaded with cargo of furs, transports of His Majesty's and ominous sloops-of-war lying farther away, the round eyes of their cannon menacing even at the distance.

Guy had many friends and they housed us and entertained us well though I put half my own time into keeping my Mohawks happy in the new setting of our camp, seeing that they were well fed and that Sir Guy Carleton, acting as governor of Quebec, kept his agreement to pay the braves as soldiers for the King. To the chiefs who asked me, impatiently: "Are we King's men or not, Thayendanegea?" I gave my answer in confidence: "We are King's men here and now while we take his penny, but we are Mohawk always and our own men so make no rash declarations to bind the nation." For though there were ever more conferences with Sir Guy and others they made us no clear offer and we progressed only from one official labyrinth to another. No man, it seemed, might ever make any decision of himself, but had to pass us on (for Guy Johnson stood with me in most things) to a superior or to an official of some special department, who, in his turn, played us the same tune and passed us on again.

We had some diversion that winter when the colonial braggart Ethan Allen led an attempt to take the city. I commanded my Mohawks in the defense while Guy Johnson loaned wisdom of frontier tactics to the regular forces. We caught the ill-organized invaders before they even struck and killed a few and captured the rest. My own heart drummed with pride then, for it was young Peter Johnson, Molly's boy just over twenty, who took Allen prisoner with his own hand and, disdaining his fellow braves' pleas to have the knave for torture, brought him unscathed to the English command.

This Colonel Allen was a brave man and a good soldier. But in all else he seemed to me to teeter to the edge of lunacy and I wondered, should the colonials achieve their daring goal of independence, what they might do with the lawless zealots who had helped win it. Allen was kept in chains and under close guard in the city. He had a comical habit, when anyone but especially an Indian approached to talk with him, of pulling his shirt open and baring his breast and crying: "Plunge your knives as deep as you will, I die for Liberty!"

The excitement of the siege buoyed me some, but then it was back to more conferences and still the English gave me replies of wind when I needed hardwood. I could not endure continuation of delay. There were other chiefs already calling that the Six Nations should make a treaty of alliance with the Congress faction. I had to know some stakes in bargaining before I could oppose them fully or bring my own influence down upon their side. And there were no such stakes to be named in Canada. Guy Johnson agreeing, the two of us made up our minds and purchased passage on the *Advocate* to England. Daniel Claus sailed with us, and Captain Tice, an English officer who had lived in our valley and whom I liked well, and Ethan Allen, below decks among the prisoners, still baring his breast and seeing assassination plots from everyone who should in natural curiosity venture down to look at him. He might have been better off had Peter Johnson yielded him to the Mohawks for the torture and martyrdom he craved.

We got to England after a voyage of five weeks which should have been fatiguing but was to me, by reason of its great novelty, all adventure. I learned to master what maritime men call their "sea legs" and walked about the ship in all weather, talking to crew men and to the captain, and watching the ever-shifting panorama of strange birds, of odd sea creatures (a porpoise stayed with our course for two days, sporting near the ship with as much playfulness as a pet dog), of the shapes of the waves themselves. Daniel Claus was sick to his belly most of the voyage and moaned that all the great, gray-green tumbling sea looked alike to him, but to me it was as various as the forest and I think, had I not been born a wilderness man, I would have liked very well to live as a sailor.

And, too, the more I looked over the waters and their vastness and variety, the more I thought all my goals (and Sir William's and the King's own) petty and insubstantial and I could understand what some English officers, widely traveled, had told me of holy men among those other Indians of India who worshipped their maker by sitting quite still, scarce breathing, and leaving God's plans for the universe to go on about them unmolested.

In London I was quartered with Captain Tice at a pleasant inn named The Swan with the Two Necks and, with Guy and Daniel, set whirling into the round of official meetings and social functions. There was a plan afoot, no sooner had I become comfortable, to move me to a grander quarters, a whole house offered by Lord Dartmouth, as more befitting my importance as ruler (so they spoke it and I would not risk my cause by argument here) of an allied Indian nation. But I liked the Swan and mostly its friendly serving people who told me more honest word of London habits and London gentry than any of my official friends, so I stayed put.

Of first impressions I remember most bells, and the swift contrast from street to street of magnificence and fell poverty. I wondered how my grandfather had found the city on his visit, for he and his fellow chiefs had been less prepared than I who had at least known something of Albany and Montreal.

I found much the same double-dealing and diversion of decisions in London as in Montreal, but a greater closeness to where some real decisions could be had. It was Captain Tice who introduced me to Mr. Sheldon, who had been an intimate friend of the notorious Lord F—— D—— and through this still retained a prodigious influence on Lord Sandwich and through him on Lord Dartmouth himself and even on Lord North. Sheldon was a foxy little man, well past sixty, but with feverish eyes of cunning and curiosity, turned out in the most rich and elegant clothing I have ever seen on any man.

He invited us to dinner right away and, with no pressing engagement, I could not refuse him though I have known a hundred men I liked better.

We ate at a tavern, but one he might have owned himself with such deference and bowing and scraping were we received, and there was a meal of ten courses and enough wine to have for once sated Tagcheunto. Mr. Sheldon sat close to my side, pressing my arm to call attention to the best delicacies, often spearing some tidbit from his own plate on a fork and passing it up to my mouth.

"Is it true, Mohawk," he asked me, midway between a serving of duck roasted in some sauce of wine and a great platter of sweetbreads surrounded by the tiniest cabbages I ever saw, "that you Indians carry a pecker the length of a turkey's neck?"

I eased my buttocks some in my chair. My belly was already swollen with food and drink and that organ he spoke of itself in discomfort from the skin-tightness of my fashionable new breeches.

"I think we are much as other men, sir," I said, and he looked saddened, "though I am cheered to count myself as long and strong as any."

"Good, good," he muttered into his stem glass of French brandy. "I had heard it was universal in the tribes. In the Orient, most men have longer pricks than Europeans and I have set it to their wearing neither smallclothes nor trousers, but letting their sex hang free and also to their constantly fingering it at work and at play and at prayer."

He gave a laugh that was graveyard raven's cackle joined with schoolboy glee.

One thing about his chosen tavern was that it could boast the fairest serving maids in the city and he had to have my opinion of them, too. They wore tight, yet low bodices laced so their breasts swelled over the tops like foam curling a fresh-drawn mug of beer and they seemed to make much of leaning by one's face as they served each new course.

"Likely wenches, eh? Likely wenches, brave?" Mr. Sheldon chirped, tweaking a maid's buttocks with a sharp pinch as she brought him more brandy. "You'd like one? Or two?" He gave a high giggle. "We've got the pick of the lot. What's the opposite of a stud farm, damme? Raise 'em and rape 'em, raise 'em and rape 'em, raise 'em and rape 'em!"

Now you will know I am not standoffish to cunny-pinching, but there was something in Mr. Sheldon's sniggering glee that blew anaphrodisiac on my desire.

"Fair indeed," I said, stroking the girl's flank, lively warm under tight-stretched muslin, "but I think not tonight . . ."

"Ah, there's a time to save it!" Mr. Sheldon said with as much appreciation as if I had offered some weighty comment of philosophy from Hume or Voltaire. "There's a time to save it, and you know when, Thaynamadippy (so he warped my war name as I winced). Keep it corked awhile for I've a party planned with my friends and you'll need all the jism you have, all the jism you have!"

"I do not know . . ." I started a refusal of any other meeting with Mr. Sheldon, but Captain Tice, himself with some cheer tickling one nipple of the lass serving him, gave me an admonitory kick beneath the table.

Mr. Sheldon had been paying me no attention anyways since he now busied himself whispering into the ear of the maid he had pinched. She gave a sickly smile to whatever he told her.

We ended our meal late and I begged a press of meetings on the morrow to leave then and return to the Swan. Mr. Sheldon bowed us farewell; the serving girl had come back to his side, carrying on a small salver one of Captain Condom's ingenious Venus's sheaths and his mind was clearly on his plans for her.

I disdained Captain Tice's suggestion of a coach, for above any city in the world London is one to walk in and we took our way back to the inn.

"And why did you kick me?" I asked him.

"You would have offended Sheldon," he said. "Look, Joseph"—he spoke seriously for all the wine he'd taken—"you may not like the man, but he has influence everywhere. This is no simple life in the Mohawk Valley any longer. The road to favor here has as many twists as a copperhead coiled to strike. If you'd serve your cause, play along with Mr. Sheldon for he can help you and you'll return soon to your own clean forest while he welters here in his voluptuous sty."

I had lied about important meetings. The whole I had to do was to meet Mr. James Boswell, a writer of fashionable trifles who had penned some paragraphs about me for the *London Magazine*. He was to take me to the portrait painter, Mr. Romney, to sit for a likeness requested by the Earl of Warwick. This Boswell was a man of flea-jumping wit, knew everyone in London and gave me good company.

In a veiled way I asked him about the importance of Mr. Sheldon and, to my dismay, he confirmed all that Captain Tice had hinted.

"He's a vile man," Mr. Boswell said, "but one to stay on the good side of, Chief Joseph. Had you never met him, there would have been no loss. But, if you have met him, keep his favor for his tongue is as sharp as an oyster knife and his influence runs as far as Westminster."

I sat for Mr. Romney, donning what Indian dress I had with me. Sometimes I carried it to his studio room and changed there, sometimes I wore it through the streets to great delight of small boys following me along and making what they thought were Indian cries at my back. I would turn then and whoop at them and, though knowing it a game, they would scatter to house stoops and behind trees, better deployed for skirmishing than most of His Majesty's regular soldiers.

After sitting, Mr. Boswell walked me about the city helping me to buy pomade and some trinkets for Molly and to order a wide gold ring that I left in the shop to be engraved inside its band: "Joseph Thayendanegea, *aet* 1742." This ring was a conceit of Mr. Boswell's when I had told how we fought, with all braves stripped pretty close to natural similitude.

"You should still have something to mark your name and station," he said. "So, if you were slain, it would be known that Joseph the Chief had died and not just another brave."

"What can that matter, if I'm dead?" I asked him.

"I'm not thinking of you," he said severely, "but of anyone who writes your history." He had a sense of such things, as a writer, and I had long admired to have a ring of fine gold, so I humored us both.

He showed me more of London than I think most visitors see, and at taverns with him pinching maids (for he was a great pincher and tweaker) I had none of the ill reaction Mr. Sheldon stirred. I think this was that Mr. Sheldon pinched harmfully and drew pleasure from a lass's cries, while Mr. Boswell pinched hopefully more to court than to wound.

"We both of us have our Johnsons, Chief Thayendanegea," he had told me when we met, "so we should be well matched." And we were. His reference was to Mr. Samuel Johnson, the famous lexicographer, and without lessening Mr. Johnson's achievement, what I heard, and later read in Mr. Boswell's own book, of his coarse manners and sometimes ludicrous affectations made me think I had had in Sir William the better Johnson bargain.

At the Swan, when I returned that afternoon, one of the servants had a note for me written upon finest vellum.

"Honored Mohawk," it read. "Let me offer you an evening of unusual pleasure in the country, at Lord Dashiell's Folly, in company with myself and Lord Dashiell and Mr. Pomeroy and perhaps for all our larger pleasure some subject of the species *virgo juvenis intacta*. If you might meet me at four of the afternoon tomorrow at my lodgings near St. Paul's, I would accompany and guide you." And it was signed in a small and spidery hand: "Billings Sheldon, Esq."

I could read it easily enough and one did not have to be Lame Crow, the Lebanon Latin scholar, to make the sense of *virgo juvenis intacta*. It was a strange sensation I had, sitting in the innocent warmth of the Swan, to find myself thinking of Captain Bull and finding him less savage than the perfumed Mr. Billings Sheldon. For Bull had raped and tormented that poor woman by the Cohocton in hot blood and primal lust, but Sheldon had turned fornication into just one more clockwork toy.

I knew that I could not refuse the invitation and did not offer Captain Tice any argument on the subject. I sat again the next morning for Mr. Romney and he remarked on my glumness, but I put it down to the slowness of negotiations. I was back at the inn early after my lunch, determined to do such justice to my toilet that, whatever strange habits Mr.

Sheldon set before me, I might meet them in gentlemanly guise.

I met Mr. Sheldon as appointed and he had us carried by litter to the riverbank and we went thence by boat, rowed and poled, to Lord Dashiell's Folly.

He kept a constant chatter all the way, and I let him talk while I observed the riverbanks, from the soiled and rubbishy congestion of London turning to fair countryside as we moved along.

"A little shrine of Liberty the like your colonials even have not in mind . . . assistance of the Fair Sex, some willing and some spirited in resistance . . . such worship as the ancients in their wisdom offered Pan and Venus and Priapus . . . no such unfortunate accidents or publicizings as shut down the Hell Fire Club of blessed memory . . . many volumes of rare and curious engravings . . ."

He spoke thus and much more. I nodded, watching the bushy bank where a small otter poked its snout cautiously to observe our stately progress before trusting itself to seek fish. I thought then, and thought later in New York port and Philadelphia, seeing a rat dart here or a shambling opossum hide there, of a kinship with these and all animals and a hope (treacherous perhaps to my own kind but strongly felt) that one day they might take back these cities of piled houses and filthy streets and humans rubbed unnaturally together. These animals were small and clever and they seemed to me sometimes an advance guard of spies, like Caleb and his companions in Canaan, delving the enemy land for its weaknesses, patient and thorough in the knowledge that one day they would have it all themselves.

It was still light when we reached the Folly, the boatman mooring our craft to a tidy dock with a neat mahogany staircase up the side better than in many a house. From the bank there stretched a good four acres of lawn clipped short, green velvet spreading to the peaky, turreted stone house above, and all along the way bushes trimmed with topiary skill to the likeness of strange animals and birds: a sphinx, a phoenix, dragons, unicorns, a basilisk. Though there was no need of his illumination, a linkboy came to meet us, a most handsome little cherub of ten or eleven in a pale blue velveteen suit and a gusset of fine French lace, swinging a lantern small as a toy, but beautifully made of brass, like a firefly at play by his side.

Sheldon pinched his cheek till he squealed.

"Ah, fairy lights to greet us, Mohawk," he said. "Fairy lights to greet us with young Dickon here. Here's a Red Indian, Dickon, come to scalp you and bugger you before your body's cold." He cackled laughter till it threw him to a coughing fit.

The poor child moved to keep distance between us and I tried to calm him, saying: "I'm an English captain, Dickon, my lad, and not like to harm a fellow Englishman," but Sheldon recovered from his cough to parry: "Soldiers are the worst kind, eh Dickon. Ah, you'd have hid in the salt house if you'd thought you'd be entertaining the military. Still chafe, still chafe from the Hessian brigadier, I'll wager. But don't fear, my angel, we've other treats for this wicked Mohawk."

Dickon was soothed by neither of us and, swinging his light pale yellow in the dusk, kept a yard or more away from Sheldon's claws and my evil repute.

When we had been let into the house by a tall footman all in black broadcloth Dickon scurried away and Sheldon led me down a corridor past standing suits of antique armor to a vast room with a round table set for dining and two men, one so round he looked from a distance like a clothed ball, the other his lean antipode, standing with their backs to a fire that roared in a great chimney corner taller than my head. He introduced me to Lord Charles Dashiell and Mr. Almer Pomeroy and I liked each of them as much as I liked Sheldon himself, but there was no backing out now.

We ate good fare, as good as in Sheldon's favorite tavern, with the difference that it was served by men though the difference ended there for Sheldon and his friends were as

free with pinching, patting, whinnying and foul suggestions as
if the men had been maids.

"Dash is our huntsman, tally-ho, huntsman!" Sheldon told
me. "Show the brave your gear, Chick."

Lord Dashiell snapped fingers at one of the servants who
went into the next room and came back with both hands full
of small whips, claw-tipped gauntlets and a varnished ferule
the cousin of the one Reverend Prouty had thwacked me with
so long ago.

"Hunts buxom game!" Sheldon cried. "And is hunted."

"I'll play either role," Lord Dashiell said. "Nobody can ask
fairer. I'll always give my partner the choice. If she wants to
be disciplined, she must discipline me. If she wants to hold
the cat, I'll flog at her."

They all laughed, even the serving men who must have
been poor souls for all their well-muscled bodies.

"And Almer is our mechanic philosopher," he said. "He de-
vises new games and engines of enjoyment when the old ones
are stale. What have you for our guest, Almer?"

"A maid," Mr. Pomeroy said, a deep voice in his thin frame
and as dry as a schoolmaster's. "A pretty, plump duckling of a
maid I've held for a week, seeing her bathed of the dirt from
the hovel her mother sold her out of, powdered and cosseted
and taught to walk with a little grace and to sing a song or
two."

"You tease us, Almer," Sheldon said. "There's no novelty to
a maid. I'm sure Prince Thaynamadingy has had many. No,
brave?"

"A few," I admitted and I felt like a reeling drunkard who,
when quizzed before the magistrate, says he has quaffed perhaps a glass of ale or two.

"But I have made our own rules," Pomeroy said. Sheldon
and Lord Dashiell leaned eagerly to hear.

"First, I have seen to it that she has been shut of any inclination for sports of Venus. She's been fed on diet of hellfire

and damnation till she shrinks to be in the same room as a man."

"Good, good!" Sheldon rubbed his hands. "Nothing sadder than a mare who outmatches her jockey's inclinations."

"Second, your brave, whose strong stiffness you've so harped upon"—he flung me a sneering look—"must enter her *per anum*. There's no great trick to cracking a maidenhead, but it takes a man, Billings, to breach a hitherto uncontested barbican. A fair test of his prowess to be an ally of the Crown, eh?"

They set to cackling with each other and I held back my crawling scorn.

"Any test you choose," I said.

So when the table had been cleared and fresh wine brought, Lord Dashiell clapped his hands and two of his sturdy menservants ushered in the girl. She was of shorter than usual height but most shapely, dressed clean and neat in country style—no, in a dissimulation of it as if a lady were masquerading as a dairy maid; the whole business as false as that. She blushed so hard one would have sworn her cheeks were painted did they not fade and recover like a reddening pulse. She carried a stringed instrument (later I found it called a mandolin) and sat to a chair before the fire as the servants bade her.

"Play, child," Mr. Pomeroy directed her.

With the most melancholy of faces, she struck a chord or two and then in a true but trembling voice sang the words she had been coached, "The Maid of Tottenham."

"An inspiration to have sung by this downy virgin," Lord Dashiell, rolling dangerously on his chair, complimented Pomeroy.

And when they came upon the plain [she quavered],
Upon a pleasant green,
The fair maid spread her legs abroad,
The young man fell between.

Such tying of the garter
I think was never seen.
To fall down, down, derry down, down, down, derry down,
Derry, derry, dino.

She came to the end of the song and bowed her head.

"Your trick now, Mohawk!" Pomeroy cried in his deep tone of a sergeant major calling drill. "Hold her for him, Plimpton, Waller!" For the maid had given a startled cry and made to run from the room.

The two servants caught her and dragged her beside my place at the table. One held her two wrists in one large boxer's paw as he pushed her head down with the other hand. The other servant had thrown back her wide skirts and now crouched holding her legs to the tiled floor. White moons of her flinching wavered before my eyes, the whole room swam in my nausea, but I thought on all Captain Tice had said and I undid my breeches.

"Stap the wench! Stap the wench, Mohawk! Stap her strong!" Sheldon was crying in his high voice, dancing at my side in lewd anxiety.

And so I plunged myself into that poor pale bundle of writhing flesh, the trembling haunches trying helplessly to sink away before me. I reached beneath, an impulse I could not check, to grip her breasts and the heart in my hands fluttered like a trapped hare, yet I could feel in my palms the hardening of her nipples as I breached deeper and heard her long-drawn sigh and the billowed tremor of response in her buttocks moving against me now.

I feel no mortal sin nor ask I absolution, Lord, against the act itself. No more was it than man has done with man since time eternal in war parties or on long hunts away from women, yet the doing and the sound of Sheldon's sniggering laughter have never left me.

For it was not in simple lust that I entered that poor maid. Nor was it lust that swelled my member for its plunge, but only cold calculation that this act was what their lord-ships desired, that this debasement should serve to elevate me in their eyes and buoy me upward in their councils. And so it was that I took the sorry wailing wench against all her will, although when I had done she turned and clung to me and kissed me and would have followed me like a dog thereafter had not Pomeroy and milord Dashiell, calling to the servants for help, hurried her into the next room to have their own sport of her the like I have not let myself to dwell upon.

I pulled my breeches up and fastened them.

"Good work, Mohawk," Sheldon wheezed. "You've won me five hundred guineas. Pomeroy held you'd not do it, but I sensed you would. I've evidence now you'd do anything, any-thing you thought might help your cause, eh? That's the mark of a stout ally and I'll say so in proper places."

I picked a tumbler from the table and gulped, but it might have been water.

"I don't expect you like me," Sheldon said. "If you did, it would have spoiled the sport. Waller, see King Joseph to the boat! I shall rejoin my friends."

I let the servant show me down the path and was in Lon-don to the stroke of one o'clock. I could not go back directly to the Swan with its candid, friendly people. I walked the streets two hours more, dodging into stews for coarse gin, lis-tening as if I could sink and lose myself in it, to the bawdy chatter.

I know not how late I returned to the Swan, but it was Cap-tain Tice who had to help me to bed and he told me I cried out sentences that had no meaning to him, shouting: "Bull, my brother, have you any ladders in your hell?" and, blasphe-mously: "Oh, Owl, my Owl, why has thou forsaken me?"

I sat the following day for Mr. Romney and ate at noon with Mr. Boswell who knew I had been to Dashiell's Folly (he knew a mite of everything that happened in London) and tried to draw me out, but gave up his pumping at my unhap-piness. An afternoon walking and looking into more shops where, in one of them, I found a vase for Molly of the glass called Venetian, something of marvelous color and variety I had not known could be worked in glass. I dined with Guy Johnson at the mansion of one of his friends and we all went after to see Mr. Sheridan's play of *The Rivals,* wonderfully played by skilled actors including the celebrated Mrs. Abington.

But for the eve to it, it should have been a grand day of the richness and satisfaction I judge possible only in London.

The next day, before I set off for Mr. Romney's, the chief Swan footman stopped me with a note he offered in a silver tray. Lord George Germain, it wrote, would be pleased to meet with me and discuss the position of the Indian Nations in the matter of the colonial rebellion. This was His Majesty's Secretary of State for the Colonies and the man I had courted to see every day since my arrival. I kept the note and I have it still among my memorabilia.

There was not then nor has been since any sure way of knowing whether my evening with Mr. Sheldon and his friends brought me this entree. The riddles of English politics were such that I might have met Lord Germain in any case through a dozen other twisting paths but it was that poor wench I thanked in memory then and thereafter.

I spoke to Lord George Germain honestly, saying that no one man could be guarantor of all Indians, but I, as much as any man, might pledge for most of them. Further, that I was myself and always should be a King's man, but that I could not throw the future of my people into either side of war without first testing which opponent could do the better for them. At the smallest, I must have assurance that the Proclamation Line would be observed most scrupulously; for real weight, some hope that the Shawnees and other nations should have redress in land or money.

We talked and bargained all one afternoon and, at the end, I had from him what I had come for. His government would bar any settlement west of the line and, should the fortunes of war go against them, make restitution in other land to all Indians who stood with its cause. The Shawnees would be helped to find and occupy and hold new hunting grounds.

This was nothing like the Indian councils I had been used to with a dozen chiefs and their hundred braves making treaty bargains in loud speeches. It was two men in a fine furnished room overlooking the Thames dueling with black pencils over a map laid open on a table. But its end was what I had desired and there was no longer any need for me in England.

Guy Johnson and I were landed, the spring of 1776, secretly and by night, at New York, where good friends I shall not even now name gave us cover and comfort.

It was a city of discord and confusion, plot and counterplot, with the same leading citizens dining one evening with General Washington and convening the next behind curtained windows to treat with representatives of our own General Lord William Howe. Known royalists walked the streets openly but sometimes in danger of attack by Liberty-shouting mobs, and some youthful Tory lads also ganged together to jostle a leading Congress man.

Guy was rowed at once to Staten Island, where he set up his own headquarters. I lingered a little longer in the city (amused at what wonder it would cause did any of the ranting patriots guess they harbored so openly vowed an enemy in their very heart) and had news of what had been passing in our absence.

My beloved valley was a maelstrom of treachery and rebel rapine, but largely over the whole country the King's cause was triumphing. Sir John had been forced to flee north to Canada and Molly had gone north, too, taking my Isaac and Christiana with her children. I myself, the time I was still sipping coffee with Mr. Boswell in London, had been seen on four separate and distinct border raids, a fearsome figure dripping with innocent blood! So before I had even lifted an ax, the legend of Brant the Brute was in full circulation.

How this image should have come about in a region where I had grown to manhood shoulder to shoulder with many whites, fighting alongside them in battles against common enemies, I cannot tell. Now I think I had been living in comfortable ignorance of growing fear among all settlers of the Indian; so concerned had I been with their encroachment on Indian lands that I had hardly noticed their changing mood. They were ripe for a Red Villain and I, with my known closeness to Sir William and wide fame for ruthless combat, stood tailored to their needs.

Some actor friends of Guy Johnson's rowed me from a New York dock across to Staten Island where I rejoined Guy. From there, helping where we could in intelligence and in direction of skirmishers, we watched happily while Lord Howe scattered General Washington's rabble and retook New York port for the Crown.

I drank a toast or two with Guy Johnson to our victories and then set off from the city to my own lands. For there had been news that cut me as sure and sharp as a knife at my heart: the murder of my father, Carrihogo.

He was an old man and did no harm, his voice no longer even very meaningful in councils. Yet he was cajoled from his safe fireside at the castle (under pretext of a message from me, his son) and then shot down as thoughtlessly as a deer in the drive of a hunt. Once I had had this news, there was no stomach for New York. I would go back to the valley and give some patriots reason to fear the name of Brant.

It was no difficult matter to slip through the guard lines of Washington's army. Nights had begun to turn chill and more sentries huddled together around forbidden bonfires than made their rounds. Once past these main forces, my travel was swift, for all through the country, despite the risk, there were still homes of gallant men and women loyal to their King who would conceal such fly-by-nights as myself.

I found the tribes in some discord, the Six Nations reft by faction. Mohawk, Seneca, Cayuga and Onondaga were ripe to take the King's cause, but the Oneida and the womanish Tuscarora saw more gain in sitting neutral and letting the white men kill one another without shedding of Indian blood. Tribes and nations beyond the Confederacy were in much the same division, some even for casting their lot alongside the liberty folk.

With Carrihogo's murder a canker of hate in my brain I had to hold myself in check against mere ranting. I marched and rode all through Iroquois country and past our borders, haranguing at large councils, talking most earnestly with single sachems and braves by solitary fires.

I went so far north as near what they now call Kingston in Canada where Molly had made a new home and, after all the affection of reunion, it was she who brought back direction to the hot madness and anger that consumed me.

"I am as much Carrihogo's daughter as you are his son, Joseph," she said, "but I learned enough from Will to keep separate private vengeance and public polity. You wear Will's mantle now. Between us, we shall never forget our father nor slacken pursuit till his slayers have had their bowels slashed and unbraided before their living eyes. But that is us. For the Confederacy, there are ends of more gravity. You have had Lord Germain's word for one price for our people's strength, now in reasonableness to every Mohawk, every other nation, you must try the Rebels to see if they may offer better."

"And if they do, sister? If they do, what then?"

"Then let the Nations turn to their side," she said, "but without us. Our path was blazed, if not long ago by Warraghiyagey, then lately by the shots that slew our father."

So I found myself holding back such hotheads as would attack the colonials at once and giving blessing to the compromise at Onondaga where the great council fire of the Confederacy burned, that it should be covered with ashes and allowed to stay cold until the Six Nations spoke with one tongue again. We kept the English flag for our banner, but I saw that word should reach the Americans (as the Sons of Liberty now styled themselves) that our course had not been set irrevocably.

Their first response disappointed but did not truly surprise me. Instead of sending any man of real bottom to treat with me they dispatched honest John Harper, a man I had long known, who had some understanding of Indian grievances but was in no wise empowered to strike a treaty with us. We had talk without substance. The only virtue of his visit might have been that he could see at Oghwaga where I had made camp, the four hundred Iroquois warriors who lay under my banner and another hundred of loyalist whites who were still straggling in from about the countryside to join me.

The next American step, delayed as long as possible, was an invitation for me to meet with General Nicholas Herkimer, another old friend and neighbor but one who by reason of his rank could carry more weight in a parley. He had moved with some four hundred of his volunteer soldiers to the edge of the Proclamation Line at Unadilla and there proposed to speak with me.

Before the conference I waited for two braves whom Molly had said she was dispatching to join me. They were Twin Duck and Aleky Bunce and they had both been witness to Carrihogo's murder. I wished them to look about General Herkimer's camp and, if they could find them there, to identify the two men who had killed my father. For, whatever the outcome of any conference, this revenge was a charge upon my conscience.

I write the word "conscience" and can hear a reader asking: Where in this pagan devotion to a blood feud is all the Christian thinking we have heard so much about? Is not this Brant just such another as so many loud-spoken Christians, a man who would practice his faith only when all circumstances make that practice easy, and abandon it the first moment it should interfere with any personal and mad desire?

There can be no defense for turning my back on God's word and His way. All man is born to sin as we well know and some of us are weaker than others. I take no pride in my thoughts and actions through these years of war, but if it were not for human weakness what need does our Lord have of a church that preaches salvation and forgiveness? Ask in your heart, reader, however placid and correct your own life, however strong your faith, what you might do with word of your father's murder? Then, if you will, judge.

We met in an open field on General Herkimer's side of the Unadilla, but in clear sight of my own followers. He had drawn up behind him the full half of his force, all under arms.

I nodded greeting to him and said: "All these men have joined you on your friendly, peaceful visit?" The first rank was close enough so that I saw among them farmers most notorious at stealing land and befuddling my people. "All want to see the poor Indians; it is very kind."

Herkimer affected not to grasp my delicate irony (a thick Dutchman, perhaps he missed it entirely), but shook my hand and made nonsense talk about what good neighbors we had been, how he remembered watching me wrestle Tagcheunto on his own threshing floor and other material to not much value.

I humored him for twenty minutes before bursting through to the reason for our meeting. "My people are in concert with the King, as their fathers have been," I told him, "but we bear no great desire to see slaughter in our own country and upon the same people with whom we have long lived in peace. What have you, Herkimer, to offer for our alliance?" I asked.

He hemmed and he hawed and this first confrontation broke apart with no meat for decision.

That night Twin Duck came to the lodge where I rested. He had seen my father's murderers in the train of a rascally settler named Joseph Waggoner who had vowed himself to slay me before the conference should be over. My war chiefs pleaded with me to loose them that very moment; we had superiority of numbers and could swarm the American camp before Herkimer's soldiery were fully awake. I remembered Molly's words and against my heart's fierce beating I held them back.

"Let me hear out the general," I said. "It was not he who killed Carrihogo. But Twin Duck, you and Aleky keep close watch on the murderers." I pricked my thumb till blood came and flicked the drops into the fire as vow these men should not escape.

The next day's conference was little better. Herkimer made familiar promises that the Americans would observe the Proclamation Line, but where the Shawnees were concerned he gave no ground, countering each question of mine with some irrelevant story of settlers slain by Indians without mention that most of the settlers had been criminally encamped on Indian land.

It was late afternoon before I gave up. I caught a motion of some few men in Herkimer's line where Twin Duck had told me Joseph Waggoner was stationed. I raised my hand and two hundred of my braves, awaiting this signal, moved nearer to the center of the meadow, crying war whoops shrill and threatening.

"I have a full five hundred braves with me," I told General Herkimer, who had gone some pale and was playing with the brass buttons on his blue coat, "all armed and ready to do battle. You are in my power, Mynheer Nicholas, but since we have been old friends and neighbors in better days, I will take no advantage of you, but let you go in peace. But for this liberty"—I slurred the word for emphasis, but I doubt he caught any wit—"I require you turn away from Unadilla and be bound home by morning light."

He began a speech of the familiar "Brother, you do me poor justice" kind, and then backed away into his own clump of staff officers. I turned my back, sure my braves could keep me safe, and strode away in dignity.

Our scouts reported Herkimer breaking camp in nervous

fear to be away. We broke our own camp, but I, with Twin Duck and two braves I had chosen for their silence in hunting, left for the borders of the American camp.

Aleky Bunce, somewhere in the middle of milling soldiers, gave forth the soft owl hoot I had set on for a signal. I lay behind bushes with Twin Duck to one side and the two braves on the other. We might have rushed into the camp and rushed out again with our prey and no one the wiser, but I wanted certainty before adventure. Herkimer's forces split into different bands, taking different trails in the darkness, but Aleky's hoot identified for us an old narrow path by which we could lie in hiding. We moved to the trail side swiftly and with no betraying sound, sunk there and waited.

Aleky had attached himself to Waggoner's small cabal in the guise of having a grudge against me and being able to lead them to me at some later and safer time. Now on the trail he loitered, taking time to piss, so that they would be a little cut off from the main body. They came abreast of us, Waggoner and four ugly rogues and Aleky, and we leaped from our ambush. Waggoner gave a cry and an oath and fled onward with about as much thought for his followers as one would expect from such a villain. Twin Duck sank his ax in the head of the conspirator nearest him and I did the same for another. Aleky and my two braves had overcome the middle men, the murderers, whom I wanted unhurt. We stuffed wadded cotton cloth to their mouths to stifle any outcry and bound them and carried them back and at the great fire with a circle of sachems and chiefs who had known Carrihogo, I had what I desired.

The two men were a trapper named Regis Mample and a drunken lout of a farmhand named Peter Pflaumer and both began to weep and snivel and plead the moment their gags were removed. They first denied any hand in Carrihogo's murder and Twin Duck and Aleky faced them and examined them most soberly before confirming again that they were the men we sought. Then they bleated long arguments that they had been forced to the act, had been put up to it by others, but Molly's informants had made certain that the deed had its inspiration in the doers' minds, whatever hopes they had of reward or fame from the Americans for doing it. And while the murderers bleated they contradicted each other, one naming one sponsor of the murder, the other another, till they were snapping at each other like curs, pushing blame to and fro.

"I have heard enough!" I said. I had kept my silence along with all the other men and grown women while they wrangled. I made a sign to Aleky and he bound each man to a stake, hands clasped behind him and about the wood, some thongs passed beneath armpits to keep him from slumping if he swooned.

"You have led the lives of worms," I said. "Whether you die the death of brave men can be your own choice." Twin Duck passed over to me a sharp knife, the fine tempering of Sheffield that I had brought back with me from London as if, even then, I sensed its future need and usage.

I will say for Mample that he made some effort toward a man's end and only broke to cries after I had stretched his guts out and lifted them up where he could look upon them. He did not linger long after that and there was little sport for the squaws and children. Pflaumer screeched the whole time he was not silent in a faint and died before I had disemboweled him properly. I felt much cleansed.

I had the heads cut off and skinned and sent to my dear sister and she may quite well have played kickball with them, as I heard outraged Americans whisper the story.

I would have gone to my tent to stay the night alone after this vengeance, but I dared not, for the cries and blood and the rich familiar excitement of war and torture and killing had gone to the heads of my men, not unaided by drink which had been brought into the camp against my command, and I was awake and busy the whole night, keeping the throng to their tents, for I wished to show the Americans that an Indian could keep his word (as they could not) and allow Herkimer to retire unmolested. And so it was, albeit sorely wearying to me.

It was never an easy matter to know how best to apply our Indian strength and in seeking the solution I joined my own forces to Colonel John Butler's rangers. I had found him in agreement with my own thought, that my Indians and his rangers could help a regular army best as scouts and spies. In any formal warfare, the regulars hampered our own tried methods as much as we blocked their classical strategies. Yet I had at my beck a thousand Indians and Colonel Butler close to a third as many able rangers. A handful of these men should suffice for all scouting needs; we were left with a force at arms and a conundrum how to use it best.

"We are little use at siege," I said, "and I even doubt our lasting strength against any disciplined army."

"This does not mean we must be wasted, Joseph," Butler said. "There is no disciplined army to counter us from Niagara east to Albany." He smoothed a map on the table where we sat.

"Even with half our force," I said, "we could keep this whole ground afire, a nagging thorn in the Americans' flesh."

"I like that well," Butler said.

"My Indians will be more than pleased at some return against the wrongs they've suffered," I said, "and your yeomen should be happy to strike the grasping farmers who have stolen their houses and imprisoned their wives."

"I do not look for any lack of enthusiasm," he said dryly. He had a nice sense of humor and in this reminded me fondly of Sir William. We clasped hands before laying our plans before the newcome English commander, General John Burgoyne.

General Burgoyne, a reluctant commander in a war he had been often heard to call needless, was slower to accept our plan.

"Burnings!" he said, his smoothly shaven face delivering a

twitch of disgust. "Burnings and scalpings are like to make His Majesty many friends, I misthink."

"If there had not been a score of Indian villages burned, sir," I said, "I might agree with you. Colonel Butler I shall leave to speak of loyalists tarred and feathered, of women and children imprisoned in the damp caverns of Connecticut mines for no crime but their allegiance to George the Third."

"Captain Brant speaks the truth," Butler stood with me. "If there were any longer, sir, a question of whether or no with regard to raiding, I should say no as loudly as any man. But American brands have set this fire, and a time comes when fire must fight fire."

General Burgoyne fingered his queue and stared at the map we had brought with us.

"How many regulars, General," I asked him, "would you count to keep this territory at a standstill?"

"Five thousand, at the least," he said with a sigh. "More likely ten . . ."

"And we can do as much with our rangers and Indians," John Butler said. "So the gift we bring you for the King is equal to ten thousand soldiers."

General Burgoyne paced a little up and down the room behind his map table. I think I have never seen any general who looked so well the part. It was early morning when we saw him, and his toilet—the barbering and the precise arrangement of his hair, the hang and fit of his red coat embroidered in gold—must have been the work of two or three hours. In England he had been a figure in Parliament, a thoughtful statesman and an orator, as well as a playwright of more than average merit. He had as little business standing here in our American wilderness as I should have had arranging a ball for the Prince of Wales.

"Colonel Butler, Captain Brant," he said, wheeling now crisply and in command of himself again. "Keep Yankee Doodle—you know the song?—well off his balance and we shall see God and King triumphant."

I spent a few days with Molly before I went back with John Butler to sow our valley with fear; stealing time to be again with Isaac my son and my young daughter Christiana. Isaac was growing into a handsome boy, all fired with tales of the conflict and questions of how many Americans had I killed and when might he join to play his part in war.

Molly gave me valuable word of plans and machinations in the American camp since a maid she had long known, Mary Skinner, a Mohawk, was now in position of mistress to General Philip Schuyler.

"She sends me as many messages as if we were lovers, not she and the patroon," she laughed. "I hated him once, for his insults to Will, but now I can be glad I planted some seed of fondness for a red skin between his blankets."

"Mary was a handsome girl," I remembered. "As lissome a body—"

"Pooh!" Molly mocked. "I can show you much better. Catherine!" she called.

I have found it strange in writing this record that some moments I have had little pride in flow easily from my pen while other events important to me and recollected with every detail clear and bright, refuse to come to life again without long poring over my paper, finicky changes of every other word. In such a fix I am where Catherine Croghan is concerned.

On Molly's call a young woman came into the room bowing her head a little to conceal a smile as she greeted me. She was tall for a woman, a good five feet six, and dressed English fashion but simply in a long, straight robe of some soft gray-lavender cambric that betrayed its modesty by clinging to her fine figure, sketching in its folds her high breasts and the warm curve of her hips, pointing with its own hue the pale lavender of her large and wide-set eyes. She wore her thick black hair simply in one bound tress that fell behind her slender, queenly neck.

"Welcome, Joseph," she said, still with that teasing smile. I had lived no celibate life since Dorcas's death, nor had I

ever been notably shy with the fair sex, but this was a time I
found my tongue turned to stammering and a sudden confusion as to what I should be doing with my hands which I first
clasped behind my back, then put to my sides where they
seemed inordinately large and strange as if they had not been
with me, there on the end of my arms, since birth.

Molly pealed a laugh.

"Come, brother," she said, "do you mean to say you cannot
recognize Miss Croghan, George's little daughter Catherine
who was used to pour your wine for you?"

Catherine laughed, too, and I joined them with an embar-
rassed laugh of my own. I remembered a bright and pretty
maid who had played boyishly on the lakeshore then when all
my own thoughts had been with Lieutenant Provost, blood
brotherhood leaving me no room for anything else. A pretty
child, a charming child whose wild hair I had teased and tou-
sled absently till she spat at me in anger and ran away, and
nothing to foretell this stately beauty.

"Catherine," I said with true inanity. "But you have
grown."

"In eight years, Joseph, I could not stand still," she said,
chiding me gently. "'Time like an ever-rolling stream . . .'"
she spoke the line from Mr. Watts's hymn with a droll carica-
ture of old age, putting out one rounded arm as if to support
herself against a chair.

She supped with Molly and me and as we talked she displayed both wit and wisdom along with her beauty, following
my and Molly's consideration of Indian and military affairs
with a quick grasp that was worthy of George Croghan's
daughter. She was staying with Molly, for all her father's beloved estate had been run over by the Tories.

We talked on late by lamp and candlelight and every sentence revealed Catherine more a paragon. She had been well
educated at the Fort Hunter school and she had used her
learning to read and study more so that I do not think, even
among the bluestockings of London, I have had such wise and

original conversations with a woman. I decided to put off my return to John Butler another day and, in fact, let the delay stretch to two days more, days and nights of enchantment and all joys but that final one man seeks with woman.

For Catherine, though Molly left us lone opportunity, would not give in to what advances I made. She put me off with none of the Puritan stiffness of Christine, but just as surely.

"I know you well, Joseph," she said, a little breathless from kissing and mauling, "even though I have not seen you these eight years. I have long admired you, but too much ever to wish to be another one of your many women. When you go back to war, I think it better you recall me with anticipation, not satiety. I have heard hunters talk for years of the one deer that escaped them, long after they had lost count of their successes."

So I went back to join my Indians and John Butler's rangers and to loyalty to my King and to revenge for my people's wrongs and there was added a new goad to my ambition, a desire to shine in the eyes of Catherine Croghan.

We had many raids that year, in the pattern we had devised to keep the New York borders ever in dread, ever uncertain.

I took my best force of Indians, a full three hundred veteran warriors, and made first strike at Cobleskill, a small village some thirty miles west of Albany, close enough to cause alarm, but sufficiently isolated for our swift attack. We set Cobleskill to the torch and the Americans who blundered into the arms of an ambush I had arranged, thinking they were en route to punish a few dozen wandering Indians, we cut down with rifle fire and ax.

From Cobleskill I moved my force back a little and for the rest of the spring we raided at will, sometimes but a small detachment firing a farm, other times my whole army as when we burned Springfield and brought back two hundred fat cattle as provision.

My name was becoming a curse and a threat to frighten

children and my raids were serving their best purpose which was to keep attention with me and away from any thought of what Colonel Butler might be planning. While my braves struck like phantoms from the forest, he organized his rangers at Unadilla. When time was ripe I turned him over more than half my own braves which left me enough men to keep my reputation alive by a strike at Minisink while Butler's army moved toward the Wyoming Valley of Pennsylvania.

I think no other action of the war has had so much slanderous embroidery as this which was a straightforward military expedition carried out with less fire and rapine than many others on either side. I, at the time demonstrably leading my own braves near Minisink, am supposed to have been there, smashing the skulls of infants for pure joy, raping innocent American maidens by the dozen, torturing prisoners right and left. Catherine Montour, that wise old woman, half French, half Huron, is said to have raged the fields of battle like a harpy, poking out the eyes of all the living wounded, her two sons capering in her bloody train. Yet at the moment, Catherine Montour was resting her aged bones in her home by Seneca Lake, no doubt taking tea in the English fashion as was her custom with some women friends in to talk of fashion and gossip.

American lies and exaggerations about the campaign were quickly to reap their bitter fruit at Cherry Valley in early winter. The English themselves have a proverb: "As well to be hung for a sheep as a goat," and the burden of its thought is clear to anyone, including an Indian. We had behaved well in the Wyoming Valley and, for our pains, been painted as monsters even as far as England. Very well.

I should have been happier about the proposed attack had John Butler been able to lead it, but he lay sick and it was upon his son, my old companion, Captain Walter Butler, that command devolved. I knew Walter Butler as a brave man and a good soldier, but he had not his father's "bottom" and he looked to this raid with a burning fanaticism that had no balance to it. He had been routed by Americans from his lands and imprisoned and suffered much from a severe illness for which he received no care. Despite great weakness he finally had made his escape and now his only ambition was to sow devastation among those who had so misused him.

Walter Butler ordered the expedition as carelessly as a boy out to hunt hares with a band of youthful playmates. There was no true plan of march, no preparation, no care for secrecy. In fact, hostile Oneidas knowing our purpose ran three days ahead of us to warn Colonel Alden, commanding the fort of his own name, and had it not been for his particular carelessness we should have been the victims, not the slaughterers, and moments I have wished this had been so.

There was sleet as we came over the crest above the valley and I remarked every tree and small bush shining with clinging ice as my warriors gave their cry and the first shots echoed back to us and settlers fled small below us, running from house to house and falling under our fire, and, even before they fell, Indians were among them, catching hair in one hand and slashing their knives with the other, so hysteric in excitement that many here were scalped alive and those who found concealment lived many years with naught but a patch of baldness to recall the battle.

There was no longer any question of command. I heard Walter Butler's voice raised in harsh, hopeless ranting and pushed past him. I heard Hiokatoo, most savage of Seneca war chiefs and in no wise softened by his having an English wife, whooping ahead of me. I reached a house and opened the door on a scene of quiet domesticity: a plump, middle-aged woman was sweeping the floor with a rush broom as if Armageddon existed only in the Book of Revelations of St. John the Divine.

"How can you pudder thus," I asked, "when all your neighbors are being killed about you?"

"Oh, we are King's people," she said in simple fealty.

"I do not think all Indians may distinguish," I said.

This news had some effect. "What shall I do?" she gasped and dropped her broom. "Has Brant the Destroyer come to slay us all?"

"I am Joseph Brant," I said. "Get yourself into bed quickly." I pointed to a pallet by the fireside.

She had no sooner pulled covers up to her quavering chin than five Senecas burst through the door.

"Flee!" I told them. "This woman has the pest and could spread death among us all!" She gibbered and shivered from fear in a frightening approximation of any dread disease and the Senecas did not look twice before retiring. When they had left I shrilled a Mohawk cry and when three of my own braves had come in gave them instructions to mark the woman with our war paint as a friend, and also anyone else within the house. (There were an old man and two children as I later learned.)

Back out into the open I found but chaos. Indians and rangers roamed about, less interested in any assault on the fort than in looting and violence. That man is closer to the Fall than to Eden was well proved that day.

I saw a girl-child younger than my own Christiana raped in succession by six men and not all Indians. I saw two infants scalped of the soft silken fleece that was their hair and too many other maimings to record. With any effort we might have taken the fort, whose soldiers fired now and again aimlessly but really did no more than watch paralyzed our burning and slaughter.

Though I saved the one family I mentioned and even some others, I shall not deny the freshly wet blood that stained my own ax. For the intoxication of killing is not so far from any other mortal addiction and I share Cain's portion of sin with every other man born. It was only moments after I had seen my fuddled old woman safe that I was into the fray myself, crouching and rushing to split a skull and peel it clean of scalp, careless in the red heat of whether ax or knife plunged into the body of a man or of a woman. There may be professional soldiers all of whose killing is done in cold blood and with calculation; I do not think I could fight always in such splendid removal from emotion. I can plan a battle, carry through many of the tactical actions, but where actual combat is once engaged, I have seen myself sometimes become another, demoniac self.

I must have been so for an hour or more at Cherry Valley. I know I had better than half a dozen scalps with their ensanguined hair hanging at my belt and in a rage at one giant militiaman who resisted both my first ax blow and a second and managed a deep hack into my shoulder with his bayonet I cut not just his scalp but prick and ballocks to throw into his dead face as I hied past him for further slaughter.

But satiety with blood or weariness worked some check on me. I caught myself trembling, leaning on a field boulder, half sick with shame, half blind with pride. I caught myself and tried to resume my role as captain and leader in the battle.

I think Walter Butler had more revenge than he had counted on. He roved the field, bleak-eyed, with me, stopping some cruelty, trying to bring some order to the taking of prisoners.

But to our every argument we had the same reply: "At Wyoming we freed enemies on their own parole and within the moon they were active against us and telling every lie they could devise." Still, we saved what settlers we could and as night fell we withdrew to our own campfires.

It was beyond Walter Butler's power or mine to restore enough discipline for a successful attack on the fort. We left the next evening, those miserable prisoners we had not prevailed upon the Senecas to release trudging with us through the snow which had by now begun a thick fall. For all tales of the evil of this raid, note that not one of our prisoners perished on the march back to Niagara and at least one maid took a husband for herself from the rangers.

I had a short leave at Niagara to see my sister and I would not deny that Catherine Croghan's presence with her had bearing on my decision. It was as good to see Catherine as I had hoped, coming upon her a little before midday as she sat in the house by the fireside helping Christiana with her needlework. I could talk about the war with her and Molly in that safe and distant house as if it all had been in another continent and another age.

It was not all rest, for with Molly there continued always to be some serious business. We never spoke of the words we had exchanged after Sir William's burial, but they were with us. Molly, in Kingston, still had messages to and from women in the tribes (and not women only; but many chiefs) and from them her sure knowledge of events, even before they happened.

There were chiefs and more than one high-placed Englishman who would have been quite willing to end Molly's widowhood, but after Sir William she saw no man she would admire to share bed and name with. She kept a good house, saw to the upbringing of her and Sir William's children and stayed close to all that concerned our Six Nations (and all Indians).

She helped me settle some things in my mind, problems of tribal discord, and Catherine offered counterpoint with lighter distractions in talk and playing on the harpsichord.

"I could stay forever," I said mournfully, the day before I had to return to Niagara.

"We could have you stay forever," Molly said, "did we not know what other calls there are upon your heart."

"I think there is but one call upon my heart," I said, looking at Catherine. "The other calls are to obligations embedded too deep to thrust away. It was just such another war as this between Englishman and Englishman that made the poet sing:

> "Yet this inconstancy is such
> As you too shall adore;
> I could not love thee, dear, so much
> Loved I not Honor more."

"Lawks!" Molly teased. "Fine language from a painted savage." But she was proud of my rags and tags of learning. Catherine would not meet my eyes and when we went our ways later to bed she only pressed my hand and avoided my attempt at a kiss.

I have usually slept well, but with the training of a warrior and a hunter so that, when she came to my room, I started from my pillow ready to grapple at an enemy.

"Hush, Joseph! Hush!" she said in a voice between a soft laugh and a sigh. "Would you have the whole house know all our business?"

There was light enough for me to see her plainly, in a long shift, as she crossed the room and, at my bedside, bent to pull it above her head and drop it in a heap on the floor as she slipped in beside me, putting warm lips to mine and finding me with innocent, insistent hands.

We did not speak, no sound but one muffled cry of hers and then both our deep breathings on pleasure, until later.

"I love you," I said, "yet I never even hoped you'd come to me thus."

"Through every night you were away, Joseph," she said, warm against me and fitting close by my side as if that other self the pagan philosophers speak of, "I felt wounded in soul and body that I had denied you. I determined to give you this, my only gift, as soon as you returned. And then, when you did return"—she giggled, all astirring against me—"I had been trapped with woman's lunar bane. Just tonight and in time it ended which means, I believe, that this was a true and an intended act."

We talked far more and made love again and plans by the hundredweight. We would be wed on my next leave, if I desired; she said she felt herself my wife in any case, but agreed that for the world and for the church (she was a baptized Christian) we should solemnize our union.

I departed that morning for Niagara with a lighter heart than in many years. Catherine kissed me hard and extravagant farewell and Molly smiled beside us, I am sure with approving knowledge of our night's pleasure. I took Isaac with me.

He was a bright, active lad of fourteen then, keeping good pace by my side. He could shoot as well as most grown men and had been at me to treat him to some share of war. I had been a soldier no older on my first campaign with Sir William, so I could not deny him. My own feelings toward war had changed and it was no longer all splendor (though it had still high moments), but a part of my work, a payment (and often a hard one) to be made for rights and benefits due my people.

But I did not try to stifle his enthusiasm with these reflections. Rather I coached him as we marched on certain tactics, the holding off of first fire or war whoop till the latest moment, so that it should have full impact of surprise, the points to aim at for the quickest kill—neck, temples, groin and heart —and such entries for a primer of belligerency. He listened intent on every word; he was my true friend that march, a sadly short memory to treasure.

At Minisink again I drew the Americans into a steep ravine where we killed with rifle and ax better than seventy in a company of a hundred. It was there, ranging the battlefield, that I came on Gabriel Wisner, a magistrate I had supped with more than once at Johnson Hall, groaning and twisted from a fatal belly wound. He rolled his eyes at my face and tried to speak but only bubbled pink froth. It was near nightfall and this field to be a banquet for wolves or scavenging dogs. I took my ax from my belt and cleaved his skull deep to quick death. As his body slumped to silence I said over him some words of the Office of the Dead for he had been a good churchman.

". . . blessed be the name of the Lord," I said. And: "Amen." I heard a snort of scorn from behind me and turned to find my son Isaac, staggering from drink and his own ax bloody in his hand, a pouch at his belt plump with loot of fallen bodies.

"Pray! Pray!" he said in mocking singsong. "Slay and pray, my 'lustrious father!"

"You're drunk, Isaac!" I said. I was not so shocked for I had sampled spirits myself as a youth, but his scorn of God I did not like. "Take some thought of what you say, son."

"'Take some thought of what you say, son,'" he mimicked me. "Isaac would as soon be Esau." He belched and, as I reached to steady him, struck with his ax at my arm and ran away down the field, a small figure lurching and seeming to my eyes desperate among all the fallen bodies.

I dreamed that night again, after long absence from my sleeping hours, of the masked caribou man and heard in the distance a great flutter of wings and knew my owl to be close by, yet to my sorrow he did not show himself to me, only that soft drumming of wings growing fainter until try as I would I could hear it no more and it troubled me much.

Next morning, Isaac was sober and surly. I made good effort to talk to him and warn him against spirits, but he listened only because he had no other choice and, sensing this quickly, I cut the talk short. What I could not tell him was a likeness I feared between him and Tagcheunto, whose death, boozy to the last, had been reported to me not long before.

While our men rested, I rode hard to return to Catherine and Molly. I had thought to bring Isaac home with me, but he said sulkily that he was a warrior and had not time or inclination for spending long leaves with women. I bid Walter Butler keep an eye on him and especially to guard against his drinking habit before I left.

Catherine and I were married in Molly's house by a proper Episcopal priest with Molly standing at Catherine's side to give her away. After, Molly set us the finest feast seen in that countryside, more like one of the long, great galas at Johnson Hall with everyone for miles about, Indian and Englishman and French eating and drinking and dancing, my Catherine the fairest woman to be seen, my sister Molly treading as light a dancing measure as any younger maid. Catherine was twenty-two and I was thirty-seven, which I think is no very large difference if the man be in good health.

I could treat myself to no long idyll and I was back embroiled in councils less than three days a bridegroom. There was discord at Niagara and I was pulled between old loyalty to the Johnsons and the shared battle experience I had with the Butlers. My Indians had taken to grumbling against John Butler and I could not hold them to him against their will. Haply, Guy Johnson was now in Niagara and Sir John joined us with a fresh willingness to face activity in the field. He retook his home of Johnson Hall and held it long enough to rally a hundred fresh loyalist recruits to his banner and his feat inspired me to a return to the castle at Canajoharie.

The thought of this place, my old home, now deserted of its Mohawks and turned to a miserable warren of patriot scavengers, had been a canker in me for too long. It stood deep in American-held lands and, if I were to revisit it, it would take some cunning beyond mere stealth of march.

To this end, I struck first farther west, toward Fort Stanwix, chasing some traitorous Oneidas to the shelter of that stronghold. I stayed there long enough to put the American command into fearfulness, and, so soon as I might be sure all attention was upon this place, I marched my men mercilessly and fast through hidden forest trails to emerge just at Canajoharie.

The first sight these settlers had of us was the smoke of their burning outbuildings raising to the sky. I had one goal in this raid, to leave standing nothing of my own memory that had been desecrated by the American occupation. We had little resistance and such as there was we shot down ruthlessly, men daring to stand in the streets of my town, to shoot from the windows of what had been our longhouses, firing on the Mohawks whose ancestral land they had stolen.

I watched and directed till I was sure every building, even including the church at whose altar I had knelt in prayer, would be consumed by flames. In this matter I offer no apology. If the Americans were to disperse my people, we could at least see that they did not move into the houses and shelters we had cherished.

But our raids were about all that went well that year. The massed English campaign from North and West had been halted and held and then broken and thrown back by the Americans, their forest-toughened western commanders turning against us the same tricks the Butlers and I had been using with such success.

Nor was the news from East and South much better. Washington's army was still plagued by mutiny and discontent, but with that stubbornness that I believe must be one mark of a good commander, he continued to make war as if he were Marlborough with the world's finest troops behind him. And, to our sorrow, he no longer felt confined to borrow all his tactics from the classic past.

There were disheartening reports from England that the Peace Party there gained new adherents every day and its partisans spoke loud in Parliament what would have been treason spoken in the streets or printed in a journal.

For me there was some counterbalance in my own life for I had found a house for Catherine in Niagara and we had there, between my absences, a life of peace and love amid the martial storm that raged the world about us. Isaac had stayed from the flowing cup and was with us, as was my pretty Christiana, and I had all the home joys any man may hope for as leaven to the rigors of the battlefield and the hardly less taxing demands of council and policy.

Red Jacket, a young yet eloquent Seneca chief, had become a small thorn in my flesh (to become a greater one as years passed) with speeches and conspiracy to bring about a separate peace between the warring portions of the Confederacy and the Americans. I cannot claim I matched him always as an orator, but the memory of Sir William had not faded from my people and, with this and the plain record of American hostility, I kept us to our bond with the King.

After Canajoharie we had planned another larger expedition on which were pinned all our hopes for a final confounding of American strength. While Major Carleton marched on Albany, my forces and Sir John's would spread familiar havoc to the west, and, at the same time, General Benedict Arnold, most skilled of the American officers but by now disgusted with intrigue and jealousy of Washington's clique, would turn over the fortress of West Point into our hands and free the whole path up the Hudson River from New York.

There are heroic tales of chiefs and captains in constant warlike action whose powers increase with each campaign like Antaeus, ever renewed at every fall in his battle with Hercules. I have known battles since my earliest youth, but I have known no men like these. Rather I have seen leading troops in the field quite human beings, obese as Hendrick, gouty and aguish as Sir William, scant of breath as Herkimer, a myriad of weary heroes scratching insect bites and complaining of headaches yet doing duty for King or country.

All this as prelude to the fierce fever that struck into my very bones almost as our march on this venture set off.

It was first a sweating of the brow well past anything to be blamed on the weather of that temperate fall. Then there came within hours a dry heat that caked and cracked my lips and had the vista before my eyes all like an underwater wavering. And, with this, pain in my elbows and groin and knees so that all movement was close to agony. I kept my pace on the march, but when we stopped that evening I could not eat and fell to a pallet of boughs that had been prepared for my night's rest so shakingly that my illness could no longer be hid from my braves. Isaac, a good son that day, knelt by my side and touched a poultice of dampened moss to my forehead as tenderly as he had been a woman.

"My father fevers," he said. "We should turn back, or rest here till your strength has returned, Thayendanegea."

"There can be no turning back," I told him. "This is the campaign of last hope to break American power. Isaac, my son, make marks by the fire and sing the Turtle song; then find and fetch me a rattlesnake."

Isaac had not been brought up in the old ways, yet he did not question me, only to ask with hesitancy of his fifteen years, "Bring back the snake alive?" and I believe he would have done so on my asking.

"No, son," I explained. "It is for a *potage*."

The fever raged and grew even the short time he was gone and when he came back with a fine snake over six feet long my voice was a girl-child's whisper as I directed him how to skin it and, discarding the head, chop all the rest to short pieces and boil them slowly in a covered pan, adding always just enough water to keep the contents a thick, oily broth. After an hour of this boiling while I fought back cries against clenched teeth, I had him feed me the broth in small sips and as hot as I might endure.

It worked its cure quickly, sending me still feverish from my pallet to stoop and shit copiously and many times. Before the night was half gone, my fever had left me and I could close my eyes in easy sleep.

The next morning I was some weak and weary, but the simple weakness of purgation and the weariness of lack of sleep were both within control and palliated by a hearty breakfast.

I tell this illness and its cure in detail since I have heard it related since as part of the story of Brant the Monster who cured a chill by catching a live rattler in his hands and eating it incontinent. It was all a milder matter than that, an old remedy I had learned from Gray Diamond, my teacher of such lore, and I do not know that it would work such swift wonders for any person not born a Turtle.

Only our second day on the trail and we had the fell news that no brew of snake or other magic might undo: the plans for West Point had fallen all awry and General Arnold had fled to the British fleet.

Sir John and I met and bested American irregulars along our route, burned settlements and saw our braves augment their strings of scalps of every size, but we could not paint our movement back toward Niagara as anything else but another retreat. I was tired to my heart of the sight of burnt houses and charred fields and the panic screams of the dying made no music to my ears. We had done our work well—slaying, as it was accounted afterward, a good half of all armed men mustered against us. And this without mention of some hundreds of stray farmers and settlers and their wives or children killed or captured, or of the stores destroyed or put to our own use and the houses and forts burnt and razed.

But the Americans seemed to renew themselves like the dragon's-teeth warriors of Jason in the old Greek tale. They were riddled with mutiny, continuous intrigue for power and noisy dissent from ranks to assemblies, yet they held their ground and grew in strength. I cannot, even now, explain it.

"Could we not stay on campaign, Father?" Isaac asked me as we drew near to Niagara. We were both on horse and a little apart from the others. "English or American," he said, "what does it matter? We can be our own men on the trail and on the warpath. We could ride on west together, beyond Detroit and into lands no white men turn to towns."

"Our lot has been cast, son," I told him, and I tried to make him see something of our bond through Sir William to the King and our need, if we were to keep our nation whole, of changing as the land changed. But he would never listen to me as I had listened to Sir William and the first night back at the fort he was in drink again and slept away from the warm house Catherine and I had with his snug bed waiting for him.

He had continued to grow into a handsome boy and with a lively manner when not gone in drink that attracted to him men and maids, too. Had he been less handsome and pleasant, he might have escaped some of his troubles and temptations, for it became a regular sport of soldiers and officers at Niagara to treat Isaac for drinks in return for his stepping an Indian dance for them or the measures of jig he had picked up from tavern friends.

I forbade his being thus tempted and made game of within the fort, but I know my orders carried only token weight. A sprawling settlement like the Niagara of those years, part fort, part wartime crossroads, with forces coming and going on campaigns, with our own Mohawks making it a halfway house as more and more took the trail to Canadian lands, could never have the enforced decorum of a castle community.

More than once I came on Isaac, center to a circle of hand-clapping tosspots, and broke the festivity apart, but with no one on whom to vent lawful spleen since most participants were ranger volunteers or English soldiers newly arrived at Niagara and claiming legitimate ignorance of my orders. And, did I scold Isaac or try to hold him to reason, he defied me or sulked, one as bad as the other.

I resumed with Catherine the good life we had built there for ourselves between a score of other raids and excursions into the summer of the next year. There was little threat then to our valley, but much disturbance elsewhere and the worst, from the view of Indian and Englishman alike, to the south and west where Major George Rogers Clark had driven back English regulars and captured such strongholds as Kaskaskia and Vincennes. It was decided I might serve best by bringing myself and the braves as I could gather for so long a journey to join with Alexander McKee and the Girty brothers against Clark.

Isaac begged to go with me, but I was bound to punish him for his wild and godless behavior of drinking and brawling about the fort so I forbid him.

What we feared from Clark was a sweep at Detroit so I went there first and made what assessment I could of its strength before turning to Sandusky across the lake.

Sandusky was abustle with meetings of tribes, McKee with George, James and Simon Girty all dancing in their war dances and exhorting alliance against the Americans. We had word (for indeed I had made sure of seeing Molly before I left Niagara) that Clark was not too strong in force and after leaving Fort Pitt he was moving slowly, waiting reinforcement from a band of Pennsylvanians under Colonel Archibold Lochry. I made a speech against further waste of time and pushed my own force of two score braves ahead of McKee and the Girtys and some rangers of Captain Andrew Thompson.

My speed was my good fortune. On a stream near the Miami we came on an advance party of Lochry's and, my braves threatening them with raised axes and even more horrid grimaces, forced them to stand where they were and entice the main force into the trap I now baited with a welcome fresh party of another two score braves led by George Girty.

It was another pitched battle doomed to be named by Americans a "massacre" as if we had descended on some band of sleeping innocents. Lochry was a frontiersman and his band of a hundred and fifty all skilled militiamen from the harsh Westmoreland hills. We caught them in full surprise, as any soldier would desire to do, and killed and took scalps and prisoners accordingly.

This was the reinforcement on which Clark had been counting, and without it he should be as easy to crush as poor Lochry himself.

We were resting with our prisoners guarded in a makeshift stockade when the remainder of our party joined us. This gave us better than five hundred men and I pressed for a quick march after Clark.

I called together McKee and Thompson and the Girtys (all but Simon who had joined a group of my own Indians in their victory celebration) and spoke my thoughts.

"We might catch Clark before Louisville," I said, "or even at the town. And, if we can defeat Clark and take Louisville, I'll wager any sum we might next move to Fort Pitt itself, gathering new allies from our success and profiting from American despondency."

McKee caught my truth at once and agreed. Thompson agreed for himself, but feared whether he could press his rangers to good speed for they were already weary and suffered from narrow rations.

"All the more cause for them," I argued. "We'll find better than green corn to eat at Louisville."

Thompson nodded and George Girty, a good fighter if not overquick of wit, spat a stream of brown tobacco juice and said he reckoned the plan made plain sense. James, his brother, said nothing, which from him meant agreement.

"We could start at dawn," I said. "I can detach a dozen braves to guard our prisoners back to Sandusky."

"I shall see to my men," Captain Thompson was saying when Simon Girty, in his usual condition of filth and drunkenness, reeled into our circle.

"What's all this, brothers?" he hooted, his speech slurred with the drink.

"We march at dawn, Simon," George told him. "We can catch Clark and end both him and his Rebel mischief for keeps."

"Arragh!" Simon grunted a syllable of phlegmy disgust. "We've marched enough. We've a victory to celebrate, booze to suck on, weary bones to rest." He belched close into my face and it was like passing windward a fire of burning garbage.

It might have been no disaster had we been able to contain Simon's rebellion in our small group; he looked not far from falling into his nightly drunken sleep. But his loud roars had brought some Indians (not of my band) close to us and he had to turn to harangue them.

"Our noble Mohawk friend has banished sleep," he said. "This bugger Brant would have us march at dawn tomorrow, so he may be sure of catching Clark for an easy victory like all the easy victories he's been used to. Here on our border, we'd rather rest and gain strength for a harder battle if need be. But I reckon hard battles are not to Thayendanegea's taste."

I held my face firm from anger.

"If Brother Girty wishes hard battles," I said, "let him march with us, for when we strike at Fort Pitt there will be trouble and glory enough for every man."

"Fort Pitt!" Girty coughed. "You think that's just another of your twig-and-plaster New York forts, Mohawk. You're on a man's frontier now, baby-killer!"

It was the last epithet that reddened my brain with rage. I had endured such accusations from the enemy, but to hear it, blown at me in Simon Girty's foul breath, in my own camp was overmuch. I cuffed him hard enough on an ear that he staggered almost into the fire.

I let my hands fall back to my sides in readiness for Simon's rush which was not long in coming. He snatched a brand from the fire and came at me roaring some boozy war cry of his own devising, poking the brand awkwardly but menacing at my eyes. I stepped to one side and caught his feet with an outstretched foot and tripped him flat.

"Go back to your pallet and rest to gain all that strength you speak of," I said. I turned away for it has always been the custom in such duellos that the first fall finishes.

"Brant!" I heard Thompson's call and I wheeled to catch Girty's full force against me. He kicked at my shins and I grasped his right hand which held an ax upraised and descending toward my shoulder. I had been able to check its fall and push him a few steps from me. Now I caught my own ax from my belt.

"One step more, Simon!" I warned him, but he was far gone in drink and rage and assaulted me again.

I parried his ax hand with my left arm, getting only a grazing cut across my shoulder, and then brought my own ax hard down upon his grizzled, greasy pate.

He fell before me, going to his knees like a man in prayer, and I saw as I drew back my ax the cleft its blade had cut and from his forehead into his hair a wide gash through bone that left air-open the pink-gray convolutions of his brain matter, not bleeding much but throbbing like a pulse of maggots.

"I am sorry, George," I said. George and James with no words came forward and, one to each side, carried their brother away.

So Simon did march at dawn, carried in a litter and with two score of Indians loyal to him, but in the wrong direction, back to Sandusky, and his whole interference cost us not just his band, but two more days to soothe and renew loyalty all through our expedition. I saw him many times after (and very civil he always was) with a grooved scar across his head you could lay two fingers in.

Our chance at speed and surprise was lost, but McKee and I still had hope. We moved down the river and to within nine miles of Louisville where Clark sheltered. We should have had Clark and the town both, but Clark himself in open council had declared his mind no longer set on a campaign against Detroit and, with this news, almost all our local Indian allies melted from us; seeing no further danger to themselves from Clark they could not be convinced to follow on and finish him. Of a thousand such lazy and careless decisions is written the loss of our Indian lands.

I made my own way home and took some risks crossing American territory, not solely for the swiftness but because I could not pass so close to my old small kingdom above Fort Ligonier without looking in upon it.

My island stood as it had both times before, rock gray and laurel green, a plinth of immemorial peace in all that ravaged land.

Resting here I lay, as before, upon the sun-touched rock and let my soul lose itself or find itself in the murmuring timeless quiet of that, my sanctuary. I saw no raccoons, but a bold gray squirrel came within a foot of my head to steal a fallen nut and shrilled a scolding cry at me as if I had not been a giant to his pygmyhood.

I took refreshment of spirit from this short visit and it quickened my pace back to Niagara. There was some praise for me at the fort for the end of Clark's designs on Detroit, but this was far from the triumph I had planned when I left. Our actions had dammed only a freshet; the full river's flood of American power flowed on unhindered.

Catherine had a fine and loving talent for shriving me of disappointment and evil moods. At home I wore the dress of an Englishman as often as Mohawk garb and I delighted in buying what fine stuffs might be had with war and its embargoes to see Catherine dressed for a great lady. I had purchased two female slaves to help her in the house (one a handmaiden for dressing and doing Catherine's personal errands), and one strong male slave, Bartholomew. We had China ware and English glass for our dining and I think there was no house, including that of the English commanders, with so civil an appearance in the whole fort region. We entertained the most notable visitors and all seemed greatly impressed—thinking, I suppose, that they were to face rude meals with a simple savage—at our neatness and delicacy and by my Catherine's wit and beauty.

Next to her, I took most pleasure with my Christiana, now thirteen years and given much to being herself a great lady, a tiny figure in fancy frocks, stepping solemn with me as I taught her a dance figure, kissing me demurely every night I was at home.

I wish I had a similar pleasure to report of Isaac, but the boy kept growing farther from me. At the fort he kept with the worst companions, boozers, rioters, renegade whites and Indians of low degree. It is true that on the warpath he showed himself a man far beyond his sixteen years, but nowhere else, and to my mind this is not sufficient to make a whole man.

I was not without sympathy for my son, for I have known myself the madness of rum and the deeper madness of giving in to war's scarlet haze. But I fought my battle against these lures and largely won it in the end. I did not require, from vulgar pride of parenthood and position, that Isaac win his battles; only that he be willing to fight them. But he chose always to let his life run without direction, in whatever runnel was easiest. I have met strangers at a distant campfire with whom I could talk more easily than with my own son, and reason. Isaac had little use for God, either my own tripartite God of the true church, or the Indian Manitou. He thought work something for a gentleman's son (in this the only pale compliment he gave me) to shun. Love was to him mere lust, and he read no books nor did he enjoy any conversation beyond battle or the hunt.

So all the connection I had with him was to try to keep him from serious trouble and to pray at night in the privacy of my study before going to my bed that he might change.

There was still action enough in our valley to keep Isaac occupied at what he might do best, and action enough there and elsewhere to keep me from home more often than I liked, not only at war but late at councils both Indian and English. The closing events of the War of Revolution now touched us vitally.

Washington, leading his French and American armies, had defeated Cornwallis at Yorktown and, had the French fleet not had other duties in the Indies, he would have taken New York. As it was he had the port surrounded and word of this had toppled Lord North's ministry in London, Lord George Germain with it. I had assurances from Sir John and from Alexander McKee that England would stand firm to promises made by Lord Germain and with these I kept some loyalty among my Iroquois, but they were not enough to satisfy my own fears. I wrote copiously to London, to my lords Germain and Sandwich, to everyone else I knew in any high position, and got back answers as discreetly worded as a flirting maid's response to a proposal.

Where they could, the Americans pressed sorely and brutally against all Indians. The poor Moravians, a hundred and more Indian converts to the gentle faith of Count Zinzendorf, were herded from their fields by Colonel Williamson and his militiamen. He made them, these simple agricultural folk who had refused to bear arms on either side, a long speech that his soldiers would take them to Pittsburgh to be held safe there until the war ended since their presence (the mere fact that they were Indians) upset the settlers. In innocence, they believed all he said and turned over to his men all their arms and even their farming tools. Wherewith they were slaughtered in cold blood at their own church house, men, women and children.

And then my greatest blow thus far. Catherine told me I paced the floor of our house like a madman, but in stony silence when the news came. The Treaty of Peace had been signed in Paris and at no place, in no paragraph of all its detailed statement of provisions and boundaries was there any mention of land for Indian people. Quite the opposite; land past the Proclamation Line was cheerfully turned over to the new nation's United States as if one inch of it had been King George's to give.

I went both to Sir John and to General Haldimand ready to break my sword and tear to pieces in their presence my proud commission (now as a colonel) in the King's forces. But for their long pleading (and Alexander McKee's shrewd Scot's question: "What land will your action bring the Mohawk, Joseph? What offers from the Yankees?") I should have. I finally held to my old allegiance and my people with me though to do the latter cost much hoarseness of breath at council.

There were dozens of chiefs to call me traitor and fool and worse. We had fought four years for the King on his minister's promise of keeping our old lands. We had lost many of our young braves in battle and no man can count the other losses of peaceful Indians wantonly slain by marauding patriot bands. Why did I still speak now to keep friendship with the English when this same King had signed a peace written as if no Indian had ever raised a tomahawk for his cause?

I hear this question still, not only from my enemies, but sometimes within myself, and I have still the same answer for it, no brave answer, no satisfying one, but the best I could find. For what else could I do at war's end to serve my people best?

When I had slowed my black pacing in our home and Catherine had persuaded me to take some food, my first thought was of Molly. Catherine understood my need to talk with my sister and kissed me close as I mounted a horse to ride north alone. It was near midnight when I got to Molly's house, but she was awake and waiting.

"Thayendanegea!" she clasped me in welcome as I crossed the threshold.

"This peace," I said, throwing my jacket to a slave. "You have heard? It is betrayal, sister."

"All of that," she said and led me to a table where she sat with me, calling for wine.

"Pontiac was right," I said bitterly.

She smiled and with the smile shed her years, once again my beautiful sister, the young, bold mistress of Johnson Hall.

"Little brother, Small Turtle," she said. "Pontiac was not right, not while Sir William lived and other men who might have seen our people fairly dealt with. You cannot mix good of the past with evil of the present, brother."

I let my head droop down into my hands folded on the table. This was my Molly and I could allow her to see defeat and desolation I would show no one else, not even Catherine. She moved close to me and stroked my head, kneading the cords of my nape that had been knotted tight in my stress. Molly was sister and mother and more, and I felt some ease moving back into my body like a slow, soft tide in summer on one of the great lakes.

When I raised my head again I could speak without ranting, if not without rancor and despair.

"You had no other choice than the one you made, Joseph," she said when I had finished blaming myself. "You have no other choice now. You say Pontiac was right, but you know, even had all tribes joined him then, defeat would have been

just as certain and the Indian settlement worse. You say Red
Jacket was right and that had all Indians stood through the
war as neutrals we would now be strong enough to push both
English and Americans back from our lands. But we could not
have been neutral, Joseph. Even had we denied our hearts,
neither English nor Americans would have left us neutral. The
Moravians were neutral, brother. All neutrality could have
brought us was a wider massacre."

"We could still strike now," I muttered.

"In force?" Molly asked. "Believe me, Joseph, this day the
only thing to light my eyes would be whole bonfires of white
men at the stake and I would be in the first row of camp
women helping the fire to feed on their eyes and char their
ballocks. But we have no such force. We are as divided as
ever and the losses of the war have left us weak suppliants,
not demanding warriors. I like this no more than you do,
brother, but it is true."

"Then let me put on woman's dress," I said, "and sue the
King and General Washington like a homeless squaw."

"Pretty you'd be!" she gave a hoot of laughter that punc-
tured my gravity. "I can see London strumpets blushing pink
with envy of you. No, brother, we must work with what we
have and all we have is England still. We have fought the
Americans and they will not, in gracious thanks, restore our
lands. England may grudge us, but the King's people have
some shame and, you play upon it properly, you may yet sal-
vage some homestead. As for the Americans, we have enough
life in us to keep them harried here and there with small
raids; and such wounds, pinpricks to the saber slashes they deserve, may win respect and fairer bargains than we'd have
otherwise."

With no good grace, I had to see the justice in reality of all
she spoke.

We talked some further of great affairs and then fell to
remembrance. I think there is no conversation (save indeed a
profound discussion among scholars) that can be so pleasant

as one remembering one thing the other has half forgotten, the other countering, and so on.

"Ah, but, Joseph, the day you leaped out Sir William's barn's top story and what you thought was a hayrick was all Enoch's piled manure!"

"I smell it yet. But do you remember, Moll, the time in the castle our mother found you with tongs borrowed of the sutler's wife and trying to make curls into your hair?"

The solemn black who served us our wine must have thought us infected with some Indian insanity. I, a man of just past forty, dressed in clean longcoat and a white ruff at my neck, Molly, three years older, in a long gown of fine brocaded woolsey, both leaning from the table with such gusts of laughter as would do credit to children sipping their first hard cider.

I slept an hour or two and then saddled to return home. For all my short rest, I rode back a man refreshed and took Catherine to our bedroom and mounted her that afternoon which time, by count of months, I think was when we must have made our firstborn, Joseph.

From Molly's wisdom and strong, gay spirit, I was enabled better to do my duties among the Nations in council. We met in a great conference in Sandusky and I told my brothers that, despite the public words of the Paris Treaty, England still stood with us in private. The English could afford no new outbreak of war between themselves and the Americans, but they would see the tribes armed and otherwise supplied to hold land against the colonials.

This kept some dissident chiefs to our side, but there were others, especially among the Senecas, who questioned whether my words had any meaning. Red Jacket spoke like a firebrand warrior, asking for action at once against the American settlers on Seneca land.

For no love of him, but bearing in mind strongly all the help other Senecas had been throughout the war years, I offered my best efforts to treating with General Haldimand for definite word of what land the King might grant us. It had been a strong part of my London agreement with Lord Germain, this understanding that, should the war go against us and the English, they would give us territory equal to what we had lost by offering them our active support.

And with General Haldimand, companion of Sir William and my old friend from as far back as the siege of Niagara, there began the dogging tribulations that, in some wise or other, have been my life almost ever since. General Haldimand had no argument against the justice of my requests. He knew I spoke truth when I repeated Lord Germain's promises. Yet, even though his position now was governor-general of all Canada, he had not power to grant us outright the land we asked. What further complicated our dealing together was that, at first, neither of us truly knew this limitation on the general. So, when he traced with me over maps and made agreement to our nations holding all land along the Grand River, a delectable country (*Pilgrim's Progress* is still with me) and almost fair trade for the valley we had lost, I took the whole matter as a deed accomplished and went back to my councils and so reported to many glad cries.

This same time, my son Joseph had been born, and we had a feast of double celebration, for his birth and for our being granted the land we sought. There were guests at our house of every rank and, out of the ranks of an English regiment, I found a red-haired Irishman who could play the harp I had helped Sir John bring back from Johnson Hall and now borrowed from him for our feast. Molly joined us from Kingston, and Alexander McKee made his long way back from Ohio. I turned down an empty glass at the seat by my right hand for honest George Croghan who had died the year before not able to see this grandchild and for him the soldier accommodated the harp to an ancient Irish lament that had even the Scotsmen wiping tears from their eyes. Isaac came to the feast and I give him credit for being only slightly tipsy and avoiding the cursing and brawling by now his familiar social manners.

It was our last dinner of any ceremony in that house, for with the peace, all was movement north to new lands. Those Tories who had stayed out the long grim years in New York, those Mohawks who had taken cover in forest and survived the struggle, all now packed what they could and made a winding, long and arduous journey north to the land we had been given to believe would be our own.

The movement of whole nations is no simple matter and indeed our taking up new lands in Canada would not have been possible all crowded into that black year of the Peace of Paris and war's end had it not begun less formally from the very outbreak of the Revolution. Most of our English friends had already established new homes here in the north and a great part of the Mohawk Nation likewise. What now remained was a final severing of old ties, a last journey for those most stubborn among us in the hard-slain hope that we might have held our ancestral valley.

I thought as I made my own plans and directed the preparations of others who sought my advice of those strong desert men of Israel, of Moses and Aaron, who led their weary tribes to Canaan. And I had (and still have) hope that if we imitate those Israelites in reverent subjection to that same Jehovah we may make here a land of milk and honey beyond even the New York land we lost.

I myself and Catherine had no easy task of moving since by now I was a man of possessions. There had been many raids in the four years gone and, in the fashion of our people, we shared booty from each raid. As leader I had always the foremost share and I may add, as a man of taste and sense, I chose well. There were in North America no such men as the famed nabobs of the true India who for their pains in war had won fortunes hardly to be counted, but, so close as one might come to being a North American nabob, that close was I. Gold, plate, glass, furniture, books, paintings, horses, plows,

carts and some ten slaves—all these I had. Catherine took su-
perintendence of the household goods, but this still left me
much work with all other effects and to bring everything together and to have bateaux available for ferrying all of it and
all of us across and up the Grand River to Loyal Village.

I had found a good house where we could stay while I built
my own on land along the river. This had belonged to a pros-
perous French fur trader and was more spacious than our
home at Niagara with a barn and other outbuildings, some
good sheds for the field slaves and twenty-five acres for tillage. Settling here and seeing to the clearing of the land for
our real home gave me much occupation and more satisfying
than the irregular tumults of war.

Also it was a good time in Isaac's life. Freed from the fort
and evil companions, given his own room in a house from
which stretched fine forest for hunting and enlargement of the
spirit, he drank but little and that no more to excess than most
other men (I should here include myself) save for the con-
tinuance that drink which made others lighter and more socia-
ble, still threw him into black moods.

But they were seldom and I felt, hunting with him for deer
and elk, recapture of the few but fine moments we had
shared, on his first war trail and later when he had caught me
my healing snake.

Catherine bloomed and was happy in our new home. It was
an easy distance from Toronto and there we both went several
trips a year for purchase of goods and material for the new
house and of finery for Catherine and Christiana and some
merry evenings of dinners and balls at great homes there.
Trade ran free again and I could buy books only four or five
months off the London presses and see an occasional periodi-
cal that might carry a sketch by my old friend Mr. Boswell.
We found cunning toys for infant Joseph, boxes that played
tinkling music at the turn of a key and dummies of caout-
chouc for his teething.

I had time to return to my work of translation and, with all the notes and material that had been with me since Fort Hunter—How long past, O Lord! another world!—made some fair progress.

There were still moments of doubt, questions I raised for myself out of my scriptural study or disappointments in council but they were slight. Even my dreams were generally calm, often of the sea, but a quiet sea (and I liked this dream for an English traveler had told me there were giant turtles that lived in such far southwestern seas), and twice my great owl came to me, shining huge and white in the dim forest of my sleep, so that I felt myself covered in a warm pale glow as though from the moon.

I was living, in some wise, the life I had envied and aimed for from my first exposure to Fort Johnson. I had wealth and I showed a good facility for adding to it for I traded well in furs and I think I have seldom sold a horse or any livestock that the transaction did not profit me well. More Indians were moving near us and settling along the river. Sir John was building a fine new home to replace his own lost estate. Walter Butler had died of an enemy bullet near the war's end, but John Butler and Guy Johnson and Alexander McKee were all alive and hearty and our friends.

I have painted all this picture to show the best of my life just then, but I was neither so self-confident nor quite so innocently credulous as it may imply. I knew there would probably be no end in my lifetime to Indian troubles with the Americans and I was prepared to be therein entangled, whatever treaties the Crown might make. But I felt some surety in my own home and in the lands Governor Haldimand had ceded us along the Grand.

In such spirit I left my home and my wife for the Great Council to be held at Niagara in the autumn of 1784 for discussions with the Americans.

I was the leading chief at Niagara, but the Americans knew my loyalties well and therefore bent their best attention on other chiefs like Cornplanter and Red Jacket, pursuing their

familiar tactic of holding nation apart from nation, tribe apart
from tribe and gobbling to their maw ever more land in the
process. No more than half the promised Americans were
there and they offered one thing one day and then, the next,
gave long explanations that, since no Constitution had been
drawn up, their United States could make only tentative
offers. I held my patience better than some (a good part of
the western Indians deserted the conference before it was half
started) and even planned to attend at Fort Stanwix where
more authority was promised but my plans fell all ajumble
with the arrival of a rider from Molly. He had two pieces of
news. First, that she begged me to take back from Niagara
her friend Mary Skinner (for some years mistress of General
Philip Schuyler and our good informant of American secrets)
who had at last deserted her military patroon and planned
now to live with Molly. This boded me no ill for Mary was
still a pretty maid no more than twenty-six and an old friend.
The second news struck me sharp: Molly said she had sound
word that the Grand River land where we were settling had
not in fact been ratified to our use; General Haldimand had
informed London of the grant, but London had chided him
that he had no power for such transfer without act of higher
ministers.

If I had felt betrayed by the Paris Treaty, now I felt both
betrayed and dumbfounded. Bad enough, in all honor, to be
trifled with by diplomatists across the sea, but here were my
very friends, Sir John, Guy Johnson, General Haldimand playing a shell game at my elbow with the future of my people.

There was no time to tarry. I sent a scout to find Phil
Schuyler's Mary, to prepare horses for both of us and to call to
my room as many chiefs of influence as he could muster. Five
chiefs showed up as I was changing clothes for travel, among
them Cornplanter, clever but prosy, and Red Jacket, a little
gone in rum since it was evening.

"I give you leave to speak for me at Fort Stanwix," I told
them, "but only where American lands are concerned. I shall

deal with the English myself and I think still this is the only dealing likely to bear fruit, even if the fruit be not all we wish."

Mary came into the room and greeted the chiefs and gave me a sisterly kiss and we were away. We rode to the head of the river and took a boat there to Montreal and on to Quebec. I had sent a runner to let Catherine know my change of plans and probable lateness in homecoming.

I had the fastest vessel I could find and bribe for greater speed but it was still a journey of weeks. Mary was a good companion, frivolous and diverting at a time when my heavy heart needed such distraction. She was still a lissome, handsome girl and General Schuyler's infatuation easy to understand, but I had no thought at all (save in the passing fancy any man might have of a pretty wench: I'll wager she'd be a fine armful in bed) of her beyond simple friendship. She told me merry scandals of the Schuylers and other sacred names high in American councils, made me play at cat's cradle with her and saw to it that we both ate better fare than I had expected on such a trip. And that was all.

I found us lodgings at Quebec and in that crowded city thought nothing that our two small rooms were next each other. There was more on my mind than womanizing.

I was received by General Haldimand at my first request and I rushed almost rudely through the niceties of reunion to get to the meat of my worries: Did we or did we not have the land so firmly promised us?

Of course we did, General Haldimand said, and then hemmed and hawed so that I could have had some pity for him were not the subject as vital as it was to my people.

Of course we did, he repeated, and there could be no doubt of it, but I must know what delays and complications rode with any decision of such importance. Only the other day he had had a letter from Lord Sydney, the Secretary of the Colonies, giving him full authority in dealings with the Indians . . .

And more. I let his speeches run their course.

"Then, sir," I said, "may I have the deed to take back to the Six Nations that they may know the King speaks as true as his enemies speak false?"

"Damn it, Colonel Brant," the General said, "don't you trust me?"

"I trust you, General," I said, honestly enough. "I saw you stand with Sir William and accept his command those years ago when General Amherst's officers would have connived to depose him. But not every Iroquois served at Niagara then and, as things are now, they require of me more than words."

His lined face lighted at the memory.

"Poor Prideaux," he said. "But old tales butter no parsnips, Colonel. You and your braves served the King and you deserve all Germain may have promised you and more. I've a tough neck like an old rooster, let me stick it out. Wait on me again tomorrow this same hour."

"A deed?" I asked.

"Something written, written and signed," he said. "It will be the best I can devise with the farthest stretching of my powers, be sure of that."

I thanked him and took my leave, still uncertain, but some cheered by the meeting.

That night I took Mary with me to dine at a tavern serving the best trade and kept my dignity as I heard whispers of: "It is Brant, the Mohawk King and one of his hundred wives."

The next day I found General Haldimand as good as his word. He must have had his scribes working into the night for he handed me an honest deed on parchment signed with his hand and to it his seal as governor-general. The Six Nations were given in perpetuity all land along the Grand River, to six miles on either bank and from its mouth at Lake Erie to its source a hundred miles inland. This occupancy was limited to Mohawks and other Iroquois who had actually fought for the Crown, but I could argue none with the fairness of such a provision. Yet I could still argue one thing.

"I, Thayendanegea, thank you, General," I said, to make acceptance formal. "And through me my people thank you. This is the land we were promised and on it we will dwell and serve His Majesty as loyal subjects."

I bowed and he bowed stiffly in acknowledgement.

"Then I spoke as a chief and my people's representative," I said. "Now, General, I must speak as one man to another, both of us grown old and weary seeing wiles and deceptions of the great world beyond the ocean."

"Yes, Joseph," he said, sadly and softly.

"Can I and my people be certain this document will stand as the King's law?" I asked. I did not like to ask it, for I respected this old man, but the question reared itself and allowed no dodging.

"I think the King and his ministers are not likely to make a liar of their appointed governor-general," he said. "That is the best assurance I can give, Joseph."

It was my turn to sigh.

"For surety then," I asked, "there is no place but London?" He nodded.

"I thank you again as a man," I said, "and not just for the deed, but for honesty. If I go armed with the deed to London, I may find the certainty my people need, and perhaps some whispers of what other aid we may expect."

I was thinking of further campaigns against the Americans and he knew my thoughts but kept discreet silence. We were once again Colonel Brant and General Haldimand.

"London is a long voyage," he said, "but only there can you get the answers you seek."

"No voyage is too long for that, sir," I said.

He offered me the hospitality of his house for a formal dinner the next night, but I gave him regrets. I could put every moment to full use, find a ship sailing the next month, buy comfits for the children and a bauble for Catherine and be aboard a boat bound home by morning.

We were back to Loyal Village in late July, half eaten in

the last days on the water by giant mosquitoes and I never felt so happy to arrive anywhere as at this my home. I had thought word would have come ahead of us, but there was no one to greet the boat save Gilpin, a surly stable slave with a carriage.

He gave grumbling monosyllables to all my questions and drove us to the house. I led Mary up the steps before me, telling Gilpin where to dispose of our bags and boxes.

There was no one in the parlor, as Catherine had taken to calling the large front room, so I called: "Catherine! Catherine! See what I found for you in Quebec!"

There is a wind called a cyclone or tornado that whirls in a furious cone with a velocity destroying to everything in its path. Such was my wife, coming in from the back hallway.

"I've heard what you found in Quebec!" she screamed in a voice I had not heard from her before. "King Brant and his hundred wives! I mark you, bitch, I mark you well, and I'll see you minced of all your charms!"

"Catherine," I said. I meant to protest commandingly, but what issued, distorted by my surprise, was a timid quaver.

"Hah!" Mary gave a cry of her own and ducked behind me. A hard-thrown tomahawk from Catherine's hand whistled by my ear and Catherine herself, with a long knife in her other hand, was swift after it, hacking and clawing at Mary. I felt on my face a spurt of blood from Mary's cheek before I caught Catherine's elbow and forced her arm down and her with it to her knees. A woman in hysteria is surprising strong, but no great feat for a fighting brave to bend and best.

"Care for your wound, Mary," I directed. "There is a pump in back."

Catherine still struggled against me as if I were a stranger or some Yankee militiaman come to rape and burn.

"Damn you, girl," I swore. "It's me. Joseph, your husband. And Schuyler's Mary bound to Molly's. What's possessed you?"

She tried to sink teeth into my wrist that held her arm and I cuffed her head away as gently as I could.

"Schuyler's whore!" she spat. "You took her to Quebec and lay with her and bought her pretties while your true wife languished in a barren wilderness."

I should find too much sorrow in repeating all that week's nightmare with any exactitude. To my shame I could not calm Catherine even enough to speak to until Mary had left the house (Isaac took her some miles away to a friend's home and from there she left to join Molly) and then there was little coherence to her berating.

She gave up biting at me, but that was all.

Little by little, I pieced out some reason for Catherine's fury.

Word had come ahead of us, but the word of a tipsy fur trader whose sole recall was having seen me and Mary in the tavern that evening and overhearing (as I had, but he with no humor) the phrase concerning Brant and his wife. No word I could say weighed a jot or tittle against Catherine's firm belief that I had played her false.

Had I had more time to soothe and talk to her things might have been better resolved, but I had chiefs to show the deed to and explain my reasons for the voyage to London, meetings with Sir John and Guy Johnson—all in themselves too much to fit into a single week without exorcising the thousand devils that seemed in possession of my wife's soul.

We have an Indian phrase that Englishes to "woman's madness" and explains the lunar variance in a female's moods. I clung a little to this, yet it could not excuse her actions fully. It was mere luck that Mary, Molly's old and true friend and with me as innocent as fresh fallen snow, had escaped with a small cut on her cheek, healing without disfigurement. Uncaught by me, Catherine would have had her parts scattered to every corner of her precious parlor. It is one thing to see wild rapine on a raid, even to kill some innocents oneself in war. It is another to enter what has been the haven of a home and find blood madness loose in it.

Catherine was composed enough to say me farewell when I left for London but we brushed lips rather than exchanging any true kiss and my mind still rankled and my heart hurt and my loins were near starvation.

FIVE

I was a month at sea, a voyage enjoyable for viewing the sights I remembered from my other journey, but weighted with the confusion and anger that would not leave me when I thought of Catherine. I tried to keep my mind filled with other things, problems and plans, and there should have been enough to fill it to bursting, yet always the rankling vision of Catherine, her fair face distorted in rage, her voice the hiss of some demented demon, found room to haunt me.

I went over all provisions of General Haldimand's deed until I could have recited it to you like a child singsonging a Bible chapter for his teacher. I recalled the sad business of the late Fort Stanwix conference where Cornplanter, taking my advice all too liberally, had signed away all our ancient Iroquois lands in Ohio and then let state representatives from Pennsylvania and New York encroach deep on what little hunting grounds we had left in those parts. This was not my real concern, for I had said I would deal with England about the Canada lands, but a squeezing of my people anywhere hurt me. If I could get some promised aid of arms in London, however secret the agreement, we might yet recover partly the western lands . . .

But she was my beloved wife, whom I trusted as completely as I had always believed she might trust me . . . Thus the haunting offense to interrupt any other chain of thought.

She knew me (as you know me, reader) capable of many things, but not of lying for my own protection. I had been entirely faithful to her since our marriage, but in honesty I could not have sworn in advance that I should always so remain. I know my own blood to be hot in passion and careless, but I knew, too, that any jade I might ever tumble away from her would be but the yielding to a passing appetite and no more hurtful to my true love than passing semen in an amorous dream.

Yet, knowing me this well, she had not even waited on any answer or explanation, but had flown upon me and bewildered Mary like a fury. Nor, in the week I passed with her had she made any slightest move of apology nor response to the overtures I made toward regaining our old warmth and understanding.

I had offered to take her with me to Quebec before I sailed and spoke of her chance to queen it at General Haldimand's table. She narrowed her eyes to the slits of a trapped weasel, saying: "So you may show Quebec another of your hundred wives?" Had we not been married in more than Indian fashion I should have turned her from the door of my house, and no tribe council would have denied my right.

Then I would swing in my brooding from hate of her to questioning of myself. Had I not let all my press of affairs distract me from what care and kindness could have brought Catherine back to reason? There were more ships than one sailing from Quebec and another week's delay would not wound fatally the Indian cause. Had I let all my great designs wait just a few days while I stayed by her side and let her spend her frenzy, we might have parted with a true kiss and not the Judas mockery we had played of brushing lips . . .

Ah, such a voyage!

The night before we docked at Plymouth, I had a return of my old troubled dream of the riven bear fur which seemed even more surely to pertain to the breaking up of tribes and the loss of our lands. And from it, after waking for an unhappy, sleepless space, I fell into that other dream of the maiden all white and this I had not dreamed for years.

I took a stage at Plymouth and went on to Salisbury where I stopped the night and dined with Colonel DePeyster whom I had known when he held command of Detroit. He set me a grand feast with rich and influential people of that town, but my chief reason for tarrying with him was for advice against whom to deal with in London. I was no longer the ignorant young brave who had had to deal with a Sheldon to win Lord Germain's ears, I was accepted as King of an allied nation and a friend who had helped England much in battle; but I could still use some friendly guidance in the mazes of English political intrigue.

Colonel DePeyster gave me letters to Lord Sydney and Lord Sandwich (no longer in the Cabinet, but still of influence) and George Selwyn who, DePeyster said, held no office but knew more of the byways of Parliament than any man that did.

I should have been just as happy returning to the Swan with the Two Necks, but I was now a personage and no longer my own master. So my London home was a house on Wigmore Street, a small but complete establishment with three bedrooms, a fine-proportioned entrance hall, drawing room, dining room, a study as well as a staff of housemaids and cooks and footmen, the whole the gift of His Majesty George III, my brother-King, for so long as I would stay in his capital!

I cannot go mealymouthed and claim I have ever been a prophet without honor in my own country, but the pomp and honors done me in London (and in Paris) have ever been beyond anything enjoyed at home. Since I am human, I have always delighted in them.

And, of all cities, London has been my favorite for beauty and variety and the concentration within its bounds of the fairest women and the most diverting and intelligent men. Further, this London of 1795 was a package of old friends:

Boswell was there, as talkative and knowledgeable as before; good George Romney, Guy Carleton and his father Charles Fox, that brilliant, unstable wit; and the Prince of Wales himself. Ah, what a galaxy!

I knew from before that in London there is no permissible way of going directly about one's business. Both commerce and politics here are battles in which the preliminaries are more important than the actual encounter. I served my letters of introduction on Lord Sydney and the others and then prepared to wait and to enjoy the medley of balls and galas and dinners that opened to me on every hand. I had an audience with the King and I flatter I bore myself well through court protocol. He was a deceptively dumpish man, only four years my senior, who allowed the brightness of his eyes to speak only when someone might talk of music or of agriculture, sitting sullen and hooded the rest of the time while great affairs of state whirred like pesty insects in the conversation about him. I pleased him by talking none of my grievances, but about our new land along the river and what plans I had for cultivation there of wheat and maize and raising livestock.

"Pigs! King Brant!" he said in a near-shout and in an English thickly Germanic. "Svine can be the Indians' salvation!"

When I had left I heard that he told his equerry that he had enjoyed the meeting and would desire to see me again before I left London. And I did see him twice after, each time talking only of pigs and maize.

His son, the Prince of Wales, became my much less formal friend. He had a lively interest in everything and chose often to take long walks, he called rambles, through the city and not neglecting its less savory side streets. I went on several such with him and Charles Fox, indulging in some gaming and more than one night coming home with the next day's sun high in the sky.

Recollection is an art without control. I am sure there are many things in a man's past he would like to savor in remembrance, but they elude him and are as lost as the song of the sirens. There are other things a man would forget, but they storm the bastions of his mind and occupy it to feed like harpies on his self-esteem. The matter of myself and Lady Frances Clifford belongs in this second sorry partition.

We met at an evening gathering, a gala of my friend His Grace the duke of Northumberland, held in my honor to introduce me further into London society. (I had met His Grace in the earliest days of the Revolution.) There were fine wines from France, long tables with every variety of food, and an orchestra of strings, clarinets and trumpets to play for our dancing. I had been in the city three days which was time enough, with Mr. Boswell's aid, for me to have bought clothes of the latest fashion, the shorter length of coat not quite to the knees (where at home we still thought long coats elegant) and a silken shirt with a black ribband tie instead of a lace jabot. My coat was of pale mustard color with knee breeches of an olive green, pump shoes with silver buckles and gray hose of close-fitting silk that gave me as good a leg as any man at the assemblage. I wore no wig, but had my hair clean combed and cut off a little below my shoulders so that I might wear it clubbed with a green velvet tie that matched to my breeches.

Until the party was filled out I stood with the duke and shook hands with an interminable number of Percys (all his kin) and other folk glad of an invitation to meet the new lion of the social season, to wit myself, and for once a lion that had known forests and the kill. Although I enjoyed such circumstances, I generally held myself (I am told) a little stiff, paying close attention to my manners since I had no wish of lowering my people in these important English eyes; in truth I do not think I noted much the faces attached to the gentlemen's hands I shook or the ladies' hands I kissed in the French manner I knew from Detroit.

I was not at my best for another reason: that afternoon I had been reminded again of Catherine, meeting at a coffee shop a young captain who had served at Niagara and inquired of her health. I mumbled him something. Till then the bustle and excitement of London had driven this sorrow from me. Now it was back in full force in all its anger and confusion.

I danced a little, but without great spirit. I was standing at a table bearing a vast bowl of punch when I felt the tap of a fan on my shoulder. I turned and saw myself quizzed by the largest, bluest eyes any woman ever had; they might have been grotesque, but that she was a tall Juno who bore them in a softly rounded face of perfect proportion in all its features, hair almost the yellow of cornflowers piled in an intricate nest above.

I looked down and had to check myself from rudely staring, for the lady's two breasts were displayed to near the middle of their nipples. They were of an exquisite roundness and firmness so that the bodice of rust-colored camelot seemed merely to outline and not support them.

"Milady . . ." I said, searching valiantly for a name I had forgotten in the introductions yet sure that, even in that daze of so many new faces, I should not have forgotten this one and all she carried with it.

"La!" she said. "We did not meet. Not till now. I have a wicked vice of tardiness and came past the hour my cousin Percy might have made formal presentation. So, and because I am a bold creature, I introduce myself, Frances Clifford. As for you, the Mohawk King needs no identifying."

I stood tongue-tied, too fascinated for a ready answer, reflecting the rare good fortune that her melodious voice matched all her other beauty.

"Come, sir!" she tapped me again with her fan. "I know you speak English and I have not known you long enough myself to master Mohawk."

"His Grace did not prepare me," I blurted. "He said nothing of such an Aphrodite among his family."

She smiled. "A compliment worth the waiting," she said. "I'm but a poor relation by marriage, a helpless widow woman he would not think to mention."

I had held out my hands and, without waiting for me to put the request into words, she took them in hers, letting the fan slip back to her wrist on its loop, and we stepped into the measure of the dance.

She was, and I cannot remember her otherwise than in the truth of my feeling, as different from other women as a fine-bred hunter from its sister horses that pull carriages. There was music in her movement whether she danced or simply walked.

I learned more of her as we danced and sipped punch and danced again and again. Her late husband, killed just the year before in some skirmish in India, had been a baronet, a distant and minor connection of the Percys. Now widowed, at but twenty-six, she found herself with a moderate fortune from his Indian findings, but, she said, unhappy as a lone woman in the whirl of London.

"There are not many men I care to be with or trust to be with," she said.

"Methinks you might have your pick," I said.

"My pick of what?" she exclaimed, and pointed three quick gestures with her fan to a macaronic effeminate, to some young country squire, red and perspiring as he danced, to a vulturine old gentleman in rusty black who practiced his terpsichore in one corner, pawing about the breasts of his youthful partner.

"A young widow is fair game in this city," she said. "They look on trying to bed me as equal sport to hunting fox. The city stifles me, King Brant, with its closeness and its simpering half-men."

We stopped our dancing and I suggested wine.

"You bring it for us to drink here," she said. We had some privacy on a couch by one wall away from the serving tables. "I had rather continue our conversation without dilution of fashionable ninny-prattle."

I went to get our drinks. I had been attracted to her from first glance, but it was seeing her again, as I returned, that turned the lock of enchantment upon me. She was in shadow, sitting back upon the couch, and as I neared her a footman passed holding high a candelabrum. Its light touched on her fleetingly, catching the yellow gold of her hair and her white face and white bosom, snow against the dark brocade of the couch, and I saw the woman of my dreams, mystery made warm and living flesh.

God forgive me, I had to have her!

I had been continent too long and after the sour taste of my farewell from Catherine I felt no fealty to marriage vows. But this is only stringing poor excuses. Had this been all the matter, I would have had myself a bawd already for London has ever been a city of great availability of Cyprians. No, it was weakness in me, but beyond that it was her embodiment of my dream, and I believe it to have been a thing laid down by Fate those many years past, even before Lady Frances could have been born, that moved perhaps the whole voyage, Catherine's rage and my reaction, all to my presence with her at the ball that night.

I gave her a drink and this time when our hands met it was something suddenly linking us. I saw she felt it, too, for she drew her hand back quickly with the glass and near spilled wine on her skirt. That moment, at least, I believe was as true for her as for me.

I sat beside her and we talked on.

"Your America!" she said. "Do you know I have dreamed of it?"

My pulse quickened, but it seemed she meant "dream" not as we Mohawks use the word exactly, but in a sense of longing and conscious thought.

"There I might find release from all that chafes me here!" she said, throwing her arms wide, that snowy bosom all atremble. "I could run through green forests and bathe in fresh streams."

Remembered and coldly set down her words were stale bait that would not deceive a starving muskrat, but heard on the heels of that candlelit image, tied to my dream, they tormented me with a rising lust I could hardly contain. Night was rushing to meet the morning; there were only a half dozen of hardy couples on the dance floor, a few seasoned drinkers still at the serving tables.

"I have a coach to my command," I said. "Let me take you home, milady."

No sooner enclosed in the coach than I put an arm behind her and buried my face in hers, my lips against her sweetly yielding lips, the rich softness of her breasts to my pounding heart. There was no doubt my kiss was returned, but she pulled away from me a little ruefully, saying: "You, too, are a city huntsman, King Brant?"

"I am a huntsman for love and not mere sport," I said.

"I believe you," she said. "For such a huntsman, I am pleased to be game." And she came back into my arms and it was her lips now pressing mine the more hotly, twisting till her tongue found passage into my mouth like a sleek adder bearing balm instead of poison.

The coach had been making its way to my house, but I rapped to catch the driver's attention and directed him to go to the Swan, where I knew I might have a room with some discretion.

"An inn?" Lady Frances questioned.

"I would not compromise you in the house I have," I said. "There are too many servants and each one has several tongues for gossip."

She shrugged and moved back to my arms, murmuring not so much words but a breathy music of prelude to delight.

At the Swan she alighted with me and smiled mischievously, putting her fan modestly to her face as I saw to our lodging. They had a fine airy room to the rear, beyond most street noise. I gave the old porter a full guinea and closed the door against his back to gather Lady Frances into my arms.

Her soft hands moved to the opening of my shirt, tore its silk in their haste, and played across my chest, the small nails biting near my nipples which I felt rising in my heat.

"Leave the one taper," she sighed against me as I reached to snuff the candles. "Nay, do not hurry. Here now we have the night and as much of the morning as a King may wish to spare."

She had slipped out of my arms and perched herself on a small table.

"Let me see you, Mohawk King," she bade. "Your body," she said as I hesitated, uncertain of her meaning.

I shrugged my fine new coat from my shoulders and followed it with my neck ribband and the torn shirt. My close-fitting breeches I unpeeled as it were, and my shoes and hose.

"Your hair," she said. "Let it fall free."

I moved as a man under enchantment and I believe I was under the enchantment of that dream. I pulled the green knot from my queue and shook my head to let my hair swing loose.

"Ah, there!" she breathed, quick panting making her breasts rise and fall in shimmering pearliness. "Red bronze and man, and man and man!"

"Stay! Wait!" she said in a choking cry as I took a step toward her. "First watch me as I watched you."

The spell still on me, I stood and stared while she caught at some fastening to the back of her bodice, released it and let the front down, her breasts as high and firm as before but all unconfined and as it seemed to my dream-struck eyes a blaze of light in that inn room. She pulled her dress down and stepped quickly from it. She wore no bustle, but only a cambric underskirt. She shed her shoes and stockings from beneath it and then let it fall to the floor by the table. She stood now and the slight candlelight, yellow itself, painted her gold and white as she took pins from her hair and let it free, thick gold upon her shoulders, shy strands of curling gold where her long legs met her body. She held her head high and smiled a narrow, curving, crazing smile as she turned and walked to the bed. I saw from the rear some goddess, tall and her rump high and swaying like two round melons as she went those short five or six steps and I was after her and around her and upon her as mad as I had been moonstruck and her madness matching mine in every direction.

"Hah! Stronger! Crush!" I heard her cry beneath me, and many other wild encouragements, and I do not know what I cried or spoke back for all this first connection was storm and lightning, an earthquake in delirium.

We lay, not sprung apart, but still sweet sweat glued upon each other, sighing, the salt sweat smarting little cuts of tooth and nail upon my chest and neck and shoulders and her shoulders and now softly relaxed breasts.

She stirred a little and slipped from under me to lie on one side, still close, but propping her fair face with a hand.

"And was the quarry worth the hunt, King?" she asked.

"If you cannot answer," I said, "what use are any words of mine?"

I think God, in nature and in all its creatures, has made nothing near so beautiful as the curve of a fine woman lying on her side. Three roundnesses, the head, the shoulders, the rump—punctuated by the deep declivities of neck and waist, and into gentle flow of thigh and calf. This was my lady Frances, stretched long and languid there beside me on the good goose-feather mattress of the Swan.

I do not count how many bouts of love we played that night, leaving such precise and frigid enumeration to professional rakes and tavern braggarts. I know the sun was not far from noon when we left the inn and we did not dress or break fast till less than an hour before we left. In ribald stories, I should at my forty and three years have wobbled staggering from our room, but truth has me walking with a proud step, nothing drained, but a man renewed in youth and vigor. Lady Frances with me, scorning her mask, tread as imperiously. It was a given matter we should sup together that night and at my house.

"Why not?" she said. "I am glad of every act I did and, if you are not also, let's call an end to it."

There was a whole two months to my unalloyed bliss. Had I

been a man on the model of Autolycus, "a snapper up of unconsidered trifles," I might have taken note of small phrases half heard, of certain looks from friends and others not so friendly, but I was living in a dream I had carried with me since my twelfth year and the real world about me (if it was a real world) had small importance. What part I may have been playing, I played it happily.

We were open in all our association this side of bed itself. I found a new lightness in my own spirit and gave in to Lady Frances's mischief, traipsing with her to Ranelagh Gardens stripped to the waist and painted for battle in Mohawk regalia. (I did not tell her on such missions I was used to wear no more above a string belt and a pecker pouch; this could have been too close to truth for even London fashion.)

And, as any man in love may tell you, I found myself refreshed and more active in all other spheres. I met with Lord Sydney and got from him the needed ratification of General Haldimand's grant. I sat with him and with General Carleton, once again governor of Quebec, to make clear not only our right to land, but our ambitions to the future. I think I never worked so well for my people's cause as when fresh from a riotous bed with Frances Clifford.

Nor, contradiction though it seem, did I neglect my long and abiding interest in God's word. I found time to seek out the offices of the Bible Society and show them the work I had done in the Mohawk signs of the Book of Common Prayer and of the Gospel According to Mark. This Gospel is my favorite among the New Testament books (after Revelations, which is beyond my skill to translate) for its brevity and clearness and I thought it a better introduction to Christ our Lord than any other part of the Bible. The prayer book may have had less necessity, but it was its words, from Reverend Prouty, that had first set my imagination on fire toward faith and its translation might serve likewise to others.

The good men I met at this Society for the Propagation of the Gospel in Foreign Parts were pleased by my efforts begun

so long ago with Reverend Stewart at Fort Hunter. I sat many
afternoons in their long office study, making clear to them
points of doctrinal or linguistic difficulty, and they undertook
to publish the whole work, handsomely printed and with fine
engravings.

I can still, old as I am (and I wrote this portion now as I
am nearing sixty), still relish each remembered moment with
my fair Juno before the fall. The Prince liked her well and she
went with us on some of his rambles. Better I can call to mind
times we took a small boat on the Thames and went water-
borne just below Greenwich to have midday meals there in
some meadow and then divest our clothes and, as she said,
"like Indians" to play run and chase and end in an exhaustion
of love. Or riding together, for she was a good horsewoman,
over that English country into Kent past Ramsgate, where five
minutes' gallop and you would never remember a city left
behind.

I thought, and even talked to her of some future. With the
friends I had in high places, divorce was not impossible. For
weeks I confess I carried a new dream added to my old, a picture of Thayendanegea holding court, a combination of Mohawk council and St. James's, with Lady Frances Clifford
queening at his side. Ah, I might have been a fuddled youth
of twenty or eighteen!

I was with James Boswell, sipping coffee and hearing out
all his gossip, when the grating voice of a woman speaking to
a man at a screened table near us pierced my ear.

". . . she says she has but to call him King and he will wait
on her like a slave," the voice babbled. "A parkin of eight
inches and the most diverting lover since she had the wild
Russian prince last year."

"But I found a little milliner," Mr. Boswell droned on.

". . . the attachment grows too cloying, she told me. What
starts out as a savage in bed, ends as another footman in liv-
ery. You must admire her versatility, Walter. She says she had
word of a veritable Ethiopian tyrant come to meet King

George this summer and she wagered me twenty guineas she'd have him twixt her legs before he leaves us. So you may call Brant"—she laughed in the same ugly voice—"a cooked goose."

"No worse than a bad cold," Mr. Boswell dissolved in merriment and I tried to laugh along with him as if I had followed all his anecdote.

To Lady Frances, for all our transports, it was clear I was no more than freakish divertisement. I could not mask my sigh.

"For gas," Mr. Boswell said, "I always advise cardamom seed. Steep them in heated wine, Joseph, and take a swig before each meal."

I thanked him and, as usual, paid for our coffee.

There should be a fine scene of my confronting Lady Frances with her insincerity and frivolity, but our meeting, after that overheard conversation, had as much dramatics as an Albany housewife telling one butcher she chose to take her trade elsewhere.

She did not raise an eyebrow. I might have raged, and felt close to it within myself, but misliked to give her another charming anecdote of passion with the Mohawk.

"Did you ever think, truly, to come with me to Canada?" I asked, like a courting boy willing to wipe all slates clean for one small assurance. In kindness she could have said: "That first night," and still ended our connection cleanly but fairly. Even this cost her too much.

"No," she said, smiling that long curved smile. "I had never had an Indian chief and you had never a lady quite so pale and fair as me. I think there was no bad bargain."

I took the bound-together notes I had prepared before we met from my pocket.

"Ah, not so fair yet," I said. "It is the London custom that a trull take home some compensation." I thrust the fifty pounds into her hands before she could withdraw, turned on my heel and left her. More money would have flattered her, less would have undervalued my own pleasure, and it was a sum I could afford for late education.

I had another month in London, but I spent it not too socially, first for my humiliation with Lady Frances, second because my dealings with Lord Sydney consumed more of my time, third, and grating my heart like a rasp on raw flesh, because I had had a letter from Catherine.

She had been delivered of our second son, Jacob, and I had not even knowledge that she carried his seed in her. She wrote that the infant was quick and bonny and then two long pages of her sorrow at our parting. "There is woman-madness in pregnancy, too, Joseph," she wrote, "and it was that which consumed me when you returned with Mary. You could not notice weight growing within me, for Jacob then was little advanced, but I felt it and burned against any other woman might be nigh you. And when I had spent my fury, bitter pride kept me from telling you its cause till you were gone and then I could weep and rail, but alone. Molly knows all this now and Mary, too. May you forgive me as easily as they and make swift pace home."

I sped about my business with Lord Sydney and got some encouragement toward England's sympathy with anything we might do, short of open war, to hold our rights along the old line. The only remaining barrier against speed was a promise I had made with an emissary of General Lafayette to visit France before sailing home and this, since France still held much loyalty along the Mississippi, might serve the Indian cause and could not be slighted.

I went, before crossing the channel to Paris, to one more ball, a masked gala that my friend the Earl Moira insisted I attend in Mohawk garb. I wore the brightest of paint and my most splendid headdress of feathers, but my mood, between the guilt engendered by Catherine's letter and my disillusionment with Lady Frances, was black as the pit.

There was every kind of costume in evidence, droll Chinese, gypsies and tinkers, nymphs from the Greek and Roman lore, knights clanking in armor, devils and bashaws of Tartary. I suppose my lady Frances was somewhere in the throng, dressed if there were any justice as Circe, but I did not seek her. I danced with a pretty niece of Earl Moira's and otherwise applied myself to the punch bowl. I was latterly engaged when a large man, guised as a Turk and with two houris in his attendance, stopped before me and gave intent examination to my war paint. When he had stared long enough to decide my true features were some kind of mask, he reached forth and tweaked my nose.

Call this some culmination to all the agony piled in me these last weeks. I dashed my punch glass shattering to the floor and raised my voice in a war cry of destruction as high as I had been in the thick forest above Canajoharie. It is some tribute to our Mohawk signals that, though I doubt anyone in the ballroom had ever known an Indian raid, my cry sent them rushing about like sheep, colonels and generals of the King's army dodging to the corners of the room as I cried again and raised my ax from my belt.

The poor Turk (and the best of the jape is that he *was* a Turk, as little in masquerade as I) fell to his knees and made some imploration to Allah, before I caught the ridiculousness of the situation and put my tomahawk back to my side. There was much laughter, nervous and then hearty, after. It was a fitting end to my London visit.

I stayed as short a time in Paris as, with common courtesy, I could. I met the King, a young man surrounded by courtiers and impressing me neither the one way nor the other (I can claim no foresight that he would fall so sorrowfully, nor can I say I was surprised), and ministers who were even more devious than my English friends. In effect, France loved the Indian and would do all she could for him . . . somehow, and someday.

This French King, I would wager you, ate bacon or ham without ever thinking that it came from that creature styled *pig* which so interested his royal English counterpart. And the same with too many of his ministers. They claimed vast lands in America still and had heard of inhabitants called Indians, but they wished the produce of such territories to be served up to them, so to speak, as ham and bacon and had no liking to learn the simple husbandry facts of pigs, or of true Indian problems.

I dined well, danced with ladies of some beauty, and was shown about the city of Paris and the palaces of the King, but there was no reason for me to tarry.

It was a much different voyage home for I was a traveler in high spirits, my pouch filled with at least as much as I had hoped to get in London and, above that for myself, that letter of Catherine's which I had read and reread till its creases were near parting. I had a new son to see, and our first son, Joseph who would be past two years old now, and my dainty Christiana, and Isaac, of whom I had had no bad report which was cheering, and Catherine for a return to all I held and hold dearest in mortal life.

Tell me, reader who has known me thus far to be a man of some devotion to truth, can you hold me blameful for not telling Catherine of my misadventures with Lady Frances? You may sit in your easy chair and put your fingertips together thoughtfully before you, saying: She is not pregnant now. There is no question of what Brant calls "woman sickness" and he has painted her, aside from this, as a wise and kind woman. She has asked him forgiveness for her lapse into fury, could he not counter by asking her forgiveness for his lapse into lust?

Such judgments are too dry. Though I described it, you had not been with me in flesh and in shocked nerves that return from Quebec. I knew enough war beyond my hearth and in my home sought only peace. I ask a reader's patience and my Lord's remission that I spoke no word of Frances Clifford on my return.

This time Catherine was at the dock to meet my boat and she had tiny Jacob in her arms and Joseph toddling behind her. I wept to meet her and her cheeks were as moist as mine the short ride to the house.

I had been gone the better part of a year and I had but unpacked my trunks and had a chance to watch my children play with their new toys and Catherine admire the brocades and silks and woolens I had purchased in London and a necklace of pearls from Paris when there were at the house messengers from every tribe and nation asking my presence at every small council but especially to the new great council called for Hurontown near Detroit.

With Catherine and myself it was as of old and as if there had never been the journey to Quebec or any ax thrown at Mary. Which made my leaving hard, but I had duty and by bateau and canoe reached Hurontown in December, where waited for me not only chiefs of the Six Nations but of every nation west, anxious to know if the English King still counted them as his children and worthy of support.

At the conference they were pleased, but I was saddened. Beyond the ratification of General Haldimand's grant I had brought them promise of some covert support from England and even, given proper circumstances, arms and encouragement from France. So there were cheers for me and my news, but I knew them, for all the stirring sound, as cheers from a scattered people, still too rent by jealousy to form the only front that might keep the Americans held back. There were all the usual fine promises and discords and patching of discords between rival chiefs and rival tribes.

I have seen settlers' wives fashion what they call a crazy quilt when there was not in the house one single piece of same-patterned cloth to make a warm bed coverlet. They take a patch of blue and a patch of red and a square of checked green and yellow and a dozen more to build something two strong men might not rip apart. But they have good thread and tight, careful stitches. I have sought all my life without finding it for some thread that might bind all Indians together. And, even times when I have thought I had such thread—a governor's promise, a king's smile, a boatload of lead and powder—I have never captured the time to make neat, careful stitches.

I have another dream now in my age, dream in the wishful sense that Lady Frances spoke the word, where the first ship of whites touches the shore and some wise Indian greets it from the sand shouting: "Plague! Pestilence!" and mustering all the lame and maimed and poxy of his tribe makes such a parade of horror on the beach that the ship turns back to Europe and, on all maps there, America is written across with warning against any landfall. So morbid are an old man's fancies. And so pleasant.

I shall speak now of some peaceful years at home but bear in mind that while I write of these years as homebound, in almost every month there were some missions to councils, some commands against American militia, some palavers with Sir John and Governor-General Carleton and Daniel Claus and others. My life does not change so much, but writing it I may have the luxury of changing its emphasis.

It was soon after the council that we removed to the new house that had been building on the curved bay of Lake Ontario. It was in every way a more spacious dwelling than any we had had before, the first house I felt nearly worthy of Catherine and myself. We celebrated with a housewarming that had every important chief of the Six Nations (barring Red Jacket, still my wordy opponent, still holding the Senecas aloof from any useful cooperation) and more English notables than many an official gala in Quebec. I danced with Catherine past dawn.

It was a double celebration for I had found a wife for Isaac, Dear Swallow, the daughter of a chief who was my Turtle brother, a buxom, pretty girl willing to endure his dark periods of intemperance and, I hoped, to steer him to a more balanced life. He seemed decently fond of her when sober and had been pleasant greeting me on my return from England. That he should have some income as a husband I saw him officially appointed as my secretary in my own position as agent for the Crown. I let him and Dear Swallow have the house Catherine and I had vacated, and there were some merry toasts regarding the extra rooms he should try to fill with children.

These years, Isaac did none too badly for all the tales told since about him. He kept his home and land well managed, took proper care of his work for me, and fathered two babes, another Isaac and (after his mother) Christine. There were still brawls, but I think he was judged more harsh being an Indian and most of all being my son, than had he been any other young man.

Catherine was pregnant again with our first daughter, Margaret, and I stood on tenterhooks fearing any recurrence of her former madness. But I think she had the same fear and held rein on herself, for there was nothing beyond reasonable unreasonableness (I rode all one night to Toronto to buy her a special dimity cloth she said she must have and came back with my horse winded to find she had forgotten the request), and she was delivered easily by a woman Molly sent us down in good time from Kingston.

Molly came to visit us little, but I took the long way to her home as often as I could for there was still no one person's counsel that I respected so well as hers. When Lord Dorchester wrote me (not even his own note but through a secretary ranked no higher than major) withdrawing hope of any real English support for the offensive we had hoped to mount against the Americans in 1787, it was she who listened out all my curses.

"All I have done," I mourned, "for England and my King to win betrayal and desertion in these times of need. I might have stayed a simple hunter, a name known only to my family and companions and none of the lies that the Americans attach to me like a cluster of leeches and the English themselves have come to part believe—"

"Those who know you, know you, Joseph," she said against

my self-pity. "No one of us can ask more. Who wins both renown and truth? Even Sir William is now better remembered in our old valley as a begetter of bastards than as the molder of a whole new land."

"You may speak truth," I admitted, "but the slurs still have power to wound."

She twisted her lips in wry humor.

"Some slurs can wound a woman even more," she said. "I've heard in the past years that I never stood faithful to Will, that I took great bribes from Lord Carleton, and worst of all that I was never fair but a blowsy, pockmarked wench who won my lord's love by dark Indian magic."

"Who says so?" I started from my chair, mindless of an old leg wound that had been throbbing till then. "I'll find him and have his head for you, Moll!"

"Nay, Joseph," she chided me. "Such things are never said by any single person, always by a nameless *they*. Better, my brother, to look on our real problems."

"Which cannot be solved," I sulked.

"I am growing to an old woman, Joseph," she said. "It is no pleasant aging to have left one's home behind to a people filled with hate, nor to see your husband's best-knit plans torn into tatters. But, if I can smile and still hope, you have no right to scowl. Where there may remain the smallest handful of Mohawks, Thayendanegea, there shall always be hope for a tribe and a nation to sweep and kill all before it. Someday, brother. Someday. Does not the Turtle know how to wait?"

"Too well," I said, knowing she was right, "but there are times he would sooner snap."

She had still her quick laughter and the sound of it lightened my heart. We turned our talk to the wedding plans for her young daughter, the fourth of her five girls to be married since they had come to Kingston, and each to a citizen of fortune and good repute. Molly, at my pleading some time before, had been baptized in the Church of England, but she still gave small attention to its rituals and made me her almoner, adviser and near her priest on all matters pertaining to religion.

In the Grand River settlement I had seen to it that a church was built even before my own new house was ready, the same church with its square tower and slim spire that stands here now. I had in it the great, black-letter Bible given by Queen Anne to my grandfather Nichaus. We had also as legacy from that good Queen a set of communion plates all in silver. And King George, who I had not thought would remember, between all our talk of pigs, that I had mentioned this chapel, sent a fine cast-bronze bell engraved with his own royal arms and with a haunting of all London in its peal.

The same year of the arrival of the bell, I had in a packet from Quebec two large crates from the Bible Society and in them, opened before my proud and amazed eyes, the volumes of Mark and of the prayer book which I had left them in my translation and which now were printed, bound and proper books.

The sight of them, so sturdily bound and fairly printed, revived ambitions that had laid still since the outbreak of war. The prayer book and Mark's Gospel should be but a beginning: I would translate all the New Testament to Mohawk and, God granting me the time and talent, the Old Testament as well. This new resolution set a task to fill all empty hours as it still does, for, despite my best efforts, I am still far from completion of even half the mission. What I had neglected to remember (in a combination of arrogance and of excitement at seeing my name upon the books) was the long, untiring help I had had from the Reverend Stewart and his friend Ogilvie at Fort Hunter. Now I had neither of them to help me and, at our Mohawk church, only a procession of transitory pastors, good enough men, but none of them scholars.

What time other duties spared me, I would shut myself into my study with my Bible and with a Mohawk lexicon of signs equivalent to English words. And I came to find in a very short time that, for study such as this, books may be said to breed books. I started off at a gallop into Matthew and was slowed before I had done the first chapter like a rider caught unexpectedly in a swamp. I could not trust myself to find exact words for our Lord's conception and, questioning my ability therein, was soon questioning every other symbol. I combed Quebec for books that might help me, and a Latin Bible spawned a lexicon of Latin and several volumes of commentaries by eminent divines, and each of these suggested other needed books, so that I was putting as much time into correspondence with London friends and booksellers to supply my cravings as into any action of translation.

Had I been translating some popular romance, I should have kept my initial gallop and let precision go hang, but this was God's work and as I felt (and still feel) in some wise a task laid upon me. I had twitted Lame Crow at Lebanon for his airs over Latin, now I wished I had studied it then myself, for to try decipherment of a strange and ancient language in one's middle years is near to torture. Not only Latin, but I needed Greek and Hebrew and I had books sent me, lexicons and grammars of those languages, and pored over them, my tongue between my teeth in concentration like a miserable schoolboy, lost between *alpha* and *alef, beta* and *beth.*

Always, it seemed, just when I felt myself at verge of greater understanding, a summons would tear me from my study.

I had tried my best at Hurontown to make clear that our Indian needs were two: Unity and Time. We could count on no English support for a real offensive and hence must limit ourselves to only such small raids as would keep the delicate balance of making the Americans uneasy yet not giving them so much fright as to move heavily against us. There had been five years since then, five years of seeing my advice ignored in almost all particulars. There were cabals against me at every other council and, where my oldest English friends (Sir John and Daniel Claus and even Alexander McKee) had turned devil's advocates, arguing to my face against any move that might turn Americans against their English Canada, my brother chiefs and sachems scorned me for not cheering every border raid. I had to bear taunts of cowardice when I did my best to influence withdrawal before even such tatterdemalion forces as Harmar's army; and more taunts when some show of force turned that and other expeditions back. To me, the point was not to show our small strength at this time. Better to let a Harmar march easily and even pillage some than chase him home and stir up a hornet's nest of revenge. So other chiefs called me old and too tied to wife and family and farm to be longer thought a leader. I could see all my power of leadership, so painfully gained, ebbing from my name. So tricksome is renown.

That spring of 1792 brought me a letter from Philadelphia, from President General Washington himself, inviting me to come there and talk and treat with him concerning Indian affairs. (Should the moral be: One's enemies remember a hero better than his friends?) It was the western raids, I knew, that had disturbed him and he must have had intelligence that the Six Nations' voice in councils, where I could still speak for my people, stood counter to this recklessness. I made up my mind to accept his invitation.

At once I had Sir John and most other of my English friends writing me dolorous letters and calling on me with long faces begging I should not make the journey. This fear of disloyalty from me who had stood firm a King's man for all my life did small credit to their perception. Nor did their inability to see that this trip (since other chiefs like Red Jacket and Cornplanter had already been feasted in Philadelphia) was necessary to holding my own position with my people.

Catherine bid me brave farewell, the parting kiss I wish I had had before London, and I reached Philadelphia, the new nation's busy capital, in late June.

The city was no London, but Washington's people had found me good lodging and treated me with a flattering respect. I was pleased to see all this noticed by the British envoys, sure to send word back to Quebec and London, too.

All these years, Washington had been to me a figure never known but long heard of, first with some scorn, later with grudging respect, never with an atom of trust. With meeting face to face at last, respect erased all the old scorn, but mistrust remained and mayhap was even reinforced.

He had me to meet him at noon in the well-appointed but small brick house he made his Philadelphia home. No footman, but a plain-faced, clean and starched maidservant let me in the door, said the President was expecting me and led me to a parlor room where I had no more than two minutes of waiting before he appeared.

He was a reasonably handsome man of a little above my own height, well dressed and coiffed, going a little jowly at his age (ten years exactly past my own) and he held himself erect and formal. He had at first an unctuousness to his manner, too much the familiar mien of a white official talking to every Indian as if to children, but this wore away immediately I mentioned some mutual acquaintances to him. Then he unbent enough to treat me as, I should not say an equal or a friend, but as a respectable curiosity.

When we had got rid of introductory niceties and before we joined some gentlemen of his Cabinet to dine, he made me a proposal of payment for actions in behalf of his nation. I should have, he told me, a thousand guineas in gold to take back home with me, a pension from the United States twice the sum I now got from the King, a second annual payment through my life of fifteen hundred dollars and the grant of United States land worth another twenty thousand dollars. He offered me, in no unclear terms, a fortune and I admired the candid coolness with which he named each figure.

He did not (or could not) conceal some shock of surprise when I rejected his offer and I wonder what gold Cornplanter and Red Jacket might have taken back from their audiences. When I had repeated, for the third or fourth time, that I wanted peace as much as he did and would work for it without payment, I think he came to believe me.

After dining, there was more conference. I brought up the subject of old boundaries with no hope of rectifying them but to listen comfortably while he made the glib American justification for theft of our lands. There was no need for him to know that I had accomplished all I wanted for my own prestige in the simple matter of having this audience. Nor any need for me to bring up (in what would have been crude discourtesy) that I knew times in the past when he had signed his own name to letters advising land company speculators (some of these companies of his own moneyed interest) to secure land well past bounds set by solemn treaty.

He is dead now, the Father of His Country, with more myths twining about his tomb than Caesar or Alexander. I have no ambition to smirch the high repute for probity he has all through the nation but orphaned truth cries out to record that as honest as he may have been with other white men, just so false did he play in all his dealings with red men.

I came home still weak from an attack of the yellow fever I suffered on the return journey and Catherine nursed me back to health with help of some simples Molly dispatched from Kingston.

As soon as I was able I went to a newly called great council at the Maumee Rapids to settle the disposition of all tribes concerning increased American militancy, that same militancy I had warned the western tribes against arousing.

After talking with Washington, I felt more than before that our only Indian salvation lay in delay, in keeping from the expense of blood and time in war till we could be brought closer together as one people, and, in this same time, to continue learning those useful arts of the white man that might make us their equal in holding to our dwindling lands.

My Six Nations stood with me, God be praised, despite every calumny and vile traducing of my foes. I, who had turned my back to a fortune in Philadelphia, was accused of being a bought man. I held my power among the Iroquois, but the western nations vacillated and allowed my old friend McKee to play on pride and stubbornness so that we had no meaningful decision from the council and when finally we did meet with American commissioners we were as split as if there had been no council; my own nations for peaceful negotiation, the Miami, Cherokee and others already rehearsing war cries.

I think sadness and disappointment may afflict a man as much as a fever. I had spoken all I could, heart, head and lights exhausted. The best I had done was to keep my Six Nations from joining in a threat of war. For the rest, I saw that bearskin of my dreams rent beyond mending. Halfway to home, riding at a parson's pace, I felt a crushing clutch over my whole chest and would have fallen from my horse had not Clear Sky, an Onondaga chief riding with me, reined close and held me erect till he could help me to the ground.

This was such pain as I cannot describe except asking you to imagine your whole rib cage pressed in a great vise and no way to release it. I lay on the grass over an hour with Clear Sky at my side keeping off mosquitoes and black flies till, of itself, the vise eased its pressure and I could breathe with less pain and hobble about on my own two feet. I disdained a litter, but managed to keep in the saddle till we were safe home.

There Catherine, who had sent me off fresh from a fever bed, put me back down in our airy room and cosseted me with broths and soft food till I had some part of my old strength back.

I was up and about in a week, but found it easier to walk with the aid of a stout cane. Catherine, sadly reluctant, now gave the news she had spared me in the infirmity of my return but which could be kept from me no longer. Isaac had killed a man, a harmless and agreeable white harnessmaker, in the village. That the deed had happened in a drunken rage was no longer the acceptable excuse it might once have been. A Captain McKeon at Niagara had a warrant against him, sworn on several reports of the incident. Isaac skulked now in his shuttered house, fuddling his guilt and fear with more drink.

I am no Roman father and I would not see my son set up against white man's law whatever his crime. I said then I would rather see him dead than held in any prison, for thus pent a Mohawk would be worse than dead.

I went first to the village and found the family of the man who had been killed, a thin, timid widow and one girl of nine years. I settled upon them two hundred pounds that diminished the dowry set by for my daughters (Isaac's own portion had been long spent and overdrawn with loan after loan, each one to be the last). The sum was well beyond anything law might give the woman and she was grateful to withdraw her own charge. With other people in the village who had made complaint I played on past favors and likelihood of my future good will.

When Captain McKeon came to the village I saw to it that he was directed to my house before Isaac's and I had waiting for him my best wine and conversation to remind him that I had been a guest at court in London and a friend to the Prince. I could show that all complaints had been withdrawn and that no witnesses were any longer sure the deed had been done without provocation. And, if Captain McKeon admired the silver-trimmed dueling pistols he kept glancing at on the mantel, I should be proud to see them as my gift in the hands of such a gallant officer.

He tore the warrant in two pieces before handing it to me and left with the pistols. I felt no more clean than once before with Mr. Sheldon at Dashiell's Folly. Yet I felt the same this instance, that there was no other action I might have taken.

I had the sullen Gilpin saddle my horse. I mounted it without his help and left my walking stick at home when I rode to Isaac's.

This had been a good house when Catherine and I had dwelt there. Now I opened the door on a room dusty and spare of furniture excepting pieces broken and askew. The young Isaac, my grandchild, played in the center of the floor, his face asmear, clothing torn and foul. Any Indian infant naked by a campfire had a better lot.

Dear Swallow, with their Christine to her breast, came from the kitchen quarters at the sound of my entering.

She made a helpless gesture at the squalor of the room.

"It is so hard, Father . . ." She let her voice trail away.

"Where is Isaac, my son?" I asked.

"His room, there," she pointed. "He is not well," she said in a helpless flurry of defense and I liked her for it.

I knocked at the door and heard Isaac mumble some obscenity from within.

"It is your father," I said, and knocked again.

"Yah," I heard him say. "The great chief. Enter, Thayendanegea."

I pushed open the door and went into something like a stews off some Cheapside alley in London. Isaac sprawled naked across a bed tangled with filthy bedclothes. He had shat about the corners of the room and the air in it was fetid with that stench and urine and vomit and dregs of cheap, harsh rum.

I lifted him from the draggled bed and kissed him on his forehead.

"You are my son," I said. "And I tell you you need have no fear, nor should my son ever have fear."

He stuttered some confusion.

"The warrant is destroyed, Isaac," I said.

He staggered away from me and caught himself from falling and sat on the bed weeping into his clenched hands.

"Ah, God!" he began to speak a little more clearly. "Thank you, Father. I had thought I saw the end of everything, but now . . . You'll see. You mark me, Father. I shall never touch drink again."

Dear Swallow had come in and moved to his side, some smile joining her sobs.

"Oh, you can, Isaac!" she said. "I know you can, my husband."

He raised his head and looked about the room as if he had not seen it before.

"All this!" he cried. "We'll clean all this! Swallow, where have we a broom?"

I pushed him back gently.

"There is much time for all that," I said. "Your words have been my reward. Now rest."

The following day it was Isaac who came to call on me. He had bathed and Dear Swallow had given some trim to his hair and his clothing was decently clean though worn. His face was still puffed with his dissipation and his eyes traced with small veinings of blood, but he was far above and different from the sorry wretch I had encountered in the bedroom.

We walked the meadow back of my house and into the trees beyond and it seemed to me that I had gained back my firstborn son and that any shaming of myself in the process was well worth this result. He repeated his resolution never to touch spirits again and we laid plans of work for him, of larger participation in my own ventures and of clearing land and adding more yieldful acreage to his own holdings. He said he and Dear Swallow had early that morning made some progress on cleaning the grime of the house.

"You have projects more important than that," I told him. "Hire some women from the village to do it." And when he looked downcast, but would not mention his lack of money himself, I pressed on him ten pounds till he should get back some stability in his life. He listened while I talked of livestock and provender, as he had used to listen to me when he was a child and my heart was filled with gratitude.

Isaac's regeneration was not the only good news of that year. Catherine was delivered of our fourth son, John, an infant bright-eyed yet grave, and through her carrying him had no more than occasional fancies usual to the condition.

But news away from home was all disastrous. Quite following my foreboding, the earlier small successes of the western tribes had accomplished only that the Americans armed to strike them in full force and under the generalship of Mad Anthony Wayne, their most puissant and subtle commander. It had been one thing to drive back listless companies of ill-organized part-time soldiers, but Wayne's expedition was another story, and for the western tribes a sad one.

He took full time to muster the men he needed, scanted not in their provision and transport, and moved through the Ohio Valley like that ponderous but uncheckable juggernaut they tell of in lore of India. He had a shrewd knowledge of my people's weakness for waiting. Thus, when they were aflame and ready for battle, he held his force quiet in unassailable positions and then, so soon as his spies brought him word of Indian impatience and desertions, plowed ahead to another victory. Thus a whole string of setbacks for the warpath tribes that ended at Fallen Timbers.

There Wayne, with his game leg wrapped in bandages, stumping about in field of fire with his troops, wrote a bloody end to Indian resistance in that whole region. And Fallen Timbers added some insult to its injury, for Indians feeling Wayne's attack had rushed for shelter to the English garrison at Fort Miami only to find that the commander, fearing any action which might again embroil the Crown in outright war with America, had the gates barred against red allies.

Despite my known sentiments, as a war chief I should have been at Fallen Timbers but for my health. I was still no well man when I had news of it, but I managed to mount horse and ride west to see what, if anything, could be salvaged from the wreckage. My sole hope was to keep the western chiefs from any negotiation with the Americans that would release more land. But even this slight ambition tumbled to failure in the fright and chaos of Wayne's victory. Chiefs who had been turned away from an English fort and back into enemy fire had no stomach for new English promises and I could not blame them. I had to stand helpless, seeing Wyandots, Ottawas, Potawatomis and Miamis sign the Greenville Treaty which gave away all Ohio and clearly offered as much land farther west as the Americans might wish to gobble when they had digested these fresh thousands acres.

Do I need to tell you I came back to Grand River with a heavy heart, seeing all I had striven for in my life lost in the frightened aftermath of one battle that need never have been fought? My blessed Catherine eased me some; she would have bundled me to bed, but I felt this was a moment of life when, should I give in to such temptation, I might never get up again. I forced myself to limping action on the farm and in the village, putting aside my cane as often as I could.

We had Dear Swallow and Isaac to dine soon after I was home and both looked clean and well. Before we sat to food, I thought I caught some old familiar reek of gin from Isaac's breath.

"Son?" I said. "I thought I smelled spirits."

"Nay, Father," he said so cheerfully I could not disbelieve him. "A glass of wine before I left the house is all. You would not have me parched of any drink?"

I laughed and was glad to agree. We had a good meal and talk of how he might in the next month go to Quebec and execute some commissions for me there. This was the last I ever held his hand in love.

It was a week later I was in Burlington Heights, finishing some business with a gentleman who claimed a new system of well-digging. I would have ridden home, but I grew weary earlier and more often now so I took a room at the town tavern. I had settled myself, not yet in bed, but in a rocking chair to read from the Bible before sleeping. It was the Book of Micah which I have often thought was as much guidance for a man's life as any part of the Scriptures. I read again and relished my favorite verse (8 of Chapter VI): "He hath shewd thee, O man, what is good; and what doth the Lord require of thee, but to do justly, and to love mercy, and to walk humbly with thy God!"

Still I felt too restless for sound sleep so I resolved to go back downstairs and have a tankard, something mulled and soporific, in the tavern to help Morpheus close my eyes.

I put the Bible down on a low chest at the foot of the bed. So placing it, my eye touched Micah VII: 6: "For the son dishonoreth the father . . . a man's enemies are the men of his own house." I gave it no thought, hummed some air remembered of Blind Kain as I went down the stairs to the tavern.

My drink was hot and nutty and I could see kind sleep in it. I had it almost half finished when Isaac came through the tavern door, with him one Blount, a trader in horses, otherwise mostly a wastrel. Isaac lurched in his stride, seeing me, but caught himself quickly to walk as straight as anyone.

"Greetings, Father," he said. "I had not thought to meet you here."

"Nor I you, son," I said, keeping my anger. "At a tavern for spirits."

"I came in with Mr. Blount, Father," he said, "just for a glass of ale and to discuss a bay gelding he has to be bought at a price below what you would believe. I could use it on my errands for you, Father."

His mistake was in coming so near me. This time I could have no doubt of the stench of gin to his breath.

"You are a liar and a weak fool gone in drink!" I cried at him. "Leave me, Isaac. I shall deal with you in the morning when I hope you may be sober, and I shall deal with you then once and for all."

He hesitated and I think would have turned away, but he saw the smirk on Blount's long face and would prefer to shame his father than to be bested in company of what he called a friend.

"I'll have the money, old father," he said, his eyes closing narrow, the ugly leer of his drunkenness no longer concealed. "You can give me it now, or I can throw your swollen carcass out the door and take what I wish when you're dead from the chest of gold you keep hid."

He reached to his side and drew a short-bladed knife.

I stood where I was and I forgot about age and my leg that still ached often and forgot even that this was my son. The old instincts that rejuvenated me were of any combat. I watched him move as I would watch a copperhead coiled or a crouched wolverine or any animal treacherous and fatal.

He held the knife well for he was no bad fighter, a brave of my own training. But before he moved he launched himself into a thick-tongued diatribe, accusing me of favoring all Catherine's children above him, of miserliness, hypocrisy and hatred.

"The great chief!" he said. "The English King's tame puppy!"

He lunged, but I had drawn my own knife from my hip and caught his blade on its handle. He leaped back, struck again, and I stopped his blade again, but this time, as I turned his thrust, my knife carried past and cut him not deep, but a good two inches across his brow and into his hair. It was a kitten's scratch compared to the ax blow I had given Simon Girty who still lives hale and foul as ever.

The cut and the little blood from it stopped him and he slumped and almost fell against Blount. My son a coward as well as a drunken deceiver.

"Take him and see that his wound is bound," I said. "I shall look in on him tomorrow." I left the tavern room and I was suddenly all old again, my poor leg throbbing painfully. The little sleep I had that night was only one dream, over and over, the hooded man I struck and thought to be my father and was not; and now I had some of its sad import in fact.

In the morning, when I tried Isaac's room, he was not there and I found he had left for home in the night. So I rode to his house to see him, but Dear Swallow at the door said he was in bed and would see nobody and I went to my own house and Catherine tried to calm me but without much success.

Dear Swallow came to us that evening in tears, saying that

Isaac would not let her dress his wound, but lay abed and took more drink and clawed at the cut with his nails.

I went home with her myself and, after some struggle, took his bottle from Isaac and held him down while Dear Swallow cleaned the cut and bandaged it. All the time I held him Isaac spewed at me a stream of foul abuse. When Dear Swallow had tied the bandage I let him drink from brandy I had brought with me, laced liberally with laudanum, so that he quickly fell back into sleep.

In the morning when he woke, he tore the bandage away again. Tragic as some moments of my life had been never was I as plagued and tormented, as close to madness as those next days. As some fever of the brain struck upon Isaac and no medicines, neither those of Dr. Callaway from Toronto nor Molly's simples, could help. As he died before Dear Swallow's eyes and mine, his frame shrunken in weight so that I thought I saw not lying, drunken Isaac but the small, quick-footed boy I had played with and the solemn youth who had asked me if I wanted a rattlesnake caught and brought to me live.

You may read in records my forgiveness by the King's authorities and by a Six Nations' council for any crime in Isaac's death, but you cannot read what is in a father's heart and should I study for a thousand years I would not have skill to write it so any other mortal might understand. It made for me a living nightmare, and one that haunts me still for in the cruel accident of killing my son I saw all the many men I had killed in years of war as the sweet children they had once been, and spoiled for myself any heroics of my own or that I read of others.

I tried some time to reason what had happened between me and Isaac. I know it is common among white men that a son may hate his father, but it had been so seldom with my own people. I had loved my own father, Carrihogo, and he had loved his father, Nichaus, and so in every Mohawk family I can recall. I think the flaw with Isaac was some white man's infection like the lung fever, and I think its seat is in how families are arranged to live. For the English pretend to honor their women and indulge them in every fancy in the home, but never heed them in council. Where we Mohawks place all inheritance through the female line and take more heed of a wise woman like Molly than of many chiefs, yet we would throw a wife across the longhouse floor if she did not have food hot and ready for her husband at his will.

Isaac grew up with no mother, with half his life Mohawk and half English (and that the English of forts and drunken soldiers and camp followers). He grew up into a split world and could not find his way in it. And so his hand was against every man's and he had envy to replace the love a son should bear his father, and it was his father's hand that struck him down. We buried him at the village.

I had not even time to mourn, for there was a summons for me, from Wyandot chiefs near Detroit that I could not deny. Emissaries of the new French Republic's ambassador to America were in the region and making some revival of French aid for Indians against both English and Americans.

They were men of much talk and little money or resources in arms, so I gave them short shrift. Still I wasted time on this trip. Any fool could have told them that, so soon upon Fallen Timbers, no foreign power could easily enlist Indian aid in war. But it could not be any fool; it had to be Thanendanegea, Colonel Brant, the Mohawk King who had just killed his own son.

I cannot even now read the Book of Kings without weeping with David for Absalom, though that son at least was killed in battle.

There were more tears to come for me. Because an Indian does not often openly show his heart before white men, there is some popular belief we do not weep and suffer as other men. Is it so bad that we should keep our deepest emotions damned in public? Let me tell you, in the still privacy within myself I have drowned mountains with my weeping and torn whole continents apart in rage and grief.

I slept at a settlement by the lake the night before I returned to my home and dreamed, as I had not in much time, of my great white owl.

It was a strange and powerful dream that began with finding myself a child again in a wilderness clearing not unlike the one of which the original owl tale was told. But I was not alone. The clearing was filled with some hundreds of persons, many faces I knew well from Carrihogo to Sir William himself to the tittering Mr. Sheldon to Tagcheunto to Lame Crow, dozens of faces that I could set a name to and dozens more that I knew I had encountered at some time, in a battle, on a London street, passing on forest trails. So great a congregation of my past.

And though I was a small child in size, I was myself grown in mind and full of desire to speak to all these people and to share some vital knowledge with them, but when I opened my mouth there came forth nothing but strange, unintelligible sounds; animal creakings and barkings, barnyard cackles, and the crowd, one by one, drew away from me and went off into the dark forest beyond the clearing, so that I cried out in my vexation and would have run after them but my small feet tripped on a snaking root and when I tried to pull myself free the root came alive to hold me fast.

And, as time swims and varies in a dream, it seemed to me I lay trapped thus for days, weakening with hunger, till at last I heard from far the beat of those great wings and my owl was alighted beside me.

A tear of his beak broke the living root and I was free.

And my speech returned as soon as the root was snapped and I cried: "Bring them back! Bring them back!"

Then, for the first time in all my dreams, the great white owl spoke.

"I bring nothing back," he said. "I send them farther, ever farther, and always I send more to join them."

I thought of all the persons I had seen and suddenly knew them all for persons dead. There had been Isaac on the verge of the crowd, seeming sober and his best self. And Ganun-dagwa . . .

"Take me with you, then, Great Owl!" I cried. "Carry me with you. I am so small a creature you may bear me easily and swiftly."

But the owl shook his beaked head.

"A far way," he said. "A far way, a far, sad time, Joseph."

He moved his huge wings and even as I ran to clasp at his talons he was soared upward and beyond me and away.

I woke clammy wet with chill sweat, had my horse saddled at once and rode home at a jarring speed.

"Molly sinks," Catherine told me and I waited only for a fresh mount to ride north to Kingston.

My dearest kin, my sister and my sib and sibyl both, lay breathing cruel rasps in the great carved bed she had shared so long with Sir William and had brought all the path north from Johnson Hall. I had ridden days and nights but I sat wakeful at her side and listening to her croaking speech as her mind roamed in delirium.

Another watcher might have seen a gaunt old woman in the bed, but all her wandering speech, sometimes sad, sometimes silly, brought to me was the straight beauty of her best years, the proud, sharp-breasted lass of bright brown eyes who could speak gravely and with wisdom with Chief Hendrick or Sir William, and take the head of the table with a visiting English lord, or romp and scamper madly all up and down the great staircase with her own children like a wise mother cat teasing her kittens to growth. Wise, beautiful, strong, powerful in anger, soft as velvet in love . . . I lose words here. This sister, sweet Molly, was my other self and part of me died that night, choking, but mercifully past pain, a frail skein of bones in my arms.

She was buried from the church at Kingston, I making all arrangements in religion as I had for her while she lived, and most persons of any importance in Canada, English, Indian and French mourned there with me.

It was just as her coffin was lowered into the cloven, yellow-brown earth of the grave that thunder broke from the scattered clouds in the sky above, the first crashes of its sound before even a drop of rain fell. Then more clouds gathered with a suddenness I have never known before and rain swept the crowd gathered for homage to Molly, scattering them into their carriages, those who had them, and others running pell-mell, clothing gathered over their heads, back along the road for shelter.

Such a storm to make children moan and tremble and grown men blench. It was as if the heavens were rent in a kind of agony and the thunder sounded with a note of tearing beyond its familiar cannon booms. The severest of rationalists, caught in that graveyard in that storm, I think would have been grateful for a charm to finger. I am not that severe a rationalist myself and I had no rosary of relic to my hand, but it was Molly's poor husk that was being laid to rest in earth so I stood my ground while the sexton spaded clods to cover the box wherein Molly rested. I stood my ground and could not help remembering Molly's fear in storms and thinking that fear in some way far beyond understanding presaged this dark troubled day of burial. I think it not impossible that some part of Molly knew this moment far before it came to pass.

I own I welcomed, early the year following, an opportunity to return to Philadelphia. My efforts now with the English were to win for our people at Grand River not further land, but enough money from the Crown to purchase the many agricultural implements we lacked and to bring into our land some European settlers (most carefully chosen) who could help us learn more of living with sensible economy on the land we had. I had more than a little memory of how I had seen Sir William turn the Mohawk Valley into rich farmland by similar methods.

But the King's agents balked at helping me, so I thought to

give them a little fright by starting rumors I planned to sell our Grand River manors to the Americans.

It was by no means so glorious a visit as I had known before. This time I had no presidential invitation (though you may be certain Mr. Adams knew I was in the city) and so saw few of the great men I had looked to meet. I stayed long enough to give some worry to His Majesty's ambassador to the United States and to meet with General Aaron Burr, the man then seeming most likely to succeed Adams as President and an intelligent and agreeable gentleman indeed. From him I had a note to his daughter, Theodosia, to call on her in New York on my journey homeward.

This visit in New York, quite barren of any political significance, was yet the most pleasant interval in my whole pilgrimage. Miss Theodosia, it devolved to my vast surprise, was a maid of only fourteen years, yet she had me to dinner with important people from the city, controlled her servants perfectly, made me small talk of everything from theology to profane verse and held more than her own with such older charmers as she had to dine. A sweet, wise child, I think I saw in her some semblance to Molly's manner, the more marked by this soonness after Molly's death.

I stopped at Hartford on the way home and had good companionship there, and at Albany, which was not so good for some Rebels in memorial of my raiding fame in those parts set on foot a plot to kill me, but I passed from the town with no harm. I hurried now, missing Catherine and our home and her love.

Job is not my favorite among the books of the Bible. I mean nothing of frivolity but I feel, with no impiety, too much closeness to that unhappy Hebrew.

It had been twelve—no, thirteen—years since that demented homecoming with Schuyler's Mary and there was no woman involved in this journey (barring the fourteen-year-old Miss Burr where my affections had been but paternal), so I had not the inkling I give you that anything would be amiss. I threw

my horses's reins to Gilpin and strode up the path to the front
door.

My greeting was a scream of terror. Plump Sophie Pooley, a
mulatto slave we had had since our first coming from Niagara,
grown with us from child to young woman, crouched by the
ingle as my Catherine, her face contorted to a mask of evil,
moved on her with a short, sharp kitchen knife.

"So, if the heat won't, *I'll* spoil your beauty," I heard my
wife say and, caught like some figure in a dream, I stood at
the door as Catherine swung the knife down and raked the
poor maid's fat cheek.

My pause was no more than seconds. Then I was at Catherine's side, but she had dropped the knife and fallen to a gibbering laughter. I pulled her back and sat her into a chair before turning to Sophie who went on screeching, shrill like the
steam whistle of a boiling kettle, not even touching the
gashed cheek from which blood fell in red beads.

I shook Catherine by her shoulders till her gibbering
stopped and had her bring pitch and a bowl of water to soften
it. In some trancelike movements she did as I bid and I applied the sticky mixture to the girl's wound. She let her keen-
ing die down to sobs while I gave her directions to lie down
and leave the pitch to set cool upon her cheek till it fell off of
its own accord. She went, still sobbing, to her quarters.

Then I faced Catherine and asked her for some explanation.

She gave me a torrent of words about Sophie refusing to
care for kettles on the fireplace crane, charging that the steam
and heat would mar her face, and Catherine deciding "to
teach her a lesson." The result was that in all she said I could
not feel my Catherine speaking.

Sophie's wound healed and left only a thin scar. She had no
beauty to begin with and I think the mark may have enhanced what meager charms she boasted. But whatever
wound Catherine bore did not heal. She had weeks and sometimes months of her old self, but without warning (no lunar
cycle nor pregnancy longer to blame) she might change into a

person in no tune with this world, ranting odd complaints, raising her hand against her own children, letting ragged lamp wicks burn high within an inch of catching fire elsewhere and destroying the whole house.

Now there was no Molly I could ride to and find wisdom from. I talked to wise men of the tribe and to English doctors and to ministers, but have had no help. They say that certain women at a certain age (these two certains neatly leaving so vast exceptions as to make their statement meaningless) give up full hold on usual sense, and so it is with Catherine, and such it is that I must learn to live with.

But why my wife? Why my son Isaac? Why my father murdered and my people uprooted from their lands?

O my Lord, why?

ᒯᒯᒯᒯᒯᒯᒯᒯ SIX ᒯᒯᒯᒯᒯᒯᒯᒯ

I write this now in 1803, taking time from the real work, the shelves of books that may someday help me complete the Bible whole into Mohawk. If this life's record is nothing else, it is something I may look over myself and with every written line I read remember enough more for another volume.

I have had everything a man could desire—fame, power, love, the esteem of the great in more than one land—yet each best thing only for a little while, and this may give a reader some armament against the transitoriness of our lives on earth. I have tried to write this history of what I have had and some of what I have lost and now I see too much that I have woefully foreshortened, and too much that I may have drawn out beyond its real importance. Let me plead only that I have tried to tell this day's truth of what I bring up, as in a net from a flowing stream, of the past.

A reader might expect now some tidying and bringing together of the many strands in what I have written thus far. I shall amend to say that a reader under thirty years might expect some such; any reader past that age, unless one of God's lucky fools, must know in nature there is no such neat binding.

I am in fair health now, as often without my walking stick as with it. I have two of my sons in Dartmouth College, the rest of my children here with me at home, my oldest daughter

Christiana wed happily and living nearby. I write that and re-
alize, after all the self-pity I have been expending, this is none
too bad a balance.

My beloved Catherine must needs be watched against those
changing moods where she could harm herself and others, but
I have Arabella, a husky woman I bought at Toronto, who
plays nurse and friend and servant with as much devotion as
if she were free friend and not slave. And this is something to
be most grateful for.

I have held us our Grand River lands against attempts to
move in upon them and I still speak with a voice listened to in
council. I know myself for an old, toothless and lamed lion,
but the world looks on a lion, however scarred and worn by
time, as a kingly, unpredictable creature that may grow new
fangs at any moment.

The years I saw myself as savior of my people grow a little
dim and I may confide in you that I am thankful for this
dimness, for what age has begun so late to teach me is that a
man may be responsible only for himself. I would not change
too much in my past (barring some closely personal acts) for I
tried to speak right as I saw it.

I think, at sixty years, I have learned something about waiting. I see the white man stealing more land rather than being
held to any line by any treaty. But God lives in a mode of
time that is eternal, and I think the Indian may be closer to
God than the white man who brought him God's word. I think
we can and will wait, like that small animal I saw so near to
London, poking its head to the riverbank as men rowed by.
Otter and marmot and Indian can wait, not easy years but
generations stretching to eons. Wood rots and piled stone
crumbles and pestilence may move quicker than quacksalvers'
cures. I cannot think God meant the fair land between our
oceans all for the white man's measuring and measureless
greed. He is a God of justice and redemption and shall we
wait in decent reverence, there will rot enough wood and

crumble enough stone and decimate enough pestilence so the land will stretch green and free and ours again some day.

I do not think I shall see it or my children or my children's children, but some spring morning some Indian above mossed ruins of Albany may look out upon the country as I did as a child and see it all open to God's creatures for their free roaming without restraint. And the ghost of poor Tagcheunto, far in some heaven, will laugh at all surveyors.

I remember my small, untouched island sanctuary in the Pennsylvania mountains and I can believe in it as some token or portent that all the land cannot be totally despoiled before a turning back to natural godly wonder. How many hundreds of years did we hold and keep America our own before the white man made landfall? We, and the forest seeds and the animals that always lurk a shadow beyond cities and towns, houses and barns, can wait as many hundreds more for redress of balance.

Meanwhile, I live. I grow more content with what I can do and less harried in my heart by what I would have done. I try to work upon my translating, but I do not waste regret for the strong suspicion that I may never reach its end. It is God's work and while I do it I am well engaged.

I think I have the same problems as any man, and perhaps heightened by the adventures of my life with more violence, more love and lust and more temptation than, say, a village sawyer.

I think more often than ever of Sir William, still able to see him and Hendrick riding forth as clearly as on the day itself. Among all things I may be grateful for, knowing him and being part of his designs (however shattered they lie now, they were glorious) has meant more to my life than any other item in account.

Even through him, for Reverend Prouty was his guest, did I come to Your worship, Lord. Even through him did I come to the schooling which has set my path on study of Thy Scriptures.

But now, in age, I find uncertainty sometimes even here. As often as the soul-staunching glimpses of Thy bosom's peace, come questionings of Good and Evil. I look back on my life and see so much red with blood, and I look presently about me and see the wicked man flourish and the widow driven from her hearth. Yet Thine is the Kingdom, and Thine is Omnipotence . . .

Now the time comes to lay down my pen, and there is this one last question, Lord, Salvation, Guide and Only Begetter that I would beg of You before I close and wait whatever end You have appointed for this my poor lamed clay.

I ask what may seem heresy, yet it is not in heresy but in humility that I beg an answer: Is it possible, Lord, to be made in Thy image, in the image of Thee who art the fire and the hurricane and the plague and all else as well as the sun and the new grass and the budded flower; is it possible, Lord, to be made in Thy awful image and yet be good?

Your divines shy away from this question with horror, and it lies now heavier than ever on my heart.

Dare I, Lord, now and ever at Thy mercy, to believe the answer may be Yes only because Thy need of my poor soul's affection and timid strength is as great or greater than mine for Thee?

I wait my owl, and Thy answer.